IMMUNITY

ALSO BY LORI ANDREWS

To Lois,
What a joy it has been to
connect through the Fortnightly!
Happy reading —
Lori Andrews

LORI ANDREWS

IMMUNITY

 ST. MARTIN'S MINOTAUR   NEW YORK

This is a work of fiction. All of the characters, organizations, and events portrayed in this novel are either products of the author's imagination or are used fictitiously.

IMMUNITY. Copyright © 2008 by Lori Andrews. All rights reserved. Printed in the United States of America. For information, address St. Martin's Press, 175 Fifth Avenue, New York, N.Y. 10010.

www.minotaurbooks.com

Library of Congress Cataloging-in-Publication Data

Andrews, Lori B., 1952–
    Immunity / Lori Andrews.—1st St. Martin's Minotaur ed.
        p.   cm.
    ISBN-13: 978-0-312-35272-1
    ISBN-10: 0-312-35272-7
        1. Women geneticists—Fiction. 2. Drug enforcement agents—Fiction.
3. Epidemics—Fiction. I. Title.
    PS3601.N5527I46 2008
    813'.6—dc22

                                                            2008020338

First Edition: September 2008

10   9   8   7   6   5   4   3   2   1

With love to Christopher,
who always teaches me something magical

IMMUNITY

PROLOGUE

After bad booze in six bars, Castro's room at the Wanderlust Motel beckoned him like the arms of a lover. At 4:00 A.M., the Vegas Strip dazzled like a dowager's jewels in the distance, while the flickering neon on his hotel looked like a battered sequin on the pasties of an over-the-hill showgirl.

He scanned the area to make sure no one was lying in wait for him. A lot of guys wanted a pound of his flesh, payback for his past acts—or just the chance to treat someone like a punching bag to batten down his demons. His tired glance registered Lil Joe, a jittery speed freak who some nights had the $15 to rent a room, but more often just paced the broken sidewalk outside the motel. Lil Joe glared at him and paced backward, away from Castro's six-foot-two, well-muscled frame. "Is cool. Is cool," said Joe through cracked lips.

A car screeched to a stop at the end of the parking lot. The passenger door opened, followed by a scream and then a thump as the car sped away. Castro got to the spot in less than a minute. Looking at the body on the ground, he realized that being pushed from a moving car was the least of the girl's problems. Her clothes were torn, her face pummeled, and a large pool of blood was soaking through the crotch of her jeans.

As he bent down to feel for a pulse in her neck, she croaked weakly, "No more, stop it." Tears pouring down her cheeks, she reached up and scratched his face with her broken nails.

Pinning her arm gently so she couldn't reach him, he said, "I'm not going to hurt you." But she didn't seem to hear him through her sobs. She curled into a fetal ball as he fished his cell phone out of his pocket. He was about to dial when he heard the unmistakable metallic wallop of a round being chambered behind him.

He put his arms out to his sides and slowly straightened up, cursing himself for not considering that the driver might park the car and double back. But when he turned his head, he saw the motel manager, a tough old broad, pointing a Beretta 9 mm.

"I didn't do it," he said.

He realized how bad this looked, what with the girl down and the scratches on his face. Lil Joe could alibi him, but the wiry junkie had slipped away. He pivoted slowly, keeping his hands up, cell phone pointed to the sky. He knew Ted would have handled it differently. Ted could sweet-talk any woman into doing anything. That man had the gift of gab. Castro could understand a woman only after months or years in her arms.

His blue eyes blazed at the older woman. "Dolores," he said, "put down the gun and let me call 911." He said it calmly, watching her image strobe in and out in the flickering light of the Wanderlust sign. If she didn't lower the gun by the time he counted mentally to ten, he would pounce and break her arm.

Her gun went down. His fingers sped over the numbers and he gave their location to the emergency operator. As Dolores bent to soothe the scared teen, he dialed Ted. "We've got another one," he said. "Black Mercedes. Nevada plates, FAN 231."

By 7:00 A.M., the man who'd tossed the girl from the car was in custody. He'd stopped for a drink after his little errand, not even bothering to clean the blood off the passenger seat.

Ted and Castro watched his interrogation through the one-way glass in the Vegas police department, where they were the DEA end of a joint LVPD/DEA investigation into a date rape drug simply called J. The women who were slipped this beauty became sedated, then aroused, then aggressive. It pushed them further than anyone would have imagined, a sick game to the men who used it. But young girls were ending up mutilated or dead.

The driver—clearly not the sharpest knife in the drawer—claimed he was just helping out a friend at the Fantasy Resort on the Strip. "The girl was like that in the hotel room," he told the interrogator. "Woulda been bad for business to leave her there."

2

Through the glass, Castro could see only the back of the interrogator's head, but he could imagine his eyes rolling at that comment. The interrogator said, "So, Joey, you're telling me it's good for business to throw one of the guests out of a moving car?"

Joey sat up straight, as if offended by the question. "She wasn't no guest. A working girl like her booking a thousand-dollar-a-night room? Get real."

On the other side of the mirror, Castro thought about whether the owner of the Fantasy Resort, Frankie "the Bayonet" DiBondi, could be moving J. Why go for the piddly markup on a drug for lowlifes when you ran a legal brothel (a million a month declared on taxes, with an unimaginable sum socked away under the radar) and owned the hottest casino on the Strip ($150 million annually with everyone from Bette Midler to Shakira wanting to play the five-thousand-seat showroom).

"Why would the Bayonet move down the alphabet to J when he could make the big bucks moving H?" Castro said.

"We still need to get on his ass," Ted said. "Could be someone else dealing inside the Fantasy."

Castro nodded. If this had occurred under DiBondi's nose, what he did about it in the next twenty-four hours could tip them off to who was selling and, more important, who was producing the drug.

When they reached the Fantasy Resort, it was barely 9:00 A.M. Castro headed straight to the casino, the surest place to find DiBondi. The 70-year-old don had a penthouse in the hotel, but was constantly in motion, greeting guests, throwing dinners for the headliners, and storming past the blackjack tables, eyeing the dealers so they didn't dick with his money. Sure, he had state-of-the-art security and a slew of ex-cops on retainer, but he was old-school.

At the bar in the main casino, Castro caught sight of DiBondi approaching a blond-haired man in his forties. Dressed in a navy suit with a prep school tie, the younger man stuck out in the casino, where the dress code encompassed either tuxedoed men escorting women in Cher-like beaded numbers or overweight Middle Americans in Bermuda shorts or sweatpants.

DiBondi put his arm around the blond man. But rather than buy him a drink, he steered the conservatively dressed man toward the exit. Castro moved into the flow of people headed out of the sumptuous breakfast buffet so it wouldn't be so obvious he was trailing DiBondi. But he needed to stay close. A valet was turning over a Cadillac with the plates FAN OO1 to the older man. Castro needed to make sure he was back in his own car with Ted before the man hit the road.

DiBondi handed his keys over to the guy Castro pegged as a businessman. That term in Vegas covered a lot of territory. The DEA agent didn't know what the connection might be to J, or even if there was any. Someone producing the drug would have known better than to show up at the casino dressed like that. And DiBondi wouldn't have been seen in public with him. But this was going down strangely enough to make them both persons of interest.

Castro's weary body, which hadn't felt sleep for nearly two days, tensed over the wheel as DiBondi and his pal pulled into a gas station outside Flagstaff, Arizona. It was their first stop since they'd left Vegas five hours earlier. Ted woke up as Castro eased on the brakes. "Fuck," Ted said. "Where the hell is he taking us?"

Castro didn't bother to respond. He switched positions with Ted and, once in the passenger seat, immediately fell asleep. When he next woke up, it was dusk and they were across the street from the Hotel La Fonda in Taos. He stepped out of the car, took a seat in the lobby, and surreptitiously snapped a photo of DiBondi's companion on his cell phone, transmitting the image to DEA headquarters for identification.

He and Ted waited until the two men got into the elevator before they approached the desk themselves, checking in as a gay couple. Each of them had now gotten a good five hours' sleep and were pumped for whatever DiBondi dished out. Ted took Castro's hand as they waited for the elevator. Once inside, Castro let go and laughed. "Next time," he said, "remind me to get assigned a woman as a partner."

"Nah, you love me," said Ted. And he was right. He was Castro's closest friend.

In the room, Castro looked out the window at the flame of the setting sun and noticed that the valet hadn't parked DiBondi's car. "Get ready to roll," he said to Ted as he grabbed a map from the desk. "They're just making a pit stop."

They took the stairs back down. Ted disappeared into the park across from the hotel for a moment, then got into the passenger seat of the car just as DiBondi and his buddy were pulling out.

Castro's cell phone rang and he maneuvered his car onto the road, falling a safe distance behind DiBondi's Cadillac. "He's not in the system," the voice on the other end said. The photo didn't match any known felons or anyone with ties to the Mob.

"Much obliged," said Castro. Then he hung up and turned to his partner.

"I heard," Ted said.

"Doesn't seem like family either."

Ninety minutes later, the Cadillac turned onto an unpaved road.

"Think he made us?" Ted asked.

"Nah," Castro said, as he cut the headlights and followed the other car. The Cadillac was still traveling at highway speed, churning up dust and small pebbles. The road passed along the edge of a quarry that was dug down hundreds of feet. "What's the map say?"

Ted took a pen-size flashlight and looked at their map, shielding the light with his hand so it couldn't be seen from the other car. "Quarry for about a mile along the road, then the map is pretty much blank for maybe ten miles."

"What's it called? Area 51?"

"Nope, nothing on it but the initials RSV."

"Here, let me see." Castro eyed the map without slowing down and the car veered sharply, bringing their right tires perilously close to the edge of the quarry.

"Shit, my man," said Ted, "pay attention. DiBondi's stopping."

Castro turned left and pulled the car behind a bulldozer. Ted pressed his night vision binoculars against his face. Castro followed suit. DiBondi and his mystery driver had stopped about five hundred feet farther up the road. They were met by four men with long, straight black hair. Native Americans.

"RSV," Castro said. "Reservation."

They were tailing DiBondi because of his possible link to the new date rape drug. But they knew the Justice Department suspected the Mob was working its way into the Indian gaming industry and now Castro and Ted were watching a possible connection.

"Whatever tribe this is, it's not doing that well," Ted said. "Look at that wooden house. Pretty run-down."

Ted took his .38 out of the glove compartment. Castro already had his Sig Sauer .40 in a holster under his windbreaker. They got out of the car and walked another hundred feet, but there wasn't enough cover for them to get closer.

Castro scrutinized the building, about eighty feet long and twenty feet wide. The arched roof consisted of bent wooden poles covered with bark. He tried to remember something from his undergraduate class on Native American history at the University of Arizona. A longhouse. The four Native Americans had gone in, but left DiBondi and his driver waiting at the door. Maybe the Indians were deciding whether to invite the men from Vegas inside. Some longhouses were a big deal, males only, peyote, and major decision making. But wait, there was something going down. Some guy had shown up on horseback and was yelling. Castro raised his night vision glasses. Guy was prepared for some sort of war dance for sure, blue stripe of paint across his nose. Chief War Paint jumped down and blocked DiBondi's path.

While the Indian was focused on DiBondi, his buddy was circling to the Indian's right, behind the horse. Castro expected the blond man to pull a gun and shoot the rider. Castro aimed his Sig Sauer at the driver's shoulder, but this would be a tough shot.

Suddenly Ted crumpled to the ground, and Castro dropped down, lunging toward his partner as he scanned the area for a sniper. Finding none, he looked at his friend, seeking out a wound. But Ted didn't seem to be bleeding anywhere other than his nose. A screechy, wheezing noise was coming from his mouth. Castro inched closer. Ted was shaking and his tongue was swollen. In the dark, Castro thought his eyes were playing tricks on him. His partner's face was swelling, distorting into some monstrous visage.

"Help," Ted spit through lips that were swelling so much they cracked. His eyelids swelled over his eyes. Blood from his nose clogged his mouth, silencing further speech.

Castro shoved his arms under his friend's, scraping his knuckles raw on the stones beneath Ted. He pulled Ted's distorted body over the gravel pathway back to the car. "Hang in there. Don't give up on me."

He lifted the man into the backseat, putting a backpack under his head so he wouldn't choke to death on his own blood. His friend was now shaking uncontrollably. He opened his blue lips in the shape of a scream, trying to suck in air around his swollen tongue.

Castro careened the car back onto the road. The tires churned up stones, but their patter didn't disguise the sound of three gunshots coming from the direction of the longhouse and aimed at his speeding car.

CHAPTER   1

Alex stepped back from the gene sequencer and looked at the four-color quilt on the computer screen that represented the sequence of the glycoprotein gene of the dengue 2 virus. Call her macabre, but stripped down to its chemical bases—the red, blue, green, and orange representing the A, C, G, and T of the genetic code—the gene was quite beautiful.

She entered the genetic letters into a computer program and a swell of music filled the room. A professor at the School of the Art Institute of Chicago, Peter Gena, had created a formula for turning the genetic alphabet of deadly diseases into musical compositions. Gena used the gene sequences of HIV, measles, and polio as the basis for his songs. When Alex ran the program on the dengue sequence, jagged notes collided with one another, with an occasional soothing tonal switch. A chilling composition, fitting the high fatality rate of dengue fever, a Southeast Asian killer.

Alex, who'd earned an M.D. and a Ph.D. in genetics at Columbia, had joined the Armed Forces Institute of Pathology—the AFIP—two years earlier to sequence the genomes of deadly epidemic diseases that the Department of Defense felt might be used in biowarfare against the United States. She also served on a government-wide commission led by the head of Homeland Security, Martin Kincade. The commission, populated with people from Homeland Security, the FBI, the CIA, Justice, and the National Institutes of Health, was charged with detecting emerging infections, analyzing the threat they posed, and initiating medical and social responses.

Her home institution, the AFIP, had more on its plate than lying in wait for possible bioterrorism. In fact, the traditional military men she worked alongside viewed her work as marginal, rather like collecting primroses or trying to find life on other planets. They were trained to deal with immediate risks—targeting the enemy or capturing a killer.

Situated on 113 out-of-the-way acres in D.C. near the Maryland border, the semisecret AFIP oversaw forensic investigations in the United States and abroad involving the military and the executive branch. Congress also gave it a blank check to develop new technologies for national security, forensics, and traditional warfare. The AFIP's equivalent of James Bond's Q—Captain Grant Pringle—oversaw a bevy of researchers just a hallway away from her. But unlike his dapper British fictional counterpart, Pringle was an overmuscled weightlifter who'd grown up in Vegas.

Alex loved her work, but felt less thrilled about her workplace. She detested the military hierarchy, the baroque rules about secrecy, and the emotionless faces of many of the men she served alongside. Her natural response was to play the civilian card—coming to work in jeans and a turtleneck, letting her personal interests dictate which research she undertook, and finding enough ways to bend the rules that they seemed like overcooked linguini when she was done with them. Her best friend and the AFIP's lawyer, Lieutenant Barbara Findlay, was often amused and occasionally infuriated by the way Alex maneuvered through the system. Alex kidded that she was Barbara's evil twin.

The music hit a particularly garish note and Alex barely heard the knock on her lab door. She opened it and admitted Captain Randolph Stone, a pathologist from Walter Reed Hospital, part of the AFIP complex. She'd met him the previous month when she was asked to give a second opinion at the hospital.

"With that awful music pouring out of your lab, I felt sure you'd be applying electricity to a body with a jagged scar across his face," Stone said.

"Did you stop by to place an order? Bride of Frankenstein for you?"

"Hmm, clone of Angelina Jolie?"

"Take a number, buddy."

Stone smiled and leaned comfortably against a counter that held the bottles of the reagents Alex had used in this latest sequence run. He looked at Alex with the sort of glance she often got on the street from men who admired her package—the long, curly blond hair, the curves of her jeans and turtleneck over her five-foot-seven frame. Most of the men at the AFIP were beyond that. They treated her like one of the guys. All except Captain Grant Pringle, who turned leering into an Olympic-level sport.

This new pathologist was around her age, mid-to-late thirties, with an engaging smile and sun-bleached blond hair that, while still short, was much longer than the buzz cuts she usually encountered in the building. He handed her a folder. "I'm here to ask you a favor."

She reached for the file. "Cloned girlfriend isn't enough?"

"Nah. I'm up to my eyeballs in autopsies and I just got a call asking if I could take this report over to DEA. There's no way I can leave the building right now."

Alex bristled. "Why not messenger it? Or use one of the eight hundred soldiers in the building?" It was bad enough that her boss, Colonel Jack Wiatt, ordered her to do things that any lab tech could do. At least Wiatt was old enough to be her dad. But surfer guy here?

"Sorry, I should explain. It's a sensitive case. A DEA agent died yesterday in New Mexico while on the job. They've convened an investigation—brought in all the big boys—to see if he was using on the job. They want it delivered by a physician in case there are questions. You may not have noticed, but it's Sunday and there aren't exactly a lot of docs in the building."

Alex opened the folder and paged through the report. Honestly, she thought, sometimes she flew off the handle too quickly. It wouldn't exactly kill her to take a drive over to Arlington to drop this off. After all, Stone was doing a huge favor for her friend, AFIP pathologist Tom Harding, who was in Australia competing in a sailboat regatta. Stone was fitting in autopsies here at AFIP while running back and forth to Walter Reed for analyses of path samples in medical cases.

Alex looked down at the final line of the report. *Death consistent with cocaine overdose.* "I don't see any tox reports," she said.

"Body just came in this morning, lab results aren't back yet. But his nasal membranes were completely eroded, just like you see with heavy users. And I found major organ failure—heart, kidneys."

Alex nodded. It was a beautiful April day, cherry blossoms in bloom, and she had a full tank of gas in her 1963 yellow T-bird. A little excursion might be nice. "What's the address?"

"DEA headquarters is at 700 Army Navy Drive in Arlington."

Army Navy? thought Alex. She couldn't escape the military even on this detour.

"Do you have a contact there?"

He moved toward her and opened the file to the second page. "Milford. He's the guy who requested the autopsy. Kept it out of the hands of the New Mexico medical examiner. Said the last thing DEA needed was publicity about their guy using coke on the job."

Alex and Stone walked out of the lab together. "Thanks, Alex," he said. "I owe you one."

CHAPTER 2

The DEA building sat alongside the federal marshals' headquarters in Arlington, Virginia. James Milford was waiting for Alex in a conference room. "Take a seat while I see if everything is in order."

Alex sat at the large marble table and looked at the framed documents along the wall. They were originals of the drug enforcement bills that various presidents had signed into law. Boring, she thought. Well, what did she expect at the DEA headquarters? Travel photos from Colombia? A poster from *Reefer Madness*?

A steely-haired man in his late forties in a gray suit swept into the room, followed by a younger, black-haired man in jeans and a brown leather jacket. The younger man was waving his bandaged hands around, saying, "No way he was using! I was with him every minute on this stakeout."

Milford tried to interrupt, addressing the older man and pointing to Alex. "Agent Galloway—"

The older man held up a hand to silence Milford and continued the argument. "Ted was cited for snorting back in the Gambrano case."

"He saved my ass," said the younger guy. "We were making a buy when it went south. Asshole had a gun to my head, practically made us as cops until Ted went ahead and tried some product."

"Guy gets a taste of it, can't go back sometimes."

For a moment, Alex thought the dark-haired man was going to slug his boss. But instead he spoke, calmly and coldly. "You son of a bitch, you didn't have any problem with it when it let you put away half the Gambrano family—"

13

"And you—what the fuck were you thinking, leaving the scene? You're watching Frankie DiBondi and his driver about to off some redskin and you leave in the middle. And for what? Ted was half dead already."

The younger man was standing ramrod straight, his eyes filled with a cold rage. He'd gone beyond reasoning with the older man. Now he just looked like he wanted to kill him.

Milford used the silence to finally get in a word. "Agent Galloway, Castro," he said, nodding at each of the men. They both looked over at Alex, as if first noticing she was in the room. "This is Dr. Alexandra Blake from the Armed Forces Institute of Pathology. She's here to report on the autopsy."

The older man bristled. "What kind of operation are you running, Milford? This isn't take-a-civilian-to-work day."

"But—" Milford started.

"Hand it over," Galloway said.

Milford passed Galloway the autopsy report. The younger guy, Castro, looked over at Alex. His eyes were an ocean blue—not the greenish blue of the calm Pacific, but the turbulent gray-blue of the Atlantic during a Nor'easter. When Alex met his gaze, his shoulders relaxed slightly. Maybe thinking she could straighten this out.

Galloway pointed triumphantly to a line in the report. "Consistent with cocaine overdose," he said.

"No way," Castro said. "I know coke heads. They're confused, irritable, twitching."

Alex hated to be the bearer of bad news about his partner. "But he did have heart and liver failure and that's common in a cocaine overdose."

"Ted had something different, really creepy. His tongue swelled, his face blew up like a pumpkin."

Alex was curious. None of that was in the report. "Do you have a photo?"

Milford took a large envelope out of the pile of papers in front of him and pushed it down the conference table toward her. She undid the silver tab at the back and dumped the photos out. This Castro guy was right. It didn't look like a traditional overdose. Thinking aloud, she said, "Looks like an allergic reaction."

Castro tilted his head slightly, considering that fact.

Galloway had an explanation for that, too. "Yeah, so, could be something they were cutting it with."

"We've got a stat on the tox report," Alex said. "It's due back tomorrow. That will settle the question."

Both of the warring men looked pleased, each sure the findings would support his position.

"When can you release the body?" Castro asked her. "His mother's got a funeral to plan."

Alex had no idea what sort of timetable Randy Stone had given them when he took on the autopsy, but now Alex's curiosity was aroused. "Why don't we wait until after the tox results come back? That way we can follow up on anything unusual."

Castro nodded. "I'll stop by tomorrow afternoon to process the paperwork for the body." He took a deep breath. "For Ted's body."

Alex watched as the rage in his eyes turned to a hollow look of loss. He moved toward Alex and picked up one of the photos of his partner. He stared at it for a moment, then turned and left the room, as if movement and action could bring his friend back.

CHAPTER 3

When she returned to the AFIP, Alex donned scrubs and entered the morgue. Randolph Stone was there, overseeing a diener, a low-level morgue worker whose job it was to sew the corpses back up. "How'd it go?" Stone asked her.

"Okay. Made me curious. Mind if I take a look at the body?"

"Knock yourself out. He's in 14."

Alex entered the adjoining room, where stainless steel compartments held the current array of corpses. She pulled out 14, and saw what Castro meant. Not only was his head swollen but his legs looked like tree trunks—Disneyesque trees of a deep blue. His toes were gnarled and broken. His feet had expanded so quickly that the bones had been crushed by the constraint of his leather boots.

Stone joined her a few minutes later. "Pretty gruesome, huh?" He pointed to a spot where the man's hairline was torn—almost as if he'd been scalped in an old cowboys and Indians movie. A sign that he was swelling so fast it actually ripped his skin.

"Mind if I take a blood sample to see if there was some sort of immune response? The swelling's pretty unusual."

Stone nodded. "Whatever you need. Day like today, I'm grateful for the help."

Back in her lab, Alex analyzed the DEA agent's blood. His T cell count was off the charts. A hyperimmune response. But what had triggered it? Why had his body's white blood cells started attacking his organs and tissues?

Alex was familiar with a whole range of autoimmune diseases—asthma, lupus, rheumatoid arthritis—in which the mechanisms by which the cells usually protected against outside invaders like viruses were turned inward to attack the person's own body. But no disease she knew acted this quickly or this dramatically. If Ted had used cocaine, perhaps it had been cut—maybe even intentionally—with something deadly. But his friend was adamant that he wasn't a user.

Then again, what do we really know about our friends? The men in Alex's life sometimes pulled tricks that would make a magician envious. Unlike her hardheaded approach to her work, she showed a surprising naiveté about relationships. Maybe Castro had similar rose-colored glasses about his partner.

But she had more than a friend's hopes and beliefs to go on. Alex could turn to the comforting familiarity and infallibility of science. When the tox screens came back tomorrow, she'd figure out what had triggered this immunity run amok.

CHAPTER 4

The guard at the AFIP entrance phoned Alex precisely at one the next afternoon to let her know that Castro Baxter had arrived. She liked that Baxter hadn't used his title, "Agent" Baxter. She was sick of the way some AFIP soldiers—even those who'd worked together for years—referred to one another as "Captain This" or "Warrant Officer That." And with all four branches of service represented here, she was still figuring out who outranked whom. A colonel in the Army—like the AFIP head, Colonel Jack Wiatt—was three ranks above a captain in the Army (with positions of major and lieutenant colonel separating them), but that same Army colonel was equal to the Navy rank of captain. Go figure. She detested titles and wanted to be called Alex by the people with whom she worked, but, honestly, sometimes she felt like calling upon her M.D. and Ph.D. and making them call her "Doctor Doctor."

Castro looked calmer today, in gray flannel slacks and a dignified pale blue dress shirt. When Alex met him at the guard's desk, he shook her hand and thanked her for helping him. He reached into his shirt pocket and pulled out a photo of Ted. "I wanted you to see the Ted I knew."

She looked at the blond man's smiling face, noting his raised eyebrow and mischievous grin. She looked up at his friend. "He looks like a man on his game."

Castro nodded. "He was always primed for the next bust, the next day, the next woman. He would have done anything for the agency. And now they're crapping all over him."

"You seem pretty confident he wasn't using. But isn't undercover work all lies and blending in?"

Castro looked at Alex, his expression a mixture of resentment and interest. "We can hand you a block of heroin and convince you it's a Fig Newton. But we never lied to each other. Ted told me some things I bet he never told another living soul. That's not to say all DEA agents are clean. But I know enough not to go on a Mob stakeout with someone whistling 'Stairway to Heaven' with a spoon up his nose or a needle in his arm. It's called survival."

His fierce conviction gave Alex pause. Still, how well do we actually know another person? "There may be another angle to all this. I tested his blood and he was having a major immune reaction."

"You mean AIDS?"

"No, sorry I wasn't clear. Like a big allergy."

Castro gave a low whistle and shook his head. "Never heard of any allergy that worked like that."

"Allergies and other immune reactions occur when the body's defenses mistakenly respond with the equivalent of an atom bomb instead of the likes of a flyswatter. The body literally attacks itself. Was your friend allergic to peanuts or cats or anything like that?"

Castro chuckled. "Ted? He was so healthy that in training at Quantico we called him the Bionic Man. Never got a cold, a headache, a bruise. Our whole class got food poisoning, didn't even bother to pull our heads out of the toilet we felt so bad. And there's the Tedster, ate the same as the rest of us, and he's ordering a pepperoni pizza. laughing his head off."

The whole picture wasn't making sense to Alex. And, if it was a hyper-immune response, what set him off? "That last day, on the stakeout, was Ted exposed to anything you weren't? Did he brush up against any unusual plants out in the desert? Was he handling any chemicals?"

He took the photo back from Alex and stared at his friend for a few seconds. Then he looked back at the blonde in jeans in front of him. "I've gone over the day in my head a thousand times. We were a few feet from each other the whole time. Nothing out of the ordinary."

"Alright," Alex said, handing him her card and taking his in exchange. "Call me if you think of anything." She nodded at the guard and used her key to open the door to the hallway. "Let's get your buddy out of here."

Randolph Stone, the pathologist, was leaning on a stainless steel counter in the morgue, dictating notes, when Alex and Castro entered. "Castro Baxter from the DEA is here to tie things up in the Ted Silliman case. Have you got the tox results back?"

Stone looked surprised to see the man, even though Alex had told him the day before that Castro would be coming by that afternoon. "Yeah, strange case. Tox screen came back negative."

"I knew it," said Castro.

"Called it over to DEA first thing this morning," Stone said. "And they told me I must have done it wrong. Damned if they didn't send their own guy over here to collect all the sample tubes and slides—every bit of tissue we had on the guy. Said they were going to run it again themselves."

Alex didn't like how that sounded. The interchange she'd witnessed over on Army Navy Drive didn't make the DEA seem like the most objective of judges. She walked over to drawer number 14, started pulling it out, and said, "At least we have the bod—"

Alex could see her reflection in the clean, empty steel drawer. She swung around and stared at the pathologist. "What happened to the body?"

"The mother called at 10:00 A.M. and authorized its release."

"No way," Castro said. "I was with her until noon today. She thought I was going to handle it."

Alex thought quickly. "It's probably just a mistake. We've had tons of autopsies."

But Stone was flashing a sheet of paper. "Nope, they signed for the Silliman body."

"Alright then, what funeral home is he at?" Alex asked.

Stone looked at the form. "Last Graces Mortuary."

Castro grabbed the paper from the pathologist and quickly pushed the buttons on his cell phone, putting the phone on speaker so they could all hear. What they learned from the receptionist at Last Graces made no sense. The day before, a "Mrs. Silliman" had stopped by with $5,000 in cash to arrange her son's cremation. When the body arrived that morning, Ted had been turned to ash.

"Whoa!" Randolph Stone said when Castro hung up. His face looked as grim as the corpses he autopsied. "Someone stole a body?"

Castro shoved Stone against the counter. "Not just a body. Ted's body."

The pathologist slumped his shoulders forward and looked at the floor.

"Castro," Alex said, "there's got to be an explanation."

Castro stepped back from the pathologist and put his hands in the air in a conciliatory gesture. "Sorry, man."

"No, no," said Stone. "Whatever I can do to help. I've never lost a . . . a . . ."

"I'm taking this," Castro said, waving the requisition form from the mortuary.

"I need to make a copy," Stone said. "Our regulations—"

"Fuck the regs," said Castro as he turned and left the morgue.

Alex looked at Stone, hoping for a better explanation. But surfer doc looked like his boogie board had just wiped out. "You'd better tell Barbara," she said.

CHAPTER   5

Back in her lab, Alex opened the door of the gleaming steel laboratory re-frigerator and removed the blood samples she'd taken from Ted Silliman's corpse the day before. The DEA had swept in and retrieved everything that Stone had removed from the body. Could they be engaged in a cover-up that included body snatching? Luckily, the DEA didn't know about her little stash. She used her fingernail to pull the labels off the samples. As with many of her temporary samples, she'd marked them with the man's initials, TS. But she didn't want them so readily identifiable if the DEA came snooping. So she took a marker and made new labels with a simple tag: 14, after Ted's final resting place, the drawer in the morgue. Unless of course you consid-ered the two hours he spent in a kiln at 900 degrees Fahrenheit.

Alex shuddered at the thought. Like most people in their thirties, she hadn't given a thought to the question of her death and the disposal of her remains. She looked out the window of her lab, at the trees blossoming in the sunshine, pushing away any thoughts of her own mortality.

The blood sample from Ted's corpse had scored high on T cells, but she wasn't sure what else she should be looking for. She'd have to think carefully about which tests to run since she had only a small amount of his blood left.

She mentally ticked off the tests that Randy had run in the course of the autopsy. He'd gotten toxicology screens on the twenty most common street drugs, including cocaine, and there was no trace of them in Ted's system. But his whole focus had been on what Ted might have voluntarily ingested. He hadn't checked for substances that might have been used to poison him, like arsenic, or toxins that he might have been exposed to inadvertently, like pollen from a plant or trace minerals from the soil.

Where to begin? Each of the tests would use up a certain amount of blood. Since she only had enough for maybe a dozen tests, she'd have to be damn sure what she was doing. Maybe Castro's investigation of what happened to Ted's body would provide a clue about which scientific questions she should ask of his blood. If they learned who'd taken the corpse—and for what purpose—maybe she could help figure out why and how he died.

She opened the refrigerator again, this time in less of a rush, and watched the President Bradley Cotter refrigerator magnet nod its bobble head. Prankster Grant Pringle had given it to her when she solved a case involving the Commander in Chief. But he'd cautioned her that she might want to take it down if Colonel Jack Wiatt—Cotter's good friend and Yale college roommate—entered the lab. She'd responded by asking Pringle to make her a bobble head of Wiatt, their boss. So far, he hadn't delivered.

She replaced Ted's samples and retrieved a petri dish containing a scraping of tissue from a dengue fever victim. There were four distinct agents that caused the disease—DEN 1, DEN 2, DEN 3, and DEN 4, all transmitted by mosquitoes. She'd already sequenced the DEN 1 and 2 organisms and now she was dotting pieces of tissue with DEN 3 into test tubes. She used the Gentra machine to pull DNA out of the tissue and then started running that DNA through the sequencer, which would soon begin to spurt out a chain of chemical letters one by one, like the beads of a necklace.

As Alex went about her work, she thought about her long-dead predecessors at the AFIP. Walter Reed, the institution's head in 1900, proved that mosquitoes transmitted yellow fever. Army General Frederick Russell, the director a decade later, helped developed the typhoid vaccine.

Alex felt a kinship with these pioneers. Although she was being paid to sequence toxins that might be used against the United States in biowarfare, her real passions were vaccine work and the treatment of afflicted patients. The doctor in her often got the better of the scientist. In Pakistan, Sri Lanka, Africa, South America, and India, dengue fever was reaching epidemic proportions, affecting hundreds of thousands of people. Her work on the genetic sequence of the infection not only would help the Department of Defense stave off its military use by terrorists; it could also lead to a treatment for people in developing countries who were exposed to the disease-carrying insects.

When she assured herself that all was running well with the sequencer, she headed to the office of her friend, Barbara Findlay. She knocked lightly, then opened the door and settled into the comfortable chair across from her friend's desk while Barbara finished a phone call.

Barbara was in major lawyer mode, but that couldn't disguise the attractive face beneath her short black hair. A descendant of slaves, her mother had urged Barbara's older brother to enlist in the Navy to get an education and see the world. He opted for a construction job and rarely made it outside the Bronx. Instead, Barbara had taken up the call. She'd risen through the ranks, attended law school at night, and now proudly occupied the office of the AFIP's General Counsel. As the single mother of a deaf teenage daughter, she'd chosen a job that would keep her in one place, without the constant moves that defined military life.

"Have you heard about the missing body?" Alex asked Barbara when she hung up.

Barbara nodded. "Dan sent a sketch artist to the mortuary to help identify the woman who paid for the cremation. But the attorneys for Last Graces closed ranks and wouldn't let him in."

"So you'll get a warrant?"

Barbara shrugged. "Not enough evidence to get the state of Virginia involved."

"What's Wiatt say?"

"The colonel's negotiating, shall we say, with some guy named Galloway at the DEA, who is claiming jurisdiction over the case. Our morgue, but his body."

Alex shook her head. "This is why I didn't go into law. There are always too damn many players—like a giant chess game where someone's always moving at you from an odd direction. You can never tell if we're going to end up the pawns or the king."

"At least we're okay from the liability perspective. We deal with Last Graces Mortuary all the time—they're a legit group. And the form the driver brought over had the signature of a Mrs. Silliman. No reason to doubt it. But the mother's already calling us, threatening suit." Barbara seemed peeved at the thought.

Alex leaned forward in her chair. "Think of how that poor woman feels. Two days ago she loses her son and then we lose him again today."

Barbara took a deep breath. "You're right, Alex. But here's my real worry. You know how the military is—one screwup like this and they'll adopt fifty pages of regulations with hoops we'll have to jump through each time we let a body out of here. It will be weeks before a body can be released. Next of kin aren't going to be too happy about that, either."

Alex knew her friend was right. In the military, the cure was invariably worse than the disease.

CHAPTER 6

Alex had worked her way through sequencing DEN 3 by 7:00 P.M., so she grabbed her briefcase—an old saddlebag—and pointed her T-bird toward the Adams Morgan district in D.C. Fifteen minutes later, she parked in front of the Curl Up and Dye Beauty Salon. The salon went out of business about four years earlier, and was available for rent when Alex moved to D.C. The monthly charge for 2,000 square feet was about a third of what residential property in the area was going for. When Alex first saw the interior, she'd fallen in love with its funky potential. She'd designed a bedroom out of the former bikini-wax suite.

Alex got out of her car and pressed a five-letter code on a keypad to slide aside the metal fencing that covered the entrance. She followed the dark hallway to another door, which she opened with a key. Inside the large linoleum-floored room, her image was reflected back from three walls of mirrors. The room featured four old-fashioned hair dryers attached to chairs, posters of what looked to be the latest hairstyles, circa 1960, and a revolving spindle with fifty or so nail polish bottles, with colors from Angel Blush to Electric Tangerine.

She deposited her saddlebag on one of the chairs, gave the spindle a spin for good luck, and walked back out of the place to find some dinner. In the bodega down the block, she thought about cooking for a change. She tried to remember her ex-boyfriend's chili recipe. White vinegar? Chili powder? She realized she'd never paid enough attention when he cooked. So instead she picked up two cans of tuna, an apple, and a slab of sharp cheddar cheese. She added a bottle of Chilean wine and made her way to the cash register. As she waited to check out, she glanced over at the *Star* tabloid. On its cover was a monstrous face with the headline ALIEN COMES TO EARTH. She almost dropped the wine bottle as she peered at the photo and text. The so-called alien had been found in an alley behind a restaurant in Taos, New Mexico.

She threw the newspaper onto the counter next to her tuna, paid for her purchases, and rushed home to the Curl Up and Dye.

CHAPTER 7

Alex dumped her groceries on the kitchen table and fished in her jeans pocket for the card that Castro had given her. The number connected her with a woman at an answering service. "Tell Castro to buy today's *Star*," Alex said. Then she realized how stupid and ridiculous that sounded.

"We're not allowed to take advertising solicitations on this number," said the woman.

"I'm not advertising. I'm a colleague of his. Here, try this instead. Just tell him to call Alex Blake."

"Will he know what this is regarding?"

Alex always found that question perplexing. If the person on the other end knew what this was regarding, he'd be psychic and you wouldn't need to call him, no? But instead of voicing that obvious, logical objection, she said, "Yes. It's personal."

After she hung up, she poured herself a glass of the Chilean red and cut up the apple and cheddar cheese to add to the tuna. A regular Emeril she was. Then she sat down at her round glass kitchen table, with the newspaper spread out beside her plate.

The corpse was holding his right hand in front of his face, palm toward him. He had less facial swelling than Ted Silliman, but his hand was more grotesquely swollen than the DEA agent's. The photo was taken in the alley, but the background obviously had been Photoshopped so that it looked like he was standing against a night sky with—as Carl Sagan used to say—*billions and billions* of stars.

Alex kept her line open, anxiously listening for Castro's call, but when a half hour passed and he still hadn't gotten back to her, she decided to take matters into her own hands. She went online and found the phone number for the Chief Medical Investigator of the State of New Mexico.

"I'd like to talk to you about the body that was found in the alley in Taos," she said when Dr. Kingman Reed came on the line.

"Ah, the man the locals are calling the alien," he said. She could envision him shaking his head in annoyance at their misperception. "Can you identify him or are you another one of those jokers itching to tell me he's from the planet Brion?"

"No, I'm Alex Blake from the Armed Forces Institute of Pathology." The second she said it, she realized how weird it sounded. Why would a branch of the Department of Defense have an interest in an unnamed corpse in a Southwestern tourist town?

"Cripes, don't tell me the locals have it right," sputtered the doctor.

"No, no. I'm a medical doctor investigating unusual immune responses. From the looks of the body, something must have triggered a hyperimmune attack."

"From the looks of the body, you say. Since when do fancy D.C. doctors subscribe to the tabloids?"

Since when do crotchety old medical examiners think they're the next Jay Leno? "Please, this is really important. Would it be possible to run his blood to see what his T cell count is?"

"I guess it wouldn't hurt anything."

Alex picked up the *Star* and thought of a dozen additional questions she could ask the doctor. "Is the body itself still around?"

"John Doe like that, no one's stepping forward to pick up the cost of burial."

"Can you hang on to him another day? I could fly down tomorrow to take a look."

"Sure, come on by. You're welcome to give him the once-over. Unless, of course, the Mother Ship comes back and picks him up tonight."

Alex sorted out the logistics with him, then hung up and booked a flight. She was annoyed that Castro hadn't called her back, but was tempering that annoyance with coffee-flavored Häagen-Dazs when the 505 area code showed up on her phone. Thinking that it was Dr. Reed calling her back to cancel, she was tempted to let it ring through to her voice mail so she could pretend she never got the message. But she decided to be a big girl and pick it up.

"Hey, Alex. It's me, Castro."

"You're in New Mexico?"

"Yeah. Have you got some news about Ted?"

"Just a slim lead. Did your service tell you to look at the *Star*?"

There was a silence at the other end, then a frustrated voice: "I drive forty-five minutes to use a pay phone so I don't break cover. And you tell me to read a tabloid?"

"The paper has a photo of a man with a swollen face. He died Saturday night in Taos. If I can figure out what killed him, I could point you in the right direction about Ted. I'm flying down to talk to the coroner tomorrow. Will you still be in Taos?"

"Yeah. Come to the bar at the Hotel La Fonda at nine tomorrow night. Act like you don't know me."

Alex wondered if all this cloak-and-dagger stuff was really necessary. But, truth be told, she was up for an adventure. She'd gone nearly three months without anyone trying to kill her. "I'll be the blonde with the Tony Lama's on."

"If Ted were around, he'd have replied, 'And I'll be the guy with the hard-on.' I, of course, was raised better than that."

The devil in Alex almost quipped, What could be better than that? But instead she said, "See you tomorrow."

CHAPTER 8

Waiting in line at National Airport the next morning, Alex programmed her work phone remotely so it rang to her cell phone and left a message for Barbara about where she was going. She'd charged the United flight to her personal credit card. The Ted Silliman case was only marginally an AFIP matter—although the body had been stolen from their morgue. But she resented the way the DEA seemed so willing to dirty this guy's reputation. Now that there was another body, Alex felt it would take at most a day or two to clear the matter up. Plus she welcomed an opportunity to use her medical skills on an immediate problem. Her bioterrorism work dealt with if, perhaps, and maybe. Solving an actual medical mystery would do her good.

She shook her head as she cleared security and walked toward the gate. She was spinning out rationalizations big-time. Why did she need to list a hundred reasons before she followed up on an intuition that just felt right? Lighten up, she told herself. Lots of women would have gotten on a plane to New Mexico just for that drink with Castro Baxter. After spending so much time living in black-and-white among soldiers who'd been trained not to betray emotions, she was intrigued by the Technicolor passions—anger, loyalty, grief—of the attractive DEA man.

In Albuquerque, she rented a car and drove to the medical examiner's office. Dr. Kingman Reed, the 80-year-old coroner, was surprised that "Doctor" Blake was a jeans-clad young woman whose long blond hair framed an attractive heart-shaped face. Surprised, but not disappointed.

"My day, we didn't have women in medical school," he said after shaking her hand. "And when we got them, they all looked like Eleanor Roosevelt. You, my dear, are a welcome addition to the profession."

Alex smiled uneasily at the compliment and then asked for background on the John Doe.

"T cell count was through the roof, just like you thought. He was brought in Saturday night, a little after nine."

About the time Ted died that same night, Alex thought.

"Guy who found him thought he was an alien because of the swollen face and the odd smell. Me, I grew up in a transient hotel with a drunken dad. I knew it was just the smell of someone who hadn't seen a bath or shower for quite a spell."

Alex put on scrubs and a mask to view the body. For an old guy putting on a homey small-town front, the coroner had the latest equipment and a good grasp of what to look for in a challenging autopsy.

"Once you suggested immune response, I tried to figure out the trigger point. I don't know the underlying etiology, but take a look at his right hand."

Alex's interest had already been spurred by the photo in the paper, which showed a hand more swollen than his head. But Alex now saw what interested the coroner. There was a gash along his palm, surrounded by a slight rash.

"What did he touch right before he died?" she asked.

"There was a Styrofoam box of leftovers at his feet from the Cactus Cow restaurant."

"What was in it?"

"Responding cops didn't think to save it. But judging by what fell on his shoe when he dropped the box, I would say it was their signature dish, the lobster and filet mignon burrito."

Alex used her gloved finger to press the man's tongue down so she could look into his mouth. No sign of an allergic reaction in the mouth itself. Indeed, as the doctor had implied, the contact point was the hand. But shellfish allergies generally weren't dermatological. Like peanut allergies or a reaction to penicillin, they affected the airways.

"No steak or seafood in his stomach contents," continued the coroner. "He was on more of a liquid diet. Rotgut-type, if you catch my drift."

Alex nodded and then gazed down at the man's toes. Another difference from Ted. This guy's toes weren't broken. "Are his shoes around?"

The older doctor pointed her to a cubbyhole in the wall. She looked at the shoes, a beat-up pair of Michael Jordan's that looked like they'd fit the basketball player himself. Way too big for the guy on the slab, which would explain why the swelling hadn't broken his toes. Alex thought about the smell, the too-large shoes, the Styrofoam leftover container. No wonder no one had stepped forward to report this man missing. He was homeless.

She turned back to Reed. "May I take some blood samples back with me?"

"No reason why not."

"Great. I can make some comparisons to the case I have there. Also, I think I can help you make an identification. We've got a computer program the Navy uses to identify drowned soldiers. We can input bone measurements to re-create a facial image without the bloating. Mind helping me?"

Reed pushed the puffy flesh in various directions as Alex tried to estimate the length and depth of the relevant features of his skull. She had an ace up her sleeve that would make the measurements more accurate. The before and after pictures of Ted showed the precise nature of the swelling. Data about the dimensions of the changes in Ted's features could be used in reverse to figure out what this poor man looked like before he puffed up.

"Tomorrow afternoon I'll send you a computer-generated portrait of him."

Reed whistled under his breath. "I thought that only happened on *CSI*."

"You'd be surprised at what we have." She mostly thought the toys created by Captain Pringle's lab were a royal waste of the taxpayers' money, but occasionally they represented a clear advance over existing technology.

"Eighty years old, nothing could surprise me," he said as he walked her out of the morgue and into the sunny Albuquerque spring. "When I first started in forensics, we kept a goat in the lab's yard. We'd inject it with human blood components and then use the goat's anti-human antibodies to test whether a crime scene stain was human or animal. Now I'm running DNA gels and they're making doctors who look like Barbie dolls."

Alex smiled and stood aside as he opened her car door. Impulsively, she gave him a hug as she thanked him. She had no trouble taking care of herself, but chivalry—especially from the likes of Kingman Reed—should not go unrewarded.

CHAPTER 9

When Alex got to Taos at seven that evening, she checked into the Hotel La Fonda and then crossed the plaza to locate the alley behind the Cactus Cow, where the John Doe had died. She was carrying a metal container a little larger than a shoebox. The plaza was dotted with people selling serapes, jewelry, and T-shirts. A bearded guy approached Alex, extending his right hand in front of his body, palm facing inward. "Greetings, earth chick," he said. "You'd look great in one of these."

He unfolded a T-shirt with a photo of the John Doe, who died making that same odd gesture.

"Beat it," she said, marveling at how quickly people circled around death to make a buck.

When she located the alley, she snooped around, but the garbage had been removed Monday morning and nothing much remained from the night of the man's death. Small groups of candles and flowers were scattered in front of a Dumpster. She was sure that, whoever this guy was, he'd have been amused at the Lady Di–level outpourings.

In the Cactus Cow restaurant, Alex ordered a filet mignon and lobster burrito, then proceeded to dump it into the liquid-nitrogen-cooled container she was carrying. She slapped a label on the cooler and took it to the local FedEx office. She knew that neither Ted nor the John Doe had died from food poisoning in the traditional sense. But she was sending the meal back to her lab to determine if the spices had triggered the John Doe's immune response.

She had a little time to kill before meeting Castro, so she wandered around, looking at the wares of the Native Americans who sat on blankets at the west side of the plaza. A Navajo woman tried to figure out Alex's totem to sell her a necklace with the appropriate animal on it. But Alex fancied a leather belt with a beautiful hand-cast silver buckle.

The man sitting on the blanket told her the price—$125. She hesitated, unsure whether she was supposed to haggle.

"You're supposed to offer me half that amount and we'll settle on $85," he said.

She laughed and pulled four twenties and a five out of her fanny pack. She slipped off her worn leather belt and rolled it up to fit in her fanny pack. Then she wove the new belt through the loops of her jeans. "It's a fabulous piece," she said.

"Zuni," he explained. "I made it myself."

By the time she freshened up at the hotel, it was nearly nine. She took the elevator down to the bar, where she took a pass on the extensive margarita menu (aptly titled "50 Ways to Lose Your Liver") and instead ordered her standard, Old Weller on the rocks. Castro came in a few minutes later, sat at the other end of the bar, and ordered a scotch. He looked different from the other times she'd seen him. Gone were the jeans, leather jacket, and casual disarray of black curly hair that marked their first encounter. His hair was stylishly blown dry and he was wearing black slacks, a black turtleneck, and a black and white houndstooth sports coat. The only connections to the previous Castros were his penetrating blue-gray eyes and the bandages across his knuckles. If she'd come across him on the street, she wouldn't have recognized him.

Castro tipped back the scotch and then, second one in hand, moved over and sat next to her. After a few minutes of small talk, he motioned her to a table in the corner. The bar was almost deserted, and their subsequent request for appetizers forced the bartender to leave the room to visit the kitchen.

"I went back to the quarry," he said, his voice lowered, his eyes shifting between her and the doorway. "No sign of blood. No spent cartridges. Maybe I hallucinated those gunshots. But the guy we thought was DiBondi's driver never came back. And our inside guy in Vegas says DiBondi doesn't use a driver. So something happened."

The bartender brought their empanadas, then returned to the kitchen. She asked Castro, "Did you and Ted eat at the Cactus Cow that night?"

He shook his head. "Didn't eat dinner at all. Barely got here when Di-Bondi started rolling again. Why?"

"The other man who died had a take-out container from the restaurant in his hand. All his symptoms are the same as Ted's, but he's got more swelling on his hand than Ted did. What was the last thing Ted ate or drank?"

Castro closed his eyes for a moment while he thought. "A few minutes before DiBondi got in his car, Ted ran over to the drinking fountain in the plaza for water."

Alex stood up and strode quickly to the mahogany bar. The bartender was still out of the room, so she let herself behind the counter and grabbed a Hefty bag. Then she ran out of the hotel. Castro threw money on the table to pay their bill and raced after her.

She approached the water fountain and waved a few kids away from it.

"What kind of goddamn stunt was that?" Castro said. "We're supposed to be undercover."

"Then block people's view of me, so I can take a few samples." She un-zipped her fanny pack and dotted various globs of this and that from the well-used drinking fountain into evidence envelopes and tiny test tubes. Then she secured the black Hefty bag over the fountain with a roll of wide tape. On an-other piece of the tape, she wrote "Broken" and stuck it onto the garbage bag.

Castro watched her put the tape roll back in her fanny pack, next to the samples she'd collected. "Man, you've got more stuff in there than I've got in my whole garage."

She laughed. "Saved my life a few times and saved my butt many more. I'll get these analyzed tonight. Can we meet tomorrow morning so you can show me the spot where Ted died?"

"Sure thing, but there's nothing there. I was all over it today. You got someplace to stay tonight? I'd offer you the other bedroom in my suite, but I'm gay."

Even in the faint light of the moon, Alex's expressive face must have show disappointment.

Castro corrected himself. "I mean, Ted and I checked in as gay couple before he died and I've got to maintain that cover." He held her gaze as she smiled up at him.

Then she walked to her car, called Dr. Reed on her cell phone, and arranged to use his equipment to run the samples she'd just collected.

CHAPTER   10

"What's the verdict on the samples?" Castro said as he got into her rental car the next morning, handing her one of the two cups of coffee he was holding.

"Good morning to you, too."

"Oh, so you're a woman who demands coffee and a salutation. Pretty high maintenance, if you ask me."

They were taking Alex's car since he'd gone to the quarry the day before in his rental car and didn't want to arouse suspicion by showing up there again. He looked more like himself today, thought Alex. Then she immediately corrected her thought. *He looks more like he did when we first met. As an undercover agent, who knows what the actual Castro is like, or if that's even his name. Maybe by now even he has no idea.*

"You're a love for the coffee," she said. "And you'll never drink from a fountain again when I tell you what was in there. Mucus, of course, a spot of baby food, pizza, and cotton candy, spermicide—seems like someone washed out a condom in there, not my personal choice for recycling—chewing to-bacco, deodorant—"

"Come again?"

"Maybe a runner who dabbed under his arm when he was splashing wa-ter on himself. We also found a variety of metals, including low doses of mercury—"

"Stop right there. Could Ted have died of mercury poisoning?"

"No. Levels were too low. Someone taking a drink would have swallowed less than one microgram of mercury. As infants, we got seventy-five micro-grams in our DPT vaccine alone. Plus, it's not uncommon to have trace metal in public fountains. The one in the plaza uses a seep hole to stop the fountain from freezing in cold weather. If the drainage system isn't just right, dirty water and minerals from the soil mix with the clean water and come out the spout. And then there were the assorted insects, animal feces—"

"You're right. I shouldn't have asked. Let me narrow the question. Anything relevant to our investigation?"

Alex shook her head. "All substances were common to fountain life. Unless it was something that quickly dissipated—or unless your buddy and the John Doe had a surprising allergy to something like squirrel droppings or baby food—the fountain is a dead end."

They rode along in silence for a bit. Then Castro started fooling with the radio dial and zeroed in on a country music station. "You don't mind? I went to college in Arizona and developed a taste for it there."

"Not at all. I've got a soft spot in my heart for rockabilly. But I wouldn't have pegged you for a Southwesterner."

"Started out in the Bronx," said Castro. "When I got to be too much for my mother, she sent me to live with her aunt, who'd retired to Phoenix."

"How'd you handle that?"

"Kicking and screaming at first," Castro said. "But Great-aunt Pearl had been a hell-raiser herself at that age. Ran away at sixteen, lied about her age and joined the WACs. With what she saw during World War II, she wasn't about to let some angry kid get away with any shit."

"Is she still alive?"

"Yep. Still driving at 81. Travels all over the country for veterans' reunions."

Merle Haggard's "Misery and Gin" came on the radio and Alex cranked up the volume and unconsciously increased the car's speed.

"Trouble with men?" Castro asked as Merle sang about a breakup.

"I'm only attracted to men who are trouble," Alex said.

Castro looked at her with interest. "Boy howdy. That's one job description I can definitely fill."

An hour later, they parked the car at a gas station about a mile down the highway from the quarry road. They each put on a backpack, looking like touristy hikers, and started trekking back to the spot where Ted had fallen. As they neared it, Alex began taking photos of the plants, the animal tracks, anything that might have set Ted off. Then Castro walked her closer to the run-down longhouse. They moved to the shady west side of the building, making it appear that they had chosen the spot to block the sun. Alex took a blanket out of her backpack, arranged some food on it, and they sat down for a modest picnic. She was bending toward something glistening like a coin on the grass when the back door of the longhouse opened. Castro gently pushed her over and began to kiss her. Yet another cover, thought Alex, but it felt damn good.

A tall Native American man walked over to the blanket and cleared his throat. When Alex opened her eyes, she saw that he was holding a large semi-automatic pistol. Castro sat up and put his arms in the air, emulating a scared tourist. "Hey, buddy, what's your problem?"

The man said, "This is private property."

"It's listed on the map as a reservation, so my girl and I wanted to visit it. Last month we were at the Grand Canyon Skywalk of the Hualapai."

"We are not the Hualapai. We don't encourage tourists. You've made a mistake, but if you leave now, no harm done."

Alex started packing up their goodies. She moved her right hand carefully, shielding the shiny object she'd found on the ground and dropping it into her backpack along with the remains of their lunch.

As they stood up to leave, Castro asked the man, "What tribe are you from?"

The man stood tall and then said in a most dignified way, "The Hakuna Makata Nation."

"Sorry to have bothered you," Castro said.

Alex and Castro hiked arm in arm back down the quarry road, playing the nervous couple. The man didn't attempt to follow them.

Back in the car, Castro said, "Well, at least we learned whose reservation we were on."

Alex burst into a sidesplitting laugh. "I can tell you don't have kids."

He looked at her quizzically.

" 'Hakuna Makata' is from a line in a Disney song. It's from Swahili for 'No worries, mate.' "

"Son of a bitch," he said. "That guy was yanking our chain."

"Yeah," Alex said, "but I did find something." She unzipped her backpack, put a round lapel pin into an evidence bag, and handed it to Castro. "Look what's etched into it."

"A wave? So?"

"Look closer."

He did. "Okay, a wave with a trademark sign at the end."

"Exactly," Alex said. "The corporate insignia for Waverly Pharmaceuti-cals."

CHAPTER 11

Alex dropped Castro back at the hotel, returned her rental car, and caught the next flight to D.C. With the time change going east, it was nearly midnight when she arrived home and fell into bed for a few hours' sleep. The next morning, she opened the FedEx package from Taos and began testing the spices and foods from the Cactus Cow. Since immune responses were often reactions to proteins in the trigger item, she used the latest in proteomics to generate three-dimensional versions of the protein molecules in the various substances from the burrito. But there was nothing that, by its nature, would trigger hyperimmunity. A few of the more problematic proteins she mixed with blood from Ted and from the John Doe. But the cells didn't react strangely. And now she'd used up more blood from Ted, meaning she could only do maybe ten more tests. She'd have to be very careful what she chose.

Frustrated by that dead end, she continued her careful interrogation of the John Doe's blood. At least she had several tubes of that, courtesy of the New Mexico medical examiner. But it would take days or weeks to search for an infectious organism's sequence in his blood and then compare it to common vectors to learn if he'd been felled by a known virus or bacteria.

Why not let the computer do some of the work for her? Peter Gena's music program recognized DNA sequences related to hantavirus, anthrax, malaria, rubella, smallpox, and dozens of other deadly diseases.

Alex spent the next two hours extracting DNA from the blood, sequencing it, and running the sequence through Gena's program, waiting for the musical symphony of a known infectious disease. But other than the hum of the fluorescent lights and the clicks of the robotic arms within the sequencing device, no sound emerged.

She paged Randy Stone and asked him to run some tox screens and antibody tests on the John Doe's blood, including ones he'd have run on Ted if the DEA hadn't cut his investigation short. Alex, ever trusting of science, comforted herself with the belief that when the results came back, the mysterious deaths of the two men would be solved.

After setting in motion the scientific investigation, she considered the events from another angle. Two men, both sick. Was there a more direct connection? Had Ted and the John Doe known each other? She'd ask Castro about any possible connection the next time she talked to him.

Deciding to focus on the identification of the John Doe, she entered her inner office to phone the AFIP's computer expert, Chuck Lawndale, a soft-spoken South Carolina corporal in his twenties. He treated Alex with a formality and respect that she found awkward. He chalked it up to his being raised in a Charleston, South Carolina, family, a descendant of Thomas Heyward Jr., a signer of the Declaration of Independence. He had gracious manners and a ramrod posture. Unlike his boss, forensic chief Major Dan Wilson, who was often in shirtsleeves, Chuck wore his full dress uniform, perfectly pressed, even when the D.C. temperature inched over 100. Alex had only once seen him out of uniform, when he went undercover in the D.C. clubs for a previous case. In black jeans and a black T-shirt, he looked more like a drummer than a soldier. His disguise had prompted one of their few personal conversations. She'd learned that he had season tickets to the opera but also liked heavy metal music. He felt that both musical forms were more complex than folk or rock. That away-from-work discussion about music was the only time he'd ever engaged her in a peer-to-peer conversation. Dealing with the likes of Alex wasn't covered in the Charleston guide to Southern-gentleman behavior.

When she phoned Chuck, he asked her to meet him in Captain Grant Pringle's wing of the building, an odd location, given that Chuck usually worked in Dan's command center for forensic cases.

As Q for the AFIP, Grant had scores of engineers fabricating the latest technologies. As she walked through the wing to find Chuck, she mentally compared Grant's technicians to a group of elves at the North Pole. She felt that most of the stuff they invented was closer to toys than useful technologies. But the mainly male Senate Committee overseeing the AFIP treated each new gadget as if it were the secret to saving civilization. Grant got a blank check and his minions got the headache of trying to produce the sci-fi creations their boss had promised the legislators.

Alex searched through the warren of project centers for Chuck. Despite his formality, she liked the young Southerner. He was new enough to the service that he hadn't seen combat, unlike most of the other soldiers—Wiatt in the Vietnam War, Dan in Desert Storm, and Grant in Afghanistan. Consequently, Chuck was less jaded and less sanguine about the dead bodies they encountered in their forensic investigations.

Chuck's specialty was all things digital. Data mining, surveillance, and uncovering military espionage, including theft of defense secrets. Guy like him could have made a fortune in the private sphere, but his family had a proud military tradition. An ancestor had fought alongside George Washington; another had served under General Robert E. Lee of the Confederacy.

She saw Chuck wave to her from a desk on the other side of an area where one of the elves was working on body armor. When she reached his desk, she noticed the *Star* photo of the John Doe propped up next to his computer. Chuck pointed to it. "Pretty creepy. What happened to him?"

"That's what I'm trying to find out."

"When you said you were sending me a photo, I didn't expect this. Gave me nightmares. Here's how he looked before he burst out of his skin." Chuck tilted his computer screen so that she could see the digital reconstruction. The man was about 50 years old, quite distinguished. She screwed up her face and Chuck asked what was wrong.

"Can you put a little more wear and tear on him? I'm sure he was homeless and I'm worried people won't recognize him from this photo."

Chuck's fingers danced across the keyboard, and the image on the screen gradually changed, almost like plastic surgery in reverse. More wrinkles creased his forehead. His nose grew a hint more red and his eyes a bit more bloodshot.

"Perfect," she said. "How about e-mailing it to me?" Then she motioned with her hands to his new surroundings. "Have you jumped ship and gone over to the dark side?"

Chuck—and everyone else in the building—knew Alex had problems with Grant. His childhood growing up in Vegas gave him a warped, fanny-slapping view of women. Not to mention that his body-building fanaticism led him to pose like a Mr. Universe every time she ran into him.

"No, I'm still assigned to computer services for forensics," said Chuck. "I'm just giving Captain Pringle's programming crew some help with a new surveillance tool."

At that instant, Grant joined them, standing in front of Alex with his chest puffed up like a rooster. "Let's rev up the Peeper and show the good doc how it works."

Grant took the wireless keyboard off Chuck's desk and started typing. On the screen, an aerial view of a city appeared. "Looks like you left your bedroom light on," Grant said.

Alex watched with shock as Grant zoomed in from a generic city scene to her block in Adams Morgan, and then to the roof of the Curl Up and Dye itself. "We've got a new satellite airborne," he said. "Does thermal imaging along with more traditional analyses."

He moved the focus frame from Alex's empty apartment down the block to a townhouse. Tapping a few more keys, he flashed an image of the house that showed all heat-emitting machinery—the refrigerator, a humidifier. Then he keyed something else in. "This looks for biologicals."

Alex's eye was caught by a small movement in the corner of the screen.

"It's a cat, ma'am," Chuck said.

Then Grant slowly panned to a larger heat signature. The movements made the image immediately identifiable. Inside the house, a couple was making love.

Alex was furious. "Grant, have you told Barbara about this? It's a gross invasion of people's privacy."

"Just making your homeland a little more secure. And this is just the prototype. I'm not going to bother the general counsel with it until we have the final version."

"And what's that one going to do?" Alex said. "Brain scans?"

"Nah. I'm more the type for pelvic exams."

Alex didn't respond. As a scientist herself, she was thinking of ways to put a cold-air filter on her top floor to keep his snooping eyes out.

CHAPTER 12

At home that evening, Alex was flipping through television channels when a map of New Mexico appeared. She turned up the volume, thinking it might be a story on the John Doe. Instead, the image of an attractive dark-haired man in his late thirties filled the screen. She recognized Elias Lightfoot Blackstone, the first Native American to make it to a governor's mansion. In the seven years since he'd been elected, the charismatic governor had turned the state around, winning him a standing ovation at the most recent National Conference of Governors. New Mexico had the lowest unemployment in the country, the fewest people without health insurance, and—judging by Alex's visit to Kingman Reed—one of the most well-financed law enforcement programs in the country. Blackstone had put in place strict environmental regulations and used tax credits to attract nonpolluting businesses to his state. He'd also managed to calm racial tensions among the diverse groups that inhabited the state. Hispanics who'd lived there for over three hundred years, ever since the region was part of Mexico. Migrant workers who arrived each year to harvest onions, potatoes, and piñon beans. Blacks in the major cities, an influx of Vietnamese in some of the suburbs, and that most vocal of minorities, Caucasians. Not to mention the sixteen independent Indian nations that operated within his borders.

On the screen, they were talking about Blackstone's best-selling book, *The American Way*, which claimed that American resourcefulness and innovation had their roots in Native American culture. Blackstone told the interviewer, "In my view, world problems can best be addressed by an indigenous view."

Controversial at first, the book was rapidly embraced by everyone from astrology lovers to business execs. When Oprah declared that following its wisdom made her calmer and thinner, the sales went through the roof.

The book was old news, though, and now came the kicker. Blackstone planned to throw his hat in the ring for the U.S. presidency. Though the election was a year and a half away, and people were generally happy with the incumbent President Cotter, Blackstone was already making a strong showing in the opinion polls. Vegas handicappers likened the governor to the young Jack Kennedy. Voters would get past his Native American heritage, just as they'd overcome their initial opposition to Kennedy's Catholicism.

The political editor of *Newsweek* was on the screen, talking about how people of all walks of life could relate to the message in the book. In describing what made America special, Blackstone was talking about *them*—in stark contrast to President Cotter, a Connecticut blue blood who was more difficult for folks to identify with. And despite his family fortune, Cotter might not be able to raise sufficient money to challenge a rival within his own party. The Indian gaming industry had deep pockets and was throwing its support to its native son. In the twenty years since the U.S. Supreme Court had decided that tribes, as sovereign nations, could legalize gambling, the Indian gaming industry had gone from profits of $100 million a year to $18 billion, a total that surpassed Las Vegas and Atlantic City combined. And there was plenty more where that came from. Of the 562 tribes in the United States, fewer than half had embraced gambling. If they all came on board, Blackstone could run a campaign with limitless funds.

The interviewer ended the segment on a more disturbing note. Red Rights, a radical Native American advocacy organization, was also supporting Blackstone. Its members expected that once he was elected, he would issue a presidential decree assuring that all previous treaties with the Native Americans would be given full legal force and effect. They wanted Blackstone to return America to the red man.

Alex shut off the television when the segment ended. She thought of the excitement that electrified the country when the first woman and the first black man were vying for the Democratic nomination for President. But everyone had known that, once in office, either would attend to business as usual. Elias Lightfoot Blackstone was a different animal entirely. He might not just chart a new future for the country; he might rewrite the country's past. She liked what she'd heard from him in the interview but, with this much at stake, she wondered about the measures people might take to keep him out of the race.

CHAPTER   13

The next morning, Alex found Chuck at his usual spot in the L-shaped conference room that served as the command center for forensic cases. He
turned to her, ready to drop what he was working on to respond to any questions.

"Go ahead, finish up," she said. She walked toward the espresso machine
in the room, a holdover from a previous time when the now-defunct commu-
nications department of the AFIP inhabited this space. Colonel Wiatt, the
new head of the AFIP, had no interest in getting media coverage for their activities. He was the original believer in the saying "No news is good news."

Alex made herself a cup of heavy black coffee and sipped. It had a slight
taste of cardamom. Coffee was a real perk of the job when she worked with
Major Dan Wilson and his forensic team. Almost every week, a different soldier on the base came back from an incredible coffee-producing venue—
Guatemala, Italy, Tanzania, or the AFIP outpost in Hawaii, which retrieved
and identified recently recovered remains of soldiers who'd been killed in action during World War II, the Korean Conflict, or the Vietnam War. Many
of the soldiers had worked with Dan across the years and owed him their
lives or their reputations. They knew of his major coffee jones and would
bring him back beans. The cabinet above the espresso machine was a regular
United Nations of caffeine.

Chuck finished the e-mail he was writing, then turned to Alex, who was
perched on the corner of his desk.

"Are you swamped?" she asked.

"Captain Pringle's new satellite program is up and running and Major

48

Wilson's investigations aren't too challenging at the moment. What have you got?"

"I'm investigating two deaths," she said.

"Homicide? Accident?"

"Too soon to tell. Definitely not natural."

"How can I help, ma'am?"

Alex cringed at his unwillingness to call her by her first name. She tilted her head as if chastising him.

"Yeah, I know," he said. "I can't get out of this whole Southern gentleman thing."

"Okay, just so it's not because of some age thing. I'm not that much older than you." She held up a photo of Ted Silliman.

"Looks like the guy whose body went missing from the morgue."

Alex was surprised. How did Chuck know about that? "You helping Dan on this?"

He nodded.

She tried to sound casual. "What have you got so far?"

Chuck regarded her for a moment. She realized that he was wary of breaking protocol with an unauthorized disclosure. She leaned toward him. "I was in the morgue when they discovered the theft. I know the mortuary's been stonewalling."

The Southerner relaxed. "The driver who picked up the body checked out. So Major Wilson's trying to find another angle. He's looking into Agent Silliman's life in Las Vegas and the District."

Today is looking up, thought Alex. First, great coffee. And now Dan. A DEA cover-up would be less likely if he were involved. "I'm trying to figure out what killed him," said Alex. "He died in the same city, the same day, with the same swelling as the guy whose image you reconstructed."

Chuck shook his head. "That's no way to go."

"I think it's some sort of immune reaction. I want to cast a wide net and search all New Mexican death records for the past week. See if anyone else had similar symptoms."

"Easy enough. Death records are computerized."

"The next part is a little trickier. Any cardiac arrest, liver failure, or immune reaction at any New Mexico hospital during that same period."

"Not sure I can get access to that."

Alex slid down off the desk. "Get up for a second." She sat in his seat, signed in under her name on his computer, and explained. "I'm on the intergovernmental commission on bioterrorism, remember? We've got access to all hospital records to spot trends that might be the early warning of an attack."

He whistled under his breath. "That's some heavy duty clearance."

Alex knew the assignment sounded more impressive than it was. So far, the commission had met only a half-dozen times. Martin Kincade, the director of Homeland Security, was the chair—efficient, but a bit too arrogant for her taste. He was a stocky, bald man in his sixties, and looked like he could be a general in the Army. But the only "General" on his résumé was General Electric, one of the many businesses he'd presided over before his political appointment. Based on her dealings with him, Alex had no doubt that he had run those companies with the strident measures of a boot camp.

But few of the other agencies involved took the commission seriously. Most of the federal terrorism watchdogs were focused on tracking dirty bombs, not lethal bugs. Even the National Institutes of Health failed to recognize the group's importance, even though it—along with Alex—would be responsible for the medical response if bioterrorism erupted. Rather than appointing one of its infectious disease prima donnas, like Robert Gallo, the codiscoverer of the AIDS virus, NIH sent a post-doc to the commission gatherings, a guy just two years out of his Ph.D. program in virology.

Alex opened her fanny pack and pulled out a small card with a twenty-digit alphanumeric password. She'd never used it before and the gravity of the situation hit her with each click of the keys.

Once her access code was accepted, she gave Chuck back his seat. He did the search and said, "The numbers are high, 5,000 admissions. Any thoughts on how to narrow the search?"

"Could you create a program that eliminates the ICD 9 codes 995 and 401?" Alex knew that she didn't want cases with anaphylactic shock due to allergy or people with a history of hypertension. "This immune response is rapid onset, with no previous symptoms."

"How do you want the data when I'm done?"

"List of patient ID numbers, so I can review their complete medical records. Then I'll be able to give you more defined search parameters. After that, I might ask you to run a few other states."

Chuck nodded. "One thing about you, ma'am, you don't think small."

CHAPTER 14

As Alex was walking back to her lab, her cell phone vibrated and she scrutinized the screen—a 202 area code with a number she didn't recognize. "Alex Blake," she said, pausing in the hallway to take the call.

"Hey, Castro Baxter here."

She smiled, which caused a passing female secretary to raise an eyebrow and flash her a smile. Boy, thought Alex, I'd be terrible at poker. I've got tells coming out of my ears.

"What's up?" she asked.

"I've got zip on Waverly Pharmaceuticals," he said. "Any chance you could you use your doctor connections to nose around?"

"Sure, give me a few hours to see what they're working on and then I'll call you back."

"How about dinner instead? We missed out in Taos."

"Sounds great."

Alex expected him to pick an out-of-the-way bar, but he suggested the Old Ebbitt Grill, a D.C. landmark known for its crab cakes and the high level political horse trading that crossed its white tablecloths. When she hung up the phone, she started humming. He'd surprised her again. And she liked that in a man.

They split the crab cakes as appetizers and sipped a Chardonnay. Castro was attentive, touching Alex on the arm and asking repeatedly if there was anything else she'd like the waiter to bring. He leaned close to her as he spoke.

His eyes sought out hers and he didn't break that bond except when his training took hold and he scrutinized the people entering the room.

He seemed in no hurry to pump Alex for information about Waverly, and she enjoyed the feeling of being on a date. During her two years with Luke, her previous boyfriend, they'd gone out to fancy dinners maybe three times. Four if you counted the one they'd had at the White House after Alex helped solve a particularly dramatic case. Mostly they ate bar food at places where Luke's band was playing or he cooked his specialties, white bean chicken chili or steak on the grill.

"Anything new on the incident near the longhouse?" she asked him.

Castro looked away, seemingly embarrassed by his failure. Then he turned back to her. "Nothing. And no leads on the mystery woman who paid for Ted's cremation. I even went to the mortuary with photos of female DEA agents to see if it was one of them. The manager gave me the runaround, so I followed the clerk home. She looked at the photos, but didn't recognize anyone."

"It's pretty bad when you don't trust your own agency," Alex said.

"Tell me about it," Castro said. "Now I'm second-guessing every order. Like why did they pull me off Ted's case and order me back to D.C.?"

"Don't tell me you're on desk duty?" She thought of the fire in his eyes and the tight energy in his body when he'd stalked into the DEA conference room arguing with his boss. He definitely was a street guy, not a desk guy.

"They're not that dumb. They know I'd be out the door if they pulled that sort of stunt. No, I can't tell if they're jerking with me or playing it straight. The assignment makes sense. There's a date rape drug called J flooding California and Nevada. Now it's hit the District."

"How does it work?"

"It's like a combo mickey and souped-up Viagra," Castro said, clenching his right hand. "Heavy sedation for the first thirty minutes and then the woman becomes a raging sex machine. Lots of women fail to press charges because they feel like the sex was their idea—even when it gets violent and mutilating."

Alex shuddered. A year earlier, she and Barbara had attended a tribute to Eve Ensler, creator of *The Vagina Monologues*. As she does at many of her performances, Eve asked women to stand if they had been the victims of violence. A sea of women rose to their feet. When they sat down, she asked the same question about rape. A few women stood, but then slowly, almost with embarrassment, one by one other women joined them. Eve talked about how some women were afraid to stand because they'd never mentioned the rape, even to their best friends. Or they saw someone from their office and didn't trust that person to keep their secret.

As Eve continued speaking, more women rose. One-quarter of the audience was now on its feet. Without looking at Alex, Barbara finally stood up. When she sat back down, Alex took her hand. But afterward, they never spoke of that night.

"Those poor women," Alex said. She reached over and touched Castro's clenched fist.

He relaxed his hand, and used it to punctuate his words. "Some of the girls were as young as fourteen. They never saw it coming."

Younger than Lana, Alex thought. "Mixed in a drink?"

"Cocktail of choice is Jack Daniel's spiked with J. Scumbags using it call it a J Jack. They brag about how many women they jacked."

Alex stared into her wineglass and imagined women getting knocked out by a casual cocktail and coming to with a rapist. She looked up at him.

The intensity of his expression sent a shiver down her spine. He folded his hands on the table and stared at them, then looked up again at Alex.

"This drug," she said. "Sounds like an important assignment."

"Yeah, but it's hard to get my mind off Ted."

The waiter came by and picked up their empty appetizer plates. Alex pulled out her folder of research on Waverly Pharmaceuticals. "I checked pending FDA applications and they've got an antihypertensive in the works and an erectile dysfunction drug for men undergoing prostate cancer treatment."

"Maybe that's it. Maybe the Mob hired him to come up with another J."

"They wouldn't need a top scientist to do that. You can just troll the U.S. patent database. The formula for Viagra and other recipes for erections and arousal are available for anyone to see."

"A regular scientific equivalent of the Playboy Channel, huh?"

Alex nodded and turned to another page of the materials she'd brought. "Here's what's in the pipeline. They've hired a new medical director—Dr. Chris Renfrew—who's got some major NIH grants. Early stage research on a diabetes cure and a potential immunization against obesity."

"Give me a break. He's got an idea for a shot that would let you eat whatever you want and not get fat?"

"Pretty much. Although in his NIH grant request, he didn't describe it quite that way." She flipped through her papers until she found an article from the *American Medical News* about his research. "He says it's for people with family histories of morbid obesity and a clear genetic predisposition. Not just your average couch potato."

She handed the article to Castro so he could read it himself. But his eyes didn't descend below the photo of Dr. Renfrew. "Son of a bitch," he said. "That's Frankie DiBondi's driver."

Just then the waiter arrived with her sea scallops and his trout. Alex waited until he left and then asked, "Are you sure? You were pretty far away at the quarry."

"True, but I was up close and personal on a chair in the lobby when he checked into the hotel. Now that I think about it, he seemed a little nervous at the time. Not your usual wiseguy."

"So why does a Vegas Mob guy deliver a pharmaceutical company executive to a longhouse?"

"That's question one. Question two is whether he ever came back."

"I'll call the company in the morning and ask to speak with him," Alex said. "If I give enough research mumbo jumbo, they'll probably put me through."

"And tomorrow I'll get some of our financial guys to check if he's in debt to the Mob. Maybe he's designing a few drugs for them."

"That doesn't explain the longhouse. You said yourself that your Vegas snitch had never seen him with DiBondi before. And why would the Mob share him with our buddies from the Hakuna Makata tribe?"

Castro cracked a smile. "Hey, I'm grateful for your help. If you hadn't insisted on seeing the scene, we wouldn't know about Renfrew."

When the check came, they both reached for it. His hand touched hers and the physical contact pleased Alex.

"Let me get it," he said. "For Ted."

Alex normally would have insisted on splitting the bill. She had a strong view about not being dependent on anyone and also not owing anyone. But he looked like a man who hadn't grown up with much and for whom this might be important. Plus, she wouldn't mind owing him a little something.

She could think of a lot of things worse than figuring out how to pay him back.

"Thanks," she said as they walked out of the restaurant. She hesitated before heading off to the Metro to go home. "Can I buy you a drink down the street?"

"Think you'll find someplace that sells your drink of choice here? Looks like a pretty fancy neighborhood."

"Hey, what have you got against Old Weller? Higher proof, cheaper price tag. Plus, my PDA's got a map of all the Old Weller watering spots in a five-state region. My equivalent of the Hollywood map of the homes of the stars."

She took his hand and led him a few blocks into a short, alleylike street. The bar she chose was dark, smoky, and anonymous. It was the type of place where old-time politicos made deals and young professionals avoided because it served peanuts instead of sushi.

Castro led Alex to the bar and gave their order to the bartender, a man in his sixties with jowls like a bulldog's. "I almost forgot," said Alex, pulling Chuck's handiwork out of her saddlebag and handing the picture to Castro. "This is what we think the John Doe looked like. Do you recognize him? Could Ted have known him?"

Staring at the photo, Castro rattled off what he remembered. "This guy was in the park the night we followed DiBondi. Ted never got within twenty feet of him."

"You're sure it's the same guy?"

"That's my job," he said. "I walk into these undercover buys with a roomful of people. I have a few seconds to scope out who's got the real juice, and who's the weak one if I need an exit strategy."

Alex looked at him skeptically. He hadn't flouted a big ego so far, but this was hard to believe.

He picked up on her doubt. He faced the bar, with his back to the room, and began to rattle off a description of the people behind him. "Guy drinking alone in the corner's got a knife scar above the right eyebrow. He's the one to watch here, because he's not about to let that happen again. The couple at the table to the right of him—they're not married, she's being too attentive. She might work for him. She came from the office and didn't have time to change out of her work clothes so she made up for it by putting on extra lipstick. The three guys near the exit work around here, probably in some bank or insurance company. Their suits are off-the-rack and the one who keeps looking at his watch is trying to catch a train out of Union Station to commute home. He's the only one drinking wine at the table. The other two have beers in front of them."

"Okay, I give," said Alex. She stood behind him and put her hands over his eyes. "Now how would you describe me?"

"Blond, heart-shaped face. Underestimate her at your peril. Shield your balls and your heart around this lady." He reached up and moved her hands away from his eyes. "Especially your heart," he said as he turned to face her. He leaned forward, intimately closing the distance between them. "Mighty fine kisser, too." They were close enough that his words created puffs of breath on her forehead.

"All in the line of duty for you," she said, looking up at him.

He shook his head and spoke quietly. "The line of duty would have meant putting my arm around your shoulders when the Indian arrived."

He pulled her close to him, tucking her under his chin. She smelled his aftershave and felt his heart beating. "Let's get out of here," he said.

She reached into her fanny pack and paid the tab. He took her hand and led her to the street. "I'll drive you home," he said.

They'd barely made it halfway down the block when his pager went off. He abruptly let go of her hand. After reading the string of words and digits across the screen, he said, "I've gotta go. A couple more girls have been jacked."

He put his hand up to flag down a cab.

"I'm more of a Metro girl," Alex said.

A cab careened to the curb in front of them. Castro handed the driver a $20 bill and opened the door for Alex. "And I'm good for my word. I promised you a ride home and here you go."

She was tempted to kiss him goodbye, but his entire face had changed its look. The playfulness and longing that had emerged in the bar had been washed away by a tightly coiled determination, his laugh lines erased by a chiseled resolve. "Good luck," she said as she slipped into the cab. But he was dialing his phone; their evening had already ended.

CHAPTER 15

Early the next morning in her lab, Alex entered the glass-walled cubicle that housed her desk and computer. She'd had a hand in designing the space and had located her office in the inner recesses of her large rectangular laboratory, rather than down the hall, to be close to her scientific experiments. She'd chosen two glass walls for the square in the far corner that was the inner office so she could easily glance over to see how far along her machines were in their sequencing efforts.

Alex sat at her desk and thought of how she'd described the wonders of the patent database to Castro. She double-checked that she was correct. On the uspto.gov website, she typed in "sildenafil," the chemical name for Viagra. She found U.S. Patent No. 5,955,611, titled "Process for Preparing Sildenafil." Sure enough, the British inventors Peter James Dunn and Albert Shaw Wood laid out in eight pages exactly how to make the drug. A scientific race was now on to find a drug for women that functioned like Viagra, but it was proving difficult. Experiments were going on with a nasal spray that acted on the central nervous system, but most women didn't respond to it. Technically, it was easy to arouse men—you just needed a drug that directed blood to the penis. Women, speculated psychiatrists, needed to be emotionally aroused as well.

Alex felt that the arousal debate wasn't all that good at capturing the desires of women like herself. The psychiatrists assumed that all women were wired the same. They wanted love notes and roses. Alex, though, was primed for sex most of the time. And rather than a bouquet of roses, a good-looking lead guitarist doing a bluesy Slash solo of a Guns N' Roses song would do just fine, she thought.

She trolled further in the patent database to look at the new approaches to women's sexuality. One, listed as coming out of Stanford, was a mix of benzodiazepine derivative, along with a variant of yohimbine, and cantharidin. Alex was amused by the last ingredient. An odorless and colorless substance first isolated from the blister beetle in 1810, it was known in legends and short stories as Spanish fly.

How geek can I get, thought Alex. I haven't even had my second cup of coffee and I'm searching through patents.

But the patent database might provide insight into the disturbing connection between Dr. Renfrew's appearance in Taos and the deaths of two bystanders. She entered the word *Waverly* in the database and got a list of twenty patents with formulas for drugs that Waverly would soon be marketing.

As she read each of the patents, nothing about their chemical makeup raised any red flags about immune reactions. The background section of each patent chronicled the results of the company's research on human volunteers. A few of the research participants in the studies experienced low level side effects—nausea, dizziness, and heart palpitations. None of these drugs seemed capable of a fatal toxicity.

The patent applications dealt with Waverly drugs that had already been found to be effective. Renfrew's diabetes and obesity studies were still in the experimental stage and might involve testing multiple new compounds. Since the studies hadn't yet paid off with a new product, the patent database didn't list the current compounds he was experimenting with.

Alex knew how tough it would be to find out how the new research was being conducted and what risks the subjects were facing. She'd been teaching at Berkeley when the scandal broke about Jesse Gelsinger, an 18-year-old boy who'd died in a University of Pennsylvania experiment testing a new gene therapy. The informed consent form Jesse signed didn't disclose the fact that two monkeys had died after receiving the gene therapy vector that the researchers were about to give him. A Congressional investigation revealed that other researchers had also covered up the risks of using that vector. Disregarding federal rules, gene therapy researchers had reported only 39 of the 691 deaths and illnesses that their experimental subjects had suffered. And when the researchers *had* told the Food and Drug Administration about the devastation linked to their gene therapy research, they convinced the

FDA that such information should be considered a "trade secret" and not disclosed to the public.

Alex fanned out the files about Renfrew in front of her, including his proposal for a six-million-dollar diabetes project that ultimately was funded by the NIH. She took a final close look. The proposal said nothing about experiments in New Mexico, which made it even odder that he'd shown up in Taos.

She needed to talk to Renfrew himself. Maybe he'd be willing to tell her more about the research. At 9:00 A.M., she called Waverly and was told Renfrew was not there. She asked to be connected with his lab. She thought she'd have better luck tracking down Renfrew if she avoided contact with the Waverly administrators and got in touch with one of the post-docs, the post-doctoral fellows, who typically performed the experiments in scientists' labs. A man answered the phone, "Dr. Renfrew's lab," reminding her of the two years she'd spent in a genetics lab during graduate school, speaking her mentor's name with the same combination of awe and annoyance. It had been strange when, as a faculty member at Berkeley, she'd first heard one of her own graduate students state, "Dr. Blake's lab." Her immediate thought at the time had been, I'm not in Kansas anymore. The pressures to break new scientific ground were wrapped up in that three-word greeting over the phone.

"I'm trying to get in touch with Dr. Renfrew."

"He's not in."

"When do you expect him?"

"Not sure."

Alex wondered how she could wrestle information from this taciturn post-doc. She looked down at the diabetes proposal, noting the name of his NIH program administrator. "I'm Victoria Goodman, his grants administrator at NIH," Alex said, crossing her fingers behind her back while she told this fib. She tried to picture Victoria and imagined her with long blond hair, jeans, and a black turtleneck, looking remarkably like Alex herself. It somehow made Alex feel that borrowing the woman's name wasn't so big a transgression.

"Yes, Ms. Goodman," sputtered the post-doc. Alex imagined he was cursing himself, wondering why he'd picked up the phone, rather than someone else in the lab.

"Is there any way you can contact him?"

"He's somewhere out in the field for the next two weeks. Something about basic botany research. He didn't leave any numbers."

Alex tried to phrase the next question so that it didn't sound odd. "When was he last in touch?"

"Friday. He worked in the lab as usual. Ah, things are going great guns with our project. We've identified a new receptor for insulin in the cells."

"And you're complying with all the terms of the grant?"

"Yes," he gulped.

Alex felt sorry for putting him through this. "I'll call back in a few days. If he calls in for any reason, find out how I can get in touch with him."

"Shall I have him call you at NIH?"

Thinking quickly, Alex said, "No. I'll be in a study section meeting the next few days." Any scientist would know what that was—a two-day meeting in which NIH personnel, aided by top scientists, determined who should be on the federal dole. Nobody would interrupt a program director when she was handing out bucks to researchers.

"Okay," he said. "Let me know if you need anything else."

But the nervousness in his voice made Alex think that the post-doc might never answer the lab phone again. And with the incident at the longhouse, she wondered if he'd seen the last of his boss.

When she hung up, she pulled her cell phone out of her fanny pack and scrolled for Castro's number. While it rang, she stood up and started pacing her lab. When he answered, she could hear the clink of dishes in the background.

"I'm at the hospital cafeteria," he said.

"How are the women who were attacked?" She walked in front of the sequencers, past the refrigerator, then turned around. Movement comforted her.

"First one died from internal bleeding, barely out of high school."

"Which school?" she asked, stopping dead in her tracks.

"Holy Trinity. What does it matter?"

A Catholic school in a black neighborhood, just like Lana's. "I've got a friend that age."

"If I had a daughter, I wouldn't let her out of the house until she was thirty years old and trained to kill by Mossad."

"Any leads yet?" she asked, walking across the lab floor again.

"Nothin'. The other victim is unconscious after her surgery. A female agent will sit by her bed until she wakes up."

"Good luck," she said. "In the meantime, here's what I know about Renfrew. He hasn't been in his lab since the day before the longhouse incident. And he's not expected back for a couple of weeks."

"Thanks. I'm working it from my end. If he's still alive, he's bound to use his credit cards or cell phone. Then I'll have him."

"Let me know how I can help." She stopped again and leaned against the lab counter, elbows on surface, propping up her head as she spoke. "And thanks for the dinner. I had a wonderful time."

Alex held her breath, waiting for a response. But she could hear someone in the background, a doctor probably, talking to Castro.

"Sorry, Alex, gotta go."

She hung up the phone, feeling slightly silly about having mentioned their dinner. Why did the start of a relationship have to be so baffling and awkward? And was she jumping the gun? Were they headed for a relationship or were they just a couple of colleagues out for a drink? She thought about how Castro looked at her. No, there was definitely something there.

Back in her inner office, she switched on the computer and saw the list of eighty-five patient IDs from Chuck. More than she'd expected. It would take all day to analyze the records.

She started with the adults because both Ted and the John Doe were adults. Since all met her broad criteria for an inflammatory disease, she looked at each person's medical history and admission summary. Looking at the charts gave her an idea.

She dialed Castro again. "Are you still at the hospital?"

"Yeah."

"See if you can have them send me some blood and urine samples from the dead girl."

"Isn't this a little out of your jurisdiction?"

"Maybe there's a connection. You and Ted were following DiBondi because of the J. There might be a link between that drug and what killed Ted."

61

"Doubtful, but I'll see what I can do."

They hung up and she was frustrated again. Well, what did she expect from the man? Romance, plus a willingness to buy her half-baked forensic theories? Well, yeah.

She spent the next nine hours reading medical charts but didn't find any with symptoms that matched the two men who'd died in Taos. She hit the vending machines for a Coke and bag of Cheetos—her idea of a nourishing dinner—and then returned to her office.

By seven o'clock her neck was stiff from poring over her computer screen trying to decipher the doctors' handwriting in the PDFs of the medical records. She was reaching her right hand up to massage her left shoulder when her cell phone rang. She was determined to continue her work and ignore the call, but then she noticed that it was Barbara's daughter, Lana. The girl's phone, designed by Grant, translated what the other person said into typed letters so that the deaf teenager could read it.

"Hi, sweetie," Alex said. "What's up?"

"I have a genetics question."

"Shoot." Alex was prepared to launch into a discussion of Mendel's peas, autosomal recessive disorders, or even RNA transcription, depending on what this high school junior was studying.

"How good are the prenatal tests at predicting deafness?"

Alex took a deep breath. Could Lana be pregnant? She wasn't quite sure what to say.

"Alex, the phone seems to be having a problem. I'm not getting any text. Could you repeat what you just said?"

Of course, Alex had said nothing, but she began a tentative explanation. "It depends what the cause of the deafness is. A recent study links mutations in the myosin VIIA gene on chromosome 11 to deafness. You can do tests for that in a fetus."

"What sort of decisions do people make once they learn the fetus is deaf?"

Alex's heart skipped a beat. This was a profound question, particularly when posed by someone who was deaf. Most parents chose to abort deaf fetuses. "It depends," Alex said.

"Not responsive," said Lana.

"You've been hanging around that lawyer mom too much."

Alex looked at her computer screen, at the long list of the names of children whose medical records met her criteria, and thought of her plan to go through them that night. She felt bad about abandoning those children, but didn't she have a responsibility for the most important child in her life?

"I'm just finishing up here," Alex said. "How about letting this doctor make a house call and explain the medical background to you?"

"Sounds great. And, oh, one more thing—"

Alex worried about what Lana would bring up next.

"Could you stop for burgers on the way? Mom's in one of her megadieting phases, which means her growing girl is being starved to death."

"Will do," Alex said. "See you in forty-five minutes." She wondered whether the growing girl was eating for two.

CHAPTER 16

Alex called in an order for two Kobe burgers at a high-end restaurant on the way to Barbara's apartment. If she was going to have a heart-to-heart with Lana, she didn't feel like she should do it over some McDonald's or Burger King special.

Barbara opened the door, surprised. It hadn't occurred to Alex that Lana wouldn't have told her mom that she was on the way. "I got a call from the Department of Child Protective Services that you're starving a young girl to death," she said.

Barbara laughed. "Did she tell you that the salad I forced her to eat had grilled salmon, strawberries, and gorgonzola cheese? The entire football team would have gotten full on that dinner."

"Ah, Barbara, you are a great mom, we all know that. But you don't seem to understand that grease is a required daily food group."

Alex looked over at the small table in the living room that served as the dinner table and also as Barbara's desk. Her laptop and papers covered its surface.

"Guess I'll have to eat in the kid's room."

"Fair enough, but you're not getting by without a toll." Barbara took the bag out of Alex's hand, walked to the kitchen, and pulled three plates off the shelf.

"Since we've got a minute alone, I can give you my latest complaint about Grant."

"Pinched a female Rear Admiral, did he?" Barbara had already sent the man to three sessions of sexual harassment training.

Alex shook her head. "Not this time. Unless you consider leering with intent to maul an actionable offense. I'm more troubled by the software he's working on."

Barbara took the Kobe burgers out of their boxes and cut a quarter off one of the towering sandwiches. "I'm on it. Grant doesn't think I know what he's up to, but there's a reason I have a candy bowl on my desk. Gets generals, secretaries, and Grant's elves all to stop in and chat."

Alex nodded. "I wouldn't see you half as much as I do were it not for the Babe Ruth bars and Dove dark chocolates."

"And here I thought it was my scintillating conversation. And my willingness to nurse you back to health whenever you put yourself in harm's way."

"You're the best, Barbara, no doubt about it."

"Grant's project's got me boning up on Kyllo v. United States—the U.S. Supreme Court case on thermal imaging," she explained.

"Ah, where cops got a heat scan of a house to find evidence that the poor slob was using high-intensity lamps to grow marijuana inside. Didn't the courts say that was okay?"

"You're right, to a point. The trial court and the federal Ninth Circuit Court of Appeals held that scanning was not a warrantless search in violation of the Fourth Amendment. Their logic was that the defendant had shown no expectation of privacy because he hadn't attempted to conceal the heat emanating from his home. But, here's the rub: The Supreme Court reversed."

"Why? The cops didn't enter the house."

Barbara took a few steps into the living room and pulled two file folders out of her briefcase. She opened one and turned to the decision. "The Supreme Court said, 'Where, as here, the Government uses a device that is not in general public use, to explore details of the home that would previously have been unknowable without physical intrusion, the surveillance is a "search" and is presumptively unreasonable without a warrant.'"

Barbara looked up at Alex and continued. "Other than your general disdain for Grant, what's got your goat on this project? You're not exactly the poster child for privacy yourself. I seem to remember you testing a certain Congressman's DNA without his consent."

Alex tapped her foot on the floor in front of her, slightly chagrined at how quickly she'd leaped to suspect her then-lover in a previous case. "He left his toothbrush in my apartment. Besides, no harm no foul. He was the only man in America with perfect dental hygiene, rinsed the toothbrush off thoroughly after he used it, no DNA in sight. If you remember correctly, he later consented to give me blood for the forensics."

"Batting your big blues at a suspect does not a warrant make," Barbara said as she handed two plates to Alex and fetched her two Cokes from the refrigerator.

"At least I asked," Alex said. "Grant's peeping into people's bedrooms with his new gadget."

Barbara's expression turned serious. "What do you mean?"

"Today he showed me the thermal image of a couple making love."

"Oh man, we might have a Griswold problem."

"Griswold?"

"A U.S. Supreme Court case which warned against police 'searching the sacred precincts of the marital bedroom.'"

Alex considered those words for a moment. "Nothing much sacred—or sinful—going on in my bedroom lately." Not since Luke had moved permanently to California the previous month. He'd mumbled about staying in touch, but Alex knew that her schedule wouldn't permit a bicoastal relationship. Plus, a musician—even one whose venues tended to small clubs and coffeehouses rather than stadiums—had too many temptations thrown in his path. She'd had a fabulous weekend of nonstop goodbye sex with him before he left, wished him well, and relegated him to her mental museum diorama of old lovers. Leonard Hayflick, the noted scientist, had proven that cells divided for a maximum of fifty-two times before they died out—unless they were put in a special culture medium. Alex's limit to relationships was two years. Despite all her scientific miracles, she hadn't gone beyond the Hayflick limit in her love life.

"Okay," said Barbara. "I'll come up with a plan to handle the Peeper."

"Great," said Alex as she left the kitchen. She walked into Lana's room carrying the feast. She pulled a comfortable old armchair closer to Lana's desk and they both balanced their plates on their laps and stashed the Coke cans on a small stretch of exposed wooden desk. She glanced at Lana's belly, which seemed as flat as ever. Lana was wearing a T-shirt with a sepia photo of four Native Americans on horseback and the caption THE ORIGINAL

HOMELAND SECURITY. Alex marveled at how quickly anything in the news, from the alien to Red Rights, could be reflected in a shirt.

Alex cleared her throat and tried to ask in the most casual way, "Why your sudden interest in prenatal diagnosis?"

Lana hadn't noticed Alex's scrutiny of her tummy. She'd been watching Alex's mouth, not her eyes. To converse, she needed to read the other person's lips.

"I have to write an ethics paper for biology class. The teacher told us about a deaf couple who wanted prenatal screening to make sure that their child was deaf."

Alex had heard the case discussed at medical meetings. In general, doctors were appalled that the couple was seeking to assure a disability rather than to avoid one. "How do you feel about the parents?" Alex asked.

Lana maximized an icon and a website filled the computer screen. A banner asking WHO SHALL LIVE? ran across the page. With a few more clicks, Lana took Alex through a series of posts. "There's a lot of people on this website that say screening prenatally for the deafness gene and then aborting a deaf fetus is genocide. They say that the deaf are like an ethnic group. We have our own culture, our own language. Yet geneticists are trying to get rid of us."

Alex put her arms around Lana in a quick hug and then pulled back so Lana could see her mouth. "This geneticist loves you very much."

Lana, dissatisfied, started moving her hands. Even though she communicated to Alex by speaking, when she was upset, she underscored her words by signing. "Now you are going to tell me the issue is more complicated than I think."

Alex smarted. She might have said something close to that. About the importance of choice and people having the right to make varying decisions. "I can't imagine a world without you, Lana."

"What do you think Mom would have done if these genetic tests had been around when she got pregnant with me?"

Alex inhaled sharply. So that was the issue. It was not uncommon for teenagers to have a falling-out with their parents. One way of establishing independence was to undercut how much your parent loved you. "Why don't you talk to her about this?" Alex asked. "She's always been honest with you."

Lana seemed to relax. "I think she would have wanted me no matter what."

Alex nodded in strong agreement.

Then Lana returned to the computer. "But on this website, there's a lot of kids whose parents just dumped them when they learned they weren't perfect. Put them in institutions or foster care."

Although, as a geneticist, Alex had read widely in the disability rights literature, the posts she skimmed now were more vehement and angry. They seemed to feel in an all-out war with the "normals," as they called them with derision. "How did you find out about this website?"

"On my Face Space page, I listed disability as one of my interests." Lana clicked over to the page. "Over a thousand kids signed up within a week to be my friend. Lots of kids in wheelchairs or kids who can use a computer but their problem keeps them out of school. A lot of them blog on the Who Shall Live site."

Alex looked at the thumbnail photos of Lana's many friends. They were teens who weren't afraid of how they looked or came across. Unlike sites like match.com, where people took advantage of the Internet to make themselves appear prettier or more handsome than they did in person, the photos here were raw and bleak. A burn victim whose face was scarred and lopsided. A boy with an arm like a fin. Then Alex began to chastise herself. Who was she to judge a person bleak just because he or she didn't look like a magazine photo of a teen? She began to understand their need for a place to be themselves.

There were several photos of a good-looking African American male, around age 19. In one of them, he had a bottle of Jack Daniel's in his hand, and, as Alex looked closer, she noticed he had his arm around 16-year-old Lana. "Who's that?"

Lana immediately switched screens. "One of my friends, but don't worry, I wasn't drinking."

Alex moved her head close to Lana's to make sure the girl didn't miss a word she said. "Listen. Be really, really careful. There's a horrible date rape drug out there."

Lana's face turned angry. "You're just like Mom. You don't trust me."

Alex took the girl's hands. "That's not true, Lana. But rape is a fact of life for every woman. And there's a new set of drugs that make it a lot easier. You have to be careful about what you drink and who you're with."

Lana pulled her hands free. "I can't sign if you do that, Alex." She pointed to the paper she was working on. "I've got to go back to my home-work."

"Okay. When I get home, I'll e-mail you the scientific article about the myosin VIIA gene."

She said goodbye to Lana and then to Barbara. But on the drive back to the Curl Up and Dye, she obsessed about Lana's Face Space page. She was less troubled by the angry teens who were lashing out at the world than the older, good-looking guy who'd seemed to be paying more attention to the bottle of bourbon than to a rapt Lana.

CHAPTER 17

On her drive to work the next day, Alex heard an NPR interview with New Mexico governor Elias Lightfoot Blackstone. "We've got what we need right here in this country, with enormous resources if we use them wisely," Blackstone said. The newscaster pointed out how Blackstone was finding support not only from liberal environmentalists but also from conservatives who liked the idea of America not needing to rely on the rest of the world.

"Can you comment on Red Rights' call to violence?" the interviewer asked the governor.

"I don't believe in violence by the people. Or by the government. Especially when turned against the people, supposedly to protect some illusive concept of freedom."

"Do you oppose an agency like Homeland Security?"

"It's not a matter of a particular agency, but the philosophy behind it. We should not have to lose our freedom to protect our freedom."

At the office, Alex had a message from Dr. Kingman Reed. She called him back. "Hi there. I was just listening to your governor on the radio," Alex said. "What do you make of him?"

"He manages to cut through the crap and get things done. In the last administration, I petitioned the state a dozen times to get the equipment I needed. No success. But when Blackstone came in as governor, he called a meeting of state agency heads and asked, 'What do you need and why?' If you gave him a straight-up answer, he found a way to make it happen."

"I believe it. Your equipment is first rate."

"When the state funds weren't enough, Blackstone got a local gambling tribe to kick in some proceeds to buy two electrophesis machines."

Alex did the math. The price would have been around $300,000. Blackstone must have some clout to have pulled that off.

"Did you call about the John Doe?" she asked.

"Your composite photo did the trick. A newsstand owner knew him as Leroy. Said he'd shown up in Taos about six months earlier, wearing a Padres cap. San Diego Missing Persons identified him as Leroy Darven."

"What can you tell me about him?" Alex asked. She'd worked the Twin Towers bombing, beginning on September 13, dealing with families who'd brought combs and toothbrushes so that she could match remains found at the scene to their dead loved one's DNA. For everyone who was killed at the World Trade Center, she'd asked the relatives what they admired about that person. Alex was trained as a medical doctor, not a forensic investigator. She was accustomed to working with people who were alive, not dead. She got to know her patients. Now she longed for information about Leroy Darven.

"Next of kin was a much younger cousin," Reed said. "She seemed genuinely sad. Said when she was a young girl, he'd carved a jewelry box for her that she thought was the most beautiful thing in the world. Told me she was going to will it to her granddaughter when she died."

Alex thought about Leroy's lonely death and was glad he'd be remembered. "Let me know if the cops find anything interesting about his last days, like any new routines—like trips to a hospital."

"Will do."

"Especially any links to a pharmaceutical company called Waverly."

"The Taos police are all over this one. It's not often law enforcement gets to work on an extraterrestrial."

After she hung up, she thought of how the pharmaceutical company Eli Lilly had undertaken medical research on homeless people, some of whom had done it just to get shelter in the Lilly facility. Leroy might have participated in research, but that didn't explain Ted. She needed information about what Ted was up to in the weeks before the stakeout. Maybe he had a medical condition that led him to try a new drug. She'd ask Dan what he'd learned about the man. Despite what Castro had said, best friends didn't share everything.

A call from the front desk alerted her that the D.C. hospital had sent over blood and urine samples from the rape victim who'd ingested J. She processed the samples so that she could analyze them using her gas chromatography/ mass spectrometry equipment. The GC/MS identified chemicals by the unique mass-to-charge ratio of their ions. The output of the machine was a series of vertical lines showing the full-scan profile of the sample. Alex watched with anticipation as the computer-generated mass spectrum appeared. The onboard software quickly compared the spectrum with known compounds in its library and found that the sample contained benzodiazepine, a class of drug commonly used in date rape concoctions. Indeed, the woman's tissue dazzled with evidence of the drug, like a drunk reeked of liquor.

Alex phoned the pathologist. "Randy," she asked, "did you find any evidence of benzodiazepine in Ted Silliman's blood? Maybe Valium or Rohypnol?"

"That's part of our standard tox screen for street drugs, and he was clean. Why?"

"Hunch that didn't pay off. He was tracking that new date rape drug, J, for DEA, and I wondered if the drug had any role in his death."

"Sorry. Let me know how I can help. I still can't believe I got tricked out of the body."

"Hey, the driver was legit, and so was the mortuary. A lot of folks got tricked on this one."

Alex hung up, booted up her computer, and turned to the medical records of the children whom Chuck had identified the day before. A half dozen, ages 8 and 9, had been admitted to a hospital near Taos the previous Saturday and Sunday. They died of heart or kidney failure. Edema—inflammation—was noted in the charts. The swelling was not as extreme as in Ted's case, and the doctors had thought it was secondary to the organ failure, which itself causes edema.

After printing off the six records so that they were easier to flip through, Alex laid out the reports on the long steel-topped counter that ran across one wall of her laboratory. She sat on a rolling stool and thought about the six little bodies. If they had the same disease as Ted and Leroy, that would quadruple the death count, from two to eight.

Two might be a coincidence, but eight was entirely different. With two adult men, it might have been caused by contaminants in illegal drugs, like

Galloway of the DEA had suggested. But, if a previously unknown disorder was reaching 9-year-olds, a new disease might be running amok.

Alex felt like an archaeologist uncovering an ancient grave. She'd need to tread carefully not to miss anything that was important. With caution, she'd sift through the dust of these people's lives to figure out what was relevant.

She decided to compare all the children's records, page by page, to see if any patterns emerged. She turned to the first page of the first chart. Kristin was the young girl's name. She'd been in fourth grade. Alex turned to the second chart, Jonathan. Same age. Both their charts noted that, earlier in the year, they'd been inoculated with the required vaccines to enter fourth grade—a measles booster and typhus. Checking showed that the other children had, too.

Alex dug further into the medical records to see if they'd all been immunized with the same batch of vaccine. But no, the lot numbers of the vaccines were very different. She checked the Centers for Disease Control website but found no adverse event reports about the vaccines, nor any indication of a significant boost in childhood deaths over the past few weeks.

She compared addresses and zip codes. They were not from the same neighborhood, not even from the same state. Like Ted, they were tourists in Taos. She looked for something else that linked these kids. Under religion, each of the children was listed as Mormon. As she studied the records, she saw that the same person had admitted them all. An elder of the church, Michael Sullivan. It dawned on Alex. They must have been on a trip for Mormon youth during spring break.

Alex looked for other connections. Five had died in the hospital. But one had died in a park. She returned to her computer and called up a map of Taos and searched for a park by that name. It was the identical square in which Ted had stopped for a drink and Castro had seen Leroy. If this child had been exposed there, probably the others had as well. The deaths had occurred between 8:00 P.M. and 10:00 P.M. the previous Saturday. Whether due to an emerging infectious disease—or a deadly crime—all eight deaths that night in Taos were somehow connected to the same park.

Alex's hand trembled as she read through the medical records of other children who'd been admitted to hospitals near the park in the days after those six children had died. She was looking for information about any fatalities between the time of those deaths and when she had closed the fountain on her Taos trip three days later. During those three days, she'd found several dozen more children who had died in New Mexico, but all those deaths were explicable—SIDS, leukemia, child abuse, and accidents. The mystery disease had made a short, fatal appearance on a single day and then had disappeared with as much stealth as it had arrived.

She called Kingman Reed back and brought him up to date. He promised that public health workers would decommission the fountain and continue the analysis of the water. That fountain could be the link between the deaths.

Alex had begun this work to clear Ted's name. Now that she could connect his death to seven others, she could start making the case that he hadn't died of a cocaine overdose. But, with the death toll at eight, Alex's search was revealing more than she'd bargained for. Was it a one-shot event, or were there others, in a different city? And, if so, what was the cause?

Alex had to consider the possibility that a terrifying new disease was emerging. If that were the case, though, who's to say the disease had stayed within state lines? She thought about where next to look. California, she told herself. With legal and illegal border crossings, plus jets landing from Asia and South America, California would be a likely outbreak point if the hyperimmunity was caused by a newly emerging pathogen. And even if, contrary to Alex's theory, Galloway was right and the trigger was an impurity in illegal drugs, California had enough users for the reaction to have shown up there.

Convinced of the soundness of her plan, she thought of how to break it to Chuck that he'd be wading through more than three million hospitalizations in that state over the past year. Bribery, she figured. She went online and found a list of upcoming heavy metal concerts in the District. Perhaps two tickets to Apocalyptica would lessen the pain of the extensive search. She typed in her credit card number and then dialed Chuck. Even though it was 6:00 P.M. on a Saturday, he was at his desk. After describing what she wanted him to do, she asked if Dan was in the Task Force room.

"Not at the moment, ma'am," said Chuck. Then, in a more conspiratorial voice, he said, "Took off a minute ago with a pack of Camels."

CHAPTER 18

Alex found Dan standing outside the AFIP building, watching a group of new recruits jog around the base. He was using the end of one smoldering Camel to light another one.

Alex approached and stood in front of him. "You know, as a doctor, I have to remind you that smoking—"

"Fuggetaboutit, as they say. My great-grandfather's still smoking and working in a factory at the ripe old age of ninety-five. It's all in the genes." Dan smiled at her. "You should know that."

Well, Alex couldn't argue with Dan. In his late forties, he was in great shape. In a fight, the younger guys had nothing on him. She'd never heard him with a smoker's cough. "Suit yourself," she said.

They watched the formation of joggers in identical camouflage uniforms. Alex knew that you could determine the world theater of war by looking at what the new guys were wearing. This was jungle camo, not desert camo. Major Dan Wilson probably knew what part of the world was the next hot spot, but that wasn't what was on her mind.

"Wouldn't put it past you to come out and look at our fine soldiers," Dan said. "But somehow I don't think that's what brought you here."

Alex nodded. "Ted Silliman. That's what brought me out here. I'm trying to figure out how he died."

"Gruesomely."

"For sure. But another man and some kids died the same way."

Dan considered that fact, blowing smoke out of his mouth in a slow, pensive cloud. Alex continued, "What have you found out about Ted?"

The major flicked an ash. "We're in a pissing match with DEA over jurisdiction. They haven't let us get to anyone he worked with or find out about his cases. Galloway over there figured we'd drop the investigation if they tied us up enough. But we're trying other angles. Seeing where he spent his time and money, what he did the week before his death."

"Anything pop out?"

"Hey, people's lives aren't what they seem. Man had this bad-boy reputation—drinking problem, slept with strippers. And a week before his death he's checking into a Connecticut bed-and-breakfast with a sweet blonde that the owner says he was crazy about. They were regulars."

"What about trips to the doctors? Hospitals?"

"Haven't checked. Why?"

"The reaction he had, maybe it was the side effect of an experimental medication."

"A new drug that causes you to split out of your skin?" He threw down the cigarette butt and extinguished it with an efficient swivel of his shoe. Then he and Alex started walking back to the building.

"Yeah, it's a long shot, but, on that last stakeout, he and his partner were following a casino owner and his companion, a pharmaceutical executive. I've got a bad feeling that Waverly Pharmaceuticals is somehow involved."

Back in her lab, Alex turned on her computer to see if Chuck had e-mailed her anything from California. Of course, his return e-mail address was nowhere in sight. She'd given him, what, twenty minutes so far to come up with an answer?

She went on CNN.com to get the latest on the date rape drug. Most of the stories had to do with the white colleges it had hit the previous day—in New Haven and Charlottesville. Far less attention was given to the eight new cases in the District.

Alex wondered what steps she might take to protect Lana. At a medical meeting, she'd heard about a British company that marketed a product called Drink Detective, a fold-out card with strips on it that young women could use to test their drinks before they swallowed. Curious about where she could buy them, she called pharmacies and hospitals, but nobody had heard of it.

She was about to give up when she remembered one of Barbara's friends, a woman named Denise, who ran a self-defense club called Jane's House.

"This J Jack thing has women signing up for our courses in droves," Denise said when Alex reminded her that she'd gone there once with Barbara. "I tell them that learning to shoot or fight isn't a helluva lot help if they're semiconscious from a date rape drug."

"So what advice do you give them?"

"Hey, I'm a firearms instructor, not a social director. But I do tell them not to go out alone. The odds are better if you have a friend to get you out of there pronto if you start feeling woozy."

"I'm looking for a product called the Drink Detective, where you can test for date rape drugs in advance. Do you carry it?"

"We haven't got it, but I know a women's clinic near American University that does. Of course, it targets the common date rape drugs and is no help against anything exotic."

"I'd still like to check it out."

Denise gave Alex directions and told her to stop by sometime. "As I recall, you were just getting the hang of that .45 Colt when you were here last."

"I don't know if I'd quite call it getting the hang of it," Alex said. "All I managed to do was shoot the target in the balls."

Denise laughed and said goodbye.

CHAPTER   19

The manager of the clinic was an African American in her late fifties. When Alex told her what she wanted, the woman took her to a glass case with an odd assortment of items. Vitamins for pregnant women, condoms for women who didn't want to find themselves in that state, calcium tablets for post-menopausal women who didn't have to worry about pregnancy any longer. And, in the far right corner, stacks of Drink Detectives.

"How much are they?" Alex asked.

"Six fifty each or five dollars apiece if you get the pack of a dozen."

"Pricey," said Alex.

"It's costly to be vigilant. And you've got to use a new one for each drink."

"I'll take the dozen," Alex said.

The manager plunked a plastic-wrapped pack on the counter.

"Could you show me how they work? I'm buying them for a teenage friend and I want to explain it to her."

The woman reached back into the display case for a single Drink Detective. When she put it on top of the glass countertop, Alex thought the front of it looked like an ad for a 1950s cocktail party. There were two glasses of wine on it, a magnifying glass, and the name of the product in an outdated type font. The woman unsealed the package and handed it to Alex. It was like an extralarge matchbook that opened up to two squares of paper and an additional strip on the top half, with extensive instructions on the bottom half.

"She'll use this dropper to put some of her drink on the top square," the woman, said, pointing to the miniature dropper in the middle of the matchbook. "If it turns blue, it means the drink was spiked with the date rape drug GHB. An orange glow on the second square indicates ketamine. And, if stripes appear on the line, the drink contains one of the benzos like roofies or Valium."

"J's got a benzo in it, so it'll work for that, too," Alex said, handing the open packet back to the older woman.

But the manager wouldn't take it. "Keep it, blondie. You just might need one for yourself."

When she got back in her car, she dialed Barbara's home number, but got no answer. That meant Barbara was out, but since Lana couldn't hear the house phone, Lana might still be there. She dialed the girl's voice-to-text cell phone and got an enthusiastic "Hi."

"You up for a visit by an old—as in thirtysomething-year-old—friend?"

"Sure. Mom's at a bar association meeting and told me I could order in deep dish pizza. If you get here soon enough there might even be some left."

"You know how I drive. I'll be there before you can finish the next piece."

With her homework spread out across the small table in the living room, Lana looked like a younger version of Barbara. Both had the same determination and grace, even though Barbara wore skirts and crisp shirts, while her daughter favored jeans and hoodies. Lana might be at the age where even the thought of having a mother could rub her the wrong way, but everything wise and wonderful about the sixteen-year-old came from her mom.

Alex worked her way through two pieces of the heavenly pizza before she came to the point of her visit. After she put the dirty dishes in the sink, she sat back down and said, "Lana, did you hear about the girl from Holy Trinity who died?"

The girl nodded. "That was horrible."

"Well, I've been thinking of how you could protect yourself." Alex took the Drink Detective packet out of her briefcase, put it on the table in front of Lana, and began to explain how it worked.

Lana pushed the shrink-wrapped pile back to Alex. "You and Mom don't give me enough credit. You think I can't take care of myself."

"Lana, it's not about you. It's like driving. It's about what the other guy will do. That's who I don't trust."

"Alex, there's no way I'm going to use this in front of my friends," she said, pointing to her ears. "They think I'm weird enough already."

Alex thought about the women whom Castro had described. Young as fourteen. "Please, Lana."

Lana shook her head. "I know my friends. We've been together since, like, second grade."

Alex moved closer to Lana. "What about the guy on your Face Space page? He's too old to have been in second grade with you."

Lana blushed. "He's a friend of a friend."

"Think about what I'm saying, Lana. Promise me."

Alex stood to leave and Lana got up and put her arms around her surrogate aunt. "I'll think about it," she said.

Alex kissed Lana on the head and said goodbye. As she walked to the door, she heard a zipper behind her. She turned and saw Lana bending down and putting the Drink Detectives in her backpack. She quietly shut the apartment door behind her.

On the drive home, Alex thought about her hippie mother, who'd raised her with tales of Free Love and Change the World. When Alex came of age sexually, AIDS had surfaced and sex turned deadly. But at least you could protect yourself against AIDS. There were condoms, screening tests. Anybody who dated today could fall victim to a date rape drug. Bartenders could make a quick two hundred bucks when a stranger asked them to spike a woman's drink. She hoped that Castro would find a way to get J off the streets and that her young friend would be able to protect herself.

CHAPTER 20

The next day, Sunday, Alex woke up and threw on a T-shirt and sweatpants. She was out the door by 6:00 A.M. for a jog through Rock Creek Park. As she ran, she thought of Dan and the painstaking steps he would take to find out what happened to Ted's body after he died. She needed to be equally diligent about what happened to cause his death.

On the way home, she stopped at a coffeehouse a few blocks from the Curl Up and Dye. She and Luke had occasionally dropped in to hear an acoustic guitar player who had a regular gig there on Wednesday nights. She was tempted to stay for their amazing espresso-steamed eggs and treat this day like other people did. Read *The New York Times,* sip a cappuccino. But eight families were depending on her. She got a dark roast to go—the largest size they had. It was going to be a long day.

After a quick shower, she fired up her laptop and got down to business searching medical databases for information on hyperimmune responses. No recent articles described symptoms as overwhelming as what had hit Ted Silliman, Leroy Darven, or the six children. She expanded her search and came across a case study in *The New England Journal of Medicine* published fifteen years earlier by Dr. Andover Teague, an associate professor at Harvard Medical School. He described a young boy, 3 years old, brought to Massachusetts General Hospital with swelling and shortness of breath. Coming from a poor family, the boy was admitted to the run-down, older wing of the hospital. His swelling started to recede almost immediately. But whenever a nurse entered the room, his symptoms reappeared.

Harvard psychiatrists—male, of course—were asked to peer into the small boy's psyche to see if his mother had traumatized him in some way, leading him to react badly to all women. But psychoanalyzing a 3-year-old was not exactly part of their playbook. And while the shrinks were in attendance, a male aide brought the boy's breakfast on a tray and, before even lifting a spoon to his mouth, the boy began to swell again.

Teague, a young internist, ordered allergy scratch tests on the boy. To his surprise, the boy had none of the traditional allergies. He was fine with cats, ragweed, eggs, peanuts—all the things that normally sent sensitive people's immune systems raging. Instead, he was allergic to any man-made materials—plastics, certain chemicals, and artificial fragrances. The nurses set him off with their perfume and hairspray. The aide, because he'd brought lunch on a plastic tray.

The boy's poverty had literally saved his life. Since his mother didn't have the requisite insurance to admit him to the newer wing of the hospital, the boy had been assigned to an unrenovated wing in a room with an old wooden dresser, worn wool blanket, and ancient feather pillow. Teague's article on the case was provocatively titled, "What Is Disease?" The boy would have been able to live completely normally a century earlier, not showing any signs of illness. But the creations of our modern industrial world literally could kill him.

She thought about the last moments of Leroy Darven. He'd touched the Styrofoam box from the Cactus Cow. She tapped her foot nervously. Then she had an idea.

She reached Castro on his cell phone. "What's the last thing Ted touched?"

He hesitated a minute, thinking back, then said, "A pair of binoculars."

Alex was excited. "What kind?"

"Steiner 8 by 56 millimeter Nighthunter Mil Spec Binoculars High Definition HD 595."

"No," Alex said impatiently. "What sort of coating?"

"Shit, how do I know? Some sort of plastic."

"Thanks," Alex said.

"That's it?"

"Yeah, I'll call you if I think of anything else."

Alex looked back at the article for more about the boy. Her guess was that he had a genetic predisposition and some environmental trigger had set it off. Once activated, the disease caused him to have a massive immune response to man-made substances. But there was disappointingly little in the case study about any genetic basis for the disease. Then again, the article had been written before the completion of the Human Genome Project.

What had happened to that poor little boy? What possible treatment could have been used? Drugs—even those made from natural components of plants—had man-made chemicals and coatings. He wasn't like the boy in the bubble—the kid with Severe Combined Immune Deficiency—who had to live in a special sterile cocoon. That bubble was made of plastic, which would be deadly for Teague's patient.

Tapping into the medical database again, Alex pulled up one other article, written a year later by Dr. Teague. He'd found nine other children around the world with the same disorder. If Teague had been older, they probably would have named the disease after him. But, instead, the medical profession chose a Latin name related to the prime symptom. *Inflatus Magnus.* Leave it to doctors to state the obvious. But there was nothing in the articles to suggest a cause for the disease—or any way to treat it.

At 3:00 P.M., her phone rang. "Alex," Castro said. She could barely hear him for the din of an engine in the background. "We've got a bead on Renfrew. He just used his cell phone."

"Where is he?"

"Near the New Mexico–Arizona border. Get this. He phoned 911 for help. He's at the bottom of a ravine with a broken leg. Mountain rescue is trying to get a copter in to him. They plan to airlift him to Albuquerque. I'm about to board a DEA jet to question him."

"I thought your boss took you off this investigation."

"It's my day off and the pilot owes me a favor. No need to get the chain of command involved in this one."

"What was Renfrew doing there?"

"Can't tell from the location. It's near a national park. No connection to the Vegas boys."

"What about Red Rights?"

The noise in the background escalated and Castro yelled out, "Who?"

"Haven't you been watching the news?"

He sounded hurried, frantic. "Too busy. The J Jack guys aren't going on *Oprah* or *Nightline.*"

"Red Rights is an activist Native American group accused of setting fire to genetically modified crops. They've demonstrated against chemical factories. Maybe they've got a beef against Waverly."

"What went down at the quarry was personal. Nobody marching with placards."

"And—"

"Alex, I gotta go. This guy's the only lead I've got. Maybe Ted and I were made on the trip to Taos. Maybe DiBondi put the hit on Ted and is now trying to knock off a witness."

"Call me as soon as you find out anything," Alex said. "And be careful."

As she hung up, she thought about how Castro had crossed a line and put his career in jeopardy. Galloway would go ballistic once he learned Castro was chasing Ted's killer and interrogating Renfrew without bringing the agency into the loop. But sometimes inexplicable events—a friend's death—required inconceivable actions. Alex knew that if anything happened to Barbara or Lana, she'd do the same thing.

After talking to Castro, it was hard for Alex to focus on her medical searches. He might have a lead, and that immediate possibility made her analysis of studies by rheumatologists, endocrinologists, and immunologists seem remote and unproductive. So many of the studies she read that afternoon focused on immune reactions that affected a single bodily system. In the deaths she was concerned about, this new disease had swamped them all. Every major organ was involved.

That evening, Alex tried to control her nervous anticipation of Castro's call by doing tasks around the house. She'd done three loads of laundry, thrown away outdated cereals from the back of her pantry, and dusted every surface in the place. In short, a set of activities she hadn't engaged in for years.

By midnight, she'd heard nothing, and now feared the worst. Castro had gone into a situation without backup. Maybe he'd let his anger over Ted's death put him in jeopardy. Maybe he'd underestimated Renfrew or the guy had a partner. How long should she wait before calling the DEA to ask for their help?

Screw it, she thought when the clock reached 2:00 A.M. and she still hadn't heard from Castro. She called his cell phone.

"Hello," he said groggily.

"You went to sleep? Why didn't you call me?"

"Don't go all girl on me."

That only angered Alex more. "Well, Mr. Investigator, if it weren't for this *girl,* you wouldn't have even known about Renfrew."

He cleared his throat as if to jolt himself awake. "It was a bust. He claims he was on a botany research trip. Fell in a ravine and broke his ankle. Denies ever being at the quarry."

"But you have a photo of him from the hotel."

"He's got a response for that, too. Says it wasn't him."

"That's absurd."

"He's lost a couple of pounds from dehydration, has dried skin from a rash. Looks five years older. I showed the doctor the cell phone photo we took of Renfrew and even he said it might not be the same guy."

"What about his registration at the Hotel La Fonda?"

"Good catch. I take back the girl remark. But there's no record of his registration there. DiBondi's name was on the reservations for both rooms."

"And the Waverly pin we found at the quarry?"

"Renfrew said there must be a couple hundred thousand of them floating around. Given out at high school science fairs, trade group meetings, even medical conferences."

"Guy's got an answer for everything."

"Yeah, but there's one thing he can't explain. Why he was so scared. Most guys would be thrilled to have been rescued. But he was nervous the whole time. He couldn't do enough to speed the interview along. I could see he was in pain, but he was turning down pain pills. He was making damn sure he didn't let anything slip when he was talking to me."

"Who do you think got to him?"

"Let's just say, if I was getting into bed with Frankie DiBondi, I wouldn't kiss and tell."

"You think he's tied to Ted's death?"

"He's hiding something. About the only thing he seemed credible on was not knowing shit about J."

Alex felt let down. Exhaustion had pushed excitement out of her body. Her bed was beckoning her. "Thanks, Castro. Sorry to wake you."

"Hey, sorry I'm in a crappy mood. I just want Ted's killer. Maybe this guy's connected, but I just couldn't break him."

"You'll find a way."

"Or maybe," Castro said, "whoever he's scared of will take him out. And we'll never figure out what happened to Ted."

Alex heard his goodbye and then a click. He hadn't even waited for her to respond.

Frustrated, she paced her newly spotless living room. The death toll was mounting and they had nothing. What tied these deaths together, other than a park and possibly a fountain?

She poured herself an Old Weller. It was late, but maybe if she read Teague's articles again, she'd figure out where her scientific investigation should take her next.

CHAPTER   21

The next morning when she entered her lab at 7:00 A.M., Alex's head ached from too much Old Weller and too little sleep. The bright overhead lights of the lab hurt her eyes and the humming, gurgling, and clacking of the lab machinery seemed an overpowering mechanical chorus. She made her way to her quiet inner office, clicked on the lights there, and turned off the ones in the main lab. She set her Starbucks down on the desk, accidentally sloshing coffee on the keyboard, then cursing herself.

Then she suddenly got silent. Here she was, not even forty, and she couldn't handle a little hangover. Those corpses deserved better than that. She gulped down some coffee and formulated her plan. Leroy Darven was the key. With several vials of his blood to work on, she had greater leeway to undertake tests that she didn't dare run on the small amount of blood from Ted. Reading about *Inflatus Magnus* had given her the idea to look more closely at the T cells themselves to determine what their target was. She knew the T cells of both men were elevated in number, but most T cells were directed against a particular invader—say, HIV or TB.

With a morning's work, fueled by frequent sips of dark roast coffee, she determined that Darven's T cells had gone generic. They'd run amok and attacked everything, including his own organs.

After that insight, though, she hit a wall. She needed to find other people with the disease to search for the common patterns. Eight deaths. One fountain. Few clues.

That afternoon, Alex got the new medical records from Chuck. Even with her narrowed criteria of patients with certain types of inflammatory disease, Chuck's search yielded 1200 California medical charts. Sadly, many turned out to be related to child abuse. She thought of having Chuck run a new search deleting that category, but she worried that this might cause her to miss a case. With all the swelling and bleeding that accompanied this syndrome, there was a chance that health care providers might mistakenly blame the parents.

By 10:00 P.M., she'd made it through the entire set of California records without finding a single new case. She was disappointed that she'd failed to get the results she wanted. Then she got angry at herself. What kind of ghoul was she? She should be glad that nobody in California had died from the disease.

She got up to stretch, and decided to walk around the base for some fresh air. At first she wandered aimlessly, then made a loop around the Walter Reed Hospital. She chided herself for being too quick to suspect an epidemic. It reminded her of being in medical school when, during the first year, she and her classmates fell into a group hypochondria. Each ache or spike in temperature convinced them that they were victims of the diseases they studied.

Despite her new medical insights, she felt she'd let Castro down. Her medical prowess wouldn't be able to prove to Galloway's satisfaction that Ted's death wasn't the result of impurities in illegal drugs. She envisioned the disappointment in Castro's eyes when she told him that this whole affair, which appeared to have claimed eight lives, was a random, isolated event, as unique and sudden as a solar eclipse.

CHAPTER 22

At home after her frustrating day, Alex thought of the dead ends that she and Castro had hit. She'd learned nothing more about the disease and he'd gotten squat out of Renfrew. When the 11:00 P.M. news rolled around, Alex turned it on, subconsciously hoping for a magic break in the case. Like a lawsuit being filed against Waverly that disclosed an immunological reaction to a new drug.

All she found, though, were commentators dissecting the presidential announcement of Elias Lightfoot Blackstone. Already, the hatchet men for the Republican Party were churning the soil, trying to dig up dirt on the man. His background was stellar, though. A scholarship to the University of New Mexico and law school at Arizona State University. He'd had the talent to be recruited by a big firm and then, just as he was about to be made partner, he left for a legal aid job on his former reservation, the Zuni Pueblo. He'd met his wife, Yolanda, there. They had three children and seemed to be a model, loving family.

Alex mused over the fact that this Democratic candidate was more pro-family than the any of the Republicans likely to emerge as contenders. Over the past few years, the Republicans' pro-family stance had come back to bite them. The Senate page scandal. The divorce of a leading Republican in which his wife claimed he'd forced her to visit sex clubs with him. Ah, thought Alex, repression and its discontents.

With so little dirt on the candidate himself, the conservative media was building an arsenal of stories about the activist Native American group Red Rights. They'd been investigated in connection with a fire at a farm that grew genetically modified corn. No one was arrested, nothing was proven. But

Red Rights had certainly spoken out against the crop. They warned about messing with Mother Nature. The news footage of their rally convinced Alex they had a pretty good grasp of the science. One member, Dale Hightower, stepped forward, a shaman's medicine bag hanging off his belt. He introduced himself as part of the Havasupai tribe who live at the bottom of the Grand Canyon and then presented data on how genetically modified seeds from corporate farms had drifted, contaminating organic crops. "What we put into our body is sacred," he said. "We do not want to be poisoned by the white man's mistakes."

The whole newscast made Alex uneasy. Dissing Blackstone because of some unproven allegations about a bunch of activist Native Americans seemed as prejudicial as saying a Catholic shouldn't be elected president because some members of that faith were part of the Mob. It was like assuming that, because Alex's mom had been an antiwar activist in the 1960s, she must have been part of the violent Weather Underground. Although, now that she thought of it, Alex wouldn't have put it past her.

Alex fell asleep with the television on, right after the news. When her phone rang an hour later, she was startled by the voices in her room until she recognized the *Law & Order* rerun.

"Alex," Barbara said, and, for a brief moment, Alex was frozen to the pillow in fear.

"Is Lana okay?"

"One of her friends got raped," Barbara said. "Lana and I are at Georgetown University Hospital. Can you get over here? Somebody needs to be with Lana while I help the girl."

Alex flung back the sheet and pulled herself out of bed. "Sure," she said, retrieving her jeans and turtleneck from the floor. Then she reached into the closet and grabbed a white medical jacket with ALEXANDRA BLAKE, M.D. embroidered on the pocket. She'd get less of a hassle at the hospital—and get more information—if she could blend in.

Sure enough, a nurse waved her through the internal ER doors and into the area where cubicles held the night's disasters. The victims of heart attacks and auto accidents lay behind curtains, while the medical staff raced through the hallways in chaos and action. Hospitals are erroneously viewed as quiet zones. But in this corridor, the clang of EKG machines, health care personnel shouting orders, and sobbing relatives reached decibel levels higher than a rock concert. Alex scanned the corridor for her friends. Outside Room 8, she saw a scared Lana sitting on the floor. The girl sat perfectly still. Without being able to hear the noise, there was nothing to distract her from her frightened thoughts.

Alex approached and then slid down beside Lana, being careful not to extend her legs into the path of an aide pushing a portable X-ray machine to the next room. Lana laid her head on Alex's shoulder for a moment. But Alex needed to know what was going on, so she slowly repositioned her body so Lana could read her lips.

"Tell me what happened," Alex said.

The girl's lips quivered and she burst into tears. "Maggie went to some sort of party and then . . ." Her sobs drowned out the rest of the sentence.

"Were you at the party, too?"

Still sobbing, Lana shook her head. Then she managed a sentence: "It's a school night. Plus Mom doesn't let me go to college parties."

"How did you and your mom end up here if you weren't part of the group?"

"Her mom called when she got to the ER because she knew my mom was a lawyer. There's some stupid white cop who's trying to make it seem like it's all Maggie's fault."

Alex could only imagine how angry that would have made Barbara. Maybe, years ago, Barbara had tried to report her own rape. Then Alex had another worry. Was Castro that cop? Could he really be that insensitive?

She told Lana to wait there, then she stood up and gently pulled the curtain aside so that she could signal Barbara to come out and talk. But she saw only a battered teenager in the bed and her mother bending over her.

She quietly closed the curtain, turned, and saw Barbara and a white D.C. cop standing next to the nurses' station. Barbara had the cold, regal bearing of a soldier. But as Alex moved closer to the two of them, she could tell that there was an abnormal tension in her friend's voice.

"You can't tell me you would be treating a white victim the way you have treated this poor girl."

"We've got to assume she consented," the police officer said. "She's sixteen. Most black girls have sex by that age."

Alex thought Barbara's head would whirl around like something from *The Exorcist* when he made that comment. Instead, she was calm and firm.

"This girl goes to a Catholic school. The gynecological exam showed a torn hymen and ripped anus. You are obviously not competent to do your job. When I am through with you, Officer, I am going to have your badge."

Just then a white man in jeans with blue eyes and black curly hair approached, signaling the officer over. Barbara said to Alex, "What kind of asshole have they sent in now?"

Alex turned to see Castro. "My kind of asshole. That's Castro Baxter from DEA."

Castro was obviously getting filled in on the case. But as the officer spoke, they could hear Castro's voice getting louder. "You did what? Just get out of here and don't go near a rape case again."

Barbara looked at Alex. "Maybe he's my kind of asshole, too."

With Castro now in charge of the rape investigation, Barbara told him what she knew and took him into the victim's room. When she came out, she hugged Lana and told her that they could go home now. Alex put her arms around them both and said she would stay awhile.

Lana walked ahead to use the bathroom on the way out. "Alex," Barbara said, "thanks for coming. All I could think of was, it could have been Lana at the party, Lana in that bed. How could I ever live with myself if anything happened to her?"

"Don't even think like that," Alex said. "But, until they get a handle on this J thing, maybe it's not such a bad idea to keep Lana in."

"That's not my main worry," Barbara said. "After what she saw tonight, I don't know if she'll ever go out again in her life."

CHAPTER 23

Within a half hour, the rape victim was admitted to a room and Castro had gotten the information he needed. When he walked through the waiting room toward the hospital exit, he was surprised to see Alex waiting in a chair.

She stood up and fell into step beside him as he walked into the night air.

"I'm sorry for what D.C.'s finest put that family through," he said. "I would've been first on the scene, but I was late flying back from Albuquerque."

He stopped suddenly and turned to look intently into her eyes. "Seeing you is the best thing that's happened in days," he said. "You wouldn't want a cup of coffee, would you?"

Alex smiled and said, "Lead on."

Castro put his arm around her and steered her down the block to an all-night diner. Inside, a hostess who seemed to know Castro pointed them toward a booth. Alex scooted along the plastic cushion on one side of the booth, expecting him to sit across from her. Instead, he told the hostess, "Bring two orders of the number five." Then he slid in next to Alex, staring intently into her blue eyes. "Now you see what we're up against."

"It's horrible. Makes me want to drop everything and come up with a way to protect those girls."

"And it's spreading. Last night, we got calls from Providence, Rhode Island, and Cambridge, Massachusetts. It's worked its way into the college towns."

The waitress brought over two coffees and two platters of waffles.

"Have your toxicologists figured out what's in it?"

"They just cracked it last week. Found three things—a benzo, a yohimbine derivative, and I'll treat for the waffles if you can guess the last ingredient."

"Something like Ecstasy?"

"No. One more chance."

Alex thought for a moment. If it already contained a benzo, that ruled out another one like Valium or Rohypnol. Then she smiled. "Spanish fly?"

Castro leaned away from her as if he'd been punched. "How'd you know? It took our lab folks a couple hundred passes to figure that out. If a victim hadn't mentioned the itching, the toxicologists would never have tested for it."

"After our dinner, I looked up arousal drugs—" she said.

He jutted out his bottom lip in a mock expression of hurt. "I'm not enough for you?"

Alex smiled. "I wasn't searching for my own use, just to check that what I told you was right. I ran across a patent filed by two guys from Stanford with a version of the combination you just mentioned. They claimed it could be a female equivalent to Viagra."

"They better not market it. The yohimbine derivative interacts fatally with any sort of upper. That's how the toxicologists figured out it contained yohimbine. A model taking diet pills died shortly after she was jacked. Ditto a high school student who'd been prescribed Adderall for attention deficit disorder."

Alex thought of the beaten husk of Lana's friend in the bed. She looked at the coffee cup in front of her, shocked at how easily a drink could be turned into a lethal weapon. She turned to Castro. "Are you any closer to tracking the source?"

"No clue," Castro said, clenching his fists.

"Maybe you should talk to the Stanford researchers. The drug they created is awfully close to the one you've described. They could fill you in on the equipment and solvents they used to create their particular combination of benzo, cantharidin, and yohimbine. Maybe you can track who's ordering the ingredients and find the manufacturers."

"How do we get in touch with them?"

"I'll send you a PDF of the patent. Their names are on the first page."

Alex picked up the syrup and smothered the waffle. Then she put a fork-ful in her mouth. "Tastes even sweeter with you buying," she said.

He was working his way through the three slices of bacon on the side of his plate, absentmindedly.

"What else have you got on the Renfrew lead?" she asked.

He lowered his voice, maybe because his little mission hadn't exactly been agency approved. "I rode out to the spot where Renfrew was found. There's no way he could have hiked out there, like he claimed. There were two sets of footprints within a couple hundred feet of the ravine, but no footprints outside of that area. There were also two sets of horse tracks. The two horses were galloping side by side toward the spot where he was found and, get this, one was leading the other on the way out."

"Someone took Renfrew up there to ambush him?"

"The someone who belonged to the other set of footprints—a pair of moccasins."

Alex thought about the Native American in blue paint Castro had seen the night Ted was killed. What could be the connection between the two men, the warrior and the driver—and how did they relate to the other deaths? Was there some sort of connection to Red Rights? "I've found six more people who died after drinking from that same fountain," Alex said.

"Are you sure?"

"Same symptoms as Ted's. And they were all children."

Castro gave a low whistle. "What a screwed-up world."

"You were concentrating on DiBondi. Could Renfrew have spiked the fountain?"

"Not on that trip. We had tight surveillance on both of them the whole time. But that doesn't rule out Mr. Moccasins. Maybe he was partnering with Renfrew and then decided to get rid of him."

"It's frustrating not knowing whether we should be looking for a disease—or a killer."

"Either way, Renfrew's a dead end right now. When he was at the hospital, he was scared shitless of saying anything."

"What did you find in his financials?"

"He gets paid nearly a million a year, with stock options worth a million more. Treats himself well. Good restaurants. Expensive cars. But no sign of a gambling debt or anything like that. I can't tie him to DiBondi."

"How about fingerprints on the pin?"

"A perfect print of a pointer finger. We didn't get a match to anything in AFIS, but that was before I found out about Renfrew."

"Maybe you can find something he's touched and compare it to the pin." Alex thought about how, in New York, cops broke a rape case by following the suspect around until he spit on the sidewalk, then testing his DNA. People left traces of themselves everywhere—fingerprints, skin cells. "Let me know if I can help."

"We'll just have to get there faster next time somebody dies," he said, putting a $20 bill on the table to cover their meal.

Alex shuddered as she slid out of the booth after him. She thought of the last, grotesque moments of Ted's life. "Let's just figure this out before that happens."

CHAPTER 24

Bleary-eyed after her late-night visit to the hospital, Alex flipped on the news the next morning and saw that in Oklahoma, members of Red Rights were rallying on a tribal reservation. They were demanding that the Oklahoma governor give them back land that had been taken from Native Americans one hundred years earlier in violation of federal treaties. Across their backs, where a previous generation might have held arrows, they carried rifles. In English and in three tribal languages, their placards read, THERE'S NO JUSTICE FOR THE INJUNS. The teenagers on the reservations hung back initially, but then took the signs they were handed and mugged for the camera.

She noticed one of the men, with shoulder-length black hair, walking into the camera's view with a more politically charged sign. GENERAL COTTER'S LAST STAND. By replacing Custer's name with that of the sitting president, he couldn't have been more clear about where the Native American vote was going.

He took tobacco leaves out of his pocket and scattered them on the ground in prayer. "Indigenous people across this country have long been the victims of the white man. In the past, they've been killed with guns and smallpox-laden blankets. They've been robbed of their lands, their wealth, their identities. Stripped of their way of life, even their bodies have fallen prey to the white culture. Unable to hunt or raise crops in their traditional ways, Native Americans have fallen prey to obesity, diabetes, drug addiction. My own tribe, the Havasupai, has the highest rate of diabetes in the world. A third of our men and over half of our women are victims of the disease."

He raised a fist, not unlike the Black Power salute of the 1960s, and said, "We won't take it anymore."

Then he gave a signal and all the Native Americans pointed their rifles to the sky and pulled the triggers. Yes, the protestors were clear about what they wanted and how they might get there.

In the cafeteria at lunch, Alex saw Barbara alone at a table. When she sat down, Barbara turned to her and said, "It means a lot to me that you showed up last night."

"Barbara, don't be silly. Of course I'd come. Tell me how Lana's doing today."

Barbara got a guilty expression on her face. "It was a lot for her to handle. I let her stay home from school. I'm planning to duck out early, after my one o'clock meeting."

"I hope things went better with Castro there. Date rape is his specialty at the moment."

Barbara nodded. "He was a lot more sensitive than that D.C. cop. I guess training makes a difference."

Alex laughed. "And what's Grant? The exception that proves the rule? Three or four training sessions haven't dampered his sexual harassment quotient."

Barbara shook her head. "I think we're going to have to dress him up like a woman and have him spend a day in our shoes."

"I'm trying to picture him in your red leather Bruno Magli heels."

"It's kinda like imagining an elephant doing ballet."

The friends fell into an easy silence while Barbara methodically chewed a salad and Alex downed a cheeseburger. Then, thinking of the news that morning, Alex asked, "Picked a candidate yet?"

Her friend lowered her voice. "I like Cotter, but there's something appealing about having a man of color in the White House."

"Blackstone's campaign isn't going to get off the ground if Red Rights scares off white support."

"Like Malcolm X frightening whites in the 1960s. And did you hear that after the Oklahoma demonstration, Homeland Security put Red Rights on the national terrorist watch?"

"On what grounds?"

"With Martin Kincade in charge, who needs grounds?" said Barbara.

"That man gives me the willies. When he was first appointed, I met with him and his general counsel to go over the constitutional restraints on what that department can do."

"You mean there are some?"

"On paper, at least. Ever since President Bush's executive orders, the agency can pretty much do what it wants. But Kincade just dismissed me. Here he's got an agency that is already basically above the law and he's aiming to take it even higher."

"Isn't he a Cotter appointee? That doesn't sound like something the President would approve of."

"Ah, Alex, for a rocket scientist, you are incredibly dense about politics. A president rarely plucks an appointee out of the air based on his or her level of competence."

"Hey, he appointed Wiatt as our boss and he's turned out to be pretty good."

"That makes my point. Wiatt was his college roommate. Not exactly a national search. And more often, a president's minions choose based on who has donated what money and who will keep a particular interest group at bay."

"Well, Martin Kincade's got the bucks, but what's his constituency?"

Barbara, a political junkie, got excited whenever she spoke of intrigue inside the Beltway. With the way she was moving her hands when she spoke, she seemed almost like Alex in her level of energy and passion. "During his campaign, Cotter floated the idea of disbanding Homeland Security entirely. After all those domestic wiretaps, a lot of citizens agreed with him. But folks in the conservative states wouldn't buy it. After he lost the South Carolina primary, Cotter did a 180 and promised a powerful leader for the agency whom the White House would leave alone."

"My, my, don't tell me Cotter is that rare chief executive who honors his campaign promises."

Barbara smiled. "Don't go canonizing him yet. The President has dealt with Kincade in his own sly way, cutting back on the scope of Homeland Security's duties. Cotter's given most of the terrorist investigations back to the FBI and CIA. The main job of the agency is the one you're involved with— monitoring bioterrorism. In fact, I was surprised Homeland Security took the lead on this Native American thing."

"Maybe the other agencies don't view the group as a threat."

"Could be. Seems to me Red Rights is exercising legitimate protest rights. Native Americans have gotten a raw deal, pure and simple."

Alex was about to pump Barbara for more details about her run-in with Kincade and his lawyers, but Chuck burst into the cafeteria and headed to their table. The excitement on his face made him look even younger than usual. "Where do you want the next batch?" he asked.

"What next batch?" Alex hadn't told him that California was a bust. He smiled broadly, proud of himself. "I tried to anticipate what else you'd want and I focused on two other Southwestern states. I played around with the parameters and I think I may have found something."

The power of music, Alex thought. Two tickets to Apocalyptica and she'd turned him into an epidemiologist. Alex took leave of Barbara and followed Chuck into the Task Force room. He'd run regression analyses on the medical details of the New Mexico victims and pulled cases from Arizona and Utah that were eerily similar. Alex looked over his shoulder as he showed her what he'd found. Two weeks before the deaths in New Mexico, seven children in Utah had died in a similar fashion. And the week before that, there were a dozen in Arizona—eleven children and one otherwise healthy adult. All had died in the same horrendous way as Ted.

Alex stood silently for a moment, struck by the kind of fear you'd feel in a cage with a lion. Despite all her training, nothing had prepared her for the terror she felt about a new, deadly disease, a potentially unstoppable pathogen.

"Are you alright, ma'am?" Chuck asked.

She realized that he was staring at her, waiting for some acknowledgment. "This is great work," she said quietly. "Could you print off these records so that I can go to work on them?"

Alex took the pile of printouts into her laboratory, laid them along the counter, and, sitting on her lab stool, began to read. As the hours flew by, her concern grew. The patients whom Chuck had identified showed exactly the same disease as Ted.

She got up and nervously paced the lab, while details of the files jumbled together in her mind. Concentrate, she told herself. Don't panic.

Returning to the stool, she started reading each file again, searching for a link among the patients. The admitting party for the children in each case was a member of the family, mainly the mother or grandmother, though one had been admitted by an older sister. What was the common denominator?

Then a pattern began to emerge. Most of the medical records in Arizona and Utah said the children had been playing outside before they were stricken. Alex quickly leafed through the records of the one adult in the group, a man in Arizona. His wife had said that he'd been jogging before he came home and fell ill in their bathroom. She'd related the nightmarish scene to the doctor. He'd applied shaving cream and a tumorlike growth had appeared on his chin. Then he'd started gasping for air and the rest of his face began to swell.

Alex thought back to the deodorant she'd found in the New Mexican water fountain, which she'd attributed to a jogger. Kids outside and a man jogging could very well have drunk from water fountains in their neighborhoods. But was the contamination natural or deliberate? And what could have set these people off? Was there something in the fountains that current scientific tests couldn't identify?

She copied down the zip codes for the admissions in Arizona and Utah. She found that all the deaths in Utah occurred within three adjoining zip code areas. Certainly they could have used the same park fountain. In Arizona, the jogger lived two zip codes away from anyone else, but his run could have taken him by the same fountain that they'd drunk from.

A disease was blooming like a deadly flower right under Alex's eyes. She wondered how other doctors had felt at the start of previous plagues, like the Spanish flu epidemic of 1918, which killed more than forty million people worldwide. Did doctors in the beginning realize that the first few cases would explode into a crippling infectious horror that decimated cities? Could they have done something differently to stop those diseases in their tracks?

Alex suddenly felt insignificant next to the lethal powers of the disease that had killed Ted Silliman and these other people. In medical school, she'd treated patients with depression and had never understood what made people just give up and lose their sense of purpose. But now the enormity of this battle with the disease—and the infinitesimal odds of being able to do anything in time—made her feel depleted, diminished.

What had she advised those patients, years ago, who'd lost their ways, whose souls had given up? Take small steps. Set goals that were achievable. That's what Alex had to do now.

She turned her stool around so that she faced away from the records as she thought about what she would do. The words *differential diagnosis* popped into her mind. That was what you learned the first day of medical school. How do you figure out what a patient is suffering from? You make a list of possibilities and then do the tests to rule in or rule out each of the alternatives.

The lab—usually her sanctuary—was weighing on her. The sequencers, the refrigerator, the mass spectrometer, all seemed to be challenging her in some way, as if they were waiting expectantly for her to start them running and solve the mystery.

Alex brought her glance back from the equipment to the records. What kind of nuttiness was this, anthropomorphizing her lab equipment? She looked at her watch and was surprised to see it was 11:00 P.M. She realized she was hungry. Shoving a yellow legal pad into her saddlebag briefcase, she took off for Dupont Circle.

In the café at the back of Kramer Books and Afterwords, Alex ordered a glass of wine and a steak salad. She began a list to help her with the differential diagnosis of this disease. She filled pages easily, pausing only for sips and bites when her dinner arrived. She ate with a pen in her right hand, scribbling as the ideas came to her, drawing arrows to indicate the steps she should pursue and their order.

When she was done, she reviewed the pages. The first one contained everything she knew about the symptoms, with thoughts of the medical specialties they encompassed—immunology, toxicology, endocrinology, virology, and so forth. That would provide a starting point for her search of the medical literature. The next few pages explored the options if it was a new disease. She'd outlined all the possible ways that it could have mutated from a common disease. Then she'd explored the possibilities that it had been transferred from animals. AIDS had hopped from primates to man. Avian flu had originated in birds.

The rest of her analysis focused on an alternative possibility. The disease could be due to something exogenous. A new pollutant. A new drug.

The final page listed the people whom she would contact. First thing in the morning, she would bring others into the loop to help her with this.

Feeling better now that she had a game plan, she looked around her and noticed that no one else was in the café. She glanced at her watch and realized that the place was about to close. Leaving a whopping tip on the table (since she'd occupied the space far longer than a normal diner), she walked out of the café and back through the bookstore.

Near the exit she saw a huge display of Blackstone's best-seller. On impulse, she grabbed a copy. The woman behind the register said, "Best book I ever read. I'm happier with my life now. Even found a boyfriend."

What a guy, thought Alex. If he doesn't win the presidency, he could always replace Dr. Phil.

At the Curl Up and Dye, Alex took the *The American Way* to bed. The Native American values Blackstone expressed did make a lot of sense. Being one with nature and not harming the environment. Paying homage to elders and caring for them, rather than sticking them in nursing homes. Learning the benefits of silence. Not exhibiting hubris. Being in the moment. Practicing tolerance and nonviolence. Not being attached to results.

Alex thought about that last admonition. As a scientist, she'd been taught practically to worship results. Every experiment was geared to getting results. Each scientific journal article had a section labeled "Results." Telling a scientist not to be attached to results was like telling a dog not to be attached to bones.

She closed the book and dropped it to the floor beside the bed. As she reached to turn off the bedside light, she heard the quiet buzz of her cell phone from her fanny pack in the living room. Annoyed, she got out of bed and retrieved it.

"Yeah?" she said.

It was Castro, his speech slightly slurred. "Goddamn bastards."

"Which goddamn bastards?"

"Milford, Galloway, the rest."

Alex recalled the explosive meeting with them when she'd delivered Ted's file to the DEA.

Castro continued, spurting out his words in an angry, clipped tone. "Tonight was the memorial service for Ted. Nobody from DEA came. Not a single one. It was just me, his mom, and a couple of friends from outside of work. He dies on the job and they're pissing on his grave."

Except, Alex remembered, there was no grave. Not with that disturbing business with the mortuary. "What the hell is wrong with them?"

Castro was silent for a moment. "Meet me for a drink."

Alex looked at the clock. It was 1:30 A.M., but plenty of times she and Luke had been out listening to music at this hour. She thought of a dozen clubs and bars that she could suggest, but Castro sounded like he'd already far exceeded his limit and was in no shape to drive.

"Where are you now?" she asked.

"Home."

"I'll come there."

Alex copied down the address. It was in a marginal neighborhood near the Capitol. Well, if Castro's job was to catch drug dealers, he could have his pick within a few blocks of his home.

On the drive, she thought about their dinner at the Old Ebbitt Grill and how she'd wanted that evening to continue, maybe even to move to his apartment or hers. They were starting from a different place now. He was angry and hurting, and she hoped she could help him. But she also knew that her going over there tonight would change their relationship. A man like Castro didn't easily let people see him vulnerable.

When he opened the door, he was still wearing a black suit, but he'd removed his tie and the points of his shirt collar were at odd angles. His curly black hair was mussed in back, as if he'd taken a short nap while waiting for her. The apartment was in an old building that had gone to seed, but he'd furnished it in a simple, sturdy way. The paint in the living room was a soothing pale blue and looked decades newer than the paint in the hallways. She figured he'd painted it himself. A building like this wouldn't have a super on call for each tenant's whims.

He walked her toward the couch and, while they were both still standing, offered her a bourbon. It was tempting, seeing as how it was her drink of choice anyway. But he'd clearly had enough. "Any chance I can make myself some coffee?"

"Life of the party, huh?" His voice had a rough edge, no trace of humor.

She shrugged and he led her into the kitchen. A small Mr. Coffee four-cup machine sat on the counter. She filled the pot with water and he pointed to a cabinet with a large container of Folger's. As she faced the coffeepot and added the coffee, he came up behind her and put his arms around her. He took a deep breath, then rested his chin on her head.

She poured a cup for him, turned around, and handed it to him. "Here. I don't like to drink alone."

When he reached for the cup, she noticed a scar on his right hand. He looked down, following her gaze. "It's my own memorial to Ted. Cut my hand on the gravel when I lifted him. Thought it was just his blood on me until some ER doc recognized I was bleeding, too."

He walked her back into the living room and they settled on the couch. "Galloway's still shitting bricks about the coke angle," he said.

Alex shifted her body to face him. "It couldn't have been something mixed with cocaine. Six of the victims were just in the fourth grade."

Castro wearily shook his head. "We've busted families with coke heads as young as seven. Brought in a guy who'd given it to his five-year-old step-daughter. Laughed at how it made her hyper, loved how he got her to suck him off."

Alex sickened at the thought. Castro looked raw and depleted. Each such encounter probably had lobbed off a piece of his soul. "Have you ever thought of leaving this business?"

His lips curled in a grin. "And do what? Ted and me were two of a kind. We'd fucked up a lot as kids, then found this thing, this undercover work that we could just nail."

Probably, thought Alex, *because* they'd fucked up as kids. Nothing like knowing how your quarry thinks as you try to trap him. "Tell me more about your friend."

He raised his eyebrows, distrusting. Resenting that she seemed to be humoring him. He reached for the bourbon instead of the coffee.

"I'm serious," Alex said. "He was more than just a friend or a partner. You admired him. Why?"

He leaned his head back against the couch and closed his eyes for a moment. Then he straightened up and faced her. "The way he listened to people. Lotta guys in this business have big egos. They need it to pull off the undercover business, to bluff their way through the buys. But Ted was never about Ted. He respected people. Could make a janitor feel like the smartest guy in the world."

With only a few questions from Alex, Castro walked her through the streetwise bravery of his friend and his magic touch with women. Alex made another pot of coffee and their discussion continued until nearly 4:00 A.M. Castro looked better for it and Alex felt like she'd met his buddy, a feeling that she cherished about anyone whom she'd first come across dead.

When it came time for her to leave, Castro insisted on walking her to her car. He opened the door of the T-bird for her, then bent his head to kiss her. Alex's lips met his. He took her full in the arms, slamming the car door and leaning her against it while he kissed her deeply.

A hooker called to him from the corner, "Castro, honey, how come you don't do me like that?"

The bond was broken. Alex accepted his thanks for the house call and made her way home.

CHAPTER 25

Her late-night visit to Castro didn't slow her down the next morning. She was in her lab by 9:00 A.M., ready to take the steps she'd outlined on her list. She headed first to the file cabinet in her office, seeking a folder she'd never expected to use. She moved aside files on medical research at the front of the drawer to one labeled ominously "Project Salvation." She pulled out a piece of paper that had been distributed at the first meeting of the Commission on Bioterrorism. It listed the direct phone numbers for the Attorney General and top public health official of every state.

She stared at the list and had a brief moment of doubt. Was she jumping the gun with her panic? Seeing connections between patients that didn't exist?

As she perused the list, she was pleased to see a familiar name. The Utah director of public health, Dr. Margo Sanchez, had lectured last year at the AFIP about public health initiatives dealing with SARS. A vibrant woman in her early sixties, she'd been a leader in child health initiatives.

With the time zone difference, Alex expected to leave a message for the woman. But Margo answered the phone on the first ring and instantly remembered Alex from the AFIP. She listened carefully as Alex explained what was going on.

"I'll put hospitals on alert and make sure they collect samples of any tissue," said Margo. "We've got a pretty good state plan in place if it does spread. But, from what you told me, it's not like SARS or other infections where we could stockpile antibiotics. You really have no idea how to treat it?"

"I'd start with steroids and antihistamines, but that's just my seat-of-pants approach. Can you send me samples of the fountain water? That's our best shot right now. That and the patients' blood."

"Anything I can do. But if the symptoms are that grotesque and that untreatable, we've got to think about how to prevent a public panic."

In her second call, the equivalent Arizona official agreed to send her samples from the fountain, but he was much more skeptical. After she hung up, Alex realized that, even if she was correct about the source of the infection, it would be nearly impossible to prove it. All the Arizona deaths had occurred on the same Saturday two weeks before Ted's death; ditto with the Utah deaths, on the Saturday a week before his demise. Even if the water fountain theory was correct, whatever contaminant caused the hyperimmune response had probably been depleted within a day.

After those two calls, she looked up and down the list of phone numbers. Where would the disease strike next? Which states' officials should she warn?

She needed help on this, manpower. She looked at the first entry on the phone list. Martin Kincade, the head of Homeland Security. He'd certainly rubbed Barbara the wrong way. But as far as Alex was concerned, he was trying to do his best with the less-than-professional commission he was saddled with.

As Alex tried to figure out where to turn next, there seemed only one possibility. She took a deep breath, dialed Kincade's direct line, and stated her name. She was sure he'd provide the backup that she needed.

"You're using this line, you must have a situation. How many deaths so far?"

Alex tallied them up. "Twenty-seven total. Eight in New Mexico, seven in Utah, a dozen in Arizona."

"Any transmission beyond the original patients?"

"Not yet. So far it doesn't appear infectious."

"So these are self-contained incidents."

Alex explained what she'd tracked down so far, describing the criteria she'd used to search the medical records.

"Hold on there. What kind of crazy soup of variables is that—edema, liver failure, ICD 9 this and that, outdoors? You put enough variables into an equation and you'll find something that looks like a pattern. It's like me saying full moon, left-handed patient, mother's maiden name Hernandez. We'd get a bunch of matches around the country. Would seem like a full-fledged epidemic when really it was just coincidence. This probably is, too."

"That's not the case. There's a real pattern here."

"If the pattern were significant, our own monitoring programs would have picked it up. You're on the commission to advise us about the makeup of organisms when we identify them. Tracking trends is our job."

"You're just blowing me off?"

"No, Dr. Blake. I appreciate the call. But we're monitoring incidents with a higher priority now. Agencies like ours, we've got to marshal resources."

Alex heard the click as Kincade hang up. Son of a bitch, she thought, getting out of her chair and pacing her lab. Sure, he could be right. It could be a series of coincidences. But that would have been more likely with two or eight. Twenty-seven was pretty high to write off as a series of random events. Even if the chance that this was an emerging infection was low, the disease was grotesquely fatal. She couldn't just stand by while innocent lives were lost. If Kincade wasn't going to take responsibility, she'd bring to bear everything she'd ever learned to get to the root of this.

CHAPTER 26

After her frustrating conversation with Kincade, Alex sat on the stool in her lab in front of the medical records from Utah, Arizona, and New Mexico. She looked at her dad's photo, propped up against a bottle of reagents. An Air Force sergeant, her dad had hardly been older than Chuck when the photo was taken. He was only 28 when he died, a casualty of the Vietnam War, leaving 5-year-old Alex and her grieving mother. Alex considered the photo and tried to look to his memory for advice. But their relationship had been one of hugs and stories, nothing to prepare her for this new specter of death.

She reached into the saddlebag she'd deposited on the counter and pulled out the yellow pad she'd filled the night before. She turned to the page on medical tests, checking off ones that had already been run. So far, the tests on Ted and Leroy had led to dead ends. But now that more victims had been identified, additional types of tests were possible. With enough blood samples, she could compare the DNA of the victims to each other. Maybe these people had succumbed to a variation of *Inflatus Magnus* that affected people later in life, rather than in infancy as it had hit Dr. Andover Teague's charges. But what was it in the fountains that had led them to react so violently to man-made substances?

Her quest was problematic because she didn't know which genetic mutation caused the disease that attacked Teague's patients. Plus, fingering a particular gene or group of genes as the cause of a disease was as difficult as finding a serial killer. There were almost thirty thousand genes in the body, which made millions of proteins and combinations of proteins. For some genes and proteins, the tests hadn't even been developed yet.

How might she figure out if a genetic mutation was responsible for the deaths? She thought about the early research identifying disease genes. The researchers would collect blood samples from people with a particular disease and an equal number from people without the disease. Then they would look for patterns. What genetic signature did the ill people have that the healthy people—the control group—didn't? When researchers found a shared genetic pattern among the ill, they would tentatively declare that the genetic sequence they had identified predisposed those people to the disease. Hundreds of blood samples were needed to avoid false associations. Say you had only fifty people with the disease and you found they all had a segment on chromosome 18 that repeated GACGACGAC. And only one of the people in the control group had that repeat. You might think that the pattern was the key to the disease, when actually it was a genetic sequence related to ear shape or eye color. There were thousands of ways in which people could be alike or different. You needed lots of blood samples to make sure that the genetic sequence you identified was the right one—the one truly associated with the disease.

Alex didn't have hundreds of people. She had only twenty-seven—the nineteen whose charts Chuck had printed off and the original eight from New Mexico. She decided to call the hospitals to request blood or other tissue samples of the victims to search for similarities to Ted's and Leroy's DNA.

She started with the seven children who'd died in Utah. The first two calls yielded nothing, since the children had died near a playground in a poor neighborhood where ambulances were slow to respond. Since they hadn't been admitted to a hospital, there were no blood samples to be sent to Alex. The rest, though, had undergone blood work in the ER before they passed away. The hospital would express the samples so Alex would get them the next day.

Arizona was more problematic. The deaths had occurred near the border town of Nogales. Two of the patients' families—apparently undocumented workers—had given false addresses and phone numbers, so there was no way for Alex to get in touch with them. Another half-dozen calls went unanswered. Alex thought of leaving messages, but didn't know how distrustful people would be of a call from a government agency, so she decided she would call back. She was able to get a few blood samples from two local hospitals. The jogger who'd died hadn't been asked for blood in the ER, according to his wife. Before Alex hung up, she remembered that he had been shaving when he'd starting swelling. The wife agreed to express Alex his razor, in case there was any blood there.

New Mexico produced the same mixed results. In total, Alex had access to samples from only a handful of the twenty-seven patients. She powered on her computer and opened up the hospital records' database, intending to figure out which states to analyze next.

She typed in her access code, but nothing happened. She figured she must have mistyped a digit, so she concentrated and tried again. Same result. She looked up the phone number for computer tech support on the commission list. She identified herself and gave the man her access code.

"I just tried it on my end and it doesn't work here either," he said. "Are you sure you've got the right code? It has to be a combination of at least eight letters and at least twelve numbers."

"I was just using it this morning. It worked then."

"Hold on. I'll check something else." He didn't wait for Alex to respond, but left her dangling with music in the background, something akin to the soundtrack of a Bollywood movie.

Great, thought Alex, they've outsourced to India the tech support for the U.S. Commission on Bioterrorism. Is a guy making ten dollars a day really the best person to guard state secrets?

The man came back on the line. "I'm sorry, miss, but your number has been deactivated. You'll have to call the chairman of the commission."

Yeah, right, thought Alex. Calling him was what got her knocked out of the system to begin with.

With no access to additional patient records, Alex redoubled her efforts to contact the Arizona relatives who hadn't answered their phones earlier. At the first house, before she could launch into who she was, the man on the other end of the line said, "¡Es Ud. abogada?"

When she was a kid, Alex's mother had parked her at camps each summer, so as not to have to deal with her. Circus camp, magic camp, soccer camp, art camp, Spanish camp. Sometimes it came in handy, like when she wanted to pull a quarter out of a young patient's ear or converse in Spanish.

A lawyer? "No. ¿Quién la necesita?" Who needs one?

"My hermana, Elena."

Why would the woman Alex was calling need a lawyer? Then she figured the woman was just taking advantage of the new American dream—litigation as a lottery ticket. Maybe someone else had figured out the connection to the water fountain and she was suing the city for her daughter's death.

There was a moment of silence on the other end. And then a younger, female voice said, "Please, can you help my madre?"

Alex asked, "May I speak to her?"

The girl spoke rapidly, hysterically. "The police take her. She's in jail. They think she kill my sister."

Oh my God, thought Alex. She tapped the fingers of her left hand nervously on her desk, like a musical concert gone awry. She looked at Dana Rodriguez's chart, open in front of her. She'd wondered why there were more than the usual hospital notes. The girl had not only had blood tests but even a postmortem X-ray. She was the only victim who'd died in Coronado Hospital. The doctors must have thought her injuries were due to abuse.

The girl on the other end was crying now.

"Where did they take your mom?"

"To jail! To jail!"

"There in Nogales?"

"Yes."

"Okay, honey, my name is Alex and I'll find out what's happening and call you back."

"My madre never hurt Dana. Nunca. Never."

"I believe you."

When Alex hung up, she called the Nogales city hall and asked to be connected to the prosecutor in the Dana Rodriguez case, Arthur Kline.

"Dana didn't die of child abuse," she told him.

"If you want to appear as a character witness, the defense is entitled to call you as part of their case."

"No, I'm not a character witness. I don't know the woman."

"Then why are you wasting my time?"

"I'm a doctor. The child had a syndrome that is fatal."

"I'm not buying it. The kid had a broken rib. What kind of so-called syndrome does that?"

Alex thought for a moment. So that's what they found on X-ray. She thought about Ted. "I bet it was the bottom rib and she was wearing a belt."

113

Kline seemed puzzled. "How did you know that?"

"The syndrome causes rapid swelling. A couple of the other people who died had broken toes because of the pressure against their shoes."

"Maybe you should come to the arraignment tomorrow. We like to be tough on child abuse, but we also like to get it right. You practice here in Nogales?"

"No, I'm in D.C." Alex thought of the amount of time it would take—some would say waste—for her to fly down to Tucson and take a cab to Nogales. Then she thought about the hysterical girl on the phone. "If I can get there tonight, can you arrange for me to talk to Elena?"

"I guess," he said. "Call me when you get here. I'll tell you what to do and where the arraignment is supposed to take place."

She hauled ass to the airport, not even stopping at home for an overnight bag.

While the plane was on the runway, she called Elena's daughter, Emilia, and said she would be talking to her mother that night. "Don't worry," she told the girl. "It's going to be alright."

At the Nogales jail eight hours later, Alex handed over her fanny pack for inspection and the guard started taking things out—her cell phone, her pen, her notepad. Each disappeared for a different reason. The phone to prevent unauthorized calls by inmates. The pen could be used as a weapon.

"Why take away the notepad?" Alex asked. "Do you think I'm going to fly her out of here on a paper airplane?"

"No pen, no good use for the paper," said the guard. He seemed sufficiently irritated by her question that he said, "I'm going to have to keep it all."

Frustrated, Alex was passed on to the next guard. "You have to sign this, warranting that you haven't keestered anything."

She had no idea what he meant.

He rephrased his question: "Any contraband up your asshole?"

Alex's mouth gaped.

The guard continued. "You'd be surprised what people bring in with a balloon up the rear. Drugs, cell phones, money. One even tried to bring in a switchblade, but it shifted in position and the guy punctured his colon."

She passed through a metal detector and was patted down by a female guard, who then led her into a large visiting room with wooden tables and chairs and a bank of vending machines against one wall. This late at night, nearly midnight, the place was deserted. Alex's wallet was in the confiscated fanny pack, but she took some crumpled dollar bills out of her pocket and headed to the coffee machine for some caffeine to speed up her brain. It was almost three in the morning her time and she had to stay sharp to find out what she needed and get Elena out of there.

The female guard stood inside the room, near the doorway. She was a stocky blonde with an ill-fitting green uniform that gapped oddly over her breasts. On her hip hung a billy club, handcuffs, and a stun gun. The inside guards were not allowed to carry real guns, though the outside tower guards were.

"Want something?" Alex asked the guard as she inserted a dollar into the machine.

The woman stared her down fiercely. "We aren't allowed to accept any-thing from inmates or visitors." She had taken her billy club off her belt and was pounding it against the palm of her left hand, ready to spring into ac-tion.

Okay, thought Alex. Maybe people become guards because they like sit-uations where the rules are clear. Or maybe, thought Alex as she listened to the slap of club against palm, they just plain love the violence.

As Alex waited for the next fifteen minutes, she felt like a prisoner her-self. She decided she would go nuts if she were forced to spend time behind bars. She couldn't handle the sensory deprivation.

Too antsy in her chair, Alex started walking around the room, but the bare walls provided no stimulation. Devoid of artwork, the walls had only one decoration—a yellowed poster of warnings. Visitors and inmates are not to touch each other. Visitors shall not pass anything to inmates. Visitors are not to use the bathroom without permission. Visitors will be searched before and after using the bathroom—in case, Alex guessed, a visitor had keestered something and tried to remove it to pass to the inmate.

A door on the other side of the room opened and in walked a thin, dark-haired female guard, Elena in tow. Alex started toward her, instinctively moving her right hand to shake Elena's hand before her brain cells registered that the prisoner's hands were cuffed behind her. The almost imperceptible gesture on Alex's part—which clearly would have violated the no-touching rule—was enough to cause the stocky blond guard to appear at Alex's side.

Great. Now both Elena and Alex had a hovering guard, ready to pounce at any indiscretion.

Elena's guard unlocked the handcuffs and cuffed the woman's left hand to the table leg. Elena rested her head on her right hand, squinting her eyes as if she were battling a massive migraine. Then she opened her eyes and stared at Alex. She managed to maintain a look of dignity despite the faded orange prison uniform, her reddened eyes from mourning her daughter, and the tangle of her gleaming black hair.

"I'm Dr. Alexandra Blake," she said.

Elena's tired eyes showed a faint disappointment. "You're not the lawyer?"

Alex shook her head. "But I think I can help you. I'm investigating a disease that might have caused your daughter's death. Why don't you tell me what happened."

Elena sniffed and wiped her eyes with the corner of her right sleeve. She gritted her teeth, massaging her temple to fight off pain.

"Have you had anything to eat or drink?" Alex asked. "Would you like some coffee?"

The woman nodded. "They give me nothing."

The guard behind Elena glared as if the woman had spoken out of turn, disclosing some state secret. Alex bounded toward the machine, prepared to create a meal for Elena. Then she realized the entrance guard had her fanny pack. She chose carefully with the limited money in her pocket. A bag of Ritz Bits with cheese—highly processed cheese to be sure, but at least it had some protein. And the coffee the woman had requested. Alex grabbed some powdered cream alternative, sugar, and a plastic stirrer.

Back at the table, Alex ripped open the bag of Ritz Bits, saving the woman the embarrassment of clumsily attempting it one-handed. Elena nodded gratefully and gazed at the packet of powdered creamer. Alex ripped that open as well. "Tell me what happened," she said.

"I push Dana on a swing and a friend come talk to me. Dana run for a drink. Then she jump up to the plastic rings."

Tears were running down Elena's face. She shook some powdered creamer into her coffee and took a sip to compose herself. "She scream and fall down.

Blood come out her mouth. I pinch her nose and blow in her mouth like in the movies."

Elena started sobbing wildly and Alex thought she had lost it over the death of her daughter. But in an instant, Elena was gasping for air. At first, Alex attributed it to her grief, but then Elena's nose started bleeding and her face began to balloon.

Alex felt paralyzed, like the first time she'd seen a gunshot victim in the ER. The room seemed to swirl around her. It was only a few seconds, but she felt like she'd lost her voice for hours. "Undo the cuff," Alex yelled at the guard closest to Elena. "Once the swelling hits her wrist, the metal will break her bones."

The dark-haired guard leaned forward to do so, but Alex's guard stopped her. "That's against the rules," she said, billy club now aimed at her sister in uniform.

Alex flung hot coffee in the aggressive guard's face, which caused her to drop the club and cover her eyes. "Do it!" Alex yelled at the other guard.

But it was too late. Seconds later, a horrible crack and a piercing wail accompanied the breaking of Elena's wrist bone. Alex squashed her paper cup into the shape of a tongue depressor and shoved down Elena's tongue, as she'd done many times for people having seizures. Elena's incisor clamped down on Alex's finger, breaking the skin. But Alex held the cup in place. She didn't want Elena to swallow her tongue and she didn't want the swollen tongue to block Elena's breathing. Blood poured from Elena's nose over Alex's hands. "Get a medic. She needs Benadryl and epinephrine right now."

But instead the angry guard pulled an alarm switch. A frightening siren filled the room and a dozen armed guards ran through the door. Two pulled Alex off the terrified inmate.

Alex fought them, but they cuffed her hands behind her back. In the melee, with no prison rules to cover the event, Alex tried biting and kicking the guards around her. "I'm a doctor. Let me help her. Get an ambulance."

But other than restraining the two women, the guards did nothing but stare as the bloated Elena gagged for air one more time and died.

CHAPTER 27

Alex spent the night in a Nogales jail cell. The hard slab of a bed was covered with a ratty sheet that reeked of urine. The toilet in the cell was sufficiently unappealing that the previous occupant must have said, Why bother? Alex started stripping the thin sheet off the bed, but the mattress proved even more disgusting. A family of insects was living in a large indentation between two prominent stains.

She suddenly lost interest in sleep. It would have been unlikely anyway, given the screeching moans of the woman in the next cell and the loud, angry conversation another inmate was having with herself. Alex tried to remind herself how, just a few years back as a medical student, she'd often gone a night or two without sleep. On her surgical rotation, she'd staff the ER at night and attend surgeries during the day, then chase down patients' test results and read up on their maladies. The adrenaline run of task after task had kept her going. But here she had nothing to distract her.

She thought of how her mother had tried to get her to take yoga. She sat cross-legged on the floor of the cell in the corner farthest from the toilet and tried to think of a good memory. But the dying face of Elena Rodriguez filled her thoughts, alongside the broken promise she'd made to the woman's daughter.

At 8:00 A.M., she was allowed her one phone call. In the confusion the night before, no one had let her know on what grounds she was being held. She'd

118

violated a posted rule by touching an inmate, but that hardly seemed the sort of offense that would lead to imprisonment. She guessed it was that little matter of assaulting a guard, or actually three. But when a male guard escorted her to the phone, he let slip that she was being held in connection with Elena Rodriguez's murder.

Holy shit, thought Alex. Then she considered her options in terms of calling a lawyer. She could call the local prosecutor who'd arranged for her visit. She'd already explained to him about the syndrome. He might believe her when she explained that Elena had died of the same disease as her daughter. But, then again, it was so early in the morning here that she would just get his answering machine. And for all she knew, he was the one preparing the murder indictment.

Alex realized that, with a homicide charge on the table, it was time for her to call in the Marines. Or at least one member of the Navy. She dialed Barbara at the office, where it was 10:00 A.M. Alex explained what had happened and Barbara said she'd have a lawyer from the U.S. Attorney's office extricate Alex immediately. This was a federal, not a state, matter, Barbara explained, in the high-falutin' lawyer voice that Alex sometimes overheard, but had never experienced addressed to her. Apparently it mattered that Alex was investigating deaths that crossed state borders.

"Just get me out of here, Barbara," Alex said. "Before I organize the loonies on my cell block to try a prison break."

When she was led back to her cell, Alex went over the events of the previous day, step by step. Elena had been taken to jail midday, before Alex had phoned her house. She'd told Alex that her jailers hadn't given her anything to eat or drink. How had the disease overtaken her? She hadn't had access to a drinking fountain. Yet Alex knew with a chilling certainty that the artificial creamer had triggered the hyperimmune response. Alex's guilt at precipitating her death was overpowering.

But what was the exposure that caused Elena to be susceptible in the first place?

Suddenly, the horrifying truth dawned on Alex. Elena had given mouth-to-mouth resuscitation to her daughter when the girl was bleeding. The disease could be transmitted through blood, just like AIDS. Maybe it could even go airborne. The Southwestern United States might be on the verge of a massive epidemic.

Alex needed to start warning people. She pounded on the bars of her cell and yelled, "Let me out! I've got to get out!"

"Yo, bitch," cried someone from another cell. "Me first."

No matter how much Alex screamed, no guard responded. With her throat sore from the yelling and her palms burning from hitting the rusty bars, Alex sunk to the floor. Please, Barbara, she thought, work your magic.

CHAPTER   28

For the next three hours, no one entered the hallway in front of Alex's cell. The vision of Elena swelling and dying in front of her haunted her thoughts. She chose to deal with the painful memory the way she dealt with any adversity in her life. She focused on science, trying to recall the genetic sequences of various inflammatory disorders—rheumatoid arthritis, asthma, lupus—and determine any possible links to what killed Elena. But that only frustrated Alex. This was not how she was used to doing science. In her lab, she would think of a sequence, look it up in GenBank, the online posting of sequences, and then run Medline searches for medical and scientific articles. She would turn to her equipment, coaxing information out of blood and other pieces of people. Here, she didn't even have a pen or pencil to write things down. Even if she had a great idea, how could she be sure she'd remember it later? This was like waking from a dream with a cure for cancer and then forgetting it by the time you finished breakfast. Only this was not a dream, but a waking nightmare.

They'd put her on suicide watch the night before, not, they said, because she was nuts, but because that's what they did with all first timers. They'd removed her belt—and also her leather-banded wristwatch, just on the off chance that she would try to slit her wrists with the tiny metallic wind-up button. At the time, Alex had thought it unlikely, considering it would be as difficult to kill yourself that way as to paint a Vermeer with a single thick black Magic Marker. But she was beginning to see how the solitude might provoke inmates to claw the walls to tunnel out of jail or saw at their wrists with a tiny button to escape life entirely.

Without her watch, she could only vaguely judge the time by the appearance of a Hispanic woman in a hairnet, rolling a cart with sandwiches on it. When she slid a sandwich through the bars of the cell, Alex opened her mouth to speak, but the woman shook her head. Apparently, fraternizing with the inmates was forbidden. No sense getting her in trouble; she'd be of no use in springing Alex.

Alex took the sandwich, feeling the scratchy, hard bread in her hand. She bit into it and tasted a foul baloney. One bite was enough to persuade her to discard it, but she wasn't sure where. If she put it in the toilet, it would clog the pipe. If she put it on the bed, the insects would have a feast. She balanced it upright on the sink, between the faucet and the wall. At least the bugs would have to do a bit of work if they wanted their lunch.

With her scientific moorings upset, Alex's thoughts leaped randomly. An image of one of the many apartments she and her mom lived in after her father died. The smell of his aftershave. A trip to the Vietnam Veterans Memorial. A Tina Turner song.

She didn't even realize she was singing the song out loud until another inmate yelled at her to shut up. Suddenly, the wails and cries of the women in the other cells started to make sense. It was a language, as legitimate as French or Swahili. A language of loneliness and despair.

Alex's second baloney sandwich of the day arrived, marking the dinner meal. Hungry, she forced herself to eat it this time, trying to fool herself into thinking it was something else, perhaps those perfect crab cakes she had shared with Castro at the Old Ebbitt Grill. Magical thinking seemed to be working. She devoured the sandwich and was rewarded with an inexplicable reprieve. A guard she hadn't seen before opened her cell and let her out. As she walked alongside the guard, someone approached from behind, yanking Alex's arms backward and pinning them in cuffs behind her. She looked over her shoulder and saw that it was the blonde she'd thrown coffee at the day before, trying to save Elena's life.

The two guards escorted her through the administrative procedure of signing out and retrieving her possessions. The blonde then shoved her out the door of the jail, almost knocking her down the steps. A man got out of his car and put up a hand in protest. The guard uncuffed Alex and pushed her his way, tossing Alex's fanny pack at her feet. "Bitch," the guard said.

Killer, thought Alex.

"That's quite an introduction, Dr. Blake," said the man, reaching down to pick up the fanny pack. Alex was rubbing her chafed wrists when he stood up and reached out to shake her hand. "I'm Bill Brown, the Assistant U.S. Attorney for the State of Arizona. I had to promise the warden I'd personally make sure you got on a plane."

"I'm more than happy to get out of here."

He glanced at her shirt, which was spotted with Elena's blood, and then at her fanny pack, which was too small to hold a change of clothes. As he walked her around to the passenger side of the car, he popped the trunk. He rooted around under fishing equipment and handed Alex a faded sweatshirt that said SAM'S FISH AND TACKLE.

At the Tucson airport, Alex made a move toward a ladies' room to change her shirt.

"Hold it," said the attorney. "I had to swear I wouldn't let you out of my sight until you got on the plane."

"I've got infected blood on my shirt."

"And I've got my orders." He looked at the line of women waiting to get into the bathroom. "You can change on the plane. Once you're on board, you'll be someone else's worry."

Alex opened her mouth to protest, but decided he'd been a decent enough guy. Instead, she walked toward a darkened bar where she could grab a coffee. "You've probably gotten a wrong impression of me," she said as they sat down.

"Accused murderer, assaulted a few guards, and I've got to let you go because you're some sort of national security asset."

Alex smiled. She'd wondered what Barbara had said to bust her out. "All that plus I make a mean margarita."

She wondered if she should ask the attorney to keep an eye out for other cases of the disease in the area, now that she knew it was transmissible. She'd noticed a small fishing rod in the trunk, probably his kid's. She thought about the panic it could cause if word got around that a deadly disease was about to run rampant through the state. She'd have to be careful how she handled this.

He walked her to the plane, depositing her as the first one to board. The first class passengers complained to each other about how she'd cut in line. She turned to him. "Thanks for the shirt," she said. "And thanks for being such a decent guy."

Then she found her seat and fell asleep before the other passengers began boarding. She didn't even wake up when the plane touched down in Denver at 11:00 P.M. and picked up more passengers.

At National Airport in D.C., at seven the next morning, she bought a toothbrush and paste, entered the ladies' room, and started to clean up. She pulled a comb out of her fanny pack and tried to untangle her mane of curly hair. Satisfied that she could almost pass for normal, she stepped into a stall and put the fishing shirt on. It would do. At least it had more character than the I LOVE D.C. shirts on the airport racks.

Even after just a short stint in a solitary jail cell, the glare and chaos of the airport concourse seemed overwhelming. But her mood was buoyant. She was free. She could do science the way she wanted. She could enlist others to aid her.

She maneuvered her T-bird to the Bethesda, Maryland, Homeland Security building where the monitoring of bioterrorism took place. It had been located there, rather than in the District, in order to take advantage of the many scientists at the nearby National Institutes of Health who might be called upon if a serious incident occurred.

Alex slid her car into a spot in the visitors' parking lot, taking advantage of the orange Homeland Security sticker she'd been issued when she joined the bioterrorism commission. As she entered the building, she was pleased to see that her commission ID card was enough to get her past security. She knew how Homeland Security prided itself on its vigilance and smiled about how they had just let a crazed blonde in a fishing shirt into their own building without asking what she was doing there.

The last commission meeting she'd attended took place three months earlier, but the facility was not that large and she readily found the director's office. Martin Kincade was standing outside his office, instructing his secretary on something or other, when he caught sight of Alex.

He looked annoyed, but motioned her into his office. "Okay, Dr. Blake, you've got exactly two minutes to explain why you're here."

Kincade remained standing and didn't ask Alex to sit. She knew that she had one chance to convince him of the gravity of the situation. The second she left his office, he'd deactivate her building pass, just like he'd withdrawn her computer access.

"This outbreak is more serious than I thought. Last night, the mother of one of the victims died. It proves that the disease is contagious. I think a good portion of the Southwest may be at risk."

"How do you even know the deaths of the mother and child are related?"

Alex half closed her eyes as she remembered the terrifying events in the jail, "I was with her when she died."

Kincade's face reddened. "Didn't I tell you to lay off this investigation?"

"Well, actually, sir . . ." Alex could have kicked herself for using that term of respect, but there was something about the way the man barked at her that made it seem necessary. "You didn't think it was a commission matter, so I felt free to pursue it." Realistically, thought Alex, she would have pursued it in any case. She was never one for lines of authority.

"These are random incidents," he said. "Based on your call, I asked my people to do some checking. The death rates in the areas where you claim the illness has struck show no significant increases over last year at the same time."

Alex, starting to feel desperate, stomped her foot and crossed her arms in front of her body. "You're talking about aggregate statistics and I'm talking about individual cases. Other than in Taos, this disease has struck in poor areas. You're right—people, on average, have a high death rate in those areas. But that's due to drive-by shootings, cardiac arrests in a public housing project that ambulances refuse to service—"

"And illegal drug use, don't forget that. We think that's the culprit. Which makes it a DEA matter, not Homeland Security's."

"Six Mormon children on a field trip? They're not exactly street drug users."

"We're investigating the man who admitted them to the hospital. He might have slipped a drug to them without their knowledge."

"That's ridiculous," she said. Then she wondered how he even knew who had admitted the students. She'd never told him who the children were. "You've been spying on my computer searches?"

"Dr. Blake, wake up and smell the legislation. This agency has authority to monitor any Internet traffic. You just made it easier by going into the medical databases using a password we issued. But I can assure you that we've followed up and don't see any threat. We are on top of everything that is coming out of the CIA, Interpol, the FBI, DEA, Mossad, the PLO, you name it. There's no indication that any terrorists have entered the country to plan a biowarfare attack."

"This may not be a terrorist attack. It's got the earmark of an emerging pathogen. But it still needs to be taken seriously. We've got to go after the virus angle or whatever materializes. At least reauthorize my computer access so I can keep tracking it. Twenty-eight deaths so far and that's just three states, Arizona, New Mexico, and Utah."

"That last thing we need is for you to be crying wolf, riling up the public."

And that was it—she was dismissed. He walked her out of his office, to the desk of his secretary. The woman quickly shoved a folder over a paper on her desk. In the few seconds before it was covered, Alex saw that it was a map, with four states colored in.

On the wall above the secretary's desk, Alex noticed the poster of Homeland Security's threat levels—green, blue, yellow, orange, and red.

"Martin," she said, dropping the *sir* and angering him by using his first name, "this is a serious epidemic and you're sitting on top of the one agency that has the resources and know-how to control it."

His secretary's mouth fell open—whether at the use of his first name or Alex's mention of an epidemic, it was hard to tell.

"Your exaggerations are the only risk here," he said. "The last thing we need is a public panic."

"If you don't start intervening soon," Alex said, "there will be more to worry about than managing the public's emotional state."

She moved over to the poster and continued. "Perhaps you should add a new color here," she said, pointing with a dramatic flourish not usually seen in people wearing fishing sweatshirts. "Black. For death."

"Nice try, Dr. Blake, but right now it's all just a fish tale."

CHAPTER 29

From Homeland Security, Alex headed to the AFIP. In her lab, she used a sterile pair of scissors to cut small pieces of bloodied fabric from the shirt she'd worn to the jail. She snipped with angry determination as she thought about the poor girl she'd talked to two days earlier. Emilia had lost her sister one day and then her mother a few weeks later. I'm going to find why this happened, Alex said, in a mental conversation with the little girl.

Some of the fabric pieces she put into evidence bags, but a few she soaked in various solvents. She could begin testing the blood to compare it to the other victims'. She'd only had a small sample of Ted's blood, and she hadn't wanted to use it up before she had more evidence to determine the types of tests she would undertake. With Leroy Darven, she'd gotten more blood. But plenty of Elena's blood had soaked into her shirt, so she had more leeway to undertake tests of things like trace metals that might seem far afield, but had a remote chance of yielding important results. Now that she knew the disease was transmissible, she'd put a high priority on tests that would allow her to determine if a new infection had emerged, like the appearance of AIDS in the 1980s.

If Homeland Security had agreed to be involved, she'd have access to the best minds in trace testing. They had people who could test the dust on an airplane passenger's jeans and tell which countries he'd visited before landing. They had testing machines that ran ten times faster than anything she had here. But she had determination, and—truth be told—some of the Walter Reed equipment was pretty good. Mostly as a result of a scandal about shoddy care at the facility. A powerful lobby of World War II vets—as well as donations from wealthy filmmakers like Steven Spielberg and Ron Howard, who'd made films about that era—had convinced Congress to update the machinery used at Walter Reed. Plus, the AFIP's chief pathologist, Thomas Harding, was back from his regatta, which meant that Randolph Stone, the Walter Reed pathologist, would have a little time on his hands to help her. He was certainly motivated, given that he'd lost Ted's body.

The autopsy, Alex thought, taking a sharp breath. She hoped Randy had taken universal precautions—gloves, goggles, etc.—because if he'd touched any of Ted's bodily fluids, he might be facing the same horrible death as Elena Rodriguez had endured. Then she looked down at the index finger of her right hand. There was a small scab where Elena had bitten her. She thought of a surgical attending at Columbia with whom she trained. He'd been infected with hepatitis C from a patient on whom he'd performed a hysterectomy. The hospital blamed shoddy surgical gloves, ordered at a discount from China, for letting the patient's blood fatally infect him. The institution had paid a whopping settlement to his family to compensate them for that poor choice.

She looked again at the scab and fought the temptation to pick it off. It was nothing, she told herself. She picked up the phone and dialed Randy. She asked him to undertake drug and toxin testing on blood taken from Elena, which she would drop off. But when she hung up, she felt frustrated that those actions would look backward, trying to figure out the puzzle of what had happened. She needed to bring in some serious brainpower to look forward, to prevent the epidemic that was brewing. If Homeland Security was going to drop the ball by not seeing the connection among the deaths, she'd approach it in a familiar way. She'd ask Dan to help her follow the trail as if a serial killer were involved. In fact, she thought, isn't that precisely what is happening? But instead of killing victims one by one, the disease was polluting fountains, causing its victims to be the vectors of the next attacks. This killer, with twenty-eight deaths that Alex knew of, would soon surpass John Wayne Gacy's thirty-three victims and the Zodiac Killer's thirty-seven.

Alex called Dan. "Glad to have you back," he said. "Thought I was going to have to send a SWAT team to spring you."

"Good to know I can call on you for that sort of maneuver." Then she turned more serious and described the body count. She ended by asking, "What else have you learned about Ted?"

"We got zip from the medical records. Until he died, he was healthy as a horse. Chuck uncovered some charges on his Visa at a clinic-based pharmacy a week before he went to Taos—vitamins, cigarettes, Advil. But it turned out to be an obstetrics clinic. Must have been there with his blonde."

"Can we get the team on this?"

"It's outside our usual parameters."

"I haven't got a lot of options right now."

"Alright then. Task Force room, 1600 hours."

After she hung up, Alex thought about how the two hats she was wearing at the AFIP—one for bioterrorism and one for forensics—were now both firmly perched on her head. With the emergence of a fatal disease with novel properties, she'd be pushed to the limit on both her skill sets.

By the time Alex entered the conference room that served as the nerve center for Dan's forensic investigations, Grant and Chuck were seated at the conference table. Dan was talking to them from behind his desk, which he'd moved into the room over a year earlier to be close to his investigators. Although Alex had come to the AFIP to sequence the genome of the Spanish flu and work on biowarfare projects, she'd been pulled into enough forensic cases to know how to present the facts succinctly. She rattled off, in chronological order, the relevant events since Ted's death and the failure of Homeland Security to pay attention to the threat. She mentioned the odd appearance in Taos of the researcher from Waverly Pharmaceuticals and Dan said he'd arrange to have Renfrew tailed. She ended her presentation with Elena's death.

When she finished, Grant whistled under his breath. "Son of a bitch. That guard should be shot for not letting you at Elena."

"She was just doing her job, Grant," said Dan. He looked at Alex. "Do you think you could have saved her?"

"We'll never know, will we?" she said. "Frankly, I have no idea what to do for these people once their immune systems have gone crazy. And there's so little time. Death occurs within just a few minutes."

"I can deploy military investigators to the sites of the water fountains," Dan said, "and track suspicious activity prior to the incidents."

"Hold on. There may not be a person behind it," Alex said.

"Come on," said Grant. "There's got to be a real live perp. Each attack occurred on a Saturday. What kind of disease does that?"

"Lots of diseases have incubation periods where it may take five days or a week for symptom to appear." Alex argued. "Besides, who'd deliberately do something like this?"

"Some sicko," said Grant. "We've seen plenty of 'em."

Well, maybe he had a point. Before she'd come to the AFIP, she wouldn't have imagined a guy like the Tattoo Killer. But once she'd seen his handiwork—the mutilation of a Navy-base librarian—she realized that the actions of certain killers were unfathomable to an outsider, even if they made a certain sick logic to the murderer himself.

"Assuming it was a person," Chuck said, qualifying his remarks so as not to offend either Alex or Grant, "why would he pick fountains?"

"Plenty of reasons," said Dan, the forensic chief. "Lets him knock off a lot of people at the same time. Plus, a stranger around a fountain wouldn't raise suspicions. It's not like wiring a bomb onto someone's car."

"But," Alex said, "why would he—or she—target kids? Adults carry bottled water. It's usually just kids who hit the fountain."

"Maybe we need a profiler," Chuck said.

Grant interjected, "Why pay the freight? It's just same old, same old from those shrinks. Hates Mom. Hates Dad. Or, in this case, could have been beat up by some bully in fourth grade and now wants to take down kids that age."

Alex usually disagreed with Grant, but she didn't have much tolerance for forensic psychiatrists. Like an earlier generation of geneticists, shrinks were full of simple explanations. The Human Genome Project had convinced Alex otherwise. Through her work on the project, Alex learned that simple explanations were rare. Traits, behaviors, even diseases were a complicated combination of interactions among genes, cells, and the environment. They were fueled by an ever-changing kaleidoscope of intentions, hormones, neurons, and emotions.

Chuck hung a map on the wall across from the conference table. He'd used a yellow highlighter to color in the states where the incidents had occurred and put black Xs on the specific cities. "Do you want me to check flight arrivals near Taos, Nogales, and Salt Lake for the few days before the incidents?" he asked Dan. "Even if someone isn't intentionally spreading the disease, it could be a kind of Typhoid Mary infecting the fountains."

Dan got up from his desk to look at the spots Chuck had marked—cities in Utah, New Mexico, Arizona. "No guarantee he flew," said Dan. "Could be he drove."

He turned to Alex. "We're better off tracking the infectious agent. How close are you to that?"

She looked down at her hands, staring again at the scab from Elena's bite, and then up at Dan. "I've got nothing so far. I'm having Randy check Elena's blood now. My tests of Ted's blood and Leroy Darven's blood didn't show any trace of a known bacteria or virus that might have caused the reaction. If it's an infection, it's transmitted by something we've never seen before."

"Who's the go-to guy on this sort of thing?"

"Pardon?"

"You know, when I've got a footprint at a crime scene, I know Sandy Tanaka is the one to bring in. Blood splatter, Bob Gaensslen. Who in medicine would you go to if you had a patient with these symptoms?"

"Someone in immunology would be a start," Alex said. "But this doesn't look like your typical immune system disorder."

"Then get me someone nonstandard," Dan said. "I'm putting my money on intentional. Think about it. The incidents occurred one week apart, in a different city, like clockwork. This guy is mobile and targeting a city a week. Fountains now. Next an entire city's water supply."

Alex looked at Dan. Could he be right? Alex wondered if they were really tracking a person poisoning the fountains, rather than a new infections disease. Either way, they'd need a lot of aid to get to the bottom of it. "There's a DEA agent who might be able to help us."

"Who?" asked Grant.

"Castro Baxter. The partner of the first victim," said Alex.

"What does he bring to the table?" Dan asked.

Alex formed a picture of the agent in her mind. Or, should she say, many pictures. He seemed a different man at each encounter. "He was with Ted when he died. He's already started an investigation. He's been back to the scene of Ted's death. And he's taken a crack at questioning the Waverly Pharmaceutical guy. But this isn't a DEA matter. None of the victims so far have had any trace of illegal drugs in their systems. He won't be able to take his investigation to the next step with the DEA."

Alex was intrigued by Castro Baxter, no doubt. But she wasn't the type to mix business and pleasure. She wouldn't want anything to cloud her mind—or his—as they fought this epidemic.

"See if he can join our meeting tomorrow morning," Dan said. "Could be he can fill in the blanks about his partner's last days."

But, thought Alex, with so many people dead, maybe Ted had never been a target at all. Just a guy in a devastatingly wrong place at a horribly wrong time.

CHAPTER 30

Back in her lab, Alex left messages for Castro at all his numbers. Then she logged on to her computer and searched through immunology articles. None of the scientists whose work she found were anywhere close to having the handle on these sorts of symptoms that Dr. Andover Teague did. He was the go-to guy Dan was seeking.

She checked the faculty website for the Harvard Medical School, but Teague was no longer affiliated with Harvard. No surprise—lots of people changed jobs. The American Medical Association didn't list him as a member— then again, only one-third of U.S. doctors joined the organization. But Alex could find no other trail for him. His publications in medical journals stopped fourteen years earlier. He didn't hold a driver's license in any of the fifty states.

Alex considered the unlikely possibility that Teague had died. He would have been, what? Midfifties now. She switched to a database with newspaper and magazine articles, figuring that, with his stellar medical record, he would have warranted an obituary in the *Boston Globe* or maybe even *Newsweek.*

Instead, Alex found an article in a 1993 issue of *Life,* complete with a photo of Andover Teague looking sternly into the camera with his hand on the shoulder of his first patient, a scared-looking 3-year-old boy who was stealing a glance up at the man. The headline, MODERN ALBERT SCHWEITZER CHARTS NEW COURSE FOR CHILDREN AT RISK, topped an article about how Teague and his high society wife of eight months, Bree Christalink, were leaving behind the comforts of Boston to create a special clinic in a remote area of Colorado. They had gathered up children with *Inflatus Magnus* from around the world and were going to live as if the year were 1860. They would wear natural fibers, eat buffalo meat (chickens and cows were fed too many artificial hormones and antibiotics), grow their own crops, and teach the children to read with century-old books that didn't use the artificial dyes of current inks.

Wow, thought Alex. In an era where medicine was turning to high-tech cures—expensive antibiotics and genetically engineered proteins that cost a patient tens of thousands a year—Teague could offer his patients a normal, healthy life without any medical intervention. But at what personal sacrifice to himself and his wife?

Alex scrutinized the photo of Mrs. Teague, heir to the Christalink banking and logging fortune. She was a glamorous redhead with her hair in a chignon. Alex shook her head. It would take an awful lot of hairspray to hold something like that in place, yet no hairspray—or other modern products or conveniences—would be allowed in the compond. Not to mention that Mrs. Teague had gone from debutante to mother of ten in less than a year. And her husband had vowed not to turn away any child, discovered anywhere around the world, who had the disease.

The clinic—or Colony, as Teague preferred to call it, protesting that these children were not sick—had been established by an anonymous bequest. Perhaps his wife's family fortune? Alex scrutinized the last photo. It showed an octagon-shaped log cabin with a wind chime of children's faces. The caption under the photo noted there was one chime for each of the ten original patients. The article explained that the camp was somewhere in Colorado, but that the location was a closely guarded secret.

"I don't want to turn this into a theme park," the doctor was quoted as saying. He recounted how the Dionne quintuplets, born in 1943, had been the subject of ruthless exploitation. The Ontario, Canada, government got a court order ousting the Dionnes' own parents and making the government their guardian. Then it turned the quints' home into the human equivalent of a petting zoo. Quintland was visited by millions of people, including Clark Gable and Amelia Earhart. By the time they were 9, the girls had been allowed outside the compound only three times. Their doctor was the best-known physician in the world.

Teague's quest for privacy made sense, but it wasn't what Alex wanted to hear at the moment. Surely there must be some way to get in touch with the man. She surfed the Web to see if any other publication mentioned the clinic. There were only two other articles. Ten years after the *Life* article, *Wired* described how a group of professors from MIT and Stanford had built a computer with all natural components so that the children at the camp could enhance their education via the Internet. The computer ran on a brilliant combination of glass, carbon, titanium, and gold chips embedded with DNA instead of silicon chips. With the four letters of the DNA code—and its ability to replicate indefinitely—the resulting machine was far superior to previous computers, which relied on only two characters, the 0s and 1s of the digital code. It had seemingly boundless storage capacity. But its klutzy size and expense put it out of reach of both the consumer and the usual industrial market. The Department of Defense had ordered the prototype. But the researchers had gotten permission to send a duplicate to the kids.

Alex phoned the MIT professor, Melinda Ingber, and explained her urgent need to reach Teague.

"Oddest thing," Ingber said. "We weren't given an address to ship to the Colony itself. Instead, we were told to send it to a contact in Wyoming. He apparently had some wood-paneled truck that he used to haul things to the Colony without the risk of contamination."

"Great. Have you got an address for him?"

"That was five years ago. Doubtful."

"What about e-mails? Once the computer was up and running, did the doctor contact you over the Internet to thank you?"

"We got an odd little e-mail about two weeks after we'd sent it. Formal-sounding, almost British in tone, expressing gratitude for the computer. I e-mailed back the next day, but the reply just bounced. Whoever sent it had already changed accounts. When I contacted Juno, the Internet provider on the e-mail, I was told the account never existed."

Alex thanked Professor Ingber. Whoever had sent the e-mail from the isolated Colony knew enough to hack into an Internet provider and get an untraceable message out. What exactly was going on in Dr. Teague's world?

Alex returned to her search for other traces of the man. The only other article linked to Teague had appeared just six months earlier. Andover Teague, M.D., and his co-author, Matthew Brunner, published an article in the *American Journal of Public Health*. Using records from the World Health Organization, they showed a marked increase in *Inflatus Magnus* across the world. Developing countries—Vietnam, Guatemala—had the largest up-surge as they moved from living close to the land to an acceptance of pesti-cides and fast food. But those countries also had the least capability for diagnosing the disease before the child had died.

Alex tipped her chair back as she considered this. If Teague was right, there was a growing childhood epidemic around the world and no one was paying attention to it. But the disease he was chronicling seemed clearly ge-netic in origin. Children were born with it. Their immunological reactions, when triggered by man-made substances like plastic, were milder, not neces-sarily fatal. How could a grown man like Ted Silliman suddenly develop similar—yet much more violent—symptoms?

Despite the differences, Alex felt sure that Andover Teague could provide some clues to help her understand what had happened to Ted and the others. He'd spent nearly twenty years of his life devoted to this type of disease.

She looked at the footnotes to the public health article, which normally would contain a way to get in touch with the authors. Their affiliation was listed as something called the Del Ray Institute, but there was no address either for Teague or his co-author, Brunner. The name seemed familiar, thought Alex. She turned back to the original *Life* article and there it was. Matthew Brunner was Teague's first patient, the scared-looking boy in the *Life* photo. Age 3 when he was diagnosed, he would now be around 18. Alex's heart swelled at the thought that he was still alive.

She wondered if the other children had likewise thrived. Isolation could have enormous tolls. These children had been wrenched from their families and taken to the middle of nowhere, away from every aspect of life they knew. It was for their own good, for sure, and most of them had been young enough not to have known another life. But once they got wired a few years back, they would have been able to access television, books, and other infor-mation sources about modern life. She wondered if any of them resented what they were missing.

CHAPTER   31

As Alex was leaving that evening, Dan asked about Castro. "I haven't heard back from him," she said. "He must be in the field."

From her car, she tried Castro's cell phone and work phone again. When he still didn't answer either one, she began to worry. He wasn't in the best shape when she'd seen him last. She decided to stop at Castro's apartment on her way home.

Castro's neighborhood looked even worse in daylight. Garbage tumbled out of cans onto the pavement, as if the garbage trucks had gone on strike. The smell when she got out of her car was overpowering, a mixture of rotting food and rotting lives. Two men in their early twenties shoved whatever they were holding into their pockets, then saw that she was just some blond woman and continued their transaction. She thought of Castro living just fifty feet away. Sometimes you can't escape from your work, she thought. It just follows you home.

She reached over to ring Castro's bell and then noticed the front door was slightly off its hinges, so there was no need for that particular step. She bounded up two flights of stairs and pounded on his door.

He came to the door with a nearly empty bourbon bottle in his hand, a couple of days' worth of dark stubble on his face, and a hard edge to his eyes. He said nothing to Alex, merely motioned with the bottle for her to come in.

"You look like shit," she said.

"Makes sense. Life's in the toilet."

"Where have you been? I've left you a bunch of messages."

Castro sobered. "Have you found out something about Ted?"

She shook her head. "No, but the body count is mounting. We've had twenty-seven deaths in three states."

"Like Ted's? Swelling and bleeding?"

Alex nodded. "The night before last in Arizona, a woman died right in front of me. Just like you said. That god-awful swelling, the sickening sound of her smothering to death, bones breaking."

Castro regarded her. His face softened and he took a step forward as if to comfort her, but held himself back.

Alex kept talking. "It's spreading, Castro. We've got a Task Force and we want you on it."

He did a drunken half bow in front of her. Alex thought he'd topple over. "'Fraid I won't be getting much of a recommendation from my current boss. Seeing as how he's recovering from a broken jaw from our last encounter."

"You decked Galloway?"

He shrugged.

Alex considered the fact. Based on what she'd seen of Agent Galloway in their first encounter at DEA headquarters, he probably had it coming. "I'll warn Dan to pay his health insurance premiums with you around."

"What would I do?" he asked as he led her into the kitchen.

"Same as you usually do. Investigate. Dan will clear it with your personnel folks."

"Why bother? I'm on administrative leave. A psych leave, to be exact."

Alex felt sorry for Castro. "It's hard to have your best friend die in front of you."

Castro tensed. "Don't give me some bullshit that you know how I feel."

His words stung her. This was not the Castro she knew. She thought of how, the last time she'd been at the apartment, he'd circled his arms around her and rested his chin on her head. Gone was any trace of intimacy.

"The only good thing for me is that the department shrink who caught my case had a roll in the hay with Ted. She knows that he lived and breathed the agency. She was ready to throttle Galloway herself when he claimed Ted was using cocaine."

"I know you want Ted's killer," she said. "Working with the AFIP would let you stay on the investigation."

"They'll just blow me off like DEA did," Castro said. "I'm not a team player."

"C'mon," she said. "We want to find out what happened to your friend as much as you do. His body was stolen from our facility."

He started pouring himself another drink, without offering one to Alex. Alex was beginning to smell disaster, or maybe it was just bourbon. She worried that she'd be spending her time standing up for Dan with Castro and vice versa. With the way both of them operated, there were bound to be conflicts. And she might be the one to get the blame.

The last drop of the bottle in his hand only partially filled the tumbler, so he reached into a plastic bag and took out a new bottle. As he did, a small slip of paper fell to the floor. The receipt. Alex picked it up, glancing at it as she placed it on the end table. It was from a drugstore in Connecticut. There were two charges on it. A bottle of bourbon and a pregnancy testing kit.

She held it out to him. "Expanding your family?" she asked, trying to sound lighthearted.

Castro took the paper from her, crumbled it into a ball, and threw it into the garbage can. He turned back around to face Alex.

"Just helping out a friend. Sintella got worried she'd gotten knocked up and didn't want to take time away from work to buy the kit."

"Sintella?"

"You know, the woman you met when I walked you to your car."

"Oh, the hooker."

Castro moved his pointer finger back and forth. "Now, now."

Alex wondered why, if he was helping a friend, he hadn't just gone to the CVS down the block. Connecticut was quite a drive to buy a ten-dollar item for some neighborhood pal. But she decided she'd pried enough already.

"Well, if you'd like the gig, we'll be in the Task Force conference room, 1508, at ten tomorrow morning. I'll leave you a building pass at the guard desk. Unless, of course, you and Mr. Jim Beam are going to crack this case yourselves."

CHAPTER   32

At 6:00 A.M. the next day, Alex was already in the glassed-in office in her lab. She'd slept fitfully, wondering if she'd done the right thing, inviting Castro into the investigation. Maybe he was too close to the whole thing. He was losing control of his life. What if Dan bounced him? That just might be the last straw for the man.

And something didn't make sense when Castro spoke of the pregnancy test kit. Could he and the hooker be lovers? Alex thought of the many faces of Castro she'd seen so far. The dapper undercover agent at the Taos bar. The angry—but still rational—tough guy arguing with Galloway the first day. The man who'd kissed her near the longhouse. The heartsick friend the night of Ted's funeral. And, last night, a dark, wounded animal. She wished she knew what magic emotional salve could calm him. But perhaps *calm* and *Castro* were not words that were easily joined.

At 10:00 A.M., Alex entered the Task Force room. Dan, Chuck, and Grant were already there, but Castro was nowhere in sight. Alex started the conversation, trying to ignore the fact that Dan was looking at his watch. "Randy Stone at Walter Reed has agreed to help with the analysis of the water from the fountains in Arizona and Utah," she said. "I'm trying to track down a doctor who was studying kids with a similar disease about fifteen years ago."

For the next few minutes, Alex spoke of the unusual doctor and his disappearance. Chuck brightened. Searching for the doctor gave him something concrete to do. "I'll check banks, the IRS, state nonprofit corporation filings, anything that might lead to Andover Teague," he said.

"Why bother with him?" Grant asked. "It can't be the same disease.

Teague's patients were born with it. These guys got it later in life. And you didn't mention any of Teague's kids passing the disease on to their parents. That's another difference."

Just my luck, thought Alex. The one time in which Grant exhibits some forensic insight—instead of just muscular flexes and a way with gadgets—he has to exercise it by pointing out the holes in my case. "That may be, but the symptoms are the same," she said. "I can't figure out what caused people to have a hyperimmune response, but that's exactly the question Teague has spent the past twenty years thinking about."

Just then, Castro appeared in the doorway, face still unshaven and his hair shaggy.

Grant turned to Alex and said, under his breath, "This is your secret weapon? He should be in a twelve-step program, not in the field."

But Dan's eyes had locked on Castro's. Each took the measure of the other. Alex sensed a familiarity there. Both men were tightly wound, determined, and used to prevailing. To his credit, Dan was willing to give the man a chance. He got up, walked over to the newcomer, and shook his hand. "Major Dan Wilson," he said. "And these are Corporal Chuck Lawndale and Captain Grant Pringle. I understand you've met Dr. Blake. Take a seat and we'll bring you up to speed."

Alex summarized what she knew about the Colony, and Castro asked, "How do they get their supplies?"

"Most modern supplies—foods, paper products, linens—would be deadly for them," she said. "According to the *Life* magazine article, they grow or catch the food they eat."

"Yeah, but things break down," Castro said. "A piece of the roof blows off and you need more wood. If they have a backup generator someplace, it will run out of propane from time to time."

Alex thought for a moment. "About five years ago, researchers from MIT and Stanford sent them a computer that runs on DNA. It was FedExed to a Wyoming address, but the researchers don't have the address anymore."

"Did you say DNA?" Grant asked. "Why put that in a computer?"

Alex was willing to defend DNA in all its mighty forms, but it was Chuck who jumped in. "Silicon chips will soon be obsolete," he said. "The number of components that can be etched on a silicon chip has been doubling about every eighteen months, but that will max out in the next decade. At that point, the chips won't be able to shrink further without electron leakage or other problems."

"So, what does DNA get you?" Grant asked.

Alex stepped in. "Richard Feynman once said, 'The inside of a computer is dumb as hell, but it goes like mad.' Computers' speed comes from their being able to quickly solve problems one step at a time. DNA is much faster. It replicates exponentially and each of the strands can be working on a different aspect of the problem at the same time. And rather than needing a billion-dollar dust-free factory to make thousands of silicon chips, I could use a single bacteria cell in a flask in my lab to produce billions more cells with the same DNA."

"And then you just pour it into a computer?" Grant asked.

For someone who headed a major technology section, thought Alex, Grant failed to grasp some of the basics of science. Were it not for his Rambo-like personality, which Congressional funding committees somehow found persuasive, he'd still be teaching firearms in boot camp, rather than working his way through a billion-dollar budget.

"The MIT/Stanford computer," said Alex, "is one hundred percent natural, which is why they can use it at the Colony. Inside its glass body, DNA is tethered to gold chips. At different points in a calculation, the surface of the chip is rinsed and the reagents for the subsequent step are added. The parallel processing of the DNA solves problems a hundred times faster than the computers now on the market."

"So, this baby actually works?" Grant asked.

"Yeah. One of the researchers got an e-mail thanks, but her reply bounced back. Whether it was Teague or one of the kids, the sender shut down that e-mail account right after expressing his gratitude."

"I'll talk to the researcher," said Chuck. "Maybe there's a way to track the IP address."

Alex should have thought of that. In a previous serial killer case, they'd been able to pinpoint the computers that he'd sent his messages from. If they learned where this magic computer was, they would know where to find Dr. Teague.

"If you find out when the computer was shipped," Dan said, "you can also pull FedEx records for an address."

"If it's as fast a computer as you say," Grant asked Alex, "why aren't we all using it?"

"Costs a fortune at the moment," she said. "Not that that has ever stopped the DOD from buying your overpriced toys."

"If you find this camp," said Grant, "I want to see the machine."

Alex looked at the pumped-up bodybuilder. Who knew what modern chemicals he used on himself to bulk up? The whole Colony might be allergic to him. "You don't have to wait that long," she said. "There's a twin to the computer at the Colony. It was bought by your favorite customer, the Department of Defense."

Grant's smile led Alex to surmise that he was about to barter some of his own new gadgets for a chance to take a peek at this million-dollar machine.

Castro walked Alex back to her lab when the session ended. "Thanks for taking a chance on me," he said. "And sorry about last night."

Alex nodded. When they stopped in front of her door, she asked, "What do you think of the crew here?"

He smiled. "The kid seems competent. The major's straight up. And I see you can't stand the bodybuilder."

Castro had hit it right on all counts. "They're a good team," she said. "Next time try to be on time."

His expression seemed serious as she glanced at him over her shoulder while she opened her lab door. She wondered if the darkness of the previous evening was still haunting him. "Are you free for dinner tonight?" she asked.

He considered her for a moment, a tall blonde framed in the doorway of her laboratory. The question seemed to inspire an unlikely amount of consternation for a man of action. She was about to withdraw the question when he shook his head. "I've got some loose ends on J to tie up. Gotta tell the Northern California agents what I know."

When he left, Alex thought how infuriatingly difficult it was to read that man. But she also felt reassured by his sense of purpose. He might still need a shave, but he was back on track, engaged, and in gear.

Alex settled into her own work, creating a chart with each of the deaths as a data point. She needed to track transmissions to the secondaries—people like Elena, who'd been infected by contact with the blood of the first generation of victims. Was the infection transformed when it reached the secondaries? Diseases mutated as they spread. Sometimes that allowed them to hop from species to species, like the avian flu, which had first affected birds but then reconfigured itself so that it could attack humans. If Elena was representative, the secondaries needed direct contact with the initial victims' blood to be affected. The CPR that Elena had given her bleeding daughter led to Elena's own death. But Dana's sister Emilia hadn't been affected, even though she had been nearby and had contact with both Dana and their mom. Less intimate contact didn't transmit the disease.

Alex thought about her tenth-grade health text. Using a stick-figure chart, it showed how one person with a sexually transmitted disease could lead to a virtual epidemic if each person he or she had sex with had sex with just one additional person. The motto of the chart was that, when you sleep with someone, you are also sleeping with that person's former lovers—at least from an infectious disease standpoint. From the risk created by one man, sixty or more loosely connected people could get an STD.

The numbers could increase exponentially for the infection from the fountains. With just a small mutation in its DNA, the disease might go airborne. Then, the limiting factors of an STD infection or AIDS—exchange of bodily fluids—would be eliminated. Instead, like TB or other respiratory threats, a single affected person on a 747 could infect the whole plane.

Alex paced around her lab as she thought of how to approach the disease. She not only would analyze how the blood of the first generation of victims differed from healthy people, but she could compare it to the blood of the secondaries, like Elena. Once she identified the cause of the disease, she could see how it was mutating.

Alex closed her eyes to think about where her reasoning was taking her. There had to be other Elenas out there. Other people in Nogales who'd been exposed to the fluids of the first victims. Maybe a spouse or an EMT worker. She took the logic one step further. Not only would there be a set of secondaries, like Elena, but the state health system would later be hit with a flood of tertiaries if the secondaries themselves infected other people.

Alex and her colleagues needed to act quickly, but they had no compelling leads. She knew nothing about the cause of this fatal immune reaction, where it would strike next, or how to treat it. But any mutation in the disease from the first to the second generation of victims might provide a clue about the disease's own weaknesses. For her analyses, Alex would need blood from the secondaries, but she knew of only one, Elena. A phone call to a hospital in Nogales led to information about other deaths. That week, ten other people had died in the same horrible way as Elena. Three of them had been admitted the day before their deaths, complaining of crippling migraines.

Alex felt a pain in the back of her head as she considered this news. She began phoning the new victims' family members and their doctors. Her fears were realized. The new victims—including an EMT worker and a teacher—had been exposed to the blood of one of the original twelve victims in Arizona. Quickly, Alex phoned the jogger's wife to warn her to get to a hospital. Answering the phone was a sobbing neighbor. The woman had just died in front of her. Alex could offer no solace, only a warning: "Don't touch the body. Call 911 and get a hazmat team there."

Alex phoned the Arizona public health director and told him what was happening so he would make sure the bodies were collected and handled in a safe way. "Maybe you should issue a warning about the disease," she said. "And let people know that the secondaries all had headaches before they died. Maybe if they got to a hospital right away something could be done for them."

"Are you crazy? The governor would have my head if I scared tourists away. And the last thing I need is every Tom, Dick, and Harriet with a headache crowding my ERs."

"At least warn your EMTs to wear gloves so they don't pick up the infection."

"Hasn't everybody heard that a million times before? The whole world's been on universal precautions since the AIDS epidemic. Besides, what would we advise them to do if they did get sick?"

Alex was silent for a moment. "You're right, of course. Until there's a treatment, all we'll do is create a panic with no solution. But promise me you'll keep people away from fountains."

"That I will do."

Alex hung up. It was a small step and maybe even a useless one. This disease or person or whatever was behind the deaths had hit only one fountain in each of the three states. A warning to the citizens of Arizona wouldn't do much good if the next target was New Jersey, Montana, or some other state.

Alex felt weary, her body heavy, her mind disturbed from all that had happened in the past seventy-two hours. She needed a nap, even a small one. Walking out of her lab, she took a corridor to a stairwell, then followed the

145

tunnels under the buildings to Walter Reed, where she sought out a cot in an area where medical interns caught catnaps when they pulled long shifts. As she laid her head on the pillow, Alex drifted to sleep thinking about how she'd been the one to set Elena off. In her dream, she was on the stand, sweating, on trial for Elena's murder. The prosecutor, a mean-spirited version of Barbara, was questioning her. "Isn't it a fact, Dr. Blake, that you knew that man-made substances would trigger a fatal reaction? And yet you gave a man-made creamer to Elena Rodriguez, leading to her horrifying death."

The jury gasped as the prosecutor held up a large photo of the bloated woman, her mouth frozen in a rictus of pain.

"I was focused on the fountains," the dream Alex responded. "I didn't think the disease could be transmitted."

The prosecutor rolled her eyes. "Let me remind you that you are under oath. Direct your attention now to your résumé, Exhibit H. M.D. from Columbia, Ph.D. in genetics, and you mean to tell me you didn't see this one coming?"

A cell phone's ring woke her from sleep. She grabbed it, and when Dan asked, "Where the hell are you?" she had trouble figuring that out herself.

"Walter Reed," she said finally.

"Grab what you need from your lab," he said, "and meet us at the van in the parking lot. There's been an outbreak in Kansas and Chuck's dropping us at the airport."

As Alex reversed her path through the tunnels, back to her lab, she thought about the dream. She might indeed be on the hook for murder—morally, if not legally. But more important, the message of the dream was a challenge: What else didn't she see coming?

CHAPTER 33

On the way to the airport, Chuck drove while Dan, in the front passenger seat, and Castro, sitting in back next to her, attempted to fill her in. They both were talking at once and she was still too dazed to take it in. Chuck looked in the rearview mirror and saw her confusion.

"Ma'am, power up my laptop and look at the news clip I saved from Kansas," Chuck said.

The on-screen FOX News reporter stood in a field in Kansas. Behind him was a huge rain-proof tent with a door flap that had been melted slightly by flames, probably from a small campfire in front of the tent. Crime scene tape cordoned off the scene and kept the reporter away from the tent itself. The field had been trampled and beer cans and other debris dotted the ground.

"Earlier today," the reporter said into a microphone, "the bodies of ten people were found in this tent, a week after a Garth Brooks concert. They were discovered when a nearby farmer realized that several cars had been left abandoned since last Saturday night. He found the tent, looked inside, and was confronted with the gruesome sight of ten bodies, swollen beyond recognition. They'd all been scalped. They died with their Western boots on, leading the farmer to report to police that the score was Indians 10, Cowboys 0."

The segment cut to a photo taken by the farmer or someone else before the cops had arrived. Ten people had fallen in various directions. Two were women, the rest were men. All of them had a huge tear where their forehead met their hairline.

They look like Elena, Alex thought.

"We'll need tox screens from those concertgoers for street drugs, if only

147

to prove they didn't take them," Castro said to Dan. "And I'll get friends at the DEA to find out whether there's a common supplier who's selling in Taos, Nogales, Salt Lake, and rural Kansas."

"We also need to get to the scene," Dan said. "It's out in the middle of nowhere. Where the hell did the water come from? Or did the transmission take another form?"

The law enforcement outpost nearest the deaths was a modern Kansas State Police building forty miles from the concert venue. The KSP let the AFIP team take over the largest room, the interrogation room, as a base for its work—with the caveat that if the police needed to question an offender, the team would have to move out.

Although it was nearly midnight, Alex drove to the community hospital to meet the local coroner. Dr. Debra Stoddard greeted her in the hallway outside the hospital's autopsy room. A slight woman in her midforties, she was about Alex's height. She looked exhausted from autopsying seven of the bodies so far that day. As Alex changed into a set of scrubs that the doctor gave her, Stoddard said, "Ten murders at once. That's more than I usually get in a year."

"Not necessarily murder," Alex said, tying on a surgical mask. "It could be a new strain of disease."

Stoddard opened the door to a small room, with just one autopsy table and not much equipment. "Check out how the scalps have been severed," Stoddard said.

Alex put on gloves and turned the head of one of the victims so that instead of resting on the back of his head, he was resting on his right cheek. "Look at this," Alex said. "All the hair is still there. The violent swelling causes a tear in the scalp that makes it look like hair's been removed, but it's just been displaced." Alex stepped back and looked around. This was not the place for a high-tech investigation. The equipment was outdated and was suited mainly for yearly physicals and monitoring people's cholesterol levels. "I think the bodies should be shipped to D.C. for analysis."

Stoddard moved between Alex and the corpse. "You walk in here and five minutes later judge me to be incompetent? I trained at Johns Hopkins and know what I'm doing. Only moved to this armpit of the country so my husband could practice law where he grew up. I finally got my chance to do something big-time and I'm not about to turn it over to you. You're welcome to watch, but that's all I'm signing on for."

"But this case is tied to others around the country."

"Until you've got proof of that, I'm sure our sheriff will see it as a state matter."

Stoddard continued to block Alex's access to the table, waiting for Alex's response. "Fine," said Alex, not out of agreement, but out of a desire for the autopsy to proceed.

As Alex watched Stoddard make the initial incision on the eighth body, she thought about calling Barbara to initiate some legal action to transfer the corpses back to the AFIP. But she put the request for legal machinations aside as Stoddard expertly removed and weighed the swollen organs. Stoddard spoke those measurements into a tape recorder. The autopsy procedure was second nature to Stoddard, and Alex was drawn in. Alex began helping Stoddard with her work. It was like dancing with a really good partner. Stoddard was leading, but Alex was keeping up with her. While Stoddard dealt with documenting the swelling of the heart, Alex was examining the liver. It was swollen, too, but there was no discoloration or necrosis. She'd need further tests to see what was happening inside the organ. If a toxin had been ingested by the victims, it would likely have cleared through the liver.

Alex could tell how weary Stoddard was by the way her body hunched forward. Stoddard had spent the day in this room, working her way through body after body. As she started on the ninth autopsy, she seemed grateful for Alex's help.

"Usually you look for anything unusual in an autopsy," Stoddard said. "Here, everything's unusual. The rapid death. The massive swelling. The involvement of every organ instead of just one or two. What do you think is going on?"

Alex was pleased that Stoddard was asking her opinion. This could open the door for Alex to get the tissue that she needed. "Well, I ran T cell counts—"

"Of course," Stoddard said. "That was one of the first things I did as well. They all were vastly elevated, as you might expect."

Alex tried not to look surprised at Stoddard's competence. She didn't need to give Stoddard any more evidence that she might have been looking down at her. "The problem seems to be a change—or manipulation—in the

T cells themselves," Alex said. "Rather than responding to a certain invader, like a particular infection, they're targeting everything. They're initially activated by contact with a man-made substance, like a plastic or some chemical."

"So instead of acting like a sniper taking out a killer, you've got the body's own cells turning into an army that destroys everything in its path."

"Exactly," said Alex. "And we need to figure out what provoked this change."

"I get it. That's why you were paying so much attention to the liver. You're interested in how it cleared the body."

"If you won't turn over the bodies, how about at least letting me take back blood samples and sections of the livers?"

Stoddard took the Stryker saw and made the Y-shaped cut in the chest of the ninth victim. When the sound died down, she turned to Alex. "Okay to the livers and blood, but I get to be a co-author on any scientific article you write about the case. Plus rights in any TV movie that comes out about it."

Alex's mouth gaped behind her mask. She would never use a forensic case for personal gain in that way. Then she put her lips back together. If that was the sort of thing that motivated Stoddard, she would appear to go along with it. She carefully chose her words: "If I end up doing something like that, I'll make sure you're part of it."

It was nearly 5:00 A.M. when Alex and Stoddard finished the last autopsy and arranged for the victims' tissue samples to be sent to the AFIP. When she got to her room at the motel, Alex saw a stem of blue flowers on the desk in a makeshift vase—a bathroom water glass. Next to it was a corned beef sandwich with a paper napkin over it. A note from Castro said, "In case you're hungry when you get back."

After spending all those hours in the morgue, her head and back hurt and her soul felt scorched by the smells and sights of death. As she scrubbed herself in the shower, she longed to knock on Castro's door and fall asleep with his arms around her. She was hungry, yes, but not for food.

She swayed slightly in the shower, head bent forward, water pounding on the back of her neck. As the water's force eased the knot in her neck, she felt exhaustion seep into her body. Her legs got weaker. Even her fingers felt cramped and tired. She dried off with a towel. Her long, wet hair soaked the pillow as she pulled the blanket up and fell asleep.

She made it to the state police interrogation room at 9:30 A.M.

"About time," said Dan.

Castro interjected, "She didn't get back to the hotel until past five."

Dan raised an eyebrow, but didn't ask how Castro knew. "Anything to report?" Dan asked Alex.

"This is the first chance I've had to witness an autopsy of one of the victims," said Alex. "The pattern of swelling and organ failure confirms my idea that the T cells have evolved or been manipulated to attack indiscriminately."

"What was the trigger here?" Dan asked. "For Leroy Darven, it was the Styrofoam container and for Ted it was the plastic binoculars."

Castro looked at Alex accusatorily. She hadn't told him of the specific trigger point for Ted and now he looked angry that she'd held something back from him. But she hadn't wanted him to feel guilty if he'd handed Ted the binoculars.

"I'll need to examine the tent to be sure," she said. "But on the news it looked like it was made of plastic. Could be our victims listened to Garth Brooks in the open field, then returned to their tent, drank some water, and breathed in particulates from the plastic. Where'd they get the water, though? And how come it didn't affect more people?"

"They were drinking from refillable jugs they brought with them," said Dan. "Chuck's plotting the likely routes the ten of them took from their homes to the concert grounds to determine where the jugs were filled."

"We need to alert Kansas hospitals to contact us about any new cases of the disease," Alex said. "If other people died of the disease in a particular hospital, the source of the water might be nearby. As a precaution, I told the public health director to decommission all water fountains throughout the state."

"We're passing Renfrew's photo around," Castro said to her.

"Why him?"

"Our tail on him followed him back to Taos on Friday night, the day before the concert," Dan said.

"Where's he now?" she asked.

Castro looked at Alex with frustration. "He went to a riding stable. Got on a horse, broken leg and all. The tail lost him. Never saw that maneuver coming."

"It's a long haul by horse from Taos to a cornfield in Kansas," Alex said.

"But easy to do in a car," Castro said.

"What could Renfrew and the Mob gain by poisoning some Garth Brooks fans?" Alex asked.

"Maybe they didn't like his music," Dan said. "And maybe the concert wasn't the target. We've don't know yet where the water came from."

"I'd like to get the water jugs and the plastic tent back to the AFIP with me," said Alex.

A sergeant from the state police entered the room. "Why bother? CBS is about to announce the killer."

Alex gave a puzzled look to Castro as the three of them followed the sergeant to the coffee room, where a small television was perched on the counter.

They impatiently watched commercials for a feminine hygiene product, a hybrid automobile, and a discount clothing store. Then the host returned with her guests, Coroner Debra Stoddard and Professor Daniel Diggs of the Seward County, Kansas, Community College.

Alex pointed at the screen. "I can't believe she's doing this." But, on second thought, Alex realized that this was totally in character with what she'd seen of Debra Stoddard.

"In all the cases I've handled," said Stoddard, "this is the only one where the killer scalped the victims."

Alex was livid. She stared at the woman on the screen, now looking much more rested, dressed in a low-cut blouse under a bright blue pantsuit. She looked like one of those female CSIs on television, who bore no resemblance to crime fighters in real life. Stoddard was a competent coroner, even testing for T cells, thought Alex, but maybe her disappointment in life in a small town created a warped desire for attention.

The host turned to the second guest. "And based on this evidence, you can authoritatively say who committed this crime?"

"The way the victims were scalped certainly points to the acts of a Native American group," said the other guest, Professor Diggs.

"People don't generally associate Kansas with Native Americans. Have tribes been involved in violence like this before?"

"Native American history is a history of violence," he said.

Alex spoke to the man on the screen, "A history of violence? It was self-defense! Think about Custer trying to wipe them out!"

The professor continued. "Kansas is home to the Potawatomi tribe, some of whom farm the land near the concert venue. They are the tribe responsible for the horrible Fort Dearborn Massacre. When 148 men, women, and children left Fort Dearborn in Illinois to march to Fort Wayne, Indiana, a band of Potawatomi ambushed them, killing at least fifty and capturing the remainder. That's the Potawatomi way."

Now Alex was nearly yelling at the screen, "That was during the War of 1812, you idiot." As a high school student in downtown Chicago, she'd often walked past the plaque commemorating the event on the Michigan Avenue Bridge. Now this asshole was making it sound like it occurred just yesterday.

Professor Diggs continued. "And the fire outside the tent, that could point to the Potawatomi as well. The tribe's name for itself is Bodéwadmi, which means 'keepers of the fire.'"

She turned to Dan. "We've got to let people know this is just bullshit. It's a disease or a poisoning, not a Native American massacre."

He didn't agree. "What would that accomplish? If you make the connection for the public that these deaths are connected, people will just blame all fifty on the Potawatomi."

Dan turned to the sergeant. "We need troopers to question people who were at the concert and confiscate any photos," he said.

"Cameras weren't allowed at the concert," the sergeant said.

Alex intervened. "There are at least a dozen videos already up on YouTube from the event. Not to mention the live footage Garth Brooks was shooting for a television special. And then there are the cell phone cameras."

"Alright, alright," said the sergeant.

"We'll question the Potawatomi," Dan said. "Where's their reservation?"

"Are you kidding?" asked the sergeant. "This is the first I ever heard of them." He led Dan out of the kitchen.

"You okay?" Castro asked Alex when they were alone. "It must have been a tough night."

Alex was tempted to step forward and lean into him. But instead she took a cup off the counter and poured herself some coffee. "I appreciate the flowers," she told him.

"No big deal," he said. "They grow around the motel." But he was smiling, glad that she liked them. He moved toward her, raised his hand to her face, and brushed a loose strand of hair back off her forehead.

Alex smiled. "How'd you know I didn't get back until five?" she asked.

His ocean blues stared at her. Today they were deep in color, less stormy than when they'd first met. "Couldn't sleep well until I knew you were safe."

She smiled. "Next time," she said, "leave the light on so I'll know you're up."

The commercial break ended and a new interview began. Governor Elias Lightfoot Blackstone said, "I hesitate to comment on the ongoing investigation of a serious crime. That is a police matter. But prejudice should be everyone's concern. I've seen no evidence to link the Potawatomi to this incident."

"What about the scalpings? Not your average street crime."

Blackstone took a deep breath, struggling to maintain composure. "There are over five hundred tribes in the United States and none of them condone scalping. It was last used a long time ago. And what were the white Americans, the Puritans, doing at that same time? They were burning at the stake as witches women who had neurological diseases that caused them to have tremors. Both of these offenses were in the past. We need to think of the world we are in today."

Alex thought Blackstone had handled himself well. Statesmanlike. Even presidential. A cynical political pundit might suggest that Blackstone's campaign had manufactured this crisis, just to have him shine in handling it. But the cantankerous anchor wouldn't let the issue drop. "In the world we live in today, ten people were scalped. And *somebody* is responsible."

Alex turned to Castro. "They've got it all wrong."

He nodded. He'd seen the effects firsthand. Ted's scalp had burst while Castro was moving him to the car, trying to save his life.

The interview cut to footage of one of the victims' families, preparing for a funeral. Alex thought that maybe she should talk to the families to set the record straight. "Scalping" was removing the hair entirely. With these victims, all the hair was still there, but there were tears in their foreheads from the swelling that made it look like hair was missing. Then she shook her head. What would that accomplish? Dead is still dead.

CHAPTER 34

The Kansas state troopers were joined by military investigators whom Dan had called in. With the investigation in full swing, Dan decided that as soon as they finished their individual tasks, he, Alex, and Castro would be better off flying back to the AFIP. He wanted to be back at his command center to handle any new outbreak. For four Saturdays in a row, people had died. Victims appeared in a new location each week.

That evening, Alex, Dan, and Grant gathered in the AFIP Task Force room. Maps lay on the table like talismans to direct them to where the disease would next strike. When Chuck arrived, he laid out a story from the website of *The New York Times*. The reporter, Brad Kendall, linked the alien, the death in the Nogales jail, and the so-called massacre in Kansas. He used the word *bioterrorism* no fewer than six times in the article. But he had no clue about the cause. There was no mention in the article about Renfrew, the Mob, or Red Rights. Kendall, like most reporters, was targeting the poor Potawatomi.

Although Kendall hadn't interviewed Alex, he had done his homework. He'd spoken to people in various states' medical examiners' offices. And he'd hit pay dirt when he called Dr. Debra Stoddard. She told him how the fatal reactions were triggered by an exposure to man-made substances. Alex could have kicked herself for sharing that bit of information with the coroner. She was concerned with how the publicity would affect the investigation. It was one thing to track a killer. It was something else entirely to do it if the entire country was in a panic.

Alex made her way to the coffee machine. Chuck was at his desk, working his way through the videos taken at the concert. "I swear, ma'am, if I

155

hear 'Friends in Low Places' one more time," he said, "I may have to quote another country western song and tell the major to 'Take This Job and—' "

As Dan approached the coffee machine, Chuck stopped in midsentence.

"Watch your tone, Corporal, or you could be using your computer skills to process payroll checks," Dan said. Alex could tell he was just kidding, but Chuck looked mortified. "Anything suspicious?" Dan asked Chuck.

"None of the footage from the concert shows a gang of Indians or even one or two, sir," Chuck said, recovering. "And there's been tons of media coverage today of Native American groups disavowing the use of scalping. The only group that's justifying the action is Red Rights."

Chuck cued up an interview with Dale Hightower of Red Rights, who was telling the anchor, "This plague is nature's punishment to the white man for polluting the earth. It will not stop until every white soul is in his grave."

The interviewer asked, "Was it the Potawatomi who killed the Garth Brooks fans?"

Hightower looked directly into the camera. "If it was, why is that more important than centuries' worth of the Indians who were killed at the hands of whites?"

Dan turned to Alex. "Our guys have interviewed everyone within miles of the cornfield. That professor was blowing smoke out his ass. There's maybe six Potawatomi left in that part of the state, most of them in nursing homes. Now, this guy here," he said, pointing at Hightower on the screen, "he might be worth investigating." He turned to Chuck. "Go over the media interviews with Red Rights from the past six months and we'll put tails on members who have gone public, like this jerk here. Find out where he was the day of the Garth Brooks concert and whether he's been near any of the fountains."

For the next several hours, Dan, Alex, Grant, and Chuck watched as the story seeped across the extreme right wing blogs. Referring to Native Americans as savages, the bloggers called upon their readers to protect members of the white race. Every opinion show on FOX was airing interviews with so-called experts on Native Americans. Not with any actual Native Americans, though, thought Alex. Congress pulled together a hearing on this emerging disease, fueling more speculation of a tie to Native American communities.

"Why would Native Americans commit these crimes in the Southwest, where their own people would be at risk?" Chuck asked.

"I think it's unlikely, too," Alex said. "Dan, I remember your work on the ETA prosecution in Spain. Whenever they blew up a building, they did it outside the Basque region where their families lived. Why would Red Rights or any other indigenous group target places like New Mexico and Arizona?"

"You're forgetting one thing, Alex," Dan said. "Even though the deaths occurred in the Southwest, none of the victims were Indians. It's not at odds with the profile of ETA."

Alex was about to respond when Chuck said, "Oh, lord." She turned to the television monitor. The disease had struck again, this time at a county fair in Oklahoma City. The water supply going into the 4-H tent had been corrupted. Not only were dozens of high school students killed, but so were their animals. Other than FOX, the networks showed some restraint by not running footage of dead people bloated by the disease, but they felt no such concerns about the rabbits, sheep, and cows. Grotesque cattle with their organs spilling out, their skin stretched back to expose their teeth in contorted grimaces of pain. And the rabbits! Not since Glenn Close boiled the bunny in *Fatal Attraction* had the death of a rabbit caused such an uproar.

"Do you want me on a plane to Oklahoma?" Alex asked Dan.

But Dan's attention was focused on the news channel that Chuck was transmitting to the large, wall-mounted Plasmavision screen at the end of the conference table. Oklahoma Congressman Danfield Fillmore was holding a press conference. He pointed out how Red Rights was suing the state to get their land back and implied that they were now escalating their tactics. "This infectious disease, this move to Armageddon, may indeed be a terrorist plot by a radical group of Native Americans."

A reporter asked Fillmore, "What do they have to gain by this?"

He explained how the infection turned fatal only if the person was exposed to a man-made material, like plastic. "If they blast the rest of us to the Stone Age," said Fillmore, "then Native Americans would be the only ones with the skills to rule the country."

"So how will you handle this, Congressman?"

The man faced squarely into the camera. "I will use all my power in Washington to put the Native Americans in their place."

Dan turned to Alex. "No," he said, answering her earlier question. "I need you here. This idiotic Congressman just gave them a reason to hit Washington."

Alex returned to her lab. She closed the door on her inner office behind her and sat in the dark for a moment. She'd clung to the idea that this was a random disease, but now she saw the hand of a killer behind it. Whoever it was, his attacks were escalating. Each fountain that had been poisoned was limited to a dozen or fewer victims. But now he'd hit a major water line. She'd had some silly notion that the disease could be contained by decommissioning fountains. But everyone was vulnerable now. Every city and every town had a water supply that was impossible to guard. Public health officials had known this since the post–September 11 anthrax attacks. Sure, you could do your best to post security at airports when the threat was a bomb on an airplane. But safeguard a country's water supply? No way.

She switched on her computer and called up the preliminary results on the tests that Randy had performed on the concertgoers' blood. Maybe she could find some sort of signature of the killer by understanding his handiwork. But, as she read the results, test after test was negative. Common and uncommon diseases, intentional and unintentional poisons—none of these showed up in their blood. What was wrong with this picture? What was out of place?

There were hundreds of enzymes, proteins, hormones, and other substances in a person's body. Most were supposed to be there. But, since Alex didn't know what the victims' blood had looked like before their deaths, she had no idea if there were more or less of those substances than before they'd been exposed.

The phrase *looking for a needle in a haystack* ran through Alex's mind. But finding a needle would be easier than what she was trying to do here. At least the needle looked different from the hay. Maybe a metal detector would be able to find it. But here, it was like looking for a random piece of metal in a junkyard when you didn't even know which piece of metal you were seeking.

She decided to focus first on substances whose levels were higher than expected. There was some mercury in the blood, but again, she didn't know its significance. Seafood, vaccinations—who knew what these folks had been exposed to in the normal course of their lives?

Randy had found evidence of a steroid that seemed unusual in its chemical composition and appeared in higher amounts than normal corticosteroids secreted in the body. That was a great find, thought Alex. She'd been wondering what had caused the victims' bones to break so readily. Usually, when muscles swelled quickly, soft tissue was damaged, but the force was never enough to break cartilage or bone.

She was excited by this new line of inquiry, but also disturbed. Who could have created this type of chemical and for what purpose? It would take a certain amount of scientific sophistication. If you wanted to kill people, even a large number of people, there were a lot easier ways than this.

The cortisone explained the breakage, but it didn't explain the hyperimmune reaction. Yet Randy had tested for chemical after chemical and the victims' blood was not registering any known toxin.

She sat back in her chair and thought of Dan challenging her to find out more about the disease. Like most people, he had no idea how amazingly complex the human immune system was, with its wealth of moving parts, all of which could trigger a problem. The immune system was like a national militia, subject to various rules of engagement. The body used certain signals to notify the killer T cells about what to attack and when. You wouldn't want to send in the infantry to attack a nonthreatening country like Canada, at least not without provocation. And you needed to make sure you got the right target, not shooting innocent civilians or soldiers in your own unit.

The immune system used cytokine proteins to announce when a battle was necessary and what the target should be. Cytokines also signaled the body when the infection was over, telling the T cells when to stop a battle and when to end the war. But when cytokines acted improperly, it was like having a stuck accelerator in a car or a platoon of bombers that couldn't be turned back. The T cells would run rampant, killing both the invading infection and the person's healthy cells.

What could a killer have added to the water supply to trigger a cytokine storm, an immune reaction out of control? Alex dipped into the medical literature online and found her answer. A new type of medical therapy, monoclonal antibodies, could have this effect. She read about how, in 2006, a German pharmaceutical company had sponsored an experiment attempting to use a monoclonal antibody to treat autoimmune disorders. The theory behind the novel treatment was that it would activate T cells that were erroneously attacking the person's own body, causing those T cells to burn out and die.

Alex felt a chill as she read the results of the experiment. The healthy volunteers who'd served as research subjects experienced a cytokine storm, resulting in massive organ failure. Not unlike what was happening at the fountains.

She searched further and found a *New England Journal of Medicine* article from March 2008. A monoclonal antibody designed to treat cancer had caused a severe hyperimmune reaction in nearly one-quarter of the patients in the South, leading to anaphylactic shock.

She got up and started pacing. Someone had discovered a near-perfect bioweapon, easily manufactured in a lab by manipulating mice to express a human protein that triggered T cells. With a monoclonal antibody, you could kill a person using his or her own immune system as the weapon.

The ring of her phone startled her. She picked it up to hear Margo Sanchez, the head of the Utah Public Health Department—one of the first people Alex had originally called. "What's this about preparing for a mass quarantine?" Margo asked her. "Did the order originate with you?"

"I don't know anything about it," said Alex. "But it doesn't make sense to round people up and remove them from their families and their lives. This isn't like yellow fever or smallpox."

"Yeah, it seems crazy to do it when the disease can't be casually transmitted. Who are we protecting? Some folks wanted to quarantine all AIDS patients when that disease first emerged, but we in public health refused. Now we've gotten a fax from Homeland Security asking us to pick a quarantine location in the state to deal with the infected. It also asked us to start ordering potassium chloride."

When Alex hung up, she wondered what the czar of Homeland Security was plotting. Small doses of potassium chloride were used in medical treatments for potassium deficiency or to replenish electrolytes when people were dehydrated. In large quantities, potassium chloride was used in lethal injections of prisoners on Death Row.

When her phone rang again, it was Dan, summoning her to the Task Force room. When she joined him there, he handed her an evidence bag with a small brown cigar in it.

"This arrived just a few minutes ago," he said. "It's a cheroot, found near the compromised water line. Can you run a quick check for DNA and then drop it off on your way home at ATF so they can follow up on the tobacco?"

She nodded and took the packet from his hands, suddenly energized by the hope of identifying a killer. In less than fifteen minutes, those hopes were dashed. No matter what she tried, she couldn't find any usable DNA on the cigar stub.

She drove to the ATF headquarters, a new building at the corner of Florida and New York Avenue. Designed by Moshe Safdie, the building's curved trellised wall made it look more like an art museum than a secure laboratory and training facility. A lab tech met her at the entrance, then she drove back to the Curl Up and Dye. Maybe a good night's sleep would allow her neurons to fire in a more useful way in the morning.

At home, she drank bourbon and caught the news. In an unprecedented evening session, Congressman Fillmore had introduced a bill with dozens of other Members of Congress supporting it. If enacted, the bill would move all Native Americans into the Grand Canyon.

Alex phoned Barbara at home. She could hear the news in the background. "Isn't this unconstitutional?"

"Sadly, maybe not," said Barbara. "Don't forget that the U.S. Supreme Court in 1944 upheld the Japanese internment camps, saying that it was permissible to curtail the rights of a racial group when there is a 'pressing public necessity.'"

"This is why the world hates lawyers," Alex said.

"The case in favor of the bill is even stronger here. The Native Americans have argued for years that they're a separate nation. That's their stance in treaties and in the bill that allows gambling on reservations. Unlike with the Japanese-Americans in World War II, Congress could take the position that Native Americans were enemy combatants who didn't deserve the rights of citizens."

"But these guys haven't done anything," Alex said.

"Neither had the Japanese," said Barbara, quietly. "Neither had the Japanese."

When Barbara hung up, Alex saw Martin Kincade's face appear on the screen. "We are determined to get the terrorists behind the poisonings, whether they are a home-grown group like Red Rights or a foreign enemy on American soil."

The anchor asked, "What are you advising people who have already been exposed?"

"Our scientists are working round the clock to help them. But in the meantime, we need a bold, new plan. These modern-day lepers could kill us all. We need to isolate the carriers to protect the healthy."

Isolate? Alex asked herself. Or did he mean *terminate*?

CHAPTER 35

Alex had scarcely opened one eye the next morning when she flicked on the television to see what doom was descending next. Mannequins dressed like Native Americans had been hung in effigy at the entrances to thirty major reservations. People were shunning the native casinos. In a particularly tacky play on the public sentiment, the Las Vegas Chamber of Commerce was running an ad on *Good Morning America* offering the "Patriotic Package"—half off the room rate at any one of a dozen casinos on the Strip, including the Fantasy.

Poised to hit the remote to shut off this macabre marketing, Alex stopped when she saw footage of the White House. Then, from the Oval Office, the calming voice of President Cotter. "The term *veto*," said Cotter, "literally means 'I forbid.' I forbid us to transform ourselves into a land of paranoia. In this time of national tragedy, we shall not add the dark specter of discrimination to the devastating consequences of a disease. I will veto any bill that Congress passes to diminish the rights of Native Americans. We will prevail, through traditional investigative means, in ending this epidemic."

By the time Alex was in her car on the way to work, the backlash had begun. The morning talk-radio shows were flooded with calls saying, "Impeach Cotter." When she heard the phrase, she changed routes, heading downtown rather than toward Georgia Avenue. She double parked in front of the imposing edifice of *The Washington Post*. But rather than enter the building, she looked for the nearest pay phone. She called Homeland Security, dialing Martin Kincade's direct line. Maybe if he saw the area code and three-digit exchange that matched those of the paper, he'd think it was an interview request.

"Hello," he said in a melodious voice, the kind that radio announcers used.

"This is Alex Blake," she said. "I'm glad you're finally taking this epidemic seriously. But we need to call the commission together to figure out how to treat and prevent this disease."

"There's no *we* anymore," he said. "You're off the commission. Your security was improperly granted."

"Hey, I'm the one who identified the problem," she said. Then the full import of his words dawned on her. "What do you mean 'improperly granted'?"

"We've determined that you are a security risk."

"That's crazy! I've got the highest level of clearance from the Department of Defense."

"Perhaps they don't know about your mother."

Alex momentarily wondered what her mother had gotten herself into this time. But she waited to see what Kincade could possibly have on the woman.

"She's got a history of terrorist acts," Kincade said.

"Because she marched against the Vietnam War? Half the country did that."

"She consorted with a known revolutionary group, the Black Panthers—"

"She helped at their free breakfast program! They were the kids in my play group when I was little."

"Your mother was photographed at a demonstration about Abu Ghraib and she recently bought an airline ticket to Arizona, where the next Red Rights rally is going to be held."

Alex was shocked by the cavalier way Martin Kincade described private information about her mother. But another part of her was suddenly fearful of the risks that her mother was facing. She was being targeted for scrutiny because of Alex. And, if Kincade was right, she was flying to the Southwest, the epicenter of the epidemic.

"Congress will go berserk when they find out how you're violating constitutional rights."

Kincade actually laughed. "Are you kidding me? This bioterrorism thing has them so scared, civil liberties are the last thing on their minds."

By the time she got back to her car, it had been ticketed for parking illegally. She dislodged the ticket from her windshield and cursed herself for wasting her time with Kincade. Well, at least she hadn't gotten towed.

In the car, she laid her cell phone on the passenger seat and tried to decide what to say to her mom. Hi, Janet, you've screwed up my life once again. But Janet could probably say the same thing. Was Alex being dropped from the investigation because of her mother or was Janet being investigated because of her daughter? Alex sped up and starting weaving between cars.

Back in her lab, she stared at the photo of her father in his military uniform, a young sergeant in Vietnam. He'd probably gotten a lot of flack for his antiwar wife. You must know how I feel, Dad, she thought as she passed the picture.

Sitting at her desk, she started dialing her mother from her cell phone, then stopped and zipped the phone back into her fanny pack. That would be too easy for Homeland Security to trace.

She walked to the Task Force room. Despite the early hour, Chuck was there.

"What's the most secure phone in the building?"

"The one with the most bells and whistles is Colonel Wiatt's," he said.

Without even making herself an espresso, Alex removed herself from the room and made her way toward the colonel's office.

His aide de camp wasn't in yet, so she sat at the aide's desk directly outside of Wiatt's office and dialed her mother using Wiatt's private line.

"Alex, I can't talk right now," Janet said. "I'm on my way to the airport."

"To Arizona?" she asked, then realized that she would have no legitimate way of knowing that.

"Good guess," Janet said. "I always knew you were a little bit psychic."

Alex sighed. She hated when her mother pulled that new-age stuff on her. The hyperrational scientist in Alex went a little bonkers when Janet started quoting astrology or offering to do her tarot cards.

"Actually, I figured you might be going to the Red Rights demonstration," Alex said. She hoped her mother would say, No, I'm heading to a Jane Austen convention.

"Don't even get me started on that," said her mother. "You're damn right I'm going there. Rounding up Native Americans to protect us. Puh-lease. I haven't seen a government go this crazy since the FBI under Hoover."

Alex sighed. Next thing her mother would say was, If you are not part of the solution, you're part of the problem. "Janet, listen. Be very careful in the Southwest. Buy bottled water."

"And support corporate hegemony? Don't you know that it's no better for you than tap water? Pepsi owns Aquafina and Coke owns Dansani. And ever since Evian started with those pink bottles I feel like they're talking down to me."

"This is serious, Mother," Alex said. Since she rarely addressed Janet as Mother, the woman got silent and paid attention. "That disease that's causing those horrible deaths in the Southwest, it's transmitted in water fountains and other public water supplies."

"Thanks, honey, but I'm sure I'll be fine," Janet said. "I never get sick. And, remember, if you're not part of the solution—"

"I know, I know—you're part of the problem."

When she hung up, she felt the same frustration she always felt when she talked to her mother. If men were from Mars and women were from Venus, she and her mother should be able to talk to each other. But with the difficulties she and her mom had communicating, it seemed like they came from distant galaxies indeed.

Alex got up from the desk outside the door to the colonel's office. With the spirited conversation, she hadn't noticed that her boss had opened his door from the inside. The colonel had been standing there listening to her. "Going somewhere, Dr. Blake?"

"I can explain," she said.

He stood aside and motioned for her to sit in one of his leather chairs. Uh-oh, thought Alex. Not a good sign. He usually let his visitors stand so that he could handle the matter expeditiously. She might be in store for some serious chewing out. She decided the best strategy was to go on the defensive.

As she sunk into the oversize chair, she said, "There's something troubling going on at Homeland Security."

"That so?" the colonel said. "Martin Kincade just told me the same thing about you."

Alex shifted uncomfortably in the chair. "He's the one dropping the ball on this new infectious disease. He hasn't called a meeting of the bioterrorism commission to help identify and treat the disease. In the meantime, hundreds, maybe thousands, of lives are at stake."

"Kincade assures me he's got it under control. He doesn't want you compromising the investigation."

"Compromising? He's the one—"

"He also suggested I should investigate the criminal behavior of some people close to you."

Alex frowned. Criminal? she thought. "My mother's protest actions? She's got nothing to do with how I conduct my job."

"Don't give me that, Blake. You violated at least five military rules by calling her on my secure line."

"But—"

"If Kincade himself weren't a complete asshole, I'd put you on administrative leave until we investigated his concerns."

Alex's mouth gaped. Just then, Sergeant Major Derek Lander, Wiatt's aide de camp, arrived to take his place at the desk Alex had vacated. She looked out of the office at him, hoping she hadn't left anything on his desk. Lander tolerated her even less than Wiatt did, and she didn't want him piling it on when she was already in trouble. He might just convince Wiatt to fire her ass.

Wiatt stood between her and the door to block her view of his assistant. "Here's the deal, Blake," said Wiatt. "Focus on the investigation of the missing DEA agent's body and let Kincade have his infectious disease investigation." He pointed to the door. "Now get out of here. I have real work to do."

Alex left the office, walking slowly past Lander with a friendly nod, as if she and Wiatt had just had a homey little chat. She repressed a grin. Sure she'd focus on Ted. Because Ted's case and the infectious disease case were one and the same.

CHAPTER 36

When Alex left Wiatt's office she headed to the Task Force room. Dan was briefing a dozen new investigators. Judging by the impatient way they stood and their intense attention to what Dan was saying, they were primed for a manhunt. But there was no target in sight. When Dan noticed her, he took her aside. "Chuck and Grant are meeting with the DOD about the computer," he said. "But where's Castro? He should be back from Kansas by now."

"I have no idea," she said.

"Why not? You're pretty tight."

"Please, Dan, can't you cut him a little slack?" Alex asked. "His partner died in front of him."

"That's no excuse for compromising an investigation. Don't you go sideways on me, too."

She started an apology: "Dan, I—"

Her sentence was cut off by Randy Stone's entrance. He strode over to Dan and Alex. "There was mercury in the Taos fountain."

"We knew that," Alex said, "but it had a seep hole. Backup of trace metal isn't that uncommon."

"That's what I thought at first, too," Randy said. "But I found the same thing in water from a modern fountain in Utah. Mercury was recovered only at the spout, not all through the fountain, like when it's from the ground water. So I did some chemical analyses of the substance. The mercury we're talking about is a by-product of Thimerosal."

Alex said to Dan, "Used in vaccines."

"And your tests?" Randy asked Alex.

"Frustrating," she said. "No evidence of bacteria or a virus. I think the killer is using something like a monoclonal antibody that's so close to natural, it's virtually undetectable."

Dan said, "English, please. This isn't the sort of weapon I deal with."

Alex said, "You know how vaccines work? Doctors inject a small amount of the infection, like measles, into you and your body starts making antibodies to fight the disease if you later get infected. Pharmaceutical companies now have an alternative. It's easy to grow the antibodies themselves in the lab to ramp up the infection-fighting properties of the body."

"Yeah," Randy said, "but monoclonal antibodies are usually devised to target one specific type of disease. Here, the victims' T cells turned generic and started attacking their own bodies."

"If someone deliberately introduced the genetic changes, it would be hard to prove," Alex said. "T cells occur naturally. These just have a larger range of targets. Once they're in a person's body, no test can detect whether they were introduced intentionally or created by a natural genetic mutation."

"It's a great way to take people out," Dan said. "Program their cells to attack them. Would that be hard to do?"

"Not terribly. Last year, drug companies tested one hundred sixty different monoclonal antibodies in people. Some of the experiments caused immediate organ failure in otherwise healthy patients."

"So, theoretically," said Dan, "someone like Renfrew or a group like Red Rights could be behind this if they had access to those mono things."

Randy asked, "But why would anyone hit these out-of-the-way places? Why not New York or here in the District? And why water fountains?"

"Could be a trial run," said Dan. "Fountains first. Then the main water line to the county fair. For all we know, Lake Mead is next."

Just then, Castro flung open the door to the room, waving a sheet of paper. He stopped short when he saw Randy, the man who'd lost his friend's body. Randy said to him, "I'm sorry about your friend."

Castro nodded, but didn't make any overture of concession. Instead he addressed Dan and Alex. "Fingerprints came back on the Waverly pin."

He flashed a search warrant.

Dan thanked Randy for his work and then walked into the hallway with Castro and Alex. When the three of them were alone, he said to Castro, "Go around my back again and you are off this investigation. Am I clear?"

"Loud and," Castro said, but Alex did not hear the least bit of sincerity in his voice.

CHAPTER 37

Dan led Alex and Castro to his Chevy Malibu. He opened the door to the front passenger seat for Alex, consigning Castro to the penalty box in the back.

"I don't think Renfrew's connected to the disease," Alex said. "He's a well-respected researcher."

Dan responded, "The precision of the attacks—they spell scientist to me."

"Yeah," Castro said. "And Renfrew's neighbors say he's not around on Saturdays. His key card wasn't used at work on the weekends."

Alex wondered if she was just being myopic about her profession. Maybe she just couldn't imagine someone like her, who'd been trained to save lives, taking them instead.

When Dan parked the car at Waverly Pharmaceuticals, he turned to Castro. "I'll do the questioning. Agreed?"

Castro tipped his head and held his hands up in front of him. "Knock yourself out."

Once inside the building, a Waverly vice president escorted them to Renfrew's lab, emphasizing that the warrant covered that space and nothing more. Renfrew, his right leg in a cast, was holding forth in front of four post-docs, leaning on his crutches and confidently gesturing with his hands.

They walked up behind him. When he noticed that his post-docs were staring at something, he turned around. His imperious tone disappeared and he swayed, leaning heavily on his crutch. "What . . . are . . . you . . . doing . . . here?" he said to Castro.

"Must have the same travel agent as you. Taos, the quarry, hospital in Albuquerque."

Renfrew's good leg began to buckle. Alex almost felt sorry for him.

"How did you get in?"

Dan stepped forward. "Turns out that your company has a hefty drug contract with the VA. Waverly decided that it didn't want to impede a federal investigation."

"Wha-what investigation?"

The post-docs looked in awe at the three visitors, who were managing to bring their demigod to his knees.

Renfrew regained his composure and looked at the post-docs. "Get out of the lab," he said. "I'm having a private conversation." He'd gotten his bravura back, at least as it applied to terrorizing those who reported to him.

When his laboratory workers had left, he said to Dan, "I know nothing about a federal investigation."

"We found your fingerprint on a Waverly Pharmaceuticals pin that puts you at the site of the longhouse," Dan said.

Renfrew looked confused.

"Lucky for us," continued Dan, "it happened to be the pointer finger. The same print your grocery store uses to identify you."

The fright in the scientist's eyes calmed slightly. "So what's the charge, even if I did drop the pin? Littering?"

Castro couldn't help but jump in. "Try murder, Ace."

"Murder?" he said. "Now I know you've got the wrong guy. Who'd I kill?"

"Nearly two hundred people and counting," said Dan. "You must get a hard-on reading about your handiwork in the papers. More victims in a week than Jack the Ripper killed in his whole career. A modern-day plague."

"But I . . . never . . ." said Renfrew. His face was so white that Alex thought she'd have to apply CPR.

Dan moved closer to the man, whether to question him or to pick him up if he fell, Alex couldn't tell. "Now let me tell you how this will go down," Dan said. "Dr. Blake here is going to take this lab apart. She'll interrogate your post-docs until she finds out what you're cooking up that's killing people. Oh, and did I tell you, you have the right to remain silent. Anything you say can and will be used against you in a court of law. You have the right to an attorney. If you cannot—"

Alex walked past an Applied Biosystems sequencer that looked like it had recently been delivered, but not yet set up. She noticed it was plated to test for 156 drug targets at the same time. That meant that Renfrew was planning to test different substances in the machine to see what impact they had on various bodily tissues.

She started paging through the laboratory notes at one of the post-docs' work station. "We'll need the computer and his access codes," Alex said to Dan. "Most of the data about his research will be on there."

"Wait—don't disconnect them yet," Renfrew said. "The liquid nitrogen tanks and incubators are regulated by the computer and I need to put in the commands to switch them to a backup generator."

Pumping his crutches, he turned quickly to the computer and hit just three keys before Dan reached him and cuffed his hands behind him. But Alex saw the lights on the incubator and liquid nitrogen tanks fade out. Castro pushed him out of the way and tried to reboot his computer. But it was as if Renfrew had pulled the plug on a terminally ill patient. The computer was flatlining. Renfrew had erased the hard drive.

With his arms cuffed behind him, Renfrew couldn't hang on to his crutches. Dan and Castro each grabbed him under an elbow and supported him. "You're under arrest for the murder of Ted Silliman, Elena Rodriguez, and a couple dozen others," said Dan.

A thin layer of sweat was dotting Renfrew's forehead. "I want a lawyer."

CHAPTER 38

Alex worked her way carefully through the materials in Renfrew's lab. The chemicals on the shelves were just what she would expect for this type of laboratory. Nothing in the bottles could trigger the responses she'd seen in the victims, nor was he stocking anything related to the creation of monoclonal antibodies. None of the lab notes talked about a T cell activator. Most focused on the obesity vaccine she'd read about in Renfrew's NIH proposal.

The approach Renfrew was taking was much like the one reported by the Scripps Institute in 2006. The vaccine would target ghrelin, a hormone active in weight gain. The notes of the post-docs chronicled experiments where weight gain in mice was cut in half with a vaccine that prevented ghrelin from reaching the central nervous system. The vaccine used the body's own immune system to target the active form of ghrelin, binding to it and preventing it from initiating the metabolic process. Could the vaccine have accidentally thrown the immune system into overdrive?

Nobody's notes discussed experiments in humans, though. Even in Renfrew's notes, the only mention of actual people was in an equation in which he'd figured out how much his stock options would be worth if one in five fat people bought his vaccine.

After familiarizing herself with the notes, Alex interviewed the post-docs individually. Each post-doc described his or her personal reactions to the "great man," as one post-doc mockingly referred to him. It was as if these were gripe sessions over a beer, rather than a murder investigation. The one female post-doc, Julianna, clearly had a crush on Renfrew. Her face flushed at the mention of his name. Alex could tell from the way the woman gushed that she and Renfrew weren't yet an item. Once you're in a relationship, you might still have stars in your eyes, but not, like this woman, a whole galaxy.

The other post-docs raised various peccadilloes. Renfrew was using their work in his publications without giving them sufficient credit. The hours were long and their personal lives were falling apart. They were stuck in this job in part because their confidentiality agreements forbade them to talk about their work, so it would be hard to convince a potential employer of their worth without discussing what they had done at Waverly and opening themselves up to damages under the agreement. Many of these concerns were familiar to Alex; she'd felt them herself when she was in graduate school. But none of the conversations brought her closer to hard evidence about Renfrew's role in the poisonings.

She finally called the four post-docs together—Renfrew's female groupie and her three male colleagues. They sat in the laboratory on stools, each at his station, but turned around so that they were facing Alex, in the middle of the room, rather than one another.

"You don't seem to understand how much trouble you're in," she said. "If your boss goes down for these murders, it'll be easy enough for the jury to believe that he couldn't have done it without you. After all," she said, pointing to one of the men, "as Buck here told me, Renfrew was all about raising the money and it was up to you in the lab to do the work."

Ms. Starry Eyes gave Buck a look like she was going to scratch his eyes out. Nobody talked about her hero that way.

Chip intervened. "Julie, you know it's true. We do all the scientific work around here."

"Hey, hey, don't lay any conspiracy jive on me," said Buck. "I just empty out the animal cages."

"*Buck,*" the other three post-docs said in unison, clearly disagreeing with his characterization of his job.

Julianna, still angry at his criticism of Renfrew, said, "Buck's the one in charge when Dr. Renfrew is in the field."

"Listen, I've been through everybody's lab notes," Alex said. Julianna's hand went up to her mouth. Buck just glared at her. Snooping around in someone's lab notes was the scientific equivalent of rape. "And other than Chip's mistake about where the most common mutation is in the gene that produces ghrelin, you're all top-flight scientists. Even the mouse man here,

Buck. So what were you or Dr. Renfrew working on that might have caused these fatal immunological episodes?"

Buck took charge. His usual role, Alex thought, just as the other post-docs had indicated. A regular Dr. Renfrew, Jr., in his bearing and pomposity. As he puffed his chest out to speak, Alex wanted to hit him over the knuckles with a ruler, like she'd seen in a play about Catholic school.

"We haven't got clinical trials going on in any of the states that have been hit so far," said Buck. "Our nearest cooperating facility is in San Diego."

"That's what's on the books, but maybe Dr. Renfrew tried to circumvent the federal research regulations," Alex said. "The first step in human research on vaccines is the Phase One trial to measure how risky it is in healthy volunteers. Could be the good doctor decided to avoid the costly process of recruiting research participants and paying doctors to administer the active ingredient. Easier to drop it in the water and see what happens."

"You're thinking MK ULTRA," Buck said.

Danny, the youngest of the researchers, looked at him questioningly. "What's that? Some computer game?"

But Alex knew it well. "From the 1950s to the 1970s, the CIA experimented with LSD on unsuspecting soldiers, mental patients, and members of the public. Trying to perfect a drug for mind control."

"Far out," said Danny. If the experiment were to be done again, he seemed ready to volunteer.

Julianne raised her hand and then realized she was not in class. "Dr. Renfrew would never do something like that. He really cares about people."

Chip muttered under his breath. "Maybe he should start at home."

Alex was beginning to feel like she was teaching a seminar that was getting away from her. "You've got a lot of research going on here. What projects are working with mercury?"

They looked at each other, confused. "None that I know of," said Buck. "And I know more of what goes on here than Dr. Renfrew."

"Isn't mercury part of the obesity vaccine?" Alex asked.

"No way," Danny said. He seemed determined to make up for his lack of knowledge about MK ULTRA. "Thimerosal, the mercury compound used in vaccines since the 1930s, fell out of favor recently because of the potential link to autism."

Alex knew the data on that issue was mixed, but there was some cause for alarm. The symptoms of mercury poisoning were similar to the symptoms of autism. Heavy metals like mercury had deleterious effects on the myelinating cells of the central nervous system, which could contribute—along with a genetic predisposition—to the manifestation of autism. "The science isn't that clear cut," she said. "There's still a lot of debate about the effects of Thimerosal."

"Who needs science when you've got the Quentin Fender challenge," Buck said.

"Who's Fender?" Alex asked.

"A multimillionaire with a child with autism," said Buck. He stood up and wrote on the blackboard:

Thimerosal (a mercury derivative)
Ethylene glycol (antifreeze)
Phenol (a disinfectant dye)
Aluminum
Benzethonium chloride (a disinfectant)

He then turned back to Alex and said, "Fender is offering doctors $75,000 if they are willing to ingest this stuff, all of which has been used in childhood vaccines. So far, he's had no takers. Even though the award money would go a long way to paying off medical school debts."

Julianna finally volunteered something. "Thimerosal was used to kill bacteria in the vaccine production process. When the European equivalent to the FDA recommended a few years ago that vaccines be made without it, we followed that advice."

"Yeah, why use mercury and lose our European market?" Buck asked. Like Renfrew, like junior, thought Alex. Focusing on the money.

But she sensed that they were telling the truth. Even though traces of mercury had been found in all the fountains, there would be no reason for Dr. Renfrew to have included the substance in any of his research products. She'd have to try a different line of questioning.

Alex pulled a small notepad out of her fanny pack. "Was Dr. Renfrew behaving any differently lately? Did he seem frightened? More secretive?"

They thought about it for a moment. Then they all spoke at once. "More annoyed." "He's always secretive." "Pretty much his same arrogant self." "He seemed fine to me."

"What about the lab routine? Anything unusual? New people coming in? Unexpected deliveries or faxes?"

"Wait . . . wait . . . wait," Danny said. "I just thought of something important."

All eyes turned to him and Alex poised her pen over her notepad.

"There was a phone call," he said.

Alex dutifully wrote down "phone call."

"A woman claimed to be our grants manager, but the real Victoria Goodman called the next day." Danny, a triumphant look on his face, turned to Alex. "I can even tell you the day she called. I remember it was the Friday after Renfrew left town."

He looked down at the pen in Alex's hand. "Why aren't you writing this down?" he asked. "You can trace back the number."

Alex obligingly moved her hand, as if she were hanging on his every word. What she wrote was the following: "I've gotten zilch from the postdocs."

CHAPTER 39

Alex usually didn't sit in on suspect interrogations. The closest she came was viewing them through the one-way mirror. But this time Dan wanted her around. Figuring out the medical basis for the poison was as important as fingering the bastard who'd dumped it into the fountains. Castro was there as well, to question Renfrew about the Taos events.

Renfrew looked older and broken in his orange jail jumpsuit. They didn't have enough at the moment to charge him on the murder, but his erasure of the hard drive gave them cause to hold him for impeding a federal investigation. His lawyer didn't look that much better. He wore a stylish, expensive suit, but seemed as out of place in the interrogation room as his client. Alex figured Renfrew called his personal lawyer. The guy probably had negotiated his employment contract and handled his will. This little gathering might be going downhill fast for Renfrew.

"My client will not be answering any questions until I can talk to your lawyer about the terms of his release," said Renfrew's lawyer.

Dan thought about it for a moment. "Suit yourself."

When Barbara entered the room and introduced herself as the general counsel of the AFIP, Renfrew's lawyer smiled like he'd won the lottery. He assumed that a young, black woman would be a pushover.

"I'm Donald Waterstone, representing Dr. Renfrew here," he said, handing Barbara a business card, which showed him to be a partner at one of the most powerful law firms in the District. "We are contesting this travesty of justice. I'd like him released immediately."

"And I'd like Oprah's bank account," Barbara said. "But this isn't the Make-a-Wish Foundation."

"You're treating a respected member of the community like a common criminal."

"Oh, we don't think he's common at all. Devious, twisted, fatal. More like a mad scientist."

"But you have no proof—"

Barbara raised her chin and spread out her arms. She started speaking, looking from person to person as if she were addressing a jury. "This is a crime as heinous as the medical experimentation by the Nazi doctors. A crime that could only have been done by someone with extensive scientific training, like Dr. Renfrew. A man who surreptitiously checked into a Taos hotel to take an action that killed six innocent children and two good men later that night. Who lied to federal investigators and, when confronted with the evidence against him, erased his hard drive in a last ditch attempt to prevent his prosecution."

Renfrew was staring at Barbara, his face turning green. His attorney sputtered, "What possible motive could he have?"

"Maybe somebody hired him to do it. Or maybe he was creating a disease so Waverly could market a cure. There's certainly a lot in his notes about stock options."

Renfrew looked down at his hands. His cheeks were red.

"Plus," continued Barbara, "do you know how much the average person hates drug companies? Everyone's been gouged by them. And if you expect sympathy for a guy making close to two million bucks a year . . ."

Renfrew opened his mouth to speak, but his lawyer raised a hand to silence him. Barbara addressed the researcher. "You could play dumb here and not give us anything, which is just going to piss us off more. Or you could stop lying and start talking. Let me remind you that you picked the wrong states to try out your fatal cocktail. Arizona, New Mexico, Utah, Kansas, Oklahoma. They all have the death penalty."

Renfrew took a deep breath. "Okay," he said, "what do you want to know?"

CHAPTER 40

Once Renfrew agreed to talk, Barbara left the room, turning the interrogation back over to Dan, Alex, and Castro.

"Start with what you were doing with Frankie DiBondi," said Dan.

"DiBondi?" Renfrew's attorney said under his breath. Obviously, his client hadn't exactly filled him in. Several different expressions crossed the attorney's face and he took a step back from his client. Alex wondered if he was concerned about how his law firm would fare in the press if linked to the Mob. A regular John Grisham moment.

"Listen," said Renfrew. "What I tell you can't go beyond this room."

"If you're worried about your safety, we have ways to protect you."

Renfrew looked befuddled.

"Someone tried to take you out in that ravine. Maybe you're worried about him coming back"

Renfrew gave a short, nervous laugh. "You've got it all wrong."

"Enlighten us, then, starting with DiBondi."

"I went to New Mexico to meet with a six-tribe conglomerate about investing in my research."

This was not an answer that anyone was prepared for. Dan asked, "Why did you need a Mob guy to hold your hand for that trip?"

"It started when I read about how one of the tribes had acquired a Swiss pharmaceutical company. Government funding was drying up. Venture capitalists had been burned too many times by biotech companies promising cures using gene therapy or embryo stem cells that never panned out. So I needed an in with some tribes with casino money."

"And where did DiBondi fit in?"

"I got an M.B.A. at Harvard right after I finished medical school there. His son was in my class. I knew the dad ran a casino in Vegas. Thought maybe he had a contact at a gaming tribe. I swear I didn't know he was with the Mob."

Dan threw up his hands. "And just who do you think runs the Vegas casinos? Mother Teresa, Inc.? What was in it for DiBondi?"

"The tribal consortium had incorporated a company called TOTEM, based just outside of Taos. They hired me as a consultant for a major drug development plan. If it worked, it would have left traditional pharmaceutical companies in the dust, Waverly included. DiBondi would have gotten a piece of that."

How do you spell conflict of interest, thought Alex. Here was Renfrew negotiating behind his employers' back. Unethical, yes. Greedy, too. But a cold-blooded killer? She still couldn't picture it.

Renfrew continued. "The tribal pharmaceutical company would be a good investment for DiBondi and his friends and a great way to fund my research. Once I was in contact with them, the tribes made me sign a confidentiality agreement. TOTEM had bought the rights to the ten most commonly used drugs in America. With the cash flow from that and from gambling revenues, they were planning to fund research on the indigenous plants on various reservations to discover their pharmaceutical potential."

That explained the drug target sequencer in Renfrew's lab, thought Alex. He planned to extract the essence of the plants and figure out what impact they had on people's health. The use of plants wasn't unheard of in drug research; digitalis, made from the foxglove plant, has been used to treat heart palpitations for more than two hundred years. Even the new date rape drug, J, used yohimbine, which was derived from the bark of a tree.

"It was an additional source of funding and I wanted to take a shot at it," said Renfrew.

"Instead," Castro said, "someone took a shot at me."

Renfrew's mouth dropped open and he turned toward Castro. "You were the idiot who was following us? You almost screwed up the whole deal for me. They thought I'd blabbed about the meeting. Gave me a minder then. A guy who followed me around when I started collecting the plants."

"And once you were out in the desert, he was the guy who pushed you in the ravine."

"No, he was helping me identify the plants. I was leaning out to slice off a piece of one when I tumbled down. It was my fault."

"If everything was hunky-dory with the tribes, why didn't your minder stay around and rescue you?" Castro said.

"If anyone suspected that the wealthiest tribes were entering the pharmaceutical arena, the stock market would have gone nuts. And the antitrust division of Justice might have thrown a wrench in the deal."

"So Chief Minder just left you there in pain?" Castro said.

"He waited until after I dialed 911 and then, before he rode off, he yelled down for me to chew on the plant I'd cut off." Renfrew smiled. "I think we've got a first class pain reliever there."

Dan put his hand up to silence Castro and took over the questioning. "So was it your idea or theirs to poison the fountains?"

Renfrew's smile disappeared. "You've got to believe me. I lied about where I was and erased my hard drive to cover up evidence of a deal with them. I had nothing to do with any murder."

Dan considered that for a moment. "At any time during your meetings with the tribes, did you see anything suggesting a Native American group might be behind these deaths?"

He shrugged. "A couple of Native Americans I met with supported what Red Rights was saying."

"How many pills do Americans take a day?" asked Dan.

Alex wondered where he was going with this. Was he still conducting an interrogation? Or was he planning to buy stock?

"Between two and nine," Renfrew said.

"So," said Dan, "if Congressman Fillmore's right that a group of Native Americans wants to blast America back to the Stone Age, and that group controlled the country's most common drugs, they could infect everyone with hyperimmunity. Or even just stop supplying needed medications and kill people off that way."

Alex wanted to take Dan aside. He was suggesting something ludicrous. Race wars in America. Reds against whites? She thought of her mother's tales of the 1960s race riots across the country. But this was the twenty-first century.

Renfrew's lawyer spoke up. "Between the gambling money and the drug sales, Native Americans have plenty of money. And if you have money in

America, you have power. You don't need to kill people. You can just buy whatever you want."

Well, he should know, thought Alex. Law firms like his represented the robber barons of today.

The lawyer put his hand on his client's shoulder and said, "You've gotten what you want from him. It's time to cut him free."

"Nothing he's said gets him off the hook for obstruction and murder." Dan turned to Renfrew. "We'll release you temporarily on one condition."

Renfrew and his lawyer looked at Dan expectantly.

"We'd like you to go back into the tribal meetings and see if you can link Red Rights or someone else to the poisonings. If you aren't behind it, then you'll have to help prove who is."

Renfrew's attorney got in Dan's face. "That's absurd. He's innocent until proven guilty. He shouldn't have to find the real killers."

"Sit down, Donald," the doctor said, perhaps thinking of those stock options or maybe of the death penalty. "I'll go back in."

CHAPTER   41

That evening, Dan and Castro coached Renfrew on undercover work. Alex headed home, bringing piles of medical articles with her. When she returned to the Task Force room at six o'clock the next morning, she found that Chuck had beaten her to work. He'd set up four televisions to monitor media coverage of the epidemic. She stood behind him to watch. On ABC, the wife of a man who'd died at the county fair in Oklahoma was being interviewed. She said that her husband might have been saved, but the doctors at the nearby hospital had walked out the night before. They didn't want to risk getting this new disease.

It was like the early days of AIDS, Alex thought. Doctors seemed to go amnesiac at that time, forgetting the oath they'd taken. Many had refused to see AIDS patients. But putting your life at risk was part of being an M.D. At the end of the nineteenth century, smallpox and typhoid ran free. Doctors succumbed as often as their patients. And what about those European men of medicine who treated people with bubonic plague? Alex remembered the mixture of pride and awe she'd felt at her medical school graduation as she recited the Hippocratic Oath: "I will apply, for the benefit of the sick, all measures which are required."

But this disease had everyone spooked. In Arizona, children and their parents who'd tried to help the bloody Dana Rodriguez as she lay dying were now themselves falling ill. The ABC newscast had a running title under the segment: THE MODERN PLAGUE.

The screen switched to a satellite feed of a hospital near Taos that was getting ready for the onslaught of secondary infections. Outside the hospital, photos of Leroy Darven were posted on telephone poles, as if he were a

185

common criminal. The text on the flyers read, "Did you encounter this man? If so, go to your local hospital immediately."

Governor Elias Lightfoot Blackstone approached and walked up the hospital stairs. He was confronted by a television reporter. "What are you going to do about the plague, Governor?"

"The entire medical community of New Mexico is united," the governor said. "This will not be another Oklahoma. We will not turn away any infected patient. Please call the New Mexico Department of Public Health if you need care."

"Your book argues that Native Americans are superior to whites. Do you believe this plague is proof of your premise?"

Strain showed in the governor's face, as he opened the door to the hospital. "I never said that. I don't make comparisons of the races. I believe that anyone can live according to the American way, which is a way of being one with nature and caring for creatures that share the planet."

The door closed behind the governor and the reporter faced the camera. "Governor Elias Lightfoot Blackstone tells others to commune with nature. But where's the first place he went today? Not out into the desert, but to a hospital. Maybe the real American way is the high-tech way. This is Manfred Danforth in Taos for CNN News."

As Alex turned away from the screen, her cell phone rang with a 505 area code. "Hey, how's it going?" she said, assuming that Kingman Reed was calling.

Instead, she heard the voice she'd just heard on television. "It's not going well, Dr. Blake," he said. "I apologize for intruding on you without an introduction. I'm Elias Lightfoot Blackstone. Dr. Reed gave me your number."

Alex moved back from the screen and sunk into a chair at the conference table. "Governor, I apologize. I thought you were Dr. Reed calling."

"He told me that you know more about this disease than anyone else," he said. "I'm trying to ready my state for the onslaught of—what did Dr. Reed call them?—secondaries. I don't want our physicians to turn anyone away, but I also don't want to hold out false hopes. Have you any idea about how to treat these patients?"

She hesitated, distressed at how little she knew. "We haven't succeeded yet in identifying the agent that's causing this immune reaction, but we know that once people are exposed, they can be triggered by exposure to any manmade substance."

"I've been thinking. Mercifully, we had a limited number of victims in New Mexico. I'm thinking of extending an invitation to the family members of those people as well as the health care professionals to be attended in a hospital on one of the reservations in our state. There would be less risk there. Fewer triggers, as Dr. Reed calls them."

It was a sound plan, thought Alex. "That makes sense. Your doctors should watch the people who have been exposed. The first symptom is a headache. Once the swelling starts, I'd suggest injections of corticosteroids, antihistamines, and maybe epinephrine."

"Thank you, Dr. Blake," said the governor. "I understand you were the first person to take this epidemic seriously. If there is anything you need from us in New Mexico, please let me know."

Alex sat for a moment, mouth gaping, after she hung up.

"Are you alright?" asked Castro, whose first sight as he entered the room was Alex sitting frozen at the table. "Who spooked you?"

She composed herself. "The governor of New Mexico. He just called, wanting my advice."

"About?"

"How to treat the secondaries."

Castro and Chuck considered that for a moment. Then Chuck said, "Well, if he gets elected, ma'am, just don't desert us to be Surgeon General."

"Not a chance," said Alex. "I don't like the uniform."

But, she had to admit, there was a slight thrill to having seen the presidential candidate on television and then talked to him moments later. She looked back at the screen, hoping to catch a glimpse of him leaving the hospital. But instead, Martin Kincade's face filled the screen. "We must eliminate the vectors of infection," he said.

It was a lot of doublespeak, thought Alex. Those "vectors" were people. The primary cases were spreading the disease to the secondaries. What exactly was Kincade planning?

The appearance of the chief of Homeland Security on television caused Alex to look at the map that Chuck had hung. She remembered the map that Kincade's secretary had taken care to hide. "Nebraska," she said.

"What?" asked Chuck.

"When I was at Homeland Security, they had a map like this, but Nebraska was colored in as well. Something must have happened there."

Chuck sat down at his computer. "Okay, we'll pull up the hospital records."

"They cut off my access."

He looked at her expectantly. "What do you want me to try?"

"Most of the fountain attacks occurred in poor neighborhoods. Why don't you run median income by zip code?"

Nebraska's average yearly household income, it turned out, was around $49,000, more than Arizona or New Mexico. By sorting for incomes less than $30,000, Chuck was able to generate a list of cities and towns that were similar to the ones where the disease had already struck.

"Now search for parks in those areas and generate a list of hospitals close to them."

The new search generated a list of six hospitals. Alex began calling them all. Sure enough, the fifth hospital she called indicated that, over a month earlier, a man had died of the strange symptoms she mentioned. A few weeks later, three more people had died of a similar disease.

"Have you seen any such deaths lately, especially of family members of those who died earlier?" she asked the hospital's infectious disease chief.

"Nah. We figure it must have been some strange allergy to insect bites. We've got a lot of critters in the rural area the patients came from. It's an hour drive from our facility."

"Do you have tissue samples from any of the people?"

"By the time they got here, they were good and dead, looking like some beached whales."

Alex put down the phone. "Homeland Security knew about the disease before I did," she said to Chuck. "Why have they been giving me the runaround?" But even as she spoke she realized that she was on thin ice, suggesting that the agency, created to protect the public, was looking the other way to further its own agenda.

"Could be they called you off because they didn't want to create a public panic until they figured how to treat this," Chuck said. He took a yellow highlighter and colored Nebraska in.

Alex put her hands on her hips. "If they were serious about a cure, wouldn't they be calling meetings of scientists to work on it?"

Chuck looked at her. "Maybe they are, ma'am. But maybe it's a cotillion where you didn't get an invitation."

CHAPTER 42

Alex took leave of Chuck and Castro and headed out the hallway and down the stairs into the tunnels that connected the AFIP and the National Museum of Health and Medicine. She thought that a few minutes with the exhibits would help her clear her head.

Doctors were always dealing with health challenges, she told herself. She could get out ahead of this disease, this new epidemic. She just needed to view the problem from another angle.

She walked past the plaque that told of Walter Reed's successful identification of mosquitoes as the cause of yellow fever. Then she wove through the museum, stopping for a few somber minutes at the exhibit of paltry equipment that filled a surgical tent from a Mobile Army Surgical Hospital, a MASH, during the Korean War. She looked at the drab olive-colored cot and imagined a soldier lying there. Every era, every region of the world, had its terrifying diseases. During the Korean War, it was hemorrhagic fever, which caused headaches, uncontrollable vomiting, bloody urine, a swollen liver, and fatal convulsions. The disease struck more surely than snipers and was responsible for 15 percent of the soldiers' deaths. When a variation of the disease surfaced in Baltimore in the poverty-stricken port area in the late 1990s, medical researchers pinpointed transmission of the airborne hantavirus from rat feces on a ship in the harbor. Destruction of contaminated rats kept the effect of hemorrhagic fever in the United States small. She needed to figure out a way to similarly contain this new infection.

Alex exited the museum and started walking along the fenced border of the base compound. She had just passed Walter Reed Hospital when she saw

Dan's car turn onto Georgia Avenue. She expected him to continue through the guarded gate. But instead, he parked across the street from the compound. A few minutes later, a black Audi pulled up behind it. From where she was standing, Alex could see an orange parking sticker in the rear window. The driver got out of the black car and Dan got out of his. They spoke for a few moments, then the man handed Dan a package. Alex narrowed her eyes to focus her vision, but she couldn't make out what was being passed between the men.

She turned left and walked rapidly to the parking lot she knew Dan would park in. She saw him slow down at the security gate, wave his ID at the guard, and then roll into the lot. Since he was a major at the base, rather than a visitor, the guard didn't inspect his trunk.

"Got something important enough to track me down?" Dan asked her as he got out of his car.

"Not really," she said. "Just out for a walk to clear my head." She looked down at the package he'd been handed and smiled. "Wasn't that a little cloak-and-dagger just to get a gift of Peet's coffee beans?"

"My buddy didn't want to sign with the guard."

She thought about the orange sticker she'd seen on the Audi. "Since when does Homeland Security offer carry-out?"

Dan looked around. There was no one within earshot. "Martin Kincade, a civilian who's never held a gun, was put in charge of securing the nation," he said. "Once he took office, he started firing anyone with military training, bringing in mercenaries. Let's just say, I've had my eye on him."

Then it dawned on Alex. The AFIP had the mandate to investigate crimes in the military and in the executive branch. Homeland Security was in the executive branch.

"We've got someone on the inside," he added.

"Dan, Kincade knew about the disease before we did. His secretary had a map with four states on it—the three we were investigating, plus Nebraska. Maybe Kincade's using this disease as a chance to manipulate the President, to play hero."

"Any evidence to support that theory?"

"Other than the map, no."

"Then get it. Kincade's trouble. There's no honor to that kind of man, who violates the rules of engagement."

Grant had joined Chuck and Castro in the Task Force room by the time Alex and Dan entered with the sack of coffee. "Martin Kincade was onto this before we were," Alex said. "Where is he getting his information?"

Chuck, as frustrated as the others, warmed to having a new mission. He began to search computer databases for people connected to Kincade. A dozen articles about him appeared on the screen at the end of the conference table, tracing his business roots from his first job, at Unilever, to his recent resignation from the board of Levanthal Industries to take the Homeland Security job.

"Levanthal? What do they do?" Alex asked.

Chuck dug further and found a dozen enterprises under the Levanthal umbrella, some of which were multi-industry entities themselves.

"Any pharmaceutical companies?" Dan asked, tapping an unlit Camel on his desk.

Lists of companies that were subsidiaries of Levanthal's main holdings flooded the screen. Some food companies, a pharmacy chain, but no drug companies.

Grant moved closer to the screen. "Check this out," he said. He pointed to Quest Entertainment.

"So?" asked Alex.

"They own a bunch of casinos in Vegas. Un-fuckin'-believable parties. Models, actresses, the whole nine yards. I try to cop an invitation whenever I'm in town."

Alex was sure he tried to cop more than that. But, for once, she could have hugged the overmuscled sexist. "Kincade's linked to a company that makes money if people stop gambling at tribal casinos!"

"Apparently," said Chuck. "But where does that get us?"

Dan let out a frustrated sigh. Alex had never seen him so perplexed. "Serial killers I get. But what the fuck is going on here?"

He put his unlit cigarette in his mouth and chewed on it for a moment, then took it out. "Okay, Alex, since we're doing such a shitty job figuring out how this disease got to the water supplies, what do you need to figure out how to fix it?"

She sat silently for a moment, then said, "I've got to find Dr. Teague.

He's been studying these types of symptoms for decades. I think I should head to Boston. That's the last place he was seen."

Alex looked at her watch and estimated how quickly she could make it to National Airport. The way she drove, under a half hour. She could catch the 11:00 A.M. shuttle to Boston. Odds were that Mrs. Teague's family had an address for the compound. But she needed to play it right. With the amount of secrecy that surrounded the Colony, they wouldn't likely give Alex the address over the phone.

CHAPTER 43

When Alex arrived in Boston, she asked her cabdriver to drop her in Back Bay in front of the gleaming, copper-colored building with the large sign saying CHRISTALINK HOLDINGS. There was a security guard checking IDs and drivers' licenses of people attempting to board the elevators to ascend to any of the corporate floors.

She paused for a moment, trying to figure out how to get through security. Consulting the company directory opposite the guard desk, she focused on the name Kennedy Bonsfeld Christalink, the patriarch of the family and Chairman Emeritus of the Board. His office was listed as Suite 101, the Christalink Foundation.

She looked around to see where the first-floor offices were. At street level, all she could see were an Au Bon Pain, a Starbucks, and a small pharmacy. Then she noticed a hallway to the right of the guard's desk that didn't require passing through the identification process. Alex followed it as it snaked around past the first-floor retail stores until she found 101. She knocked and was welcomed by a gray-haired woman in her late sixties.

"I'm here to see Mr. Kennedy Christalink," she said.

The woman looked at her jeans and replied, "Of course you are." She pushed a button on her phone and said into the receiver, "Are you accepting applicants?"

A gruff voice barked back, loud enough for Alex to hear, "Yes. We'll take tea."

The receptionist hung up and directed Alex, "Just down that hallway and to the right."

Alex started walking before the secretary finished speaking. She had no idea what she was supposedly applying for and didn't want to wait until the woman keyed in on that fact.

Christalink, a man in his eighties with a floppy, thick moustache, sat in an overstuffed chair in front of a jade-inlaid Chinese screen. He was reading Warren Ripley's book on Civil War artillery. On the wall to the left hung an exquisite portrait of his redheaded daughter, Bree, painted when she was in her twenties. No other pictures or paintings graced the room.

He rose to shake Alex's hand, then motioned her to a doorway that opened outside to a charming private garden. They sat under a portico on lovely silk-covered armchairs, with a view of the Charles River. Christalink chose a chair next to a table with a much younger walrus-moustached photo of him cradling a red-haired toddler on his lap. In the photo, he held a book in front of him. *Alice in Wonderland.*

The receptionist arrived moments later with two individual Japanese tea pots and matching cups, a small plate of madeleines on the side. She put the tea service on the table between them.

"I wondered why you didn't claim the penthouse office at the top," Alex said to Christalink. "Now I know. This is amazing."

He smiled. "The first office of Christalink Logging, as it was called then, was in an old Victorian house, with a small garden in back. As a young boy, I'd go to work with my grandfather. When he needed to hold a private business meeting, I'd play in the garden."

A boat on the Charles River caught his eye for a moment, then he continued. "I had all manner of adventures in that garden. I was a pilot, a dragon slayer, a king. That garden developed my imagination. When I took over the company in the 1960s, everyone was touting specialization. I chose diversification. I was early into the satellite industry, cable television, biotech. I could see the promise of many different approaches to earning money."

"And now you're devoting some of your wealth to philanthropy."

He nodded. "Another reason for the first-floor office. I'm not interested in funding the big guys—the American Cancer Society, Mothers Against Drunk Driving, the Neuropsychiatric Institute. Fresh ideas interest me. And I don't want people who need seed money from me to practically be strip-searched just to get in the building."

Alex thought about how risky it might be for the man listed as number forty-five on the *Forbes* list of the wealthiest individuals in America to be this accessible to kidnappers or rivals, with an office that didn't require visitors to go through security. His receptionist—who'd probably been with him since the Korean War—could hardly fend off trouble. "Aren't your advisors worried about your safety, with you being so accessible?"

"If I listened to my so-called advisors, I'd still be building log cabins and probably be living in one as well. The only people who really cared about me are dead and gone."

Alex considered that for a moment as she brought her cup of tea to her lips. The directory had listed a number of Christalinks, including the current Chairman of the Board, his son. It didn't bode well for corporate dynamics if the family itself was in turmoil. But she didn't want to pursue the issue further and risk upsetting the man before she got a chance to ask him a favor.

He sensed her hesitation and said, "So tell me about yourself and your ideas."

"I'm Dr. Alexandra Blake and I have an M.D. and a Ph.D. in genetics."

He clapped his hands together. "Ah, genetics, the wave of the future. I like that. Now, are you seeking money for basic research or a pilot project or epidemiological work?"

"No, no. I'm not here to request a grant. I'm seeking information. I'm looking for a way to contact Dr. Andover Teague."

Christalink started to choke on his madeleine. Alex stood up and slapped his back. He turned his face to her and sputtered, "That vile man. He killed my daughter."

CHAPTER   44

Kennedy Christalink's anger at Andover Teague was overpowering. But when he said that Teague killed his daughter, Alex thought he was speaking metaphorically. After all, Teague had taken Bree away to a secret, remote location, removing her from the Christalink family orbit.

"What exactly do you mean?" Alex asked, as she settled back into the other armchair.

"It's all my fault. Bree was taking a year off between college and graduate school, working for me. She wanted to be a social worker but frankly she had much better business sense than any of her brothers. I was hoping to interest her in the work of the company, so I could groom her for the chairmanship. Instead, she was taken by one Andover Teague."

It dawned on Alex what had happened. "He asked the foundation for funds."

Christalink nodded. "He wanted to develop a vaccine, save kids around the world. It would be a perfect philanthropy project. Plus, there might be a commercial component. Since no one could diagnose which infants would be afflicted, all newborns would have to be vaccinated. Four million a year in the United States alone."

"But then the plan changed and Teague took your daughter away with him."

He nodded. "It was just supposed to be for a year or two. He said he was close to a cure. But my sense is that when he got there, he liked the life. The kids were fine. The pressure to 'fix' them was gone."

"And how did Bree feel about that?"

"She was lonely and overworked—like some common chambermaid. She lost a lot of weight. Couldn't take it after eight months and turned around and came home. But she still loved her husband and it drove her crazy that she'd given up. She couldn't forgive herself."

"Is there any way I can talk to her?"

Christalink shook his head, his mouth a tight grimace. "She was back only four months when she went into kidney failure. Maybe if she'd been diagnosed earlier, if she hadn't been out there in the middle of nowhere, she could have been saved."

Christalink picked up the picture of himself reading to a young Bree. Alex thought he would hand it to her, but he was lost in his memories of his daughter.

Alex knew from the articles that Bree was 23 when she went to the Colony. Quite young to die of kidney disease. "Any family history of kidney problems?"

"None. And the women in our family live forever. My mother died at the age of ninety-six."

"I can see why you would hold Teague accountable, but I need to contact him. All those people dying in the Southwest have a disease that looks a lot like what those kids had. Maybe he could help save some people."

"What? By flying them off to Neverland? When I met him, I thought he was a doctor, not some circus master."

"Surely you can at least give me an address, a bank contact, a cell phone number."

"Even if I were willing to help, I don't have any way to get in touch with him. When Bree died, her mother hired a private detective to track him down, hoping he'd at least come to the funeral. He couldn't be found."

"Can you think of anyone else who could reach him? His own family? Parents of the children, maybe? Colleagues of his at Harvard?"

Christalink stared out at a sailboat, his eyes filled with sadness. Then he turned back to Alex. "I have no idea who might have that information. I'm sure those would have been the first people the private detective contacted. But if you do manage to find Teague, tell him I hope he burns in hell."

After leaving the philanthropist's office, Alex wandered through the streets of downtown Boston, wondering what to do next. The number of people lining the sidewalk in the center of town made her expect a parade. Then she realized they were queuing up to enter a department store. "What's going on?" she asked one of the waiting women.

"Didn't you hear the guy from Homeland Security this morning? This is an epidemic triggered by man-made items. We need to buy feather pillows and muslin shirts. I'm trying to figure out how to cook the weeds in my backyard."

"But the disease hasn't hit anywhere near Massachusetts," Alex said.

"Suit yourself," the woman said. "I'm taking care of my family."

Alex didn't have the heart to tell her that her tactics would be futile. The weeds in the yard probably had traces of man-made pesticides. Feather pillows might be stitched together with nylon thread. Instead, Alex moved on.

Catching the Green Line D train to the Longwood Station, she walked past the imposing marble steps of the main building of the Harvard Medical School and entered the Countway Library. With the type of research Teague had been doing, he probably logged some serious time there. Maybe someone would be around who remembered him and stayed in touch.

The student at the circulation desk pointed her toward the office of Mr. Peter Schoenfeld, who looked the right age to have known Teague. Schoenfeld apparently didn't get many visitors. He seemed prepared to launch into a description of every book that Teague had ever checked out, every article he'd requested. To hear Schoenfeld tell it, Teague would have been nothing without him.

"He must have been grateful for your help," Alex said. "I assume you've kept in touch. I'm wondering if you could tell me how to reach him or perhaps pass a message on from me."

"Oh, I think he must be past his prime by now," he said. "No publications for a decade and then an article for some public health journal, not even one of the big three."

Alex knew what he was talking about—the trifecta of medical journals: *Lancet, New England Journal of Medicine,* and *Journal of the American Medical Association.* The most prestigious places to publish.

Schoenfeld harrumphed further. "Even that little ditty was probably written by his co-author. But I do have something better than a current link to him. When he left, he donated all his papers to us. I was so sure he'd be another Harvard Medical School Nobel laureate, like Baruj Benacerraf—"

Alex nodded. "The doctor who discovered how genes regulate immune responses."

The librarian stood up and took Alex to one of the private reading rooms. "I'll have my assistant bring in the boxes that Teague left us. Those documents are the link to the old Teague, who had a lot more on the ball than the current one, wherever he is."

Fifteen minutes later, Alex had stacks of documents spread out across one of the long reading-room tables. From the circulation card glued to one of the boxes, she saw that Teague's papers had been requested frequently in the two years after he'd moved to Colorado. Even the *Life* magazine reporter had wanted a peek. But since then, interest in potential origins and cures for *Inflatus Magnus* had dwindled. The dust on the top of the boxes signaled Alex that they hadn't been opened in years.

The first box held case notes on the first child he'd seen, Matthew Brunner. There was a birth certificate with his mother's name, father listed as "unknown." The second box contained lab notebooks and copies of articles about the development of vaccines for typhus and yellow fever. Alex was familiar with the history of those medical triumphs, both of which had their roots at the Armed Forces Institute of Pathology in the early 1900s with the work of the AFIP directors Walter Reed and Frederick Russell.

As a researcher herself, she was thrilled to come across what appeared to be Teague's laboratory speculations about the origins of the disease and a possible route for vaccination. The only drawback was that Teague, like many scientists, had used his own shorthand—abbreviations for patients, substances, and body systems. He'd been working alone on these theories, so there was no compulsion to make his notes accessible to anyone else. Alex set these precious papers aside while she worked her way through the third box.

At first she thought she'd hit pay dirt. These were the documents related to the establishment of the Colony. A copy of a check made out to a real estate broker in Wyoming. Perhaps he represented the owner of the Colorado property. Or could the compound actually be in Wyoming instead, with a little white lie told to *Life* to augment the security? An exhaustive search of the box revealed no land deeds or other identifying information about the

Colony. But she did find a startling stack of documents. All the parents of the children, including Matthew Brunner's mom, had signed over their children to Teague in legal adoptions. That didn't sound like his plan had been temporary. And Alex started to wonder what a grown man had been doing for fifteen years alone with a bunch of kids.

She poked her head out of the reading room, Teague's lab notes in hand, and located Schoenfeld's assistant. "I'd like to photocopy a few pages, please."

The woman looked at her as if she'd just suggested lighting a bonfire with Vesalius's original sixteenth-century *De Humani Corporis Fabrica.* "Documents from the private collection do not circulate, nor may they be copied," she said. The glare that accompanied the woman's statement convinced Alex that there was no appeal from this position.

As she walked back to the reading room, Alex wondered why they were being so protective about the materials. Perhaps Schoenfeld's crew thought that if Teague won a Nobel Prize, they'd be sitting on some hot property with these notes and Knopf would pay a fortune for the book rights. Wasn't that what had happened with *A Beautiful Mind?* She bet that Schoenfeld was already figuring out who would play him in the movie.

Back alone in the room, Alex started copying down all the names of the children who'd been adopted, their parents' names, and the courts in which the adoptions had been approved. Then, certain that no one was watching, Alex yanked the bottom of her turtleneck out the back of her jeans and slid Teague's lab notes and a few other papers under the back of her shirt. She tucked the shirt in and slipped into her leather jacket.

Before leaving, she stopped to thank Schoenfeld, hoping that the papers wouldn't make a detectable crinkling sound when she shook his hand. But Schoenfeld didn't notice her transgression. He said, "Haven't thought about Teague in years, and then two of you coming looking for him within a few months."

"Two? Who besides me?"

"I didn't think to ask his name. He was Caucasian, late thirties."

"Maybe a medical resident interested in his work?"

The librarian shook his head. "Harvard supports diversity, but I've never seen a doc here with a tattoo on the back of his neck."

"What kind of tattoo?"

"Some sort of number. Maybe 186 or 187, something like that."

"Did you get any other information from him?"

He shook his head. "Soon as he heard I had no means of contacting the doctor, he just stormed out of here. That's when I got a glimpse of the tattoo."

CHAPTER 45

When she got back to the AFIP at 7:00 P.M., Alex was surprised to find Dan, Chuck, Grant, and Castro smiling in the conference room.

Castro said, "I was telling the guys what a Wonder Woman you are."

"Thanks for the recommendation, but my trip to Boston was practically a bust."

"Yeah, but you hit it right on J."

"What are you talking about?"

"The patent you sent me."

Alex was still perplexed.

"Remember how two Stanford students made a bundle by starting Google?" Castro said.

She nodded.

"Well, that set the bar. Two other students designed a female alternative to Viagra—complete with Spanish fly—but had to pull their FDA application when a few of the test subjects died."

"Those two guys on the Stanford patent were students, not professors?" Alex asked.

Grant interjected, "What's next? Extra credit for a meth lab?"

"And the chemistry students gave you some leads?" Alex asked.

Castro smiled. "They were the leads."

"They were behind J?" Alex asked.

"Once they saw their *legal* market disappear," Castro said, "they started selling it to the club crowd."

"Unbelievable," said Dan.

"Yeah. The first one—straight-A student with a heart of stone—gave us some bullshit about market equilibrium. Said if rapists weren't using this, they'd just be using something else. But the other one rolled easily. Laid out the whole structure. DEA's arrested dealers in three states."

Alex sighed. One less thing to worry about for Lana. Still, it might have been a lot easier for the girl to avoid J than to avoid the plague now spreading across the country.

At the agreed-upon time, Chuck switched on a small toaster-size device with speakers so they could receive a transmission from Renfrew about his first day back at TOTEM. He'd been issued a cell phone designed in Grant's lab with episodic encryption and transmission that could not be picked up by electronic eavesdroppers, but they had to listen to it with a special minicomputer on their end.

"What have you found?"

"Nothing much," said Renfrew. "These guys are behaving like venture capitalists. They have accountants and me advising them on the worth of different pharmaceutical companies. All I can say is, if their new company goes public, be sure to buy."

Castro stood up and started to pace, looking frustrated. He said to Dan in a loud voice, so Renfrew could overhear, "Let's pull him out if he can't do better than that."

"No, no," said Renfrew. "Just tell me what you want me to look for."

"What chemicals and laboratory potential do they have?" asked Alex.

"Right now, nothing's up and running. They bought a couple of sequencers, but the wet labs aren't built out yet. They're moving slowly, getting their business plan in order."

"And what are they saying about the deaths?" Dan asked.

"Nothing more than what you would overhear in a bar. It's a tragedy. Who could be doing it, et cetera. There's nothing that suggests they were involved."

"Do any have ties to Red Rights?" asked Dan.

"If anything, the head of the group, Chief Brave Sun, would like them to disappear. He thinks their radical ways are going to tar all Native Americans and make it, quote, 'less likely we could attract foreign business partners.'"

"Anyone in the group disagree with him?"

"Not aloud. Sometimes in a side conversation, his younger brother, Donald Sun, will express some interest in Red Rights' slogan that America should be given back to the red man. But what businessman wouldn't like to make a killing in real estate?"

Dan looked one by one at Castro, Alex, and Chuck. "Any more questions for Renfrew?"

They shook their heads.

"Okay," Dan said, "call us as soon as you have something."

Chuck turned off the device.

"Sounds like a dead end to me," said Alex. "They haven't got the scientific know-how to pull off something like this."

"Maybe Refrew doesn't know what to look for," Chuck offered.

"He's a researcher," Castro said. "He should know exactly what to look for."

Chuck, the most conciliatory of the group, said, "He'll do better next time."

Castro rolled his eyes and Alex changed the subject, filling them in about her visit to Teague's father-in-law. "Oh, there's one other thing," she said. "A man in his late thirties came looking for Dr. Andover Teague at the Harvard library a few months ago. The librarian had no other description than a tattoo on his neck, with a three-digit number, something like 186 or 187."

"What do you think?" said Chuck. "Gang affiliation?"

"Maybe a military unit? 186th Battalion?" said Grant.

Castro laughed. "You guys got to get out in the real world a little more. It was a 187. And our guy's from California."

Alex looked at Castro. "How do you know?"

"I've seen those tattoos on the West Coast. It's a badge of honor. Means the person killed someone, probably did time for it."

"How do you get that from a three-digit number?" Alex asked.

"With help from the state," Castro said. "California Penal Code 187 to be exact. The provision of the criminal law that applies to murder."

"Okay," Alex said. "Let's think this through. We've got a guy who's committed murder and he's looking for Teague. If he's behind the fountain poisonings, he probably hit the same dead end I did. So maybe he's found another doctor to help him out."

"If he's from California," Chuck said, "why wasn't California hit?"

"Could be he's building up to it," Dan said. "All he'd need to do is hit one or two major water supplies and he could bring the state to its knees."

"I'll warn the state's public health director," Alex said. "They can start testing the water. I don't know much about the infectious agent but there's been mercury in each of the fountains."

"Wasn't there a big anti-GMO protest by Red Rights near Sacramento recently?" Chuck asked.

"You can follow that angle," Dan said.

"If he got the tat while he was in prison," Castro said, "they'd have it on his release photos. Could be hundreds of guys with that tat, but I've mainly seen it on the biceps, not the neck. Maybe the librarian will recognize a photo."

CHAPTER   46

The next morning, Alex entered the Task Force room just in time to meet Debevoise Rienne. An agent with Alcohol, Tobacco and Firearms, Debevoise was a light-skinned black with a slight lilt in his voice that signaled a link to the French West Indies, possibly to Martinique or Guadeloupe. The brownish stains on the pointer and middle finger on his right hand indicated he appreciated tobacco personally as well as professionally.

After being introduced to the team, Debevoise teed up his first slide, a photo of the cheroot near the Oklahoma water main. "Did you know that the Spanish word *tabaco* is derived from the Taino language in the Caribbean meaning a roll of leaves? That's exactly what you're looking at. A cheroot is made of a roll of tobacco leaves. It's a cylindrical cigar where the ends aren't crimped. We actually see a lot of them these days. They're cheaper to produce than the traditionally shaped ones."

Alex could tell that Dan was getting annoyed at the history lesson. "Anything special about it that would allow us to track where it was purchased?" Dan asked.

"Everything about it is special," Debevoise said. "But that doesn't translate into any leads. It was homemade. There must have been DNA on it where the maker licked the surrounding paper."

The team looked at Alex. "No luck there. He sealed it with water rather than spit."

"What kind of tobacco?" asked Grant. He was just the sort of guy Alex could picture buying the issue of *Cigar Aficionado* with the bulked-up

Arnold Schwarzenegger on the cover. Or making his date suffer through an after-dinner session in one of those smelly cigar bars.

But Debevoise beamed at him as if he were a prize student. He clicked to his next slide, which indicated the types of tobacco used in the United States and the chemical comparisons of each of them to the cheroot. There were at least eighty different tests.

"Wow," Alex said. "How does ATF have such advanced tests for tobacco composition?" It struck her as ironic that so many tests had been created for tobacco and so few to predict and prevent lung cancer.

"Lot of money in counterfeit cigs these days, what with the huge tax on each carton. Knockoffs are cheap to produce and easy to unload."

He used a laser pointer to circle the screen image of tests for known brands. "You can see by the graph, there was no similarity to the name brands, mainly because the cheroot at the scene was pure tobacco, no additives or preservatives." He advanced his slides. "So we started to look by tobacco genus. These days, people prefer lighter tobacco, like the Brightleaf kind grown in Virginia. But this cheroot contained shade tobacco. The early colonists learned the habit of smoking it from the Native peoples. The Puritans had a name for it—evil weed."

"There's the tie to Red Rights, right there," Grant said.

Castro added, "Native American shamans overdose on tobacco as an entheogen—basically a hallucinogen that provokes a spiritual experience." Alex wondered if he knew that from his DEA work or from his earlier studies at the University of Arizona.

"Hightower's been sprinkling tobacco at the ceremonies," Chuck said. "And he wears a shaman's medicine bag."

"But," Alex said, "we've seen hours of tape of him and never seen him smoke." She turned to Debevoise. "You said the early settlers used it. That doesn't conjure up the Southwest or even the South to me."

"Now, ma'am," Chuck said, "don't forget that South Carolina was one of the original thirteen colonies."

"Point taken," she said. "But is there any way to tell where this stuff was grown?"

"Of course," Debevoise said. "I personally prefer a Perique cheroot, from Saint James Parish, Louisiana."

Grant said, "Alex, that's like the Maserati of tobacco."

"But shade tobacco has its origin in the colder, less vibrant Northeast," Debevoise said. "It's grown in Connecticut and Massachusetts."

"That doesn't sound like a tobacco of choice for a member of a tribe from the bottom of the Grand Canyon," Alex said.

"We're getting ahead of ourselves here," Dan said. "So far, there's nothing to link that stogie to any particular individual."

"Not to mention that there were a couple hundred thousand people at the fair," Alex said. "Maybe the cheroot doesn't even belong to our guy."

Debevoise clicked back on his first slide. "The part of the water pipe that was tampered with was pretty isolated. Twenty, thirty workers might have had access."

"No one saw anything suspicious?" Alex asked.

Dan shook his head. He had slipped a Camel out of its pack and was tapping it rhythmically against the conference table. "No guards in the area. The water main was unattended most of the time."

"Still, he's taking risks if he chose someplace without the constant activity of a park, where he could easily blend in," Alex said.

"He's also escalating," Dan said. "More water, more victims."

"And we've got squat on where he'll strike next," Grant said.

Dan thanked Debevoise, stood up, and said, "I'll walk you out."

When they left the room, Alex mused that she'd never seen Dan be quite that polite before. Then it dawned on her how all that tobacco talk must have made him want a cigarette real bad.

Back in her office, Alex went through the slim sheaf of papers she'd accumulated about the medical aspects of the case, including the three articles by Teague and the materials she'd "borrowed" (she didn't like to use the term *stolen*) from the Harvard library. When she glanced at the author line on the public health article, she reread the reference to the Del Ray Institute. She went on the Web to find out about the institute. She got no hits. She could find lots of towns in the United States named Del Ray, including one in California, but no foundations or scientific think tanks with that name. She expanded her search to include Spain and South America, even looking for a Del Ray Instituto, but found nothing.

She leafed through the other papers, including the adoption papers of all the children. She noticed that all the adoptions had occurred on the same day—March 9, 1993. Matthew Brunner's form echoed his birth certificate—a mother listed, Julie Brunner, with father unknown. Julie's age at the time of the adoption was 22. Alex looked up from the page. A mother at 19, no partner, and a child with a terrifying illness. Alex's heart went out to her.

As she looked down again, an additional detail popped out at her. Matthew's original address was 19 Del Ray Street. As an 18-year-old writing for a public health journal, he'd probably made up the institute just to sound more credible.

She then spread Dr. Teague's early notes out on her desk. Realizing that she should be careful with this property of Harvard, she made a copy of them.

She sat back down and started to mark familiar terms in red pen on the copy. An hour passed and she'd managed to translate only about one in ten words. He'd made lots of references to a substance called GH, but she had no idea what that could mean. When she Googled it, all she got was a link to the website of the country of Ghana.

All she'd accomplished so far was to give herself a headache. Well, maybe it was unfair to blame her pain on Teague's poor penmanship and odd abbreviations. In the Nogales jail, she'd been shoved around by prison guards and tried to sleep sitting up with her head resting on a jail cell bar. Not exactly ergonomically correct, she thought, as she tilted her head to the side to relieve a knot in her neck.

When Castro arrived with the photos of the inmates he'd received from the California Department of Corrections, they e-mailed them to the Harvard librarian. They waited together in Alex's office until he'd looked at each one. But the librarian had no imagination. All the photos showed the guys in short, prison haircuts. The man who'd come to the library had longer hair, so he couldn't make a definitive ID.

CHAPTER   47

At eight that evening, the air in the Task Force room smelled of the remains of tuna sandwiches. Even good-natured Chuck was speaking in an angry tone, as lack of sleep and lack of leads weighed on all of them. From a single victim in Nebraska, the first state that it had hit, the toll had mushroomed to 120 lives in Oklahoma alone. And who knew how many secondaries were now nearing death?

Alex left the conference room to nab some chocolate in Barbara's office. She knew her friend was working late.

"Turns out that putting a civilian into an undercover job entails filling out a million forms, not to mention buying life insurance for him," Barbara said as Alex popped a dark truffle into her mouth.

"Sorry," Alex said, her word partially garbled through the chocolate.

"I hate to ask this, because you're probably as busy as I am, but is there any way you can run by the house to see Lana? She's still having a hard time with that thing with Maggie."

"Of course."

As Alex drove to Barbara's apartment, she thought about how Barbara had referred to what had happened—"that thing." Is that how she thought about her own rape? Was *rape* too horrible a word to speak?

Lana motioned for Alex to follow her into her room, where her computer desk was covered with papers. Lana sat at the desk and Alex perched on the corner of her bed.

"They caught the guys who were producing J," Alex told her.

"That's not going to help Maggie," Lana said sharply. "Her life is already ruined."

Alex saw the pained expression in the girl's face. What could she tell her to reassure her? "You're right that it's a horrible, life-altering experience. But women do go on and get degrees and jobs and continue to live." Like your mother, thought Alex. But it was Barbara's choice when, if ever, to tell her daughter about her rape.

Lana remained silent, skeptical.

"Is your friend back in school?"

"Yeah," said Lana. "We're trying to pretend nothing happened. But it's hard."

"And how are you doing? Did I ever tell you that my best friend in junior high school got very sick and died?" A brain tumor, Alex recalled. The reason why she'd become a doctor.

Lana's eyes got large.

"I thought I'd never be able to concentrate on my schoolwork again," said Alex. "I didn't want to be there. It all seemed so trivial and beside the point."

Lana nodded. She looked down when she spoke. "I finally told myself, if Maggie can go back, I should be able to go back, too." Lana was obviously troubled, maybe feeling selfish that she herself was hurting when the violence had been directed against her friend.

Alex put her hand on Lana's chin and tilted the girl's head so that she could read Alex's lips. "That's all you can do. Take one day at a time."

Lana was only half following what Alex was saying. She had turned away from Alex's eyes to look at her fingers. Until that point, Alex hadn't realized that she had been tapping nervously. She wondered how Lana had noticed, given that she couldn't hear the soft pats of her fingertips against the table.

"What does it mean, pointer, pointer, ring finger, pointer, pointer?" Lana asked.

"You noticed—and memorized—my movement out of the corner of your eye?"

Now it was Lana's turn to be surprised. "Of course. Doesn't everyone do that?"

"Well, actually, no," Alex said. "People don't process movement in that way."

Lana cocked her head. "But movements tell a lot about people. You know, like when someone leans in to talk to you. That means they are especially interested in what you are saying, or want to get to know you."

"You're right, Lana. In fact, there's a whole field of investigation, kinesthetics, that deals with interpreting movement. As to my tapping, sometimes I don't even realize that I'm doing it, like just now. It's a way my subconscious tells me about a genetic sequence of relevance. I tap it out with my fingers, each representing a letter of the genetic code."

"And the gene you were tapping just then?"

"Tell me the sequence again?"

Lana repeated the order of taps that Alex had made.

"That's funny. That's one of the alleles that they look at in paternity tests. I'm not sure why I thought of it just now."

When Lana finished describing her upcoming French assignment—writing an additional chapter for the book *The Little Prince*—Alex tried to ask casually, "So, how did the teacher like your prenatal screening paper?"

"She liked it. I got an A. But now I've gotten her into trouble."

"I find that hard to believe. What'd you do?"

Lana looked down at her hands and shifted in her chair. "I got the great idea of having the other kids try out being deaf. So the teacher bought a bunch of earplugs and told the class to wear them for the evening, to see what it was like."

"What a great assignment—like when they make students put on that heavy fake belly to understand what it feels like to be pregnant."

"Yeah, nobody had a problem when we pretended to be pregnant. But this time, all sorts of parents complained to the principal. They didn't like their teacher turning their precious kids into defectives. Said their kids could have gotten run over by a car. Even my friend Chloe blamed me. With the earplugs in, she couldn't call her friends or watch TV."

Alex thought about how isolated Lana must have felt when her friends couldn't identify with her. "I'm sorry, sweetie. Sometimes people just don't get it. Are you okay?"

Lana graced Alex with the faintest of smiles and said, "My Face Space friends made me feel better."

On Lana's home page, Alex saw the photos of a burn victim, a child with a limb deformity, and a twelve-year-old in a wheelchair. In solidarity with

Lana, they'd all covered their ears in goofy sympathy. One had a pair of Mickey Mouse ears on, with Kleenex stuffed in them. A young boy on crutches had exaggerated, oversize earphones perched on his head. Still another wore a tightly wrapped turban. A pretty blue-eyed girl, bald from cancer chemotherapy, had pencils sticking out of her ears, eraser side in, and was holding up a sign: CAN YOU HEAR ME NOW? NO, 'CUZ WE WANT TO BE LIKE LANA.

"Quite a sense of humor your buddies have," Alex said.

Lana nodded. "Yeah, we gimps and deaf guys are a regular laugh riot. That's something most people don't understand. They're so afraid of being disabled that they can't imagine how it's possible to be different and still have a sense of humor."

Alex nodded, then looked back at the photos on the screen. A girl in a hospital bed was smiling broadly. She was holding up a picture she'd drawn of Lana wearing a Wonder Woman suit. What an amazing community, thought Alex. While adults fumbled around trying in a well-meaning way to ignore these kids' differences, the kids themselves were able to help and comfort one another.

Alex looked at Lana. "I thought this website was just for people in high school. Some of these photos, like the girl in the hospital bed, are of people who can't be in school. How do they get into the loop?"

"Well, they can be brought in as friends of people who are already on Face Space. Or, there's lots of kids under the category of home schooling."

Alex tapped her foot excitedly. Lana pointed to Alex's boot and said, "You're thinking of something big and I think you are going to ask me to help you."

Alex hugged her. "You nailed it, honey. I'd like you to show me how it works with the home schooling section. I've got a list of kids and I'm trying to find at least one of them. They have a special sickness and they can't go to school. I don't have all their names with me, but I do remember at least one of them. Matthew Brunner."

Lana typed the name into the search box. In just a few seconds, a photo emerged of a handsome boy with long, dark hair and a billowy muslin shirt on. His home page had a logo, as did Lana's, indicating that he was part of the Who Shall Live listserve.

"Wow," said Lana. "He looks like Johnny Depp in *Pirates of the Caribbean*. And he's one of us!"

But Alex hardly heard the comment. She reached over and took the mouse from Lana's hand. For the next ten minutes, through clicks and links, she read the entire opus that Matthew had posted. A half-dozen poems, stunning photographs of his adopted siblings, and a series of scientific formulas. The pharmacological properties of plants. Complex genetic tests for immunodisorders. His own lab notes about progress toward a treatment. Inserted in those notes was a question: "Should I be playing God?"

Alex carefully read each posting. She couldn't believe he was just 18. He had a sophistication about immunity that many top researchers would envy. And the experiments that he had carried out! Alex was impressed with the breadth of Matthew's knowledge. He'd read widely about the birth of medicine in Ancient Egypt nearly two thousand years ago. He'd learned hieroglyphics so that he could translate ancient prescriptions that used alcohol or fat to extract medicines from plants. He'd replicated some of those early experiments and then begun exploring the medicinal potential of insects near the Colony. He'd discovered that a resinous substance used by bees in their hive, propolis, could treat bacterial infections like strep. And that the peptide polyfensin, produced by common flies, was both a powerful antibiotic and a potential treatment for immunological disorders.

She handed the mouse back to Lana. "I want you to write to him. I need to find out where he lives."

Lana refused the mouse. "Alex, you're talking crazy. There's no way someone will give their address on Face Space."

"This is really important. It's about a case."

Lana crossed her hands in front of her. "And I thought you were here to see me. You and Mom, all you care about is your work. When you were going out with Luke, at least we'd all do other stuff together."

The comment stung. "I am here to see you. But this isn't some game. This is about the Southwestern Plague. This boy lives with the one doctor in the world who might be able to save people."

"If that's true, why don't you call the doctor?"

"We haven't been able to locate him."

"So you want me to try to get this kid to trust me. Like, hey, I'm disabled and so are you, so I must be a good guy?"

"No, this has nothing to do with disability. Can I send a message to him directly?"

"Face Space only allows other Face Space users to log on."

Alex wondered if it was time to call in the cavalry—i.e., Barbara. But she didn't want to start a riff between mother and daughter. She tried to still her body parts so as not to lose Lana's trust with some unintended gesture. She looked imploringly into the girl's eyes. "How about this? I draft an e-mail from me and then, if you're comfortable with it, you send it on to him?"

Lana thought about it. She was clearly pained over being at odds with her surrogate aunt. Then she stood up so that Alex could sit at the computer. "Okay, let me take a look at what you want to say."

In a Word document, Alex wrote, "Dear Matthew, I am a doctor who read with interest your article on *Inflatus Magnus* in the *American Journal of Public Health*. I have a patient who is exhibiting symptoms of the disease and it would help me tremendously to talk to you or Dr. Teague. Please get in touch with me at"—Alex started to type her AFIP e-mail address, but then she realized that the suffix afip.osd.mil, a military one, might be confusing or threatening to him. She instead put in a personal address from her Yahoo account.

Peering over Alex's shoulder, Lana read the note. "This makes it sound like you're a real doctor."

Turning back over her shoulder so that Lana could read her lips, she said, "But I am."

"Technically, yeah. But who's your patient?"

Alex stood up and faced Lana. "A friend of Castro's died of the disease. I'm trying to learn what killed him so that I can prevent other deaths. Just do me this small favor."

Lana sighed and sat down. "Okay, Alex. I guess there are worse things in the world than entering a digital conversation with a clone of Johnny Depp." She typed a gracious note to Matthew, referring to Alex as her "amazing aunt," and then pasted in the typed request.

"The second you hear anything, let me know," Alex said. Maybe the boy would write back that night, making Alex's task an easy one. If not, Grant and Chuck would be able to find him soon enough. Now that Matthew had entered the global village of the Internet, it would be as if he were living next door.

CHAPTER 48

The next morning, when Alex entered the Task Force room, she saw her colleagues excitedly hovering around a machine. "Do you believe that DOD just had this baby in storage?" Castro asked her. "But the kid's got it humming now."

Chuck looked at Alex, annoyed at being called the kid.

"Don't look at me for sympathy," she said. "Now you know how I feel when you call me ma'am."

At first, Alex was going to make a comment about boys with toys, but as she neared the machine, she, too, was drawn in by its simple splendor. The combination of glass, gold, and DNA gave it the appearance of a work of art, rather than a descendant of the original IBM computing machine. It responded to spoken commands, did its computations at record speed, and had been programmed to use a neural-network-based artificial intelligence to find what it needed on the Web to answer virtually any question.

So far, Matthew hadn't responded to Lana. Alex had called Chuck earlier that morning to say they might need to get into Face Space.

"Sam here broke through all the security measures in about ten seconds flat," said Chuck.

"Sam?" Alex asked. "The computer has a name? Like HAL in *2001: A Space Odyssey*?"

"Uh-huh," Chuck said. "Nicknamed after the two institutions that worked on him. Stanford and MIT. S and M. Sam."

"Okay, let's take a look at Matthew Brunner," Alex said.

Chuck said aloud, "Sam, find the current Face Space page of M-a-t-t-h-e-w B-r-u-n-n-e-r."

Two seconds later, a disembodied voice said, "There is none."

"That's nonsense," Alex said to Chuck. "I was just on it last night."

The voice said, "Do you wish to refine your search? You asked about the current page. You did not ask about last night's page."

"Yes, Sam," Chuck said. "Show us last night's page."

A page opened up and Alex saw exactly the material she had viewed on Lana's computer. The boy must have taken his page down after getting Lana's e-mail.

The computer, which Alex had a hard time thinking of as a Sam, spoke again. "Would you like to learn more about Mr. Matthew Brunner?"

Not wanting to get into a chat with a machine, Alex quietly nodded to Chuck.

"Yes, Sam," Chuck said, "please do a full search on that person, eliminating other people of the same name to the best of your ability."

Sam replied, "What do you mean, to the best of my ability? I have not been built with limits."

Grant guffawed. "You gotta have some limits. You mean to tell me, you can have sex?"

Sam used a slightly condescending voice now. "What is sex but a way to replicate your DNA? I do that thousands of times a day."

Grant looked chastised, but kept up a good front. More to the group than to the computer, he said, "If you are doing it that many times a day, you might be in danger of going blind."

"No," said Sam. "I can see just fine." The Brunner page disappeared from the screen and a current image of the five of them in the room appeared. Alex was transfixed by the video. Grant looked a bit surprised, she looked tired, and Castro, damn him, looked as seductive as ever.

"Okay," Alex said, not quite believing she was talking to a computer. "You've had your fun. Give us any other information you have about Matthew Brunner."

A light in the panel above the monitor dimmed for a second and Alex thought the computer was about to shut down. Then she realized that it was Sam's equivalent of a wink. Rome was burning, people were dying of this disease, and now she had to put up with a comic of a computer. Yep, that was just her luck.

But then the information started spewing across the screen at high speed.

Not just the materials that Brunner had chosen to load on his Face Space page over the past year, but every e-mail he'd ever received. When Chuck sorted them by sender, they saw he'd corresponded with dozens of other kids on Face Space, as well as forty or so professors with .edu addresses, mainly about his scientific theories or with queries about their articles. And he'd received an e-mail from someone named Jeffrey Ossing with an AOL account.

Chuck used the large screen on the wall to display the e-mail that Ossing sent to Matthew Brunner. I WANT TO SEE YOU AGAIN. REMEMBER THE BLUE TRIKE. The date on the cryptic e-mail was two months earlier. Before the incidents in the fountains started.

"Blue trike?" Alex said.

"Could be a street name for a drug," Castro said. "We've had blue heavens for depressants, blue devil for methamphetamine, and blue kisses for an Ecstasy precursor."

From hanging out with Luke's musician friends, Alex knew songs that referred to heroin as brown sugar. But she hadn't heard the nicknames for this rainbow of other drugs.

"I'll go through the e-mails from scientists to see if 'blue trike' comes up there or anything useful about Teague," Alex said.

Grant said, "If you're trying to find this Matthew character, why not just look up the IP address for his computer? All computers have one so they can hook to the Internet."

Chuck turned to Grant. "It was the first thing I tried, but the IP address is obscured somehow. Probably because the prototype was developed for the Department of Defense. They wanted to be able to hop onto the Internet without leaving any trace."

"So you want to find Nat?" the computer asked.

Chuck and Grant looked at each other, their faith in the machine plummeting. "No. Remember, we told you we were looking for the location of Matthew Brunner and Andover Teague," Chuck said.

"Yes," said Sam, his tone once again condescending, "but they are with Nat."

"Who the hell is Nat?" Grant asked.

"He is my twin."

CHAPTER 49

"Like many firstborns, I was slightly larger and knew a little more," said Sam, the DNA-based computer. "When they made my twin, they wanted to reverse the initials to credit the MIT group first and call the machine Mas. But that is not even a name. I moved the letters up one, M to N and S to T, and came up with Nat and that's the name that stuck."

Alex excitedly asked the machine, "Do you know where Nat is?"

Sam said, "Negatory. I have been in storage for five years. The administrator who commissioned me left the Department of Defense for private industry a month before I was delivered. No one knew how to use me. According to studies funded by the Human Genome Research Institute, DNA frightens people."

"Not, uh, Alex here," said Chuck.

Alex appreciated the effort that Chuck had put into using her first name. Maybe she'd talk to Castro after all about not calling Chuck "the kid."

"I'm a geneticist," she said to Sam. "I work with DNA all the time."

"Pleased to meet you. I will inform you if I need servicing."

"Stand in line," Grant said, leering at Alex. "A lot of men want to be serviced by the doc."

Castro gave Grant a sufficiently crippling look that the bodybuilder seemed to deflate. Then Castro addressed the computer. "So what can you do to track down your duplicate?"

"I need to process that problem," Sam said. "I will start with the data that shows twins have a special affinity and ability to communicate. In one study at the University of Minnesota, three hundred twins who were separated at birth—"

"Enough, Ace," said Grant. "Just tell us where he is."

"Does that mean I am officially part of this investigation?" asked Sam.

"Yeah. You can even have as your partner Castro Baxter here," Grant offered.

Alex turned to Castro to watch his reaction, but he was fine with it. "Pleased to have you on board," Castro said. "A regular Sam Spade, you are."

The computer cycled for a moment. "Sam the shovel?"

Castro laughed. "No, it's the name of a famous fictional detective. In your spare time, read a Dashiell Hammett book. But only *after* you find the guys we're looking for."

"Will do."

Castro stood and looked at Dan. He wasn't asking for permission to leave, but merely giving Dan the heads-up that he was on his way out. "I'll see if there's a new drug called blue trike. Have the kid try to get a bead on Jeffrey Ossing." Castro was out the door before Dan could point out that he was the one who gave orders here.

CHAPTER   50

Primed now that they were finally getting somewhere, Alex told Chuck to call her as soon as he found out the location of the Colony. Then she returned to her lab and started reading the e-mails that scientists had sent to Matthew. Many of Matthew's pen pals were well-known academics. Alex had even heard some of them speak at medical meetings. The boy seemed to have picked up the mantle from Teague. He was corresponding with them to find out how to cure *Inflatus Magnus.*

The tone of the scientists' e-mails indicated that they didn't realize they were corresponding with someone so young. It would have astonished them to see the boy's photo on his Face Space page. She took a few notes on theories about anti-inflammatory drugs, but didn't come across any reference to "blue trike" or any hint of the location of the Colony. Nor any indication that these scientists were even marginally related to the fountain deaths.

As she mulled over the significance of the scientific posts, Alex studied the compelling photos that Matthew had taken. Sunflowers that he or Teague must have crossbred with other plants so that they had luminous purple leaves. A wonderful shot of a carved wooden door with a small window through which you could see a working laboratory with mice in cages. And the most magnificent portraits of his siblings, capturing in black-and-white an astonishing radiance and hope. She printed off a half dozen of the children's photos and hung them in the office of her laboratory, the place where she felt most at home.

Worrying that Chuck may have had a breakthrough, but not called her, Alex entered the conference room at 3:00 P.M. Dan turned to her and asked,

"Where's the cowboy?" Dan conveyed the clear impression that Castro was on probation and could be dropped from the group at any time.

"I'm sure he'll be here soon," Alex said, then chided herself for always rising to defend him.

"I've got some bad news," Chuck said. "Even though we've got copies of all e-mails going to Matthew, we can't read his responses."

Perhaps with the help of Nat, Matthew Brunner had managed to wipe all trace of each message moments after he'd sent it. From Matthew's end, there were just whispers and shadows.

Castro bounced into the conference room. "Sorry I'm late," he said to the group, and Alex could have hugged him for apologizing. "No luck on blue trike, but I found Matthew's AOL buddy." He shot a photo down the table toward the end, where Dan was sitting, but he didn't take a seat himself.

It was a mug shot. From the side angle, they could see part of the tattoo on the back of his neck. A one and an eight.

"Three months ago," Castro said, pacing, "he got out of prison, where he served ten years on a felony murder rap, homicide in the course of a drug deal. Probation officer in Los Angeles makes him check in every other week on Wednesdays, but he didn't show up last Wednesday."

Alex thought about it. A killer was in the mix. But how was the killer linked to the Colony? "If he's checking in on Wednesdays, that still gives him time to poison the fountains on Saturdays and get back to Los Angeles."

"Okay," said Dan. "Chuck will search his credit card statements for trips to the Southwest. The disappearance doesn't look good. He's planning something."

Castro looked at Dan. "I've got an address for his apartment, but his landlord hasn't seen him for a week. I think one of us should do the search, rather than the local cops. Unless there's a big vat labeled 'poison,' they won't know what they've found."

"If he's involved, you'll need a hazmat team," said Dan.

"Now that Homeland Security's pursuing the Red Rights angle, they'll never authorize one," Alex said, "and CDC won't make a move without Martin Kincade's okay."

"Why don't you come with me?" Castro asked Alex. "I can go through all the other evidence and you can advise on any chemicals."

Dan looked from Castro to Alex, trying to see if this was a setup.

"I'm hazmat qualified," Alex reminded him. "And I can download the rest of the scientists' e-mails to my laptop to read on the flight. That way, I won't lose any time."

"Okay, kids," Dan said. "But this is strictly business."

Alex was quietly offended, but Castro was angry. "Ted is the one who keeps me going on this. I'm not about to let anything get in the way of this investigation."

"Just bring us back some evidence," said Dan. "What you do after the case closes is your own business."

CHAPTER 51

On the drive to the airport, Alex listened to reports on the radio of the esca-lating race wars. A school on a Cherokee reservation had been burned to the ground the night before. In retaliation, young Cherokees had defaced graves in the back of an Episcopal church.

When they boarded the plane, Alex saw that she had the aisle seat and Castro had the middle. "Here, I'll get in first. You've got longer legs."

In the half-empty plane, no one arrived to claim the window seat, so they had the privacy of a row to themselves. They put their faces together and, in hushed voices that could not be overheard, tried to figure out Os-sing's link to the epidemic in the Southwest.

When Alex sought out the restroom an hour later, a flight attendant smiled at her and said, "You two look awfully cozy up there."

"We're just discussing business."

The woman smiled. "Don't give me that. I've seen how he looks at you when he doesn't think you're looking. That man is into you big time."

When Alex returned to her seat, Castro stood and kissed her lightly on the forehead before he let her pass to the middle seat. Maybe the flight atten-dant was right.

"You're a new breed for me," he said after they'd both sat down. "A straight shooter. You live by the truth. It's a novel idea for me."

"It's good for the soul," she said lightly.

"In my line of work, the truth could get me killed."

The apartment was a small one in East L.A., in a neighborhood not unlike Castro's. But, it being California, the sidewalks were just a little bit cleaner and drug deals were made, even in this run-down neighborhood, amid the scent and color of bougainvillea.

They had a federal warrant, but the landlord would have let them in anyway. He was worried that Ossing might have skipped town. If the cops could pin something on the guy, it could make it easier for him to toss Ossing's stuff on the street and rent the place to someone else without all that headache of notice and a hearing.

Castro insisted on going in first. "Why should we both get blown to bits if he's left a shotgun primed to take out intruders?"

"People actually do that?" Alex asked in a whisper as they went up the stairs, Castro with Sig Sauer drawn.

"Don't know about L.A., but certainly in Jersey."

He put a finger up to his mouth to silence Alex and indicated with his hand that she should wait on the second-floor stairwell, until he scoped out the third-floor apartment.

A few minutes later, Alex's curiosity got the better of her and she walked up the last flight of stairs. Castro heard her and opened the apartment door. "All clear," he said, and she followed him back inside.

They locked the door behind them and started in the bedroom. It was minimally furnished, with just a few shirts and pants left in the closet. A pair of running shoes and a pair of work boots. A few sweatshirts on the closet shelf.

Castro ran his hands over the sheets. "Guys just out of prison get unannounced visits from their probation officers, so they don't leave anything in plain view. But probation officers are pretty lazy. Won't take a place apart if a guy looks like he's toeing the line."

He pulled off the bottom left corner of the sheet and mattress cover. There was a small tin.

"He hides breath mints?" Alex asked.

Castro popped open the tin. "Ecstasy. Our buddy Ossing was probably making a little extra cash."

She nodded and then started searching in the bathroom for something related to the poison. The room smelled faintly of men's aftershave, a pleasant smell that was at odds with the general mess of the room. Crumpled clothes on the floor. Flecks in the dirty sink from shaving. If she'd needed his DNA she would have collected some hairs, but all California felons had to give DNA when they were released from prison, so she already had access to a national forensic bank that contained Ossing's genetic profile. She took the top off the toilet tank but nothing was taped inside the basin.

In the medicine cabinet, his entire pharmacopoeia was a half-used tube of acne cream, an unopened box of Pepto-Bismol tablets, and an empty bottle of Empirin with Codeine, apparently prescribed by a dentist for someone with a different name.

The kitchen offered up a lot more. Under the sink was a large bottle labeled vinegar, but it didn't have the familiar smell of that substance. Castro entered the room as she was using her hand to waft some of the scent toward her to figure out what it was.

He looked from the bottle to the burnt pan on the stove. "Looks like we've got a ketamine lab."

He leaned over toward the bottle Alex was holding. "He could make a lot of dough with that much stuff, cooked down to a powder. From Los Angeles, it's easy enough to drive down to Mexico and buy the liquid form from a veterinarian."

"It's a dissociative drug, like PCP, no?"

"Yeah. Some people like to do what they call kitty flippin'—combining ketamine with Ecstasy. It's generally sold in club venues. We can start asking around at the clubs near here."

Castro opened the freezer and found a packet of twenties in Reynolds Wrap under a box of TGIF frozen potato skins. "Looks like he's planning to come back," he said. "We'll have to get a guy on surveillance."

Alex put the vinegar bottle back under the sink and stood up. She started opening kitchen cabinets, but other than a can of baked beans and a stack of papers, the cupboard was bare.

"We've tested the water from the fountains for all the common street drugs," she said to Castro. No residue of either Ecstasy or ketamine. There's nothing here he could have used in those attacks."

"Maybe he makes it someplace else. Or he has a partner. Or he took it with him."

Alex took the papers off the shelf and put them on the dented metal card table that Ossing used as his kitchen table. Travel brochures. At first she was disappointed because she didn't see ones that related to Taos. But then she realized she might be looking at his future plans, rather than his past ones. "I think I found his next targets," she said quietly.

Castro walked over and put his hands on her shoulders. He rested his chin on the top of her head and watched as she turned the brochures over one by one. Every one of them was about either Universal Studios or Disneyland.

She reached her left hand up to touch his hand. "Do you know how many people go to either of those places in a day?"

She finished rifling through the brochures when she got to a piece of paper folded in half. She opened it up and realized she had seen this before. She had taken a duplicate out of the box at the Harvard library.

It was Matthew Brunner's birth certificate.

CHAPTER 52

Alex and Castro took the red eye back. She fell asleep next to him, her head dipping slightly to rest against his shoulder. When she woke up, she straightened herself immediately, but he said, "Felt good having you lean on me."

They went directly to the AFIP and entered the Task Force room at the same time as Barbara. Dan was behind his desk, on the phone, while Grant, Alex, and Chuck were sitting at the conference table.

"They called with their decision," said Barbara, a grim look on her face. "Universal Studios closed today for a few days, but Disney is not willing to shut down their theme park."

"But we've got the brochures and today's a Saturday," said Alex.

"I'll call Sandy Mendez at ABC," said Grant. Alex knew that, during a previous investigation, he'd tried to seduce the reporter by promising her a tip in exchange for a date. Alex had gotten the sense that it hadn't worked. Mendez was a pro and had managed both to get the story and to keep Grant at bay.

"Why not leak it to Brad Kendall at the *Times?*" Alex asked Grant, knowing full well he'd never give a scoop to a male reporter.

"Hold it right there," Barbara said. "Nothing leaves this room about Disneyland. They've promised they've got it under control. They've shut off the fountains and are testing the water in the restaurants for any trace of mercury. They've even managed to make a product placement deal out of this threat. They've convinced Purestream, the Canadian company, to give away their bottled water for free for the rest of the week, told them it could knock Evian out of the park."

"You're usually all over us about informed consent," Grant said to Barbara, seeing his dinner with Sandy Mendez slip away before his eyes. "Shouldn't we get this out to the media so that people can choose whether or not they want to take the risk? For all we know, the guy's moving from water to the soft-drink fountain."

Barbara faced him. "What you're saying makes some sense—"

"For a change," Alex cut in.

"—But I've got a preliminary injunction from an Orange County judge telling me not to meddle in the company's business or face a suit."

"So?" said Grant. "The public would be on the AFIP's side."

"A move like that, there might not be an AFIP," Dan said. "Figure they get 30,000 visitors a day, who spend at least $100 a head, what with entry fees, food, and souvenirs. That's over three million dollars lost for each day that we scare customers away."

Barbara nodded at Dan gratefully. "Disney has made a concession. When the park opens in two hours, they'll use facial recognition software to try to identify Jeffrey Ossing. They'll also relay video coverage of the entrances to us, in case we notice something they don't."

Dan looked at his watch. "That means we've now got one hour fifty-eight minutes to set up our equipment and test the feeds."

CHAPTER   53

Grant's kingdom had the best monitors for multiple feeds. When the park opened, Dan, Castro, Chuck, Barbara, and Alex took front row seats in Grant's conference room. Alex knew she should be in her lab, thinking of another string of tests to undertake on the victims' blood, but she couldn't escape the hope that Ossing would walk through a turnstile and be wrestled to the ground by Disney security or an FBI agent dressed like Snow White. Then maybe the nightmare would be over.

Thousands of admissions later, Alex was bleary-eyed with the kind of headache one can only get by an overdose of the song "It's a Small World After All." Or at least she hoped her headache was from the song.

At entry turnstile 3, a minor showdown seemed to be brewing. A handsome Native American man was being turned away by a guard. His daughter, a 10-year-old beauty in a Pocahontas costume, was crying as the guard barred their entrance.

Barbara put the phone on speaker and dialed the head of Disney security. "What's the deal with the Native American in lane three? Has he made some sort of threat?"

"No, we're just being cautious. It's a preventive step."

"Let me get this straight," Barbara said. "You're turning him away because he's a red man? Since when is discrimination 'preventive'?"

"Now calm down, missy. We don't want to upset any of our visitors by having Native Americans here."

"You're a public park. You're violating federal and California law by discriminating on the basis of race."

"And you're getting this feed as a courtesy, not to meddle in the way we do business. So shut up or I'll pull the plug."

A stunned Barbara bit her tongue.

"That's more like it," said the security chief. Then he hung up the phone.

Barbara turned to Dan. "I'm sorry. I almost blew this investigation. I just—"

"You were in the right, there," Dan said. "When this whole thing is over, tee me up to testify against them." But Dan, as everyone else, was getting impatient. "Grant, can you follow up on the feeds? I could use a smoke, and if someone can grab sandwiches, we can reconvene in the Task Force room in fifteen minutes."

Alex placed a tray of sandwiches on the conference table. Castro was alone in the room, intently studying the photos of the victims arranged on the wall to the left of Dan's desk. As Alex approached, she saw that he was staring at the photo of his friend.

He turned around sharply when he realized someone was approaching, as if embarrassed to be caught in this private grieving. He saw it was Alex and his shoulders relaxed. Their blue eyes connected. They didn't touch, but it was their most intimate moment since the flight from California.

Then machine-gun fire echoed through the room and Castro threw his arm around Alex's shoulder and pulled her to the floor. The room quieted but their hearts were still pounding.

Just then, Dan walked in and saw the two of them lying in front of his desk. "Get a room," he said with disgust.

Castro pulled himself to his feet and said, "It was that damn computer."

"Is that any way to talk about your partner?" the computer said.

Alex was tempted to ask Sam to replay the shooting noises, but Dan was wearing his gun and she didn't want to get accidentally shot in the crossfire. "Tell Dan what you just did."

"Well, from the way my partner and Alex were looking at each other, I endeavored to play the sounds of fireworks. But, since I was programmed by the DOD with actual battle sounds from various wars, it was easier to find the noises of M-16s and AK-47s from the Vietnam War battle of Dak To."

"This is an investigation, not a frat house," Dan said to Castro.

"Tell him to cut it out," Alex said, pointing at the computer.

Dan rolled his eyes, then picked up a folder off his desk and headed back out the door. Just then Chuck entered, carrying a large tray. "I brought us—"

"Sandwiches?" Alex asked, pointing to her tray on the table. Chuck looked chagrined, but Alex continued. "We could be here all night. The more sandwiches the better."

Chuck was staring at Alex. In the past, his Southern politeness had prevented him from even looking her straight in the eye. She looked down at her black turtleneck. There was a huge gob of dust from hitting the floor in front of Dan's desk. She brushed it off and then said to Chuck, "Sam here blasted us with the gunfire from the Battle of Dak To."

The Southern gentleman smiled softly. "Don't tell me you fell for that."

"Well, yeah. Thanks for warning us."

"He's programmed with every battle where there is recorded audio," said Chuck. "The Department of Defense intended to reanalyze the sounds to find out what went wrong. In Dak To, we lost nearly four hundred men and another thousand were wounded."

"Do you want to hear it over?" asked the computer. "We didn't even get to the part with the 151,000 artillery rounds, 2,096 tactical air sorties, 257 B-52 strikes."

"No way I'm going to say, 'Play it again, Sam,'" Alex said.

As Dan left the room, he motioned to Alex to follow him. In the hallway he said, "I just got word from my Peet's Coffee buddy."

"Something's up at Homeland Security?" Alex said.

Dan nodded. "He's heard rumors about an off-the-books operation. SWAT team, toxic gas. But he's the guy who runs the finances and he hasn't found the money trail."

"Can't we do something to stop Kincade?"

"One government agency against another? So far, we've got nothing on Kincade that couldn't be explained away. For all we know, he's gotten executive clearance for a clandestine operation."

"Executive? Cotter would never allow it."

"Things like this don't go all the way to the top," Dan said. "The President needs deniability."

Castro was glaring at the two of them, not happy to be cut out of the conversation. Chuck was glancing back and forth between television monitors. When Alex saw that CNN was showing the Red Rights rally in Arizona, she moved quickly back into the room, toward the monitor. Was this rally Kincade's target? She scanned the crowd expectantly. Less than ten feet away from Dale Hightower was her mother.

Alex saw Janet clapping wildly as Hightower spoke. "That's my mother," she said.

"The dark-haired one in the purple sari?" Chuck asked.

"She's beautiful," Castro said. "You take after her."

Alex was surprised. She'd always felt that she favored her father, who had not been prone to the emotional excesses of her mom. But as she focused on the energy and determination of the woman on the screen, she clued in on what Castro had noticed. She was stubborn, just like her mother.

Hightower was using the anti-Indian sentiment of the proposed interment camp to recruit not only young Indians but hundreds of white American college students. "This is the Civil Rights Movement of the new millennium," he said. He was planning a march in Texas the following week. That state had been chosen because of its liberal attitude to the open display of weapons.

"I will end our ceremony with a Cree Indian prophecy," said Hightower. "Only after the last tree has been cut down, only after the last river has been poisoned, only after the last fish has been caught, only then will you find that money cannot be eaten."

Alex saw her mother ecstatically agreeing.

CNN cut away to a reporter outside the Homeland Security headquarters. He said that Homeland Security had its agents, the National Guard, and the Texas State Police on readiness status.

Would the showdown occur in Texas? Or was something under way for Arizona? Alex looked from screen to screen, hoping that they would bring back the picture of her mother, so she could assure herself the woman was alright. She thought of a million things she should have told her. Then, as usual, her concern became tempered with anger. Why hadn't her mother ever bought a cell phone? Janet had said she didn't want to give up her privacy to the government-monitored airwaves. But right now Alex would have given anything to contact her mother and tell her to leave Arizona and get out of what might become the line of fire.

CHAPTER 54

Alex paced the Task Force room and followed the news, awaiting more coverage of the Arizona rally.

"Why don't you call her hotel?" Chuck said.

"I have no idea where she's staying."

"How could you not know?" Castro asked.

She looked at him intently. "That would take more than a few hours to explain."

When all three news channels were on commercial breaks, she took the wrapping off a sandwich. Castro joined her at the table, but she hardly noticed him. She was staring at the map on the wall. The states that were the targets were colored in. Arizona, Kansas, Nebraska, New Mexico, Oklahoma, Utah. What did they have in common? They all circled Colorado.

Alex's thoughts kept returning to the e-mail in which Jeffrey Ossing had told Matthew he wanted them to "meet again." Matthew fretted on his website about "playing God." Could Matthew and the tattooed parolee be behind the fountain poisonings?

Alex had a fleeting thought of calling in a profiler to psych out Matthew based on his writings. But then she remembered that Castro had mentioned a DEA shrink that he seemed to respect. "I'd like to talk to that psychiatrist you mentioned from the DEA," she said to him.

"Isn't your timing a little off? We're in the middle of a case and you want to find your inner child?"

"It's about the case," she shot back. "I need to talk to her about Matthew Brunner."

Castro flipped open his cell phone and pressed one button. He sweet-talked the receptionist into fitting Alex in that afternoon for an appointment with Dr. Emilie Londine. "You can fax her what you have on the boy."

Alex thanked him. She was curious to meet this woman anyway, who was also a tie to Castro and Ted. A woman whom Castro had on speed dial.

When Alex entered the psychiatrist's office she saw that Emilie was indeed different, as Castro had said. She was one of those thin, attractive French-women who had more ways to tie a scarf than there are knots for sailors. Her office didn't have a couch. Instead, there was a mahogany bar that looked like something from a neighborhood tavern.

"Aren't you supposed to calm people down and help them over their addictions?" Alex asked.

"DEA agents are not a group of men who include calm in their reper-toire," she said, her voice a soothing melody. "The men open up with me be-cause they sit next to me at the bar and talk to me as if to a friend. I try not to put too much distance between me and them. And I try to create an at-mosphere that is not too different from that which is familiar to them."

Alex looked up and noticed the multicolored boxes behind the bar. Teas of various sorts, rather than booze.

"I'm having green tea with mango," Emilie said. "Would you care for some?"

Alex nodded, and while Emilie was making it, she pictured Castro and Emilie sitting next to each other at the bar, an image too cozy for her. "Aren't you worried about transference? If you're sidling up next to someone at the bar, isn't there a risk they will view you more as a woman than as a counselor?"

Emilie walked around the bar and stood next to Alex, handing her a cup of tea. "Ah, Castro told you about Ted. My one slip. Once it was clear we were headed to an affair, I referred him to another psychiatrist. I also dis-closed our relationship to the agency director and offered to quit. He wouldn't let me. The older men who'd filled this position had gotten nowhere. The DEA agents who go undercover do so because they have problems with au-thority. The last thing they need is some old Freudian patronizing them."

She chose a stool next to Alex and waited calmly for Alex to begin. Alex had come to talk about Matthew, but her curiosity about Ted—and Castro—was overwhelming. "Were you still seeing Ted when he died?"

Emilie looked away for a moment, composing herself. "No. After all that Sturm und Drang with my supervisors to win the right to see him, he flatly dropped me about six months ago."

The therapist seemed to retreat for a moment into a memory that brought a smile to her lips. Then she continued. "But it was hard to stay mad at Ted. Plus, he seemed genuinely happy with this woman, whoever she was."

Alex thought about Castro's description of the funeral. He hadn't mentioned a new love. And Dan hadn't had any luck identifying the woman Ted was seeing. "Do you happen to know her name?"

Emilie shook her head. "He said there were complications. I think she was married."

Alex took that in, wondering what to make of the fact. "Castro is so sure that Ted hadn't used cocaine, and the medical tests I've done support that. What's your assessment?"

"Castro didn't know Ted as well as he thought. Ted liked living on the edge in far too many ways. Clandestine affairs. Perhaps a little too friendly with the men in the drug world. Ted hid many of his demons from his friend. But Castro's certainly seen enough cocaine users to judge that Ted was clean. Plus, that fits with my view of the man. Danger was Ted's drug of choice, not cocaine."

Alex sipped and then said, "I appreciate your seeing me."

Emilie opened a file on the counter. "My pleasure. It's an interesting case."

Ah, thought Alex, the worst words you can hear from a shrink. Often, it means that psychiatrist is interested more in writing about the patient than in treating him. "This has to remain confidential, of course."

Emilie nodded. "You sense that I am thinking of him as a case study. That's an occupational hazard, of course. But I take the idea of patient privacy seriously. Especially for a boy like Matthew Brunner, who already has such a strong desire to be normal. The last thing he needs is to be viewed as some circus sideshow."

Alex watched as Emilie laid out a few of Matthew's postings on the coffee bar. "His early poems portray a childhood wonderland. But they are quite formal in tone, even to the point of using words like 'twas."

"Initially, everything the Colony children learned came out of books printed before 1860, which didn't use modern dyes."

"Ah, that explains it. Then, when he got linked to the Internet, the posts changed. For the first year or two, he was struggling with the language, feeling awkward, making missteps. It's like the child whose parents dress him in an outdated way for school. There's a mortification when Matthew learned how different he was from everyone else. But he also has a confidence and a strong sense of self that you don't usually see in a teen. Rather than hide the poems that he wrote prior to getting wired, he's put them up on the Internet for anyone to see. His whole life is out there. He's saying, Here's who I am. Accept it or not."

"And who exactly is he, today?"

"Take a look at these photos he's taken of his younger brothers and sisters."

Alex was already familiar with them. She'd printed them out and hung them in her office. She was feeling attached to, and responsible for, the young ones in the Colony. If Emilie had been analyzing her, the psychiatrist might have linked Alex's desire to be a guardian angel for those children to the death of her father when Alex was 5. "It's clear he loves them."

"Yes, yes, but more than that. He feels responsible for them. And—look at the beatific way he's posed them. As if they were angels."

"And what do you make of that?"

"When he speaks of playing God, I think he means that he will do what it takes to protect them and better their lives. But there is a tension. His latest poems show a longing on his part—almost an obsession—to move into the outside world. But he is scared of what he'll need to do to achieve that goal."

"He's of the age where most teens are leaving their parents, entering a life of their own."

"Yes, but how will he effectuate that? If he feels his life is worthless if he stays there, maybe he will think his siblings are without a future, too."

A chill ran down Alex's spine. "You're not envisioning something like a Jonestown massacre, are you?"

Emilie shrugged. "When someone uses the phrase *playing God,* I have to take seriously all the possibilities. Think of how he came to be in the Colony. For his own good, his mother banished him from the outside world. If that is his view of love, he may wake up one day and lovingly hasten their escape from their current world."

"Or maybe," said Alex, almost to herself, "he will break out of the Colony to establish his independence and see the outside world."

"What would happen then?"

"It would be like the boy in the bubble, the child with Severe Combined Immune Deficiency. When he finally came out of the bubble at age twelve, he died fifteen days later."

Alex's visit to Emilie made her even more concerned about Matthew. When she returned to the AFIP, she screwed up her resolve and headed slowly down the hallway to the office of the general counsel.

Barbara, as ever, was on the phone when Alex entered her office. That was another thing that Alex would have detested about practicing law: too much wasted phone time—at a desk, no less. Alex liked the sense of movement, progress. When she was in her lab, she darted between the sequencers, moving her hips to the Razorbacks' rockabilly songs when she was running her experiments. She wandered out of the building to pursue some idea when the mood struck her. The road not taken, if marked Law Street, held no interest for her.

"You must be upset," said Barbara after she hung up the phone. "I think this is the first time you've ever been in my office without raiding the candy dish."

"Who's the best defense lawyer you know?"

Barbara tilted her chair back, considering the question. "For you? Or did your new flame beat up another DEA boss?"

"He's not my new flame—yet—and I'm not talking about either of us. I'm beginning to think Matthew Brunner is behind the murders."

"That poor boy?" Barbara's face grew grim. "He's hardly older than Lana. And what possible reason—"

"I'm thinking Congressman Fillmore has the right motive, but the wrong suspect. He thinks Red Rights is behind this as a way to blast us back to the past so Native Americans can rule the country. But what if Matthew wanted to make other people more like him? He might be able to get someone like Ossing to poison the fountains for him. Then everyone would have to put aside man-made chemicals and he could just walk out of his prison and join the rest of the world."

"Is he capable of that?"

"Morally, I don't know. But scientifically, sure. From what I've seen on his Face Space page, Matthew has got one of the best grasps of immunology and pharmacology that I've seen outside of a Nobel laureate. I'm almost positive the agent that was used in the fountain was a monoclonal antibody, and Matthew's got everything he needs to make one at the Colony. His photos clearly show a mouse colony."

"Mice? Why is that a tip-off?"

"Monoclonal antibodies are made by taking a cell from a mouse that has been engineered to make a human antibody and fusing it with a cell that keeps dividing indefinitely, producing huge amounts of the antibody in a flask in the lab."

"Wouldn't you need to administer that intravenously?"

"Not anymore. Herceptin, the monoclonal antibody used to treat certain women with breast cancer, is given in an IV. But some drug companies are testing monoclonal antibodies that can be administered orally. It's tricky. You need to coat them in some sort of lipid so that they can enter the bloodstream and aren't just digested in the gut."

"How sure are you that a monoclonal antibody was even used? Did you find any evidence?"

Alex sighed in frustration. "Antibodies and lipids are common to the human body. I wouldn't be able to tell the difference between ones that were added and ones that were active in the patients before they were exposed."

"You mean someone could inject me with a mouse-made something and there would be no way to tell another species was involved?"

Alex tapped her foot excitedly. She thought of how Kingman Reed had described the old days, when medical examiners kept goats in their yards to produce antibodies to see if a crime scene stain was human or not. "Barbara, you're a genius. I've been so focused on how to measure the effects of the monoclonal antibody on the victims, I didn't even think to see if there were any mouse antibodies in their blood."

Barbara seemed pleased at the compliment, but was still skeptical. "Even if Matthew was making this stuff, what could he offer Ossing to get him to dump it in the water?"

Alex waved her hands in the air as she tried to come up with an answer. "Some new hallucinogen? He's systematically studying the properties of plants. Maybe he's found a legal equivalent of marijuana."

"Ah, something like salvia."

Alex nodded. *Salvia divinorum,* a type of mint plant, was routinely used by gardeners as ground cover. But college students had discovered an additional use for it. Chewing or smoking it led to a psychedelic trip. YouTube videos chronicled kids tripping out on it, causing some states to ban the plant entirely.

"You're making a good case against the boy," Barbara said.

"But he's been out of the mainstream world in an isolated environment. Couldn't a good lawyer argue that he's not guilty by reason of insanity?"

Barbara straightened a pile of papers on her desk, as she chose her words. The papers seemed in perfect order already to Alex, but Barbara was apparently bothered by the corner of a sheet that was slightly misaligned. "That's going to be a hard sell to a jury. For all we know, he was well cared for by the doctor, so he can't claim abuse. The poison had to be placed in the fountains by an accomplice, which shows a level of planning that doesn't come with an insane flare-up. Plus, the test is whether he knew wrong from right. With the level of stealth involved, it will be hard to argue that he didn't know what he was doing was wrong."

Alex slumped in her chair. If only Matthew had been healthy, she thought. Then his scientific genius could have developed in a less sinister way. But then she corrected her thoughts. If he'd lived on the outside, in a normal way, he wouldn't have been Matthew. The isolation, life with the doctor, perhaps even the quest to free his younger "siblings"—all of that made him who he was.

Noticing that her friend had shrunk into herself, Barbara pulled open a drawer and handed Alex a card. "He's the one," she said.

"Pardon?"

"He's the lawyer I would call if I ended up behind bars."

Alex stood. "Thanks, Barbara."

"You want off the case now that it's taken this turn?"

Alex shook her head. "No, I'm going to see it through, no matter where it takes me."

CHAPTER 55

In her lab, Alex separated the blood cells from the serum of Leroy Darven, preparing them so that she could add an anti-mouse immunoglobin antibody with a tracking enzyme linked to it. Sure enough, when she completed the immunoassay process, the sample lit up, indicating the presence of a mouse antibody.

She practically ran to the Task Force room. Chuck, Dan, Castro, Grant, and Barbara were fixated on a map, trying to predict where the disease would strike next.

"I owe you an apology," she said to Grant.

"Well, that's a first," he said.

"You were right. This was never about a disease. There was a person behind it from the beginning. I found definitive evidence that a monoclonal antibody was used to spike the water."

She glanced at the map and couldn't get her eyes off the flat, squat state of Colorado, squarely in the center of all the action. If Matthew was working with Ossing, it would have been easy enough for Ossing to drive from Colorado to each of the adjoining states to spike the fountains. "Maybe Ossing is getting it from the Colony." She couldn't bear to point the finger at Matthew quite yet.

"Or what's to say Red Rights isn't behind it?" Grant asked. "There's no love lost for us white guys."

"Have you seen how the mainstream Native American tribes are trying to distance themselves from Red Rights?" Chuck said.

"Wouldn't you?" Castro asked. "Some lunatic with guns shows up, acting

241

a lot like he's planning to wipe out the white guys. Tourists would be nuts to visit the casinos now."

"This whole conflict in the Native American community between Blackstone and Red Rights makes me think of how my parents used to talk about the 1960s," Barbara said.

"How's that?" Chuck asked.

"The black community was divided between a nonviolent leader, Martin Luther King—"

"I bet that's who your mom supported," Alex said.

Barbara nodded. "—And Huey Newton, whose Black Panthers wanted to seed a revolution."

"That's exactly who my mom supported," Alex said.

They were about to launch into a political discussion when Chuck said loudly, "Dr. Blake, you'd better see this."

The vigil that Hightower was leading outside of an Arizona chemical plant was turning into a free-for-all. The protestors were maybe five thousand strong, with a few of the Native American teens carrying rifles, but now a dozen private security guards in riot gear had exited the building and, along with National Guardsmen, plunged into the crowd. Alex searched frantically for her mom. There she was, just twenty feet away from Hightower! Then Hightower disappeared from view and a security guard started flailing a billy club at the man standing next to her mother. Janet put up her hands to stop the man, and the surging crowd lurched in her direction, knocking her to the ground. Alex lost sight of her for a moment as the camera turned to a young woman who'd fallen and was bleeding from the head. Then a cloud of tear gas filled the screen and the sound of ambulances and police vans flooded the background. An explosion knocked the cameraman off his feet; his camera crashed to the ground, abruptly ending the feed.

Castro turned to Alex. "We'll find her," he said.

Alex was shell-shocked, staring at the television, waiting for the picture to return. Which worked about as successfully as trying to find significance in a television test pattern. Barbara put her arm around her friend.

"I'll generate a list of hospitals and police stations and we can start calling," said Chuck. His computer and printer hummed as he went about the task.

"I'm going to the airport," said Alex, intent on catching a plane to

Phoenix. But just then the CNN anchor announced that the governor of Arizona had the state on lockdown. The airports would be closed. And since the governor didn't want the state swollen with Native Americans from border states joining in the protest and perhaps inciting violence, roadblocks would be put up on the highway borders.

"What's next?" said Castro. "A Berlin Wall around the state?"

Alex knew that she should be thinking about the larger political ramifications, but she was instead focused on her mother. If she couldn't get in and Janet couldn't get out, what were they going to do?

"Oh shit," Chuck said, and Alex worried that something had come across the Internet about her mother. But then she noticed the strange bleep on his monitor that had distracted the Southerner. A major diversion in the GPS on the cell phone they had given Renfrew. Dan hadn't trusted him enough to let him loose without a way of keeping track. "Renfrew's left New Mexico," said Chuck. "He's on a flight."

"Son of a bitch," Dan said. "Where's he going?"

Chuck tapped a few keys on his computer as Dan looked over his shoulder.

"Dulles?" said Dan. "The guy was stupid enough to book a ticket in his own name?"

Dan motioned to Castro. "Let's roll. He's landing at Dulles in forty-five minutes."

CHAPTER 56

Back in her office, Alex started dialing all the phone numbers that Chuck had generated. The state and local police stations had the same response: They were processing hundreds of arrests and wouldn't know for hours who they had in custody. It could be days before the names were entered into any sort of electronic database that Alex could search.

She'd chosen to call the police stations first because she knew if her mother ended up there, at least she hadn't been seriously hurt. In fact, Janet would see it as a badge of honor to have been arrested for her activism.

The next call was more difficult. Alex dialed the first of the ten hospitals on the list. Since she wasn't sure of the location of the chemical plant, she called hospitals in alphabetical order. At Allendon Hospital, the clerk in the ER said, "We've got a dozen folks being airlifted here for the burn unit."

"Burn unit?"

"Yes," the clerk said solemnly. "One of the storage buildings on the plant grounds exploded."

"That's what knocked over the cameraman."

"I guess. I haven't had time to watch the news."

Alex tried to figure out her mother's distance from the plant and from the cameraman to determine whether she, too, had been harmed by the explosion. "Do you have a patient named Janet Blake?"

"Honey, these folks aren't coming in with IDs. We're just getting bodies and doing our best to keep them alive."

Alex's sharp intake of air alerted the woman to her concern.

"Listen, we've only got a few here. Most of the wounded were taken to Pilsen Medical Center. Chances are, if your friend was hurt, she's there."

At Pilsen, all calls were being referred to the chief executive of the hospital, Colin Barnaby. "Yes, I can confirm that approximately eighty people are currently being admitted to the hospital."

"How do I find out if my mother is one of them? Her name is Janet Blake. She's a dark-haired woman in her fifties."

"That's easy. Just have her sign a HIPAA statement authorizing me to provide information. Then, if she is admitted, I can alert you."

"No, you don't understand. I'm her daughter. She would want me to have that information."

"Ah, you don't know how many people say that. When we had a Major League Baseball player as a patient, literally dozens of people called up posing as his siblings."

"Okay, how about this? I fax the form to you and, if my mother comes in, the admitting staff gives it to her to sign."

"Well, you can fax it, but I can't promise anything. We're awfully busy here with all these admissions. And patients have to come first."

Alex hung up the phone in frustration. She thought of calling the Arizona director of public health. But what could she say? He had enough on his hands with the secondaries from the fountain cases. He couldn't afford to waste resources, especially since it might turn out that her mother was back at her hotel discussing the Cree prophecy over margaritas.

Frustrated, Alex paced her lab, but felt guilty as she passed the photo of her dad. Why didn't she have a picture of her mother anywhere? Maybe she needed the reminder of her father because he'd left her life when she was so young. Perhaps she took her mother for granted because she knew she could always get in touch with her. Although today, that no longer held true.

She went back into her office and sought out her mother's faculty page at Oberlin. The smiling face of the attractive brunette filled her screen, along with the list of courses she taught, like the history of social movements. The photo calmed her. Whether Janet was in police custody, on an ER gurney, or discussing politics at her hotel, Alex was sure she was doing it with flair and passion.

———

Alex rejoined Chuck in the conference room just as Dan and Castro were pushing a frightened Renfrew through the door. The cast on the man's right leg was grimy. His clothes looked like he'd slept in them. Renfrew looked imploringly at Alex. "You've got to help me," he said.

Alex looked at Dan for permission to approach the man. He nodded. She walked Renfrew to the table and sat him down. She was in major doctor mode now. "Are you hurt?" she asked. She tried to take his jacket off him, but he clung to it as if it were a coat of armor. He sat shivering. Alex worried that he might be in shock. She sat next to him, used her hand to turn his face toward her, and looked into his eyes. His pupils were not dilated, but his skin looked clammy. Alex moved her fingers to his wrist and counted silently. His pulse was regular, if a bit high, as was his respiration.

"What did he tell you?" Alex asked Dan.

"He claims he was headed here," said Dan.

Renfrew reached out and grabbed Alex's arm. "I need protection," he said, lips quivering. "Somebody killed Chief Sun."

"Who killed him?" Dan asked.

"Some other Indian." The words came tumbling out. "Last night, I realized I'd left my data stick in one of the computers. So I went back to the office near Taos about 10:00 P.M. I was near the board room when I heard loud talk in some Native American language, then a scream. When I opened the door, a guy with a knife was jumping out the window and Sun was on the floor, bleeding to death."

"He wasn't dead yet, when you entered the room?" Dan asked.

Renfrew shook his head. "He was trying to say something to me. It sounded like 'not soupy.'"

Alex's left fingers tapped the table. "Could it have to do with the poison? Something about the consistency of the poison?"

Chuck was more practical. "Did you call an ambulance?"

Renfrew sighed. "By the time my brain registered what was going on, he was dead. It all happened in less than a minute. Then I just got the hell out of there."

"Were there any guards in the building?" Dan asked.

Renfrew shook his head.

"Did you call the police?"

Another negative.

"I ran to the foyer of the building, saw a car tear out of the parking lot, figured it was the killer, and hoped like hell he'd been working alone and I wasn't gonna get my throat slit by his partner on the way to my car. Drove clear to Albuquerque, caught the first flight to Dulles this morning, and here I am. You gotta protect me. When he cleared the window, the guy might have looked back, seen me with Sun."

Dan had been hovering during the conversation. Now he sat down at the conference table across from Renfrew. "If you fled the scene of the crime, you might have more to worry about than the killer."

"What do you mean?"

"You're an outsider. You failed to show up there this morning. Who knows who saw you go into the building late last night. A surveillance tape at the office could have caught you going in, but not the guy who came through the window. You're the A-number-one suspect for murder."

Renfrew sat up straight, as if steeling himself for blows. "That's why I took this," he said. He reached into his coat pocket and pulled out a crumpled handkerchief. Now Alex realized why he had been reluctant to part with the coat. He carefully unfolded the handkerchief on the table. As he turned back the white petals of cotton, a large clump of black hairs was revealed. "Chief Sun took a pretty big chunk from his murderer."

Dan was torn about how to handle Renfrew. He asked Chuck to monitor all law enforcement bulletins, but nothing was reported on a killing in an office building in Taos.

"What if he's still alive?" Alex asked Dan.

"No way," said Renfrew.

"Still," Alex said to Dan.

The major then got on the phone with the local police, asking them to check to see if there had been some altercation there. Dan didn't give away any details. Twenty minutes later, the cop called back.

"Everything's fine," he said. "A guy named Donald Sun was there, took us through each room. Nobody else was around. Everything seemed in order. I noticed a little bit of glass on the floor near the window, but Sun said it was from a broken light bulb."

Dan hung up and turned to the astonished Renfrew.

"I swear," the researcher said, "what I told you is true."

Chuck said, "Well, they did have time for a major cleanup. And maybe these Native Americans wanted to handle the crime their own way, not get the white men involved."

"Or maybe they were in on it." She turned to Renfrew. "Could Donald Sun have killed his brother?"

"I'm sure it wasn't him. Donald has short hair. The guy who went out the window had shoulder-length hair."

Alex looked down at the foot-long strands of hair spread on the white handkerchief. That description fit the evidence.

"Chuck and I will take Renfrew's statement," Dan said to Alex, "and then find him a place to stay here at the base."

Renfrew looked relieved.

Alex reached for the handkerchief. "I'll take these and try to figure out who they belonged to."

In her lab, Alex turned on the radio for news of the protests. Then she put the hairs under a microscope to determine if any had enough skin attached to support a DNA analysis.

As she looked through the microscope lens, she flicked through the magnifications. At a magnification of 100X, she noticed something strange at the proximal end of each strand, near the root. There was a small area, about half an inch long, where all the hairs were a lighter color than they were at the distal end.

"I'll be damned," she said aloud. This man had dyed his brown hair to make it appear black. There was something jolting about that fact, something out of sync with the Native American creed of choosing the most natural approach.

Looking at the hair was informative, but her DNA run was a bust. His genetic alphabet didn't match that of anyone in the CODIS database. No big surprise. Native American justice was a world unto itself. With reservations having the legal status of separate nations, they also had separate justice systems, and their own ways of dealing with those who broke the law. Because many Native Americans felt their religious beliefs precluded the giving of blood for DNA banks, there were few Native American samples to compare to the DNA from the murderer's hair. And Native Americans seldom made it to traditional courts, so there was no ready set of mug shots to show Renfrew for comparison. It might be that Sun's killer was going to get away with murder.

"Any luck with the police or hospitals?" Chuck asked when Alex rejoined the team in the Task Force room.

"No. They've got a lockdown on information. Most of the injured protestors are at Pilsen Hospital, but they aren't releasing the names. It's frustrating not to be able to get in touch with her to see if she needs me." Then she realized how strange these words sounded to her own ears. She'd spent so much time as a child taking care of her mother that she'd been grateful for the distance of the past few years. Now she'd give anything to have her mother call and ask for her help.

"I've got an idea," Castro said. He dialed his phone, putting his hand over the receiver and saying softly to Alex, "I've got a secret weapon."

Alex looked at him quizzically. Then she heard him say, "Aunt Pearl, I need your help. A friend's mom may have been admitted to Pilsen Hospital and my friend can't find out anything. How about moseying over there to see if they've got a Janet Blake, midfifties, wearing a purple sari, brought over from that chemical-plant protest?"

Castro was silent for a moment, listening for the response. Then he shrugged. "What do you mean, what kind of purple? How many Janets could there be wearing saris?"

Another silence and then he said, "Yes, more like amethyst than lavender. And thank you, Pearl." He hung up and said, "She'll call us as soon as she finds something out. And she's offered to take your mom back home with her if she needs a place to stay."

"That's great," Alex said, clapping her hands. She looked around the room. Dan was eyeing her impatiently. He wasn't one for family issues on the job. So she turned her attention back to the AFIP matter at hand.

"Shouldn't Renfrew be in touch with someone in Taos? He's a prime suspect since he up and left right after the murder."

"Hard to figure who he should call," said Dan, looking relieved that she was now back in work mode. "His contact was the top guy, Chief Sun, who's the one who got himself killed. At this point, we can't even tell if the others might have been in on it. If what Renfrew says is true, there's lots of money at stake."

"Sounds like Chief Sun was also a conservative, keeping them from getting involved with Red Rights," Alex said. "Maybe they've joined forces now."

"Or who's to say they weren't working together earlier?" asked Chuck.

"Doubtful they would have poisoned a fountain in Taos, their own backyard," Alex said.

"We can't rule out that Renfrew is pulling a double-agent trick on us," Dan said. "Maybe the group sent him here to see what we know."

"The Star-Spangled Banner" quietly filled the room and Sam spoke. "Do you want to know the latest on Red Rights?"

Alex exchanged glances with Chuck. "You were eavesdropping?" she said to the computer.

"I am programmed to respond to voices," Sam said, "whether or not they are directed to me. Sometimes people don't know what they want to know and I have to be able to figure it out. Whenever I do that, I am programmed to play relevant music first, so that I don't confuse people by just entering the conversation."

Chuck moved over to the chair in front of the computer. "And you have something to tell us?"

Sam's screen flashed CNN. Martin Kincade was holding a press conference. "We have found a conclusive link between another Native American tribe and Red Rights. This photo shows a member of the Zuni tribe of New Mexico welcoming Dale Hightower to their reservation."

The picture showed video footage of Hightower with a Native American on either side of him, presumably from the Zuni tribe. Dan walked closer to the screen to see the footage.

"That's shot at an odd angle," Alex said. It was cropped so that you could see the three men just from the chest up.

Dan switched channels, with the hope that another station was running it from the beginning. Sure enough, CBS was showing the footage.

Dan pointed to Dale's arms. "Welcoming, my ass. Look at how his arms stretch backwards. I bet they've got him cuffed."

"A little bit of tribal justice?" asked Alex. "Hightower's statements to the media certainly aren't helping the Native American cause. People are avoiding their casinos like the plague." She winced when she realized how she'd phrased that.

The phone on Dan's desk rang. Once he realized who was calling, he put it on speaker. "I just saw the news," said Chris Renfrew. "That guy in the middle is the one that killed Chief Sun."

When Dan hung up, Alex and he sat around trying to decide what to make of it. What was his motive? What were the Zuni going to do with him? And who the hell was he, actually?

CHAPTER 57

After Renfrew's accusations, Dan sent federal investigators from Albuquerque to the Zuni Pueblo to attempt to question Hightower.

An hour later, a frustrated Dan updated his group. "The Zuni won't let any federal investigators on the reservation. Wouldn't even talk to my guys at all."

"Do you blame them?" Alex said. "Would you trust a government that's trying to move you to an internment camp?"

"Guys," Grant said. "Don't slip in that liquid on the floor from our bleeding heart here."

Alex glared at him.

"They may be bent out of shape for a good reason," said Dan, "but now it's interfering with a homicide investigation. So, Alex, how do we get our hands on Hightower?"

All eyes focused on her. The question hung in the air while Grant shifted his body to better show off his muscles.

Chuck, the consummate Southern gentleman, opened his mouth to fill in the silence. But Alex interrupted him. "We can ask Governor Blackstone to help us."

After her rash suggestion, Alex decided to make the call from her office. She wanted to think about the best approach and, truth be told, she didn't want her colleagues watching if she crashed and burned or if the governor refused to take her call.

She walked into her lab, past the pile of folders containing the medical records of the victims, past the machines that had failed to identify the disease that had claimed them. In her inner office, she sat at her desk and looked at the photos of the children living in the Colony, astonishingly beautiful angels whose images Matthew Brunner had captured. She studied their faces for solace, trying to forget the dark shawl of death that the files in the lab represented.

Alex went on the Internet and found listings for Blackstone's office, for the governor's mansion, and for the chief of staff, but she wondered how she could work her way up the food chain to talk to him. Then she remembered that a 505 number had shown up on her cell phone when the governor called her. Dare she call him on what might be his cell phone? She scrolled back to that number and pressed Send.

"Elias Blackstone," the voice answered.

"This is Alex Blake from the Armed Forces Institute of Pathology," she said. "We need your help."

"How might I be of service?"

"We are trailing a man, Dale Hightower."

"Ah, the Red Rights activist."

"Yes. He apparently has been taken into custody by the Zuni Nation."

"My people?" he said quietly, as if to himself. "The Zuni are a religious people. They're planters and farmers, not hunters."

"Could you contact the reservation? We need access to Hightower."

A silence followed. Alex wondered if Blackstone was weighing the ramifications of this request.

"That's a tall order," the governor said. "Putting aside the political landmine for me to be seen as trampling a tribe's sovereign rights, it may appear vindictive for me to take action against a man who, while seeming to support me, is scaring people off."

Ah, politicians, thought Alex. They never change their stripes, even if their faces are a different color. He was just like any other politician. Thinking of himself first.

"Well," said Alex. "Thanks for your time." She prepared to hang up.

"Dr. Blake, I believe you've gotten the wrong impression. In our last call, I offered to help you in any way I could. I am a man of my word. Now tell me what questions you have of him and what makes you think he is at the Zuni Pueblo."

Alex recounted what they had seen on the broadcast. She told him they had a reliable source who had linked Hightower to a murder. And the more they talked and he asked questions, the more her confidence grew that he was indeed a man of his word.

CHAPTER 58

While they waited for word from the governor, Alex, Barbara, and the rest of the team—minus Grant—discussed other angles. "You got nothing on the DNA tests?" Dan asked Alex.

"No matches to the hair DNA in CODIS," she said, walking over to the espresso machine. She measured out coffee, this time Peet's in honor of the Homeland Security source. But before she started grinding it, her cell phone rang.

"I asked at the Pueblo and they do not have the man you seek," said the governor.

All eyes were on Alex. "How can you be so sure?" She could see Dan mouthing the word *shit*.

"Ah, Dr. Blake, I believe they speak the truth, but I can also see with my own eyes. I watched the video and there are many aspects that point away from the Pueblo."

"What do you mean?"

"The land is wrong. It is too lush. My people live in a place where the soil is dry. The landscape is not of the right elevation and there's no angle with the sacred mesa in the background. And the men who are with him are too young. If he had been brought to the Pueblo, the elders would have met him."

Alex sighed. "We think he is the key to what's going on. I felt sure you could put us in touch with him."

"If you need him, he will be brought into your life at the right moment."

"I'm frustrated that I can't hasten that moment along."

"I know this sounds odd, Dr. Blake, but may I speak a Native blessing to you?"

Alex thought about it. Anything that might help. "Yes, I'd be honored."

"May you have the strength of eagles' wings, the faith and courage to fly to new heights, and the wisdom of the universe to carry you there."

"Thank you, sir. I'll try my best."

When she hung up, she explained to the group, "The video's apparently a setup, not shot at the Zuni Pueblo at all." She ground the coffee and put it in the machine. Then she paused, thinking, before setting the machine to brew.

She whirled around and faced Dan.

"Not soupy!" she said. "That's what Renfrew heard the Chief say. But he may have been saying 'not Supai'—that the killer was only pretending to be a Havasupai."

"What would Dale gain by misrepresenting his tribal background?" Barbara asked. "Red Rights is open to people of all tribes."

"Maybe Hightower isn't Native American at all," Alex said.

"What else could he be?" Barbara asked.

"Someone like me," Castro said. "A plant, an agent, a guy working undercover."

Barbara got animated. "It's brilliant. Put an undercover agent into Red Rights, get him to espouse violence, and you can shut down the whole Native American economy in a heartbeat. Casinos, tourist visits to reservations . . ."

"Even a presidential candidate," Dan said.

"But why wouldn't the Havasupai have outed him if he wasn't one of them?"

"Nobody asked them," said Castro. "There's just a few hundred of them left, and you need to take a burro to the bottom of the Grand Canyon to enter the Supai village."

"We've got to find out who he really is," Alex said.

Barbara left a message on Lana's cell phone that she wouldn't be home for dinner. For the rest of the evening, they found out everything they could about Dale Hightower. Chuck analyzed every videotape in which Dale appeared. Rarely did any other member of Red Rights appear with him. And now that they'd begun to scrutinize them closely, they found that there was something unusual about the way he spoke. The vowels weren't as open as in much Native American speech. Yet he still didn't speak as if English had been his first language.

And his features. His nose was not as flat as the typical Native American's. Alex was astonished at how, previously, everyone had just taken cues from the bright-colored tribal clothes he wore and his self-professed membership in the Havasupai Nation. Alex thought about how Americans were used to seeing whites playing Indians. After all, no one raised an eyebrow when Sal Mineo played a Sioux in a Disney movie that Alex saw as a kid on television. Did anybody really know what a Native American looked like?

Alex remembered an article published a few years earlier by Stanford researchers saying that male Native Americans had a distinctive genetic region on their Y chromosomes. She headed back to her lab and ran a test for that gene on the DNA from Hightower's hair root. It came up negative. He did not show the segment on his Y chromosome that was common to many Native Americans, but Alex knew that this was not definitive. The data was still shaky on that connection. Some Native Americans didn't have that genetic segment. But her further tests did find that he had a genetic allele, linked to certain thalassemias, that was generally found only in the Arab Negev Bedouin community.

She brought the news back to her colleagues. "Hightower may have been the descendant of an indigenous group," she said. "But it had its roots in the deserts of southern Israel and not the Southwestern United States."

"Okay. If he were planted in the group, when did it happen and why?" asked Barbara.

Chuck was running videotape from more than two years earlier, showing demonstrations by Red Rights. "Dale Hightower didn't show up at a single rally until six months ago. He wasn't part of the sit-in at the nuclear power plant. He wasn't around for the first protest against genetically modified crops."

Alex looked closely at the photo of Dale Hightower, with his shoulder-length hair. "The other Native Americans in all this footage either have long hair, to their waists, or short hair."

"The short-haired ones probably work outside the reservation," said Chuck. He ran his hand over his head. "I know about having to cut your hair for work."

"Maybe he grew his to go undercover," Alex said. "But it probably took almost a year to grow his hair like that, and his first videos with Red Rights started six months ago."

"The fountain incidents started two months ago," said Barbara. "And Blackstone's presidential announcement came just a few weeks ago."

"But," Alex said, "Blackstone's book came out nearly two years ago, about when Hightower would have started planning to go undercover. Maybe he—or whoever sent him in there—was worried about Blackstone's power even then."

Barbara was excited. "I buy that. It's like COINTELPRO. When the Black Panthers started getting political power, including a following of white radicals, the FBI sent informants in who posed as members of the group. They espoused violence and gave firearms training to the group. Not that the Panthers were always angels themselves, but the FBI guys pushed the group to be even more violent. The goal was to give the government a reason to eliminate the Panthers."

The word *eliminate* hung in the room for a moment. Then Alex said, "Like the Department of Homeland Security is trying to do with certain Native Americans now?"

Barbara nodded.

"Who's pulling his strings?" Dan asked. "Who's got the most to gain?"

"Vegas," said Castro. "Business is up tenfold with people scared away from Indian casinos."

"They're not the only ones," said Alex, who hated to voice what she was thinking. "President Cotter gains, too. The backlash against Red Rights is wiping out his chief political opponent."

They sat silently, considering that for a moment. As employees of the Department of Defense–based AFIP, Cotter was their boss's boss, their Commander in Chief.

"Doesn't need to go that high," said Barbara, the consummate D.C. analyst. "Homeland Security's got a lot on the line. President Cotter's been cutting back their power more and more since Kincade took office."

"You think these boys manufactured an epidemic to stay in business?" Castro asked.

"Have you ever met Martin Kincade?" Barbara asked Castro. "He acts like Homeland Security is above any law."

Alex shook her head. "Maybe Kincade is capitalizing on this epidemic.

That I could believe. But I don't think he started it. I've been at a bunch of commission meetings at his agency. There's no one affiliated with Homeland Security who has the scientific background or—dare I say it—the cojones to do something like this. Most of the scientists on the commission are a bunch of government hacks."

Barbara grinned, and Alex realized that by joining the AFIP, she'd presumably joined the ranks of the hacks herself. In her mind, though, she was a free agent. She could always go back to academia. She didn't need to toe the line to make sure she made it to the next government pay grade.

"Hightower wasn't undercover for so long," Alex said. "There could be a record of him somewhere."

"You'll never find him," Castro said. "When I joined the DEA, the first thing they did was delete all computer records of me."

"Records might be one thing, but images are another," said Chuck. "I doubt Hightower had plastic surgery to make him appear to be a Native American."

"You're right. It would be too difficult to change his skin color," Alex said.

Chuck said, "Then there's got to be a photo of him somewhere that's linked to his real name. A yearbook picture. A security photo from an airport."

"You're talking months of work and a detail of twenty guys or more," Castro said.

The theme song from the 1970s TV cartoon show *Underdog* filled the room. "That," said Sam, "or the facial recognition software that I contain."

Great for this investigation, thought Alex. But who knows how many privacy laws Grant would later break with this machine.

"Hightower's face has been all over the media," Chuck said. "Maybe we'll match it to some past photo of him."

"Precisely," Sam said. The computer posted Hightower's face on the left side of the screen. Within seconds, a dizzying array of faces sped by on the right. In less than three minutes, they got a match. His name was Farim Mohammad Patterson.

Dan read the information on the screen. "He's a second-generation Arab in the United States. Headed private security at Levanthal Industries until six months ago."

"The company with Martin Kincade on the board," said Chuck. His fingers swept the keyboard as he followed a trail. "But I don't see him listed now with Homeland Security. In fact, I can't find him anywhere at all."

Grant burst into the conference room and Alex feared that Disneyland had been hit. But, instead, Grant turned on the television in the room and said, "He hit an Amarillo high school."

Three hundred kids had died, boutonnieres and bouquets dotting the heaps of bodies as if they were a funeral pyre.

CHAPTER   59

Throughout the night, Dan was in constant touch with investigators across the country. Military police, FBI agents, and state and local law enforcement were tracking information about the possible suspects. About the only agency that was not directly in the loop was Homeland Security. The suspicious two degrees of separation between Farim, Levanthal, and Kincade—plus the concerns raised by his man on the inside—made Dan suspicious of including them in the investigation.

Past contacts of Farim and Ossing were being interrogated. The tail whom Dan had assigned to Farim had lost him in the chaos of the chemical plant explosion. Details of Farim's life were surfacing, such as previous jobs in the security industry and evidence he'd given up his apartment in New York and sold his condo in Vegas six months earlier. Ossing hadn't gone back to his California apartment since Castro and Alex had searched the place.

Survivors of the Amarillo High School bloodbath had posted photos of their dying classmates on the Web. While the news media by and large had been reluctant to show the victims, the students' macabre competition to post from their cell phones and PDAs meant that some families learned first of their son's or daughter's death through Face Place and text messages.

Near 4:00 A.M., Dan had sent Alex to Walter Reed to get a few hours' rest. "Promise you'll call me if anything changes at all," she said.

He nodded, but his attention was on the two phone calls he was on simultaneously—one on his desk phone and one on his cell. They were taking turns sleeping in two-hour shifts, but Dan hadn't yet assigned himself a turn.

After a short rest, Alex returned to more bad news. Powerless to deal with the disease directly, Members of Congress were lashing out crazily. Bills were introduced to close all schools, inter Native Americans, increase the power of Homeland Security, and impeach President Cotter. And then there was the racial violence, which erupted out of the malice that accompanied prejudice and the terror of an untreatable disease.

"Please," Alex said to Dan, "let Chuck work with me for just a few minutes. We need to find the Colony." To Alex, all roads pointed to that hidden community.

Chuck sat at his computer, waiting to hear the major's answer.

"What's the angle?" Dan asked.

"We know Ossing was in touch with the Colony. And whether he or Hightower is distributing the toxin or not, we need to stop the disease. We're already starting to lose as many people to the violence as to the infection. If we had a treatment, we could at least combat the fear. And Teague might be able to help us treat it."

"Okay, Chuck, help her out. What do you know so far?"

"I tracked down the parents of that first set of kids who went to the Colony," Alex said. "Matthew's mom died in a car accident shortly after she gave him up to Teague for adoption. The other mothers were mostly young women. One hung up on me after saying that she hadn't told her husband about her defective kid and wasn't about to. A few others begged me to let them know if I found their children. But none of them had a clue where the Colony was."

"What about the doctor? Where'd he come from?" Dan asked.

"Teague's parents died when he was young. He ended up at an orphanage with his older brother Tommy when he was seven and his brother was nine. Apparently, he was a skinny kid with glasses who took a lot of shit from the other kids. Tommy protected him. And get this—his name was Andy at the time, short for Andrew. He changed it to Andover when he applied to Harvard. Thought it made him sound more Ivy League."

Chuck was searching databases as Alex spoke.

"No luck with the brother in the driver's license database," said Chuck. "No income taxes filed or Social Security paid in the past fifteen years."

"He dropped out about the same time Andy did?" Alex asked.

Chuck nodded. "I've also hit a dead end on where in Wyoming the computer got sent. MIT doesn't save its FedEx receipts that far back and the company itself is making a fuss, requesting a warrant."

A sharp whirring noise rang out from the side of the room, followed by the first few bars of the Pete Townshend song "Who Are You." And then Sam the computer said, "Do you want me to help you?" Without waiting for an answer—since, after all, humans were so predictable—Sam said, "I have combined three interests of yours—finding Nat, finding a FedEx label, and finding someone else's brother. When my creators shipped Nat, they had me prepare the label."

The printer next to Sam started to disgorge a page. Chuck retrieved it. It was a copy of a FedEx label addressed to Thomas W. Teague at 150 Old Granger Road in Humphrey, Wyoming. After the researchers designed a computer of DNA and natural substances that wouldn't harm the children, the computer had been shipped to Andover Teague's brother.

This could be the Colony! Alex thought. It could be in Wyoming after all! "Have Sam check the Internet to see if he's got a phone," Alex said to Chuck.

"Do you not respect computers?" asked Sam. "Why do you talk about me as if I were not here?"

"Sorry," Alex said, rolling her eyes at the idea she was apologizing to a computer.

"I saw that," Sam said. "You swirled your eyes."

Castro spoke sternly to the computer. "Come on, partner, I know she can be annoying, but we're in crime solving mode now. So cough up the phone number."

"He hasn't got a phone. Do you want other references to that address?"

"Yes, please," said Chuck.

"There is a deed registered on the Wyoming property in the name of Thomas Teague. Property taxes are paid in person each year—"

Now it was Castro's turn to roll his eyes. "We may have to send you to Quantico. Anything of relevance to the investigation?"

"Ah. Does it count if someone searched Google maps for that address this morning?"

Castro was up out of his seat like a shot, moving toward Sam. "From where?"

"The requester went online at an Internet café in Los Angeles at three o'clock this morning. He asked for the route from a motel at 11245 Del Monte Road in Brentwood, California. He signed on as Jeffrey Ossing."

"Maybe Ossing and Teague's brother were partners," Alex said. She didn't want to voice the other half of her thought. Maybe Matthew was working with them. Maybe "blue trike" was a code name for the toxin planted in the fountains.

Chuck turned to Dan. "Do you want me to call the local police in Humphrey and Los Angeles?"

"Yes to L.A.," Dan said, "but chances are he's already on the road. No to Humphrey. This is our first real lead. Maybe the brother and the ex-con are running this show, being paid by who knows who. Maybe Red Rights. Here's our chance to get them both at once. Grant, you and I will pick up Ossing's trail. Alex, Castro—you can take the brother."

"Let me grab some stuff from my lab so I can test the toxin if either of them have it on them," Alex said. And, she thought, grab some ephedrine, cortisone, and antihistamine, if she had to make a last ditch effort to treat someone whose body was blowing up and shutting down.

Dan looked at his watch. "We launch in a half hour at 700 hours, at Andrews Air Force Base."

Castro shot out of the room before the others, but then turned on his heel and ducked back in. "Much obliged, Sam," he said as he left.

CHAPTER 60

Grant sat in the hangar at Andrews Air Force Base on a duffel bag that he'd brought with him. Alex wondered what he had in it. From the size of it, either he had enough artillery to stage a military coup or he was carrying his weightlifting equipment. Her packing was a little more modest. She'd grabbed her gym bag, which had a change of clothes and underwear, and stuffed it with the drugs and portable testing equipment she might need. Dan was pacing the hangar, systematically smoking Camels. Two pilots, a man in his early fifties who was watching *Jeopardy!* on a small television set and a woman Alex's age who was eating an apple and leafing through the Armed Services newspaper *Stars and Stripes,* were waiting patiently for Major Dan Wilson to give the order to go.

"Where the hell is he?" Dan asked, of no one in particular, but Alex knew his question was addressed to her. "If I find out he's pulling a Rambo and trying to settle this score alone, I will kick his ass right into an obstruction-of-justice charge."

Alex looked out the hangar door for about the hundredth time. Truth be told, she wouldn't put it past Castro to try to get there first. He was on this case because of Ted and he'd already thrown away one job to avenge his buddy. He had no particular loyalty to the AFIP. Maybe Alex had just deluded herself that at least he played it straight with her.

Alex realized she was getting a headache. She touched the scar on her finger, where Elena had accidentally bitten her. Then she tried to put that threat to her life out of her head. She took a sip of bottled water. Maybe she was just dehydrated and exhausted.

The vibration of Alex's cell phone in her fanny pack led to a frantic unzipping in the hopes it was word from Castro. Instead, Barbara's number popped up.

"Are you near a television?" said Barbara. "Take a look at CNN."

Alex took a few long steps toward the pilot and told him she needed to switch channels. Out of curiosity, Dan and Grant followed her.

The newscaster was telling the audience that a dozen modern-day Typhoid Marys had been rounded up by Homeland Security and were being taken to a secure treatment facility to protect the public. Mug-shot-like photos of the twelve of them held steady on a screen behind the anchorman. One of them was Castro.

"Where have they got him?" Alex asked Barbara.

"I checked out redeployment orders for NIH physicians. About twenty have been reassigned to a new facility on the NIH campus. My bet is that he's in Bethesda."

Alex hung up and looked up at Dan. "We need his help," she said.

Dan shook his head. "We're not going to delay this mission to pay a hospital visit. Let's go."

Alex looked at him with pleading eyes. "Look. Ossing asked for directions for his nine-hundred-mile drive at three this morning, California time. There's no way he's in Humphrey yet. And, if they're in it together, Tommy Teague won't leave until Ossing gets there. Just give me an hour or two to get Castro out."

"And let him infect us all?" Grant said. "Weren't you listening to what CNN had to say?"

"That's bullshit," Alex said. "It's like AIDS. You need to be exposed to blood. Chances are that Castro doesn't have the disease. Not everyone exposed to a dying patient gets it. And even if he does, think about it. If he was infected by Ted, he's got just a couple of days to live."

She looked Grant in the eyes, then Dan. "Would you want to spend the last two days of your life locked up in some leper colony instead of closing in on your partner's killer?"

Dan threw up his hands. "Okay. You've got two hours. We'll take off now and have another plane waiting for you at Dulles heading straight to Malmstrom Air Force Base in Great Falls, Wyoming. I want you on that plane by eleven whether or not you've got Castro in tow. If you have to leave him behind, I'll team you with an MP I know at the base and you can brief him on the drive to Humphrey."

Alex threw her arms around Dan in a hug. Then she turned to the female pilot, who was about her size. "I'll trade you the clothes I've got in this bag for your uniform."

The woman looked down at the gym bag that Alex was carrying, then up at Alex. "Let me guess. Inside it you have a black turtleneck and jeans." That was precisely what Alex was wearing. Pretty much what she always wore to work.

Alex nodded. It didn't seem like much of an exchange when she looked at the well-tailored navy-colored skirt and the Air Force jacket with an array of ribbons signaling combat in Iraq and a promotion to major.

The woman smiled. "Okay if you throw in the belt."

Alex looked down at the hand-tooled belt she'd bought in New Mexico, with the silver buckle made by a Zuni. "Deal," she said.

The men turned around as the female pilot donned Alex's clean clothes from the gym bag and Alex put on the suit off the woman's back. As Alex bent down to shove her worn turtleneck and jeans into her gym bag, she noticed that Grant had been watching their reflections off the nose cone. The entire maneuver took less than five minutes. Within ten, Alex was in her T-bird, on the way to the National Institutes of Health, her hair tucked up into a jaunty pilot's cap.

CHAPTER 61

On the Bethesda campus of the National Institutes of Health, Alex bent over to rifle through the trunk of her car. She heard a whistle behind her, turned, and caught the smile of a bicycle messenger as he rode past. She wasn't used to wearing a skirt and had been bending a little too far, she figured.

She kept preprinted forensic forms in the trunk, which allowed her to check off the types of tests she wanted done on biologicals—blood, semen—that she found at crime scenes. She fastened a few of those sheets to a clipboard. They looked enough like hospital forms that she figured she could blend into the facility. She took a pen out of her fanny pack and wrote "Experimental Protocol 7432" on the top lab form. Then she shoved her fanny pack into the leather saddlebag briefcase she pulled out of the trunk. Somehow, the major's uniform didn't quite make it with the fanny pack. She looked down at the name tag sewn into her uniform. DUSTER. She needed to remember the name she was now using. Mary Ellen Duster.

With her gym-bag strap over her shoulder and her briefcase in her hand, Alex was about to close the trunk when she noticed the box of laboratory masks she used at crime scenes when they were dealing with unknown substances. She put one on. She'd been in projects with some of the NIH docs and wanted to elude recognition. Although the mere fact that she wasn't wearing jeans was probably a disguise enough.

She walked toward the front of her car just as a twentysomething-year-old Slavic man put a business card under her windshield wiper. As she grabbed it, he motioned toward the hearse parked discretely on the other end of the lot, with CHESTERFIELD FUNERAL HOME ornately inscribed on the outside.

Vultures, she thought. He was hanging around, waiting for the patients to die, hoping to sell his service to the next of kin. She started walking toward the building, then doubled back, pulled the mask down to expose her mouth, and spoke to the man. "How much are they paying you for this?" With his high Slavic cheekbones and the clothing of a recent emigrant, she didn't think he was one of the Chesterfields.

"Fifty dollars a day," he said. "And a bonus for each body."

"What's your cell phone number?"

Excitedly, he pronounced the numbers for her, and she entered the digits into her own phone.

"Here's a down payment," she said, reaching into her briefcase and handing him a twenty. "I might need you soon." Who knew how a hearse might come in handy? He could create a diversion, or block the exit to the lot once she and Castro left.

He reached out to shake her hand, then, watching her pull the mask back up, thought better of it.

A loud siren announced the approach of an ambulance and her new pal looked expectantly at the east side of the building, where another patient— or, he might say, another potential customer—was being unloaded.

Alex approached the main entrance of the building and was amazed when a guard waved her through. This often happened in supposedly secure medical facilities, such as locked psychiatric wards. So much attention was paid to keeping the patients in that there was little focus on keeping others out. Whether the inmates were crazy or contagious, shortsighted administrators just assumed that no one in his right mind would want in, unless they had some legitimate business. All effort was placed, like at the Hotel California, in making sure that the patients didn't leave.

The building had a smell of new paint and disinfectant. It had been hastily put up and was small for a medical facility. Alex wondered why Homeland Security was betting that the disease could be contained with just a couple of hundred admissions. Or maybe, she thought, they were readying stadiums for the infected, just as the Superdome had housed people in the wake of Hurricane Katrina.

Alex knew that Homeland Security was being wrongheaded. Finding

Thomas Teague, Jeffrey Ossing, and Matthew Brunner was the key to stopping the disease, not quarantining people in a modern-day sanitarium.

Past the guard's desk, the facility branched into three hallways. One was probably for labs, another for the patients, and a third probably led to the morgue. She bet, with the way the disease was progressing, that there was as much space for bodies in the morgue as there was for patients in the wards.

Alex stood for a few seconds at the juncture where the three hallways met. She looked down each, trying to discern which had the most activity. A woman with an EKG machine was heading down corridor three. Alex bet that she was heading toward a patient's room, rather than away from it.

The corridor turned after a hundred feet and Alex saw that she'd made the right choice. Another fifty feet farther was a nurses' station. And to her right was a room, about the size of a large living room, that served as a sort of staff lounge. She peeked in and saw the medical hierarchy in all its splendor. The doctors were wearing hazmat suits, looking like strange astronauts with stethoscopes jutting out from their necks, resting on the inflated suits like a gold chain necklace worn against a beer belly.

The next level down in the hierarchy, the nurses, wore masks not that different from Alex's and gloves. They had surgical booties over their shoes and lab coats made out of a raincoat-looking material. The aides, whom Alex identified by the bedpans and water pitchers they carried, had none of those protections.

Alex sighed. It was all completely backward. The aides were the ones most likely to be exposed to the patients' bodily fluids, yet they were the least protected. Ah, doctors, thought Alex. So good at taking care of themselves.

An alarm sounded and Alex thought she'd been found out. But a voice came over the PA: "Code Blue in 1701. Code Blue."

Two of the hazmat docs exited the lounge, along with two nurses, and headed down the corridor. Alex's heart started pounding. What if Castro was dying?

She'd worked alongside him for weeks now and hadn't seen any sign of the disease. But maybe she'd been deluding herself. Other than her headache, Elena hadn't looked sick before she'd swelled up in front of Alex.

Her feet felt heavy as she forced herself to walk down the corridor toward 1701. The door was open, and a nurse was coming back out. "Nuh-uh," she was saying back into the room after her. "I'm not getting paid enough for this."

Alex peeked into the room the nurse was leaving. Inside, a gray-haired woman was swelling up and spewing blood. One of the doctors was speaking to the remaining nurse, his voice muffled through the clear hazmat faceplate. "Sondra, do something about this." Then he closed the door from the inside so that Alex could no longer peer in.

There were twenty-five more rooms on the corridor. She didn't have the time to go into each one to find Castro, so she doubled back to the nurses' station. An elderly man in a hospital gown was pounding on the glass window that protected the nurses from the patients. "I'm perfectly fine. I don't know why you've got me here. At least let me go someplace and have a smoke."

The nurse on the other side of the window looked as terrified as if a lion had gotten out of its cage at the zoo. But come to think of it, the nurses were the ones in cages here, Alex thought.

The nurse just kept repeating into a microphone that allowed her to be heard on the other side of the glass booth, "Get back to your room, Mr. Dante."

Finally, the man turned around and shrugged at Alex. "This is the damnedest place," he said, as he wandered back to his room.

Alex approached the glass and put her clipboard up against it so the nurse could see the top form. "I'm transferring one of the patients," Alex said.

"Come around to the side," said the nurse.

Alex walked down the corridor between the nurses' station and the lounge and the nurse buzzed her through a door. Inside, Alex saw a wall of monitors, charting the vitals of every patient—EEG, EKG, and a third line of information she couldn't figure out.

"That's attached to a stretchy band around the patients' arms," the nurse explained. "It alerts us to any swelling."

Alex looked at the data from 1701. The third graph was escalating rapidly and the line for her EKG was highly erratic.

The nurse noticed her gaze. "There's not much we can do for them once they hit that stage."

"That's why I'm here to pick up one of the patients. He volunteered for an experimental protocol of the military."

"Which one is he?"

Alex looked more closely at the monitor and noticed the patient's name was in small letters in the upper right corner. She quickly scanned the other monitors and found Castro in 1704. His EEG showed him to be almost comatose. "This guy," Alex said, pointing to his monitor. "What's with his vitals?"

"He's a fighter. Had to be restrained. He's slowed down because of the heavy sedation."

"Well, I'll just get him and take him out of here," Alex said.

"I'm sure the rest of the staff will agree with me that you are welcome to him," said the nurse. "Although he is sort of cute. Let me just check on protocol. I'm sure there's some form for you to sign."

The nurse left the station and walked back down the hall toward the building entrance, where, Alex guessed, the administrative offices had to be. Alex took a quick look at all the monitors. Castro was just a few doors down from the room with the Code Blue. She looked at the numbering on the monitors and identified the one associated with the room farthest down the hall, 1751. Then she bent down swiftly and switched the lines, so that Castro's vitals were showing up on the screen marked 1751.

Alex had no desire to wait until the nurse came back since she was sure no administrator would let her take Castro out of there. She opened a few cabinets that held equipment, found a scalpel, and then took it quickly from the nurses' station to Room 1704. Once inside, she shut the door behind her. She nearly burst into tears when she turned around and saw Castro, pale as a cloud, spread-eagled on the bed, hands and feet tied in rubber restraints to the bedposts.

If Alex had harbored any doubt about busting him out of there, the restraints changed that all. Even with just a little swelling, the rubber would have cut off his circulation and killed him. Were doctors or sadists running this place?

Castro opened his eyes and strained against the restraints, then fell back on the bed, eyes shut. Alex slit the restraint holding his right wrist, then leaned clear over him and slashed the left. Then she slashed the ones holding his ankles.

A buzzing sound came from across the room and Alex wondered if she'd triggered an alarm. But she saw it was Castro's cell phone. She picked it up cautiously and waited for the person on the other end to speak, "Castro, honey, it's Pearl."

"This is Alex. Did you find my mother?"

"Sure did. She's got a slight concussion, but she's resting comfortably in the guest room. Did you want me to wake her?"

"No," said Alex, as relief flooded through her, "but tell her I love her."

"Sure thing. And tell my great-nephew that the color was closer to magenta than to amethyst."

Pearl was a pistol, thought Alex, just like Janet.

Alex stuck the phone into the pocket of her borrowed skirt and then took it out and laid it on the bedside table. No reason to provide a way to trace them. She approached the bed. "Come on," she said to Castro, using her fingers to hold up his eyelids while she spoke to him. But he just flopped his head to the side and drooled.

Her visions of him running out to her car with her were going south fast. She opened the door a crack to see if the coast was clear to push him someplace. The doctors and nurse who had responded to the Code Blue would probably be wheeling that dead patient to the morgue any minute now.

Alex didn't see anyone in the immediate hallway so she stepped outside the room and looked past the nurses' station. Damn, she thought. The nurse from the station was coming down the hall about a hundred yards away. And with her was Martin Kincade's secretary. Alex was doomed. Even with her hair up, a mask, and a uniform, that old biddy might be able to recognize her.

Back in the room, she wrenched the pillows from under Castro's head. He was too far gone to protest. She put them on top of his midsection and then added towels and a washbasin, then plopped onto his body and bed anything else that wasn't nailed down in the room. She pulled a sheet up over him and tucked it tightly around three sides of the bed, covering him as if he were a bloated corpse, but leaving the sheet flapping free at the edge above his head so that he could breathe. Then she pulled out the leads to his EKG and EEG. She heard the alarm sound. Then a voice: "Code Blue in 1751."

Through a crack in the door, Alex saw the nurse and Kincade's secretary run past the room toward 1751. The doctors from 1701 soon followed.

With that distraction in place, Alex rolled Castro and his bed out of the room, grabbing his chart from outside the door and shoving it under the sheet. As she pushed him in the opposite direction from where the others had run, she used her cell phone to call the guy with the hearse. "The loading dock, now!" she said.

She raced behind the guard's desk, but he didn't even turn around. He was looking out the entrance as an ambulance screeched into the lot, apparently to drop off someone else. She turned down hallway one, which she guessed was the one with the morgue. Based on its direction, she assumed it dead-ended into the loading dock.

She was right. There was a young guy in black jeans and a black goth T-shirt, thumping on a desk in tune to the music from his iPod. He took the earbuds out for a second when she approached.

"Dead man rolling," she said, motioning down at the seemingly bulging figure under the sheet.

"Can I peek?" he asked.

Great. Leave it to her to run into a necrophiliac. "That would be medically inadvisable," she said. "Sometimes these bodies just bust open and spew blood."

He nodded. "Awesome."

From the tinny earphones she heard the sound of a Megadeth song as he pushed the button that opened the exit to the ambulance port. You gotta love a guy who's perfect for his job.

When the door opened completely, Alex saw that her Slavic buddy was already backed up to the loading dock. She was able to wheel the hospital bed right into the back of the hearse and hop in after it. As she closed the back door of the hearse behind her, she saw Martin Kincade's secretary yelling down the hall after her. It didn't take a lip reader to know that the woman was saying, "Stop her!"

CHAPTER 62

Alex was nearly crushed by Castro's hospital bed rolling inside the hearse. As the driver flew over a speed bump in the parking lot, Alex thought Castro was going to fall right off. Luckily, he was tucked in so tightly that he didn't tumble out. Once they'd cleared the bump, she managed to bend down and engage the brakes on the bed. She then sat on the floor next to the bed and rubbed her thigh where the metal bed rail had hit her. "To Dulles," she told the driver.

Dan and Grant would be in the air right now, so she called Barbara. "I've got him," she told her friend.

"I hope you know what you're doing," Barbara replied. "I don't want the liability case if your guy infects the entire state of Wyoming."

"Barbara . . ." Alex scolded.

"Alright, rescuing the hunk was the right thing to do."

"I need a couple of favors," Alex continued. "First, have Chuck get my extra set of car keys from my desk and cab over to NIH to get my T-bird."

"What makes you think he'd be willing to do that?"

"I've seen the lust in his eyes when he passes her in the parking lot. Ferris Bueller's got nothing on him."

"Okay, then."

"I also need to know what runway to meet the plane at."

"That's easy. Once you get to Dulles, take Aviation Drive across the bridge to the terminal on Wind Sock Drive. That's where the private planes land. The plane is waiting for you in the east section. You can drive right up to it. That is, if you had a car."

"Yeah, that's my third favor. I may need you to write out a little check to Chesterfield Funeral Home."

The man in the front seat spoke up. "No, to me. To me."

Alex put her hand over the receiver. "What's your name?"

"Miles Kovic," he said.

Barbara spoke from the other end of the line. "I heard him. Tell him where to stop by and pick it up."

"You're the best," Alex said to Barbara.

She hung up, took out one of her cards, scratched out her name, and put in Barbara's. She reached across the seat to Miles. "Just go there and pick up your check." Then she repeated Barbara's directions about where they were to meet the plane.

That bit of business done, she peeled back the sheet to see how Castro was doing. He was still out of it, but she smoothed his hair back. "I thought we were a real Bonnie and Clyde, what with this getaway," she whispered. "But that Miles character in the front seat, he's a true highway robber."

CHAPTER 63

When they reached the private landing strip at Dulles, Miles and three cargo handlers lifted the hospital bed with Castro atop it up the stairs to the plane. The copilot, an Air Force lieutenant in his early forties, helped Alex use straps to secure the bed against the wall in an open cargo area at the back of the passenger section of the plane. A flash of an image went through Alex's mind. Her father, an Air Force sergeant during the Vietnam War, flew missions like this, with men dead or dying in the rear of the plane. She said a silent prayer that Castro would survive.

The lieutenant waited until she was safely seat-belted in and then returned to the cockpit for takeoff. After their altitude stabilized, Alex got up, changed in the small bathroom into the jeans and turtleneck she'd shoved into her gym bag, and stood beside the hospital bed. As a doctor, she'd seen patients die, but no one she'd been involved with at this level. Her father's body had been decimated by a bomb in Vietnam, so there was no chance to say goodbye and no casket to grieve next to.

"Talk to me, Castro," she said. "I didn't break you out just to watch you sleep."

But the man didn't respond. His breathing and pulse were slow and labored. She leaned over the bed, repeating a whispered mantra: "You're going to be alright."

A figure came up behind her and she assumed it was the lieutenant. Just then, Castro opened his eyes and said groggily, "I think I died and went to heaven."

Alex followed his eyes, turning around to see who was behind her. Major

Mary Ellen Duster, dressed as an Alex clone. She spoke to Alex. "Since I was already familiar with this mission, I decided to hang around and fly you out."

Alex pointed to an empty seat over which she'd draped the major's uniform. "Thanks. It did the trick."

Mary Ellen looked at the neat blue jacket, not much the worse for the wear considering its recent adventure. Then she looked down at the Zuni belt she was wearing.

Alex followed her gaze. "Hey, that's okay, keep it. You probably saved his life."

The major scrutinized Castro, whose eyes were open but slightly glazed over. "Based on what you're heading into," she said, "I'd say it's out of the frying pan, into the fire."

The major walked a few steps so that she was closer to Castro's head. "Darlin'," she said. "We are going to start pouring coffee down you. We need you back on your feet pronto." She showed Alex where the supplies were in the small galley and then returned to the cockpit, leaving the two alone.

Alex pulled out his chart to see what knockout drug they'd used in the IV. Lorazepam. Great. A central nervous system depressor, lorazepam could impair physical and mental abilities. She looked over at Castro, who'd managed to pull his arms free from the sheets and push the button that raised the top section of the bed to a sitting position. The exertion from that one small activity had sent him back into a stupor. She wondered about the other side effect of the drug. Some people got hyperaggressive with it. Then, she thought, given Castro's usual level of aggression, would she even notice?

Another page of the chart showed the blood work that had been done. She was surprised he had any blood left, given the number of vials they'd collected. She'd better get him hydrated fast.

On the last page of the chart, she saw an official-looking proclamation of Homeland Security. It said that when the patient died, the body became the property of the agency.

What kind of insane order was that? People, no matter what they died of, had a right to determine what was done with their bodies. Cremation, burial, a tomb. Orthodox Jewish individuals believed the body needed to be buried whole. Native Americans felt that their spirits wouldn't rest until the body was in the ground with the proper burial ceremony.

Alex could think of no medical or public health reason why the patients in Bethesda couldn't be afforded the same rights. There was nothing in the nature of the disease that indicated that it would pollute the soil or endanger the pallbearers. Alex's thoughts turned more cynical. If Homeland Security owned the bodies after death, Kincade could do whatever he wanted to the patients while they were alive. No one would be the wiser.

She thought about the order for potassium chloride. What if the new hospital wasn't trying to care for the patients but trying to eliminate them? Was Martin Kincade running his own equivalent of a gas chamber? If so, how could they get the evidence to prove it?

She opened a small carton of orange juice and put a straw in it. Approaching Castro, she touched him gently to wake him, then told him to drink. Two cups of coffee, a gallon of water, and a carton of orange juice later, Castro became more animated. He turned his head to show Alex where he'd been hit by a Taser in the AFIP parking lot as he was getting into his car. She told him that Martin Kincade of Homeland Security was behind the roundup.

"Once I catch Ted's killer," he said, "I'm going to pull Kincade apart, limb by limb."

Then Castro reached up to Alex and pulled her close to him. They knew that if he had the disease, he had almost no time left to meet those goals.

CHAPTER 64

The next time Major Duster entered the cabin, Castro, looking a bit ridiculous in a paper hospital gown, had left his hospital bed for a legitimate seat and was discussing tactics for the current mission. Mary Ellen said, "Risen from the dead, have you? Just in time, too. We'll land in Cheyenne in about thirty-five minutes. I radioed ahead and they'll have a car ready for you."

"What about other supplies, like a gun?"

Mary Ellen reached into an overhead compartment. "Major Wilson made sure you were fully stocked." She took a case down and opened it to show a Sig Sauer, night binoculars, a knife, a pair of handcuffs, flares, a Wyoming road map, and an untraceable cell phone.

"Well, happy birthday to me," Castro said.

"Clothes are a different matter," said the major. "No one expected you to show up dressed like that. I'll radio ahead to the base. What size?"

"Large shirt; thirty-three waist, thirty-three inseam."

"Make sure they're pure cotton," Alex said. Then she turned to Castro and said, "Let's not take any chances."

He stared at Alex. "Good thing you're all natural."

The major returned to the cockpit and Castro got up and started walking down the aisle of the plane, trying to get his sea legs back. With only the slight cover the paper gown provided, Alex caught glimpses of his strong back, with a scar. Mostly likely a knife wound. His legs were well muscled but seemed not to be following his mental orders. He tottered along, grabbing the back of a seat every few feet.

"You're looking pretty pitiful," Alex said. "I'm the designated driver for sure. I just hope you can shoot better than you can walk."

Castro changed quickly when they landed. Alex got behind the wheel of the car and he grudgingly let himself into the passenger side.

"I'm fine," he said.

But Alex could see he was not. She told herself his fatigue was from lorazepam and the tests he'd undergone—blood tests and bone marrow draws, a biopsy of his spleen. But she also knew there was a chance the disease was kicking in. She glanced at him again.

"You've got a guilty look on your face," he said.

"I'm wondering if I did the right thing, busting you out."

"I was going nuts in there," he said. "Strapped down like an animal."

"It might have been safer."

"Yeah, like that's how I live my life."

She thought of the governor's book, *The American Way.* "From what I've seen, the Castro way isn't long on safety."

He put his hand to his temple, as if easing a headache.

Alex tried to calm her concerns. None of the secondaries died this early, she told herself. But *early* was a relative term. If he was affected like Elena had been, he basically had another few days. Some people, though, were fine, even if they were around man-made substances a few weeks after their exposure to the dying patient. Alex had a morbid, horrible thought, wondering if the doctor in her was treating him like a data point for analysis, going through this countdown and stakeout not just as a friend and partner but also as a medical researcher, waiting for symptoms to appear so that she would better understand the disease. She banished those thoughts. No time for psychoanalyzing herself today. She might be nearing the Colony.

She turned on the radio to catch up on the news. There'd been race riots in towns along the Mexican border, with blacks and Chicanos weighing in on the side of Native Americans. When the news report was over and the station turned back to music, Alex switched channels and heard the now-familiar voice of Governor Elias Lightfoot Blackstone.

"This is not the time to pit brother against brother, citizen against citizen," said Blackstone. "Now is the time for us to open our hearts to the afflicted and work together to end this reign of terror. I do not know if the monster behind these murders chose this path to bring suspicion on Native Americans and deter me from seeking office. But, if that is the case, I will not put others at risk. I have sought the counsel of my elders, who reminded me that the pursuit of one man should never be put before the needs of a people or the concerns of a nation. Today, I am irrevocably ending my quest for the presidential nomination."

"Didn't see that one coming," Castro said. He turned to Alex. "Guess you won't be Surgeon General after all."

"Don't joke," Alex said, turning off the radio. "He's making a big sacrifice. And maybe for no reason. The deaths could be completely unrelated to his candidacy."

They drove in silence for a few miles, then Castro said, "Let's talk strategy. I don't think we should worry about the doctor. He's lived with a bunch of kids for years. He hasn't exactly been doing target practice. We've got to keep our eye on Mr. 187 and the doc's brother. If they're running the poison, they're going to be well armed so that nothing will blow their plan."

"I wonder what the Colony looks like," Alex said. "There's one photo of a log cabin, but Teague vowed not to turn any patients away. And the children have grown up. They'll have wanted independence, some space of their own. It's got to be some sort of community now."

He glanced at the road map. "Old Granger Road—is what the kid said?"

Alex smiled at his reference to Chuck. "If he helps us through this whole thing," she said, "I think you should call him by his given name."

"Hell, if he helps us get out of this, I'll call him the Dowager Queen if he wants."

They turned off the main highway, rode for about fifteen minutes more, and then found Old Granger Road. Within ten minutes, the road gave out, seeming to disappear into thin air.

"This can't be the Colony," Alex said. "Where's the octagon-shaped building?"

For the first time since Sam had come up with the address for Teague's brother, Alex's adrenaline-boosted hope faded and she realized how hopeless their whole enterprise was. Find the Colony? Figure out a disease? Yeah, right.

"Hey, step at a time," Castro said. "The Colony could be around here. Even if it's not, this Tommy Teague can get us there."

Alex stopped the car, realizing they'd have to head up on foot. She turned to Castro to ask if he could make it, but he'd already leaped out and begun his ascent.

When she got out, she saw what had caught his attention. Just off the road, behind a clump of trees, sat a wood-paneled truck, about the size of a UPS delivery van. Castro pried open the back door and stepped up and inside.

Alex peered through the door of the van. "Shouldn't we head to the cabin first?"

"Needed to make sure Teague and Ossing weren't in here, making an escape."

She stepped inside. The four walls of the van's storage area looked like a general store from a previous era. There were shelves on all sides and wooden crates bound to the walls by heavy, strawlike rope that looked like it might have held up the mast of an old clipper ship. Alex saw an old doctor's kit, with glass vials inside. They were empty, but had been emptied recently. Probably into containers at the Colony itself.

Castro picked up a leather-bound volume from the floor next to one of the crates. As Alex came up beside him, she felt the warmth of his body. His face was slightly red. Each movement created more of a strain than he was letting on.

The pages were made out, one after another, with lists of supplies and costs and dates. Castro carefully turned to the last page. It was dated ten days earlier. It listed a variety of purchases. Pure linen. Unprocessed honey. And, at a cost of $380.51, a liter of Thimerosal, the mercury additive to vaccines.

They jumped out of the truck and started up the hill in what they assumed was the direction of the house. The broken branches covering the path made Castro's unsteady journey even more difficult. "Maybe we should wait for Dan and Grant," Alex said.

Castro straightened his back. "I'm fine."

They reached a clearing where the vegetation was more trod upon. A few Marlboro butts dotted the path and, farther along the path, a small pile of butts surrounded a tree. As they reached the position where the smoker would have stood, they saw the outline of a cabin a few hundred feet away.

Castro looked down at the footprints in the dirt. He put his shoe alongside them. They were bigger than Castro's shoes.

He turned to Alex. "Why would a guy with a view of God's country look back at his house while he took a smoke?"

They both knew that he wouldn't have. He'd had a visitor, one who'd done some serious surveillance on the house. Could it have been Ossing? If he was in this with Tommy Teague, why would he have snuck up on the house? Or was there a third person spying on them both?

"Wait here," Castro said, as he stepped out toward the house.

Alex touched his arm, stopping him. "No. I should go instead. If Tommy Teague's there, you might spook him."

"What? And watch him or one of his buddies blow your head off instead? No way."

He continued in the lead, with Alex a few steps behind. He stood to the right of the main front window, swiveling his body quickly for a few seconds, then pivoted back abruptly. "Alex, stay out." He tried to open the front door, then took a few steps back and rammed the door full tilt, banging his shoulder against the old wood and knocking it in.

Alex was right behind him. Greeting them in the middle of the room was a freshly mutilated body. Around the body was the makeshift equipment of a torturer.

"Stay back and down," Castro told her. He swiveled his body, Sig extended, into the bathroom.

"All clear," he said.

Alex, nauseated and dizzy from the sight of the dead man, solemnly approached his body. His hands had been bound by his own belt and his pants and boxers were around his ankles. Frayed electrical wires had been applied to his testicles.

Three of his fingers had been cut off. Judging by the pattern of the blood, they'd been removed one by one. His eyelids had been hacked off. The killer had wanted him to see what was happening next.

"Tommy Teague?" Alex said weakly. She took a deep breath. She'd been so sure that Teague and Ossing were partners. "It's a lot of violence for just a disagreement on a deal," she said to Castro.

"Some guys get off on it."

She knelt next to Teague's chair. "No, it's more like someone wanted something from him. And he held out a long time," she said, pointing at the pile of three fingers. "It would have taken five, six minutes to cut off each one."

Alex looked at the color of the blood, the flexibility of the arms. The body had not gone into rigor yet. Then she choked back tears, looking accusatorily at Castro. "If I hadn't—"

He knelt next to her and put his hands on her shoulders, trying to calm her. "I know, Alex. If you hadn't broken me out, you might have gotten here in time."

Alex removed his hands from her shoulders. She thought about her stubborn streak, always doing what she thought was best. But she'd never had to face such grim consequences of a decision.

"I owe you my life," Castro said. "But I also owe Tommy Teague. We're gonna get the man who did this."

But Alex knew she'd have to find her own way to atone. She stood up and started furiously pulling open the drawers of the desk, trying to find anything to identify the location of the Colony. But there was nothing. No maps, hardly any paper. The cabin was just that one big room, with a bed at the back, plus the small bathroom. Along the wall hung a menagerie of metal animals. As she approached, she saw they were sets of wind chimes.

She looked at the body. He'd been part of it from the beginning. He'd made the wind chimes of the children's faces that Alex had noticed in the *Life* article. Above the stove was a recent photo of the man next to an older fellow who must have been Andover Teague. They were standing in front of that same barn-shaped building with the face chimes. But now there was a pen of sheep to the side, bordered by flowers with a sunburst pattern of white leaves surrounded by purple leaves. Columbines, the state flower of Colorado.

Alex called Dan's cell phone. "Where are you?"

"About a half hour from the location, at a juncture Ossing will have to pass."

"He must have beat you to it." She told him about the body and asked him to send forensic techs to the cabin.

Then she called Chuck, who was holding down the fort back at the AFIP. "I need you to use the Peeper," she said. "There's a newspaper article on my desk. It's got a photo of an octagonal building with a wind chime on it. I need you to find it for me."

"The article?"

"No, the real deal. That building and wind chime are somewhere in the Colorado countryside and I need to know where."

As she returned to Castro's side, Alex had to fight the desire to cover Tommy Teague's body with a blanket. She knew it would disturb the evidence. Whatever he'd been up to in the past few months, he'd protected and cared for his brother and the kids all those years, and now she felt the need to protect him.

"We've got to go," she said to Castro.

"But where? We haven't sifted through the evidence here."

"Dan's got a team on the way but right now we need to follow the killer. I think he's heading to the Colony and I think it's in Colorado. Get in the car and I'll explain."

Castro wasn't listening. He was looking through the drawer of a hand-made bedside table. "A Webley Mark IV," he said.

Alex saw the broad smile on his face as he lifted the revolver and a box of bullets out of it.

CHAPTER   65

After they crossed into Colorado around 4:00 P.M. local time, their new cell phone rang. Alex heard Chuck's excited voice. The Peeper had found the Colony. Chuck gave her the coordinates of the Colony—seventeen miles west of Stevenstown, four miles north of Wander Gulch—and told her how best to approach the site. "I've got some bad news, though," he said. "Ossing flew United, connecting through Vegas, to Cheyenne. We picked up the ticket on his credit card. He might have already made it to Tommy Teague's."

"He did," Alex said. "And now Teague's dead."

She said to Castro, "We're about three hours from the Colony. Chuck says the best entrance road is a mile north of Carterville, off Mercer Road."

"Ask him what the security situation is," Castro said. "Any guards? Gates?"

Alex conveyed the question. When she hung up, she told Castro, "There seems to be an electrified fence at the perimeter of the property. It's a little over forty acres. Maybe we can throw something into it and short it out."

"Not likely," said Castro. "Electric fences don't short out. Not since the 1960s."

Alex looked at him. "And how exactly do you know that?"

"A friend of Aunt Pearl's raised cattle in Arizona. Only about fifty head. Today, most of the cattle ranching there has been taken over by the megaranches, herds of a couple thousand. Electric fencing is big business."

Alex pictured a person getting shocked. She thought of how electricity caused people's muscles to contract, usually knocking them down. "So how do we break through it?"

"Those fences are designed to keep animals out, not people. Sometimes there's a kink in the wiring and tossing a hammer at it can break it completely. Or the wire's been stapled and a section has shorted."

Alex's phone rang again and she expected to hear more from Chuck, but instead it was Dan. "We're all looking for a green Sebring, Wyoming license plates 958 LAG. Ossing rented it in Cheyenne and Wyoming State Police found Sebring tracks in the mud on the approach to the cabin. The car was last seen going across the Wyoming/Colorado border."

"He's heading to the Colony," Alex said.

"Affirmative," said Dan. "We're about a half hour behind you. We'll meet you with Colorado State Police at the Chevron station five miles west of the Colony on Mercer Road. We'll approach the Colony together."

When she hung up, she looked at Castro. She knew he'd never agree to wait for the rest of the cavalry.

"I'm not waiting, either," she said. "If Ossing enters the Colony with his modern-day clothes or deodorant or who knows what, he'll end up triggering a reaction that could kill them all. We'll need to get the doctor to come outside to talk to us."

Twenty minutes later, Alex and Castro passed a small, private airport. A mile farther down the road, Alex pulled into an out-of-the way gas station to fill up the tank. Maybe during ski season it might have been busy, but the first week in May, they were the only customers. She went inside the attached mini-mart, found a detailed Colorado map, and picked out a Denver Broncos baseball cap. She saw a revolving stand of sunglasses, mostly with plastic frames, but a twirl of the stand revealed a pair with a wire frame and tinted glass, covered in a thick layer of dust. The glasses were big and rectangular, the type that had fallen out of fashion in the 1950s. Perfect, she thought.

She opened her fanny pack to remove a credit card to pay for the purchases. Then she realized what a stupid move that would be. The last thing she needed was to give Homeland Security a way to trace her and Castro. She forked over the money—$52, including the charge for the gas—and hoped she had enough in her wallet to buy the gas for the rest of the trip.

She got back into the car and handed Castro his new disguise.

"What, no Ray-Bans?" Castro said. "Any self-respecting fugitive wouldn't be caught dead in these."

Alex didn't want to spend too much time thinking about the operative word in that sentence, *dead*. "Put 'em on. Your face was all over the news when you were captured. And once they learn you've busted out, you're going to get a shot at another fifteen minutes of fame."

Castro obliged, then tipped the rearview mirror his way so he could assess his new look. But his next reaction was to take off the hat and glasses, reach for his gun, and open the door. He crouched on the side of the car. "Drive slowly to that strip mall across the road. When I signal you, come back and park alongside that car." Then he moved away from the car, heading toward the back of the gas station.

As she readjusted her mirror, she saw what he had seen. A Chevy Impala had pulled up to a pump on the side of the station. On the passenger side sat the head of Homeland Security, Martin Kincade.

She followed Castro's request and drove the car across the street. She opened the glove compartment, took out the Webley Mark IV, and loaded it with bullets from a dusty cardboard box that Castro had found in Teague's nightstand. She laid the gun down on the passenger seat and turned to look out her window. From her vantage point in the strip mall, Alex could see the driver get out of Kincade's car, start the pump, and head to the other side of the station, where the bathrooms were. She saw Castro sneak up behind him with a gun, but the man swiveled around and knocked the gun from Castro's grip. Alex's hand flew up to her mouth. She watched as they struggled with each other. The man's arm reached around and gripped Castro's neck in a choke hold. Castro brought his leg up around the other guy's and knocked the man to the ground. But the man's arm didn't leave Castro's neck and the two fell backward into the men's room. She saw legs sticking out as they wrestled, flipping each other over. Then the bodies lurched forward, disappearing farther into the bathroom. Alex strained to see what was going on. Then she looked over at the Impala. The Homeland Security director was no longer in the car.

The passenger side of her car opened. Martin Kincade grabbed the Webley and then sat down, pointing the gun at Alex. "I need a new driver," he said. "Start the car."

She did as he said. But she started backtracking to the border.

"Not that way," said Kincade. "Toward the Colony." He put the gun close to her face until she turned the car around and headed in the opposite direction.

Nervously trying to avoid any potholes, so that he didn't accidentally pull the trigger, she said, "How did—?"

Kincade laughed. "Your investigative skills led me right to it. Like you told your colleagues at AFIP, the Colony was the key."

A chill ran down Alex's back. Was there a mole at the agency? Had Wiatt sold them out in some way? That seemed unlikely. And she'd trust Dan, Chuck, and even the annoying Grant with her life. Who were the outsiders? Castro? But he would never have gone over to the dark side. He had one focus—avenging his dead friend. What about Randy Stone? This was the first time he'd gotten involved in a case. If he was working with Homeland Security, that might explain how he'd managed to lose Ted's body.

"Who did you get to?" Alex asked.

"Not a who, but a what. When your man Pringle petitioned the Department of Defense to release a computer from storage, I figured it related to the investigation. We had our computer experts examine it, but they couldn't even figure out how to turn the damn thing on. It was easy enough, though, to slap a bug on it. Everything you said in that room with the computer was relayed directly to me. You must be proud of the way you broke this case."

Proud was the last thing Alex felt at the moment. Castro was lying in a men's room, probably dead. The director of Homeland Security was forcing her at gunpoint to drive to the Colony. The photos of Dr. Teague's charges, those beautiful children, flashed through her mind. "What do you want with the Colony?"

"You're dumber than I thought," he said. "The toxin's the perfect bioweapon. And with this outbreak in the Southwest—the entire world is terrified by it. America would be a superpower again if we held this in our hands."

"You can't go in there," she said. "All the children will die."

"In times of war, men and women die all the time for their country. Plus, you don't think we'd actually let them live, do you? That boy might sell the formula for the toxin to one of our enemies."

Alex thought about Dan's buddy at Homeland Security warning of the off-the-books mission. So this was it. Kincade would get the toxin and then destroy the Colony. And who would ever find out? The Colony was a mirage, a fiction, a place that was hidden from view. "These aren't soldiers who've volunteered to risk their lives," she said. "They're innocent civilians."

"They're modern-day lepers, nothing more."

Alex looked at this man without a conscience, this man who failed to ob-serve the rules of engagement. She knew that no matter what risk she had to take with her own life, she wasn't going to let him near the children.

CHAPTER 66

As Alex drove, she considered her options. Martin Kincade was holding a gun on her, but he was getting weary, tilting his body toward her and pointing the heavy Webley Mark IV at her head. He eventually moved his gun hand to his lap, with the weapon still aimed at her. "Keep both hands on the steering wheel or I'll shoot you."

Although he had the upper hand, Alex saw that he was sweating. Maybe he realized that if he shot her as they rolled along at seventy miles per hour, the car could careen out of control, possibly killing him as well.

She looked around for a highway patrol car, but saw none. The road, pine trees on either side, was deserted. She sought something to bash the car against. Maybe if she rammed the passenger side into a tree she could knock him out of commission or at least get him to drop the gun. Being in control of the car, she had the element of surprise on her side. She could brace herself, but he wouldn't know what was coming.

Her eyes were fixed on the road ahead, but every few seconds she stole a glance to the right, to see if there was some way she could veer off the road without turning the car over in a ditch. Or should she just point the car in the direction of the ditch and open her door and bail before the car sped downward? At gunpoint, she'd started the car without buckling her seat belt. She had some mobility. But landing on a highway at seventy miles per hour wasn't exactly conducive to survival.

Up ahead, the road intersected with a rural highway. On the right, Alex noticed a car, an Impala, parked at the light. She didn't see a person in it.

Then suddenly her car careened wildly as a tire blew out. Kincade looked at her in a panic. She gripped the wheel tightly, took her foot off the accelerator, and fought her frightened desire to brake.

Kincade dropped the gun on his lap as he tried to brace himself by putting his left hand on the dash and his right hand against his door. Alex grabbed the gun with her right hand. Her inattention to the road caused the car to spin around, barreling down the highway in the wrong direction in her former lane. Luckily, there were no oncoming cars. Still gripping the gun, she positioned her right hand back on the wheel and maneuvered the car to the side of the road. The car slowed enough so she could finally brake. As she did, the Impala pulled up next to her passenger side. As Kincade tried to pry the gun from her, a battered and bleeding Castro exited the Impala and threw open Kincade's door, pulling him away from Alex.

Kincade turned to him, swinging. Castro belted him in the face with the Sig, knocking him out. With the seat belt constraining his body, the director of Homeland Security fell sideways half out of the car.

"Give me a hand," Castro said.

Alex's heart was racing from the encounter. Her left hand was glued to the wheel, her right hand pointing the gun at Kincade. "Is he dead?"

Castro put his hand under the man's nose. "Still breathing."

Alex exhaled deeply and then walked around the car. With her aid, Castro was able to pull Kincade out of the front seat of her car and shove him into the back of the Impala. When they moved him, the Broncos hat and sunglasses he'd been sitting on fell out of the car. Alex picked them up.

"Let's go," Castro said to Alex as he climbed into the backseat after Kincade and held his gun on the dazed man. "The keys are in the ignition."

Alex popped the trunk of her car. She grabbed her briefcase, her gym bag, and the case that Major Duster had given them. She pushed those across to the passenger seat of the Impala and started the car.

"You shot out my tire?" Alex said angrily. "You could have killed me!"

"Alex, baby, I've seen how you drive. You're practically a stuntman."

Her adrenaline started to ebb and she looked in the rearview mirror at her passengers. Kincade's dazed body had slumped. Castro pulled the seat belt from the side, slashed a section of it off with his knife, and used it to bind Kincade's hands behind him.

"How did you get up ahead of me?" Alex asked.

"Took a back road and drove like a banshee," Castro said. "Now double back to the airport."

"We can't go there," she said. "That's probably where he landed. It'll be swarming with Homeland Security agents."

"It's the best place to find another car. Plus, they're looking for a man and a woman in a car, not three people."

He pulled Kincade's body upright and put the Broncos cap on the man's bald head.

At the airport, Alex saw the A-3 Skywarrior jet with a federal seal on the tail. Two men with guns were guarding it.

She drove past the employee parking lot, which required a key card to enter, and turned into a lot with meters.

Castro said, "I need one with a lot of money on the meter, so we know the owner won't be back anytime soon." He passed the dependable Sig Sauer over the seat to Alex and reached for the Webley. "If he stirs, shoot him."

Castro opened the door and made his way up and down the aisle of cars, limping from his beating at the gas station. She saw him stop abruptly and was convinced they'd been spotted. But, no—he'd stopped to grab on to the side of a car to steady himself. Then he walked halfway down another aisle and broke into a Range Rover. He parked the SUV next to the passenger side of Alex's rental car and pulled Kincade out of the car and onto the backseat of the SUV. The Broncos cap dropped to the ground. Castro was huffing from the physical exertion.

Alex grabbed the gun and the map and moved their bags once again, cramming them into the passenger seat of their new wheels. She picked up the baseball cap. Castro moved into the backseat of the SUV, lying down next to Kincade so that it looked like the car contained only a woman.

Alex put the cap on to hide her long blond hair and hopped into the front seat. As they sped away, Castro rifled through an array of camping gear in the back. He tied Kincade's hands and ankles more securely with nylon rope he found among the gear. She saw in the mirror that his face was contorted in pain. "Are you okay?" she asked Castro.

"Just drive," he said.

The rural highway gave out a half hour later, leaving nothing but a dirt road approaching a mountain, then circling it like a ribbon. As Alex started driving on that pocked road, she marveled at the choice of a site for the Colony. The snow on the top of the mountain probably provided a good water source, and from that altitude you could feel like you ruled the world.

As they drove around the mountain out of the blue-spruce-lined section of the road to more of a clearing, Alex saw that the road, like strands of Christmas tree bulbs, circled several more times to reach a higher section of the mountain, where she could see the electric fence.

On the next-higher stretch of road, Alex thought about Castro's list of things that could go wrong with an electric fence, but this one looked quite invulnerable. Gleaming wires, with posts every twenty or thirty feet. She saw a prairie dog take a run at a section of it and bounce back in pain.

"Looks awfully secure up there," she said.

Castro stared out the window. "People think they're creating a sturdier fence by putting the posts close together, but it actually makes the fence more vulnerable," Castro said. "You want the wires to work like a rubber band. If animals or people run into the fence, you want the fence to bend, not break. These posts are too close. Ramming them could knock the posts out of the ground and break the insulator."

"Ramming them with what?"

"We'll figure that out when we get there."

As they rounded the cone-shaped mountain, their journey took less time as each rotation took them higher. The Range Rover was coming out of the shadowy back side of the mountain into glaring sunlight when Castro said, "There he is!"

Alex saw the Sebring on a stretch of road a half mile or so farther up the mountain. They'd have to go around another time, maybe thirty minutes' worth of driving to catch up with him. She swerved and started driving off-road up the mountain.

The Range Rover bounced as it traversed a dry riverbed. When it hit an unexpected dip in the ravine, the car lurched violently. Kincade slid across the backseat of the vehicle. Castro grabbed him just as he was about to hit his head against the inside of the door. The man woke from his stupor and tried to bite Castro's arm.

Castro let go, and Kincade's head came close to hitting the door, but he managed to move his tied legs diagonally and propel himself away from it. "Keep your hands off of me," Kincade said.

"Fine way to talk to someone who's trying to keep you from getting a concussion," Castro said.

Kincade was becoming more alert, struggling against his restraints and bringing himself to a sitting position. He sputtered, "This is treason. You'll be hung."

Castro ignored Kincade. "What do you think, Alex? This guy is threatening us."

"But if he's the only witness against us . . . ?"

"You're right. Let's just knock him off, leave him out here to be eaten by wolves. I'm sure no one would miss the asshole."

Kincade was ashen.

"Whatsa matter, Martin, no stomach for the action?" Castro said. "A simple little ride through the country's giving you an ulcer?"

"Untie me or I'll have you arrested."

Castro laughed and waved the Webley. "You're in no position to negotiate. Maybe I should've just let you bite me. Get a good dose of those germs they're calling the modern-day plague. That plane you've got standing by could take you right into isolation."

Kincade shut up. Then he tried another tack: "Listen, we can handle this. We've got the best research doctors looking into the disease. I'm sure there's hope for you. Just turn yourself in so that you can be treated in time."

Alex maneuvered the SUV back onto the road, racing after the Sebring. "If your docs could save his life, they would have given him the cure when you had him hostage in Bethesda—"

"Maybe they've just discovered it," Kincade said.

"Yeah, and maybe the check is in the mail and my dog's just sprouted wings," Castro said.

"And maybe we've got Jennifer," said Kincade.

"Fuckin' bastard," Castro said, grabbing the man by the shoulders and ramming him against the car door.

"Jennifer?" asked Alex. The sound of her voice caused Castro to let go of Kincade.

Despite the blood trickling from the back of his head, Kincade flashed a triumphant look. "You mean you haven't told your partner here about your wife?"

Alex felt suddenly light-headed and involuntarily let up the pressure on the gas pedal, then pushed back down a few seconds later. But it was enough for Castro to feel the change in speed.

"I'm sorry, Alex. We were separated, on the road to divorce, when I met you. She was living out of state with her sister. Then, after Ted's funeral, she called and told me . . . well—hell, I never let anyone outside the DEA know about her."

Alex felt her cheeks grow hot. Was that what she was? A mere "outsider"?

"He's right," Kincade said. "She was hard for us to discover. Then I talked to Ted's mother about how we were going to give Castro here a commendation for his great work and wanted to invite everyone who was close to him. She wanted to make sure we got in touch with Jennifer. Quite a beautiful woman, your wife. Although a little naïve."

He reached over to the passenger seat and picked up Alex's cell phone. "I'm sorry," he said again.

He dialed his wife's home number and then her cell number. She didn't answer either. "Where is she?" he demanded of Kincade.

"It was easy to persuade her to come to the ceremony on your behalf. We sent a plane to Connecticut for her. Now she's in one of those cells where we torture the Guantánamo rejects."

"You son of a bitch," Castro said, striking Kincade across the cheek.

Kincade regained his smug look. "Unless you let me go, your wife will come to a very unpleasant end."

"Get her on the line," demanded Castro.

"Untie me and I'll make the call. We'll let her loose once you take me to my men."

Castro positioned the Webley under Kincade's chin and cocked the hammer. "Give me the number or I'll blow your head off."

Kincade must have recognized the madness in Castro's eyes as a force to be reckoned with. He blurted out the number.

Alex clutched the steering wheel, her foot paralyzed on the gas pedal. She tried to drive as smoothly and uniformly as she could so that a jerk of the car didn't cause the Webley to fire accidentally. Holding her breath, she listened intently to the short beeps of Castro's cell phone as he used his left hand to hit the digits, never removing the gun from Kincade's flesh. She heard eleven numbers being pressed but didn't hear the click of the Send button. Castro was figuring out what to do.

Alex's mind was spinning. There was no reason to believe that Homeland Security would let Castro's wife go even if they were given what they wanted. This had to be a mission that the agency could say never existed— and a wife who'd been kidnapped couldn't be counted on to keep her mouth shut.

Alex's emotions were a tangle. The obvious question—why hadn't Castro told her?—was dwarfed by the stakes of this particular call. On one side was a woman and on the other side was the Colony full of people. But if she were to condone sacrificing Jennifer for the good of the children, she wasn't any better than an agency that might be planning to kill the carriers of a disease to protect the rest of society.

Castro closed the cell phone without transmitting the call, then set the phone on the passenger seat. "Okay, asshole, here's how it's going to go down. You're going to tell me where my wife is being held or I'm going to kill you."

Alex stole a glance in her rearview mirror. Kincade looked a little ashen but his color did nothing to diminish his bravado. "Then you'll never see her again."

She watched Castro exchange the gun for a hunting knife. Perhaps he'd realized the lunacy of firing an old gun in a closed car moving at high speed. Who knew how the bullets would ricochet and who they would kill?

Castro pulled Kincade's bound arms from behind his back and out to the side, then yanked them straight. The man squirmed and yelped, but a quick flick of the knife toward his neck cowed him into a stiff silence.

In a flash, Castro moved the knife downward and slashed the fabric of Kincade's jacket and shirt, exposing the vein in the crook of his left arm. "I'll ask you one more time. Where are you keeping Jennifer?"

Kincade couldn't take his eyes off his own pounding vein. It was as if this body part of his had mysteriously appeared. As if he'd never noticed it before. His eyes stayed on the vein, not daring to look at the knife.

"Castro, don't," Alex said.

His blue eyes were gleaming. He paid no attention to Alex. With a quick swipe of the knife, he made a clean cut.

Blood gushed out and Kincade screamed. "Help me!" he yelled to the back of Alex's head.

But Castro responded instead. "Maybe, *maybe* Dr. Blake will dig into her medical bag of tricks and sew you up if you give us what we ask."

"You'll pay for this," said Kincade, wincing.

"I already have. You screwed with my job and fucked with my family. Haven't you heard of pay it forward? I've already paid; now I'm just collecting on what you owe me."

The blood continued to squirt and sputter. With his hands tied behind his back, Kincade couldn't curl up his arm to put pressure on the wound to stop it. With effort, he shifted his arms behind his body to try to press the wound against his back to stem the bleeding. Castro pulled the rope around Kincade's wrists, yanking his arms to the side. A geyser of blood shot up the window. Kincade looked at it with horror.

"Take me to a hospital," he pleaded. "I'm going to bleed to death."

Alex spoke from the front seat. "Just tell Castro where you're keeping his wife." That last word tasted strange on her tongue. Bitter.

"No."

"In a few minutes, you'll start to feel light-headed," Alex said. "That's because blood supplies the oxygen that your brain needs to function. Next, you'll . . ."

Kincade's lips became a tight line. His eyes darted about as if looking for a way to escape.

Castro made a slit in the other sleeve of Kincade's jacket. Kincade jerked his arm away, but Castro caught the man's wrist and poised the knife over the vein.

"She's in the basement of headquarters," Kincade said.

Alex picked up the phone and called Dan. "Homeland Security kidnapped Castro's wife."

"You must be breaking up, Alex. I thought you said Castro's wife."

"Can you find a way to get her out of the basement of the Bethesda headquarters? She's probably being held in the area where they interrogate suspected terrorists. I'll put Castro on so he can tell you what she looks like."

Alex tried not to listen, but she found that she was inordinately curious.

"She's a five-foot-two-inch blonde, in her thirties," Castro said. "She has green eyes. And she's three months pregnant."

CHAPTER 67

They drove in silence for a while, Kincade slouched down in his seat, whimpering. Alex wished she could stop the car and check on the man, but she couldn't afford the time. Ossing already had too much of a head start.

Each time she glanced in the mirror, Castro's eyes seemed blue-black, hard-edged, and clear. He had a look of madness about him. Alex remembered what he had said in the bar. You figure out who's the most dangerous person in the room. Right now, he was that person, the one whose behavior Alex couldn't control or predict.

A truck passed them and the driver leered at her. Usually, she'd give a guy like that the finger, but right now she'd rather have him look at her than notice the bloody Jackson Pollock design across the window of the Range Rover.

"Castro," she said quietly, "he's lost a lot of blood."

Castro leaned forward and dipped his head wearily so that his forehead touched the back of her head, as if contact with her body would soothe him. She felt him nod.

"We might need him," Alex continued. "So here's what I want you to do. Take some more of that nylon rope and tie it around his upper arm for a tourniquet."

She felt Castro's head pull away from her, saw him reach, robotlike, into the camping equipment. As he went through the motions of aiding his enemy, Alex found herself hoping against hope that Dan's men would reach his wife in time.

The noise of the approaching helicopter distracted Alex from her thoughts of Castro's wife. Kincade revived slightly, used his nose to hit the Open button on his window, and thrust his head out the window to get the copter pilot's attention. Castro had him back inside the car in seconds.

The copter's shadow eclipsed the car and, without slowing her speed, Alex reached for Castro's Sig from the passenger seat beside her. She held her breath, waiting for the copter to land in the road in front of her, with men descending from it in an all-out assault.

"How'd they find us?" Castro asked.

The shadow passed over them. "They're not after us," she said. "They're after the Colony. We've got to stop them."

"Fat chance," said Kincade, weakly but with conviction. "An hour from now, there will be nothing left."

Alex turned a sharp left and the Range Rover again lurched up the mountain to the next level of road. She sped around to the other side of the mountain and saw the Sebring parked ahead. Ossing was out of the car, looking at the electrified fence. He threw a stone at it. The stone bounced back.

He got back into the car and Alex saw the car shake as he started it up again. He then got out of the car, picked up a rock, and bent back into the car, lodging it on the accelerator. He snapped back from the car and the Sebring lurched forward, picking up speed. It crashed through the fence, breaking the wires. The man then ran up the mountain toward the Colony.

Alex pushed the accelerator farther and pulled up in front of the hole that Ossing's car had made.

"We've got to get him before he gets into the building," Alex said. She handed Castro his weapon and took the Webley.

"I'll go after the helicopter crew," Castro said. Sig Sauer in hand, he ran toward the field where the chopper was likely to land.

She saw Castro disappear into a cornfield. One man against a SWAT team. What could he do?

A slight breeze blew and the sound of chimes drifted in the air. Up ahead, Alex saw the building from the original *Life* magazine article, with the wind-chime faces of the original ten children. At the side was the pen with sheep and the flowering columbines. In front of the pen was a spotless twenty-year-old Toyota Camry with Massachusetts plates and a Harvard Medical School parking sticker. Alex tried to process that. Why had Dr. Teague brought his car here?

Ossing was running toward the building. He threw open the door and Alex ran after him. The log cabin had one giant room, like a barn. But there was no one in it.

Alex wondered if the Colony had surveillance technology that she hadn't noticed. Had they fled the building? Ossing had already run out the back when she ran through.

On the other side, she saw a beautiful glass castle. Inside was a young man, facing out.

Transfixed by the sight of Matthew Brunner, she didn't notice Ossing, who snuck up and grabbed her from behind, pinning her so tightly that she thought her bottom ribs would break. Her gun arm was pointed down and she tried to swivel her wrist so that she could aim the Webley at her attacker.

Ossing let go for a millisecond, grabbed her right arm, and brought it down full force so that the gun in her hand slammed against her right knee. She dropped the gun, cupping her hands around the knee and wailing in pain. Her knee gave out and she fell to the ground on her other knee. She gasped in pain as Ossing shoved her shoulders and knocked her on her side. Within seconds, he had the Webley in his hand.

"Stop it!" the boy yelled from behind the glass.

Like a wild animal whose attention had been diverted, Ossing turned toward the boy.

Alex used her right arm to push herself into a sitting position. She rocked back and forth in pain. She ran her right palm over her damaged knee and cursed herself for her stupidity. Her leg was beginning to swell. She'd have to try to stand so that it wouldn't lock in its bent position. If it did, she wouldn't be able to see this thing through. But getting up would draw Ossing's attention. And now he had a gun, thanks to her incompetence.

"Let me in, Matthew," Ossing said.

"What do you want?" asked the boy. He was wearing the same billowy muslin shirt as in his Face Space photo. He seemed to have stepped out of a long-ago era.

An incapacitating wave of pain came over Alex as she tried to bend both her legs in front of her to get up. Nausea overcame her and she almost didn't hear what Ossing was yelling through the glass.

"I want *you*," said Ossing. "I'm your dad."

Alex fell back into a sitting position as she tried to process that new information. Was it true?

"I've come to get you," Ossing said. "You'll be famous. We'll make a bundle."

Alex now realized why Ossing had brochures of Disneyland and Universal Studios. He was going to turn Matthew into an oddity on display, a modern equivalent of the bearded lady in a freak show.

"Keep him out," Alex shouted. "Protect the children."

Alex sensed that Ossing was turning toward her. She rolled to the side just as he fired his weapon, pinging the ground with a bullet on the spot she'd just occupied.

"No!" said the boy.

Ossing suddenly turned back to the castle and fired into the glass, just to the side of where the boy stood. Matthew disappeared and Alex feared he'd been wounded.

Then she realized that he'd never been there. They'd been talking to a hologram.

"Matthew," Ossing yelled. He ran to the wall and used the butt of his gun to knock out more of the glass, creating a hole large enough to pass through.

The children! Alex thought. They would die if he got close to them. She clenched her teeth in pain as she lay down on her back and inched toward the building, scrambling like a wounded crab, two arms and her good leg pulling her along. When she reached the building, she brought herself to a sitting position, with her back against a sturdy section of the glass. Using her good leg, the left one, she pushed down hard to start raising her body, her back inching its way up against the glass. Finally, she was standing on her left leg, her back flush with the glass. She tentatively put weight on the right leg as well, and tears of pain flooded her cheek.

She pivoted on her left foot and faced the hole in the glass. She lifted her right leg and moved it to the inside of the building. But she knew that it wouldn't bear her weight if she tried to put her left leg through the hole in the glass so that she was completely inside the building. She pulled the sleeve of her black turtleneck down over her left hand to shield it. She would sacrifice the skin of that hand since she needed the right one more. Then she grabbed a section of the jagged remaining glass with her left hand, breaking her skin through the fabric and drawing blood as she used her hand to provide the leverage to bring her left leg over the glass. She broke off a piece of sharp glass and slipped it into her pocket. She could use it as a weapon.

Inside the glass castle, hallways ran in three directions. Ossing was striding straight ahead. As his back disappeared in front of her, Alex thought of the expression on Matthew's hologram face when Ossing had announced he was Matthew's dad. Matthew hadn't recognized him. How could Ossing and Matthew be getting the toxin out if Ossing hadn't come here before? Matthew couldn't live in the outside world.

Alex thought about the torture of Tommy Teague, the three fingers that were cut off. He'd held out for a long time, protecting his brother and the children, keeping the Colony address a secret from Ossing. And now the whole Colony was about to come crashing down.

CHAPTER 68

Alex was about to follow Ossing when she noticed a prism on the ceiling, which had helped create the illusion that the boy was standing behind the glass. She turned to the right to find Matthew and started hobbling down another hallway. Each step was an exercise in agony. She felt the pressure of the swelling in her right leg and saw the lump around her knee as a growing bump in her jeans.

As she moved away from the glass entrance, the hallway got darker, no longer illuminated by the early evening light from outside. She was bracing herself with her right hand against a wall, touching it every few feet to take some of the weight off her bum leg as she labored along. She was careful not to disturb the wood-framed portraits of the children that hung every few feet. Some seemed to have been made with a pinhole camera, creating the illusion of light beaming down on these residents of the Colony. But where were the children? Would Ossing reach them first?

She was paying so much attention to balancing herself on the right wall and looking at the children's faces that she almost missed a glass window on the left wall that was framed with the same sort of wooden frame as the portraits. Behind the glass stood Matthew.

"Go away," he said. "We're not allowed to have visitors here."

"I need to talk to you. My niece, Lana, e-mailed you about me."

He looked curious, torn. "The pretty, deaf girl."

"Yes. I saw your posts about playing God. I can understand your wanting to change the world to be more like you and your—" Alex searched for the right word, "brothers and sisters. But you've started an epidemic."

The boy look confused.

"What did you put in the fountains?"

"I don't know what you mean."

"Your experiments, the things you talked about on your Face Space page . . ."

"I watched the animals and what plants they ate when they were sick. I made some simple medicines to help my brothers and sisters. That's all."

An older male appeared behind him. "Get away from the glass, Matthew," said Andover Teague.

Alex was shocked at his appearance. He looked so much older than she'd expected. His speech was slightly slurred. Maybe he'd had a stroke. "Dr. Teague," Alex said. "I need to talk to you. People are dying from a disease like *Inflatus Magnus*. I'm a doctor from the Armed Forces Institute of Pathology."

Teague tilted his head with interest. He probably hadn't had a conversation with another doctor in nearly twenty years. He turned to Matthew. "We have to get the Colony ready. We have another child arriving. Uncle Tommy is meeting the helicopter at the clearing."

"Your brother is dead," Alex said to Teague. "Matthew's . . . biological dad killed him."

"That can't be," the doctor said. "We just got a message from Tommy."

"How did he contact you?" asked Alex. "Was it the same way he always does?"

Matthew spoke up. "Usually he calls. This time it came over the Internet."

It dawned on Alex that this was how Homeland Security would gain access. They were pretending they had a child to deliver to the Colony!

"It's a trick, from Homeland Security," said Alex. "They're going to infiltrate the Colony."

"What would they want with us?" Teague asked.

Alex said, "The toxin. They're coming for the toxin."

"My vaccine?" he said.

A chill went through Alex's body. She'd been blinded by the connection between Ossing and Matthew. She hadn't even considered the possibility that Dr. Teague could be leaving the Colony and poisoning the fountains. "Vaccine?" she said. Then she thought about the GH that appeared repeatedly in his coded notes. It was a transposed way of writing the symbol HG, the chemical name for mercury, which in Teague's time was invariably a component of childhood vaccines.

She limped toward the window, putting her face within inches of it. She pressed both palms against the glass. The coolness of the glass soothed the gash on her left hand. Her blue eyes stared at the doctor, a sickly shadow of his photo in *Life*. "Come out here, Doctor. Let me tell you what is happening."

The doctor stared at Alex for a moment. In his right hand he held an unrecognizable pistol with an exceedingly long barrel. Any gun he'd brought into the Colony would have been crafted in the seventeenth or eighteenth century, before the use of modern chemicals and plastics.

He walked closer to the glass and put his left palm on the other side of the window from her right palm. Then he pointed the gun to his left. "There's an entry farther down this hallway. Wash off in the decontamination chamber and I'll meet you on the other side."

Alex walked to the entrance as quickly as she could, propelling herself with her hand against the wall. She was nearly to the door when her right leg locked up and she fell, the jagged glass in her pocket cutting into her abdomen. She bit her lip to suppress a moan, got up, and limped on, before Teague had a chance to change his mind. She realized that she might be walking into a trap, but that possibility didn't slow her steps. She thought of the children whose photos were arrayed in her office. She had to protect them.

She flung open a door and saw a makeshift version of the type of shower that she'd used when she'd worked on a project in one of the Berkeley labs. The ones that were used when entering—and especially when exiting—a P4 containment facility where genetically engineered organisms were being created that might be hazardous if let out in the world.

Here, the concerns were reversed. It was crucial to scrape away any vestiges of the modern world before you entered the facility. She pulled her turtleneck over her head. With her swollen knee, she couldn't bend down to remove her boots and jeans. She moved soaps and supplies from a wooden bench and sat on it, struggling to take off her boots and socks. Then she slid out of her jeans and hung them on the bench next to her, draping her bra and panties next to them.

She dug into her jeans pocket, pulled out the shard of glass, and entered the shower stall. Inside, she reached for a yellow sponge and put the glass in its place, so that both hands were free to wipe herself down. She brought the sponge close to her face and saw it was a honeycomb sea sponge. There were two metal chains in the shower, marked 1 and 2. She pulled the first chain and a torrent of water came down on her. She moved out of the flow and lathered up with the soap, which had a grapefruit smell. Walter Reed Hospital had started using soap with grapefruit extract to launder sheets because of its antibacterial properties. As she ran the sponge down her body, she steered clear of the cut in her abdomen and washed gently over her swollen knee. A fine mess she was.

She stepped back under the water, washed her hair, and scrubbed her whole body. She then tried the other door to the shower, to go into the Colony, but it was locked. She was now completely wet, with towels tantalizingly in view on the other side.

She pulled and pulled but the door wouldn't open. Finally, she looked at the other chain, labeled 2. Maybe it opened the door. She pulled.

A gas filled the shower cubicle, burning her eyes and stinging her skin. She felt like a million bees were attacking her. She wanted to scream, but she feared that opening her mouth would cause the substance to fill her lungs.

Then, the gas dissipated. Her skin still stung, but she heard a loud click. The shower door opened and she exited the stall, the glass shard in her hand. She reached for a towel, then realized that, other than for her hair, she didn't need it. The gas had dried the water off her skin. In the thin metal that formed the edges of the shower, she could see her reflection. Her body was red, as if she'd been dipped in boiling water or Easter egg dye.

She saw muslin jumpsuits and robes hanging opposite the shower. A jumpsuit would be more practical, but with the limited range of motion of her cut left hand and her swollen right leg, she could only manage a robe. She cinched the fabric belt around her and slipped the glass into the pocket.

This was what Tommy Teague must have done when he came in and out of the Colony. And now he was gone. That poor man.

She saw a pair of wooden clogs and put them on. They were big and Alex was disheartened. Her bad balance was even worse now, but going barefoot wouldn't work, either. Ossing would soon catch on that he was headed in the wrong direction. She could hardly battle Ossing like this. What was she thinking, charging in here without waiting for Dan? And where was Castro?

She had to figure out how to make sure the children stayed safe.

Dr. Teague had a gun. At least that was a start. If she could just prevent him from using it on her.

There was a knock on the wooden door leading out of the room and Alex opened it. Dr. Andover Teague moved the gun from his right hand to his left and reached out to shake her hand. "Dr. Blake," he said. "Welcome."

His graciousness seemed wildly out of place. Shifting the gun back to his right hand, he offered her his left elbow as she negotiated the walk down a short hall to a large room that served as his laboratory. The far side of it had three windows that faced a meadow of sunflowers with iridescent purple petals. Just inside the door of the room was a large ashtray on a stand, the kind used in fancy hotels. Crushed in the sand of the ashtray were three cheroot butts.

Teague motioned her to sit at a chair alongside a desk. Then he said to Matthew, "Get her some ice for her knee."

Matthew opened the laboratory refrigerator and Alex craned to see what was inside it. Unrecognizable cultures and liquids and tiny petri dishes holding budding plants. He put the ice in a cotton dish towel and handed it to Alex.

As Alex applied the ice to her knee, she noticed from the corner of her eye a glass/gold/DNA computer, Sam's twin. A cardboard sign with a child's lettering pasted to the side of the computer said PROPERTY OF THE DEL RAY INSTITUTE.

"Hello, Nat," she said.

Matthew smiled at her familiarity with the computer. "This is Alex," he said to the machine.

"Pleased to meet you," Nat said. Alex knew at once he was the younger twin, the second machine to be crafted. While Sam had a slightly tinny computer voice, Nat's voice was full and clear, like an astronaut's or commercial pilot's. A calming, commanding voice, which asked her, "Are you friend or foe?"

Matthew looked at her shyly but didn't offer a response. "Friend," she said.

Then she turned to Teague, who was standing in front of the windows, facing her. Behind him she saw the copter hovering in the sky. She wondered why it hadn't landed yet. Maybe the pilot was waiting for a signal from Kincade. Or perhaps the crew was waiting until the dimming evening lights turned to a dark nightfall.

"We've got to destroy the toxin and all of your notes about it," Alex said.

"That's what Homeland Security is coming here for. It's the perfect weapon for biowarfare."

Teague looked puzzled. "This is my greatest triumph. The vaccine against the disease. I leave the Colony once a week to inoculate people."

"By putting the vaccine in fountains? That's killing people."

"Public health is always a trade-off. Vaccines harm some children while protecting others. This vaccine caused deaths, yes, but think how many other people who drank from the fountains were immunized."

Alex hadn't considered that possibility. "It's not up to you to decide how many to sacrifice for what you consider the greater good. That's not how human research works."

He waved his gun as he spoke. "Who are you to lecture me? I've devoted my life to science, to curing a deadly disease, to letting hundreds, maybe thousands of children live normally. This is exactly how science works.

"You're from the AFIP, you say. A century ago, when the AFIP director, Walter Reed, wanted to prove mosquitoes transmitted yellow fever, he tricked people into getting bitten by the deadly bugs. Don't look at me like that, Dr. Blake. I'm doing science exactly as our heroes did it. When I die, there will be a hospital named after me."

Matthew quietly approached. "Dad, you didn't do this, did you?"

Alex flinched at his use of the term *dad* to address the doctor. But what else could he call him? Teague had been the only parent figure for most of Matthew's life. He'd legally adopted the child.

The doctor put his left arm around the boy, but kept his right hand tightly on the gun.

Alex looked at Matthew. "Where does he keep the vaccine?"

But instead of responding, Matthew turned his head abruptly to the left as the door burst open. Alex dropped the ice from her hand and stood up.

Jeffery Ossing, gun in hand, was pushing Martin Kincade into the room. Both were still dressed in their street clothes. Ossing must have blasted his way in through the shower entrance.

"Stand back," Alex said to Ossing. "You haven't been decontaminated. You'll kill your own son. Any man-made material triggers the reaction."

The weakened Kincade was still bound at the wrists, but Ossing must have removed the man's ankle binding so he could walk. Kincade spoke as if he were in charge. "Dr. Teague. Hand over the toxin."

Ossing said to Matthew, "I saw him in the car and recognized him from TV. He's a big shot. He's the hostage we need to get us out of here. He called his friends in the helicopter and told them to fly us out."

Alex gazed out the window as the copter drifted down to land. Then she confronted Ossing. "Don't you understand? Matthew can't leave here."

Kincade's eyes were on Teague, but Alex noticed Matthew looking at the cabinet above the desk. That must be where the toxin was.

Teague and Ossing were at a standoff. Both had their guns aimed at each other. There was a good ten feet between Alex and Ossing. She, Teague, and Ossing formed a perfect triangle. Kincade was standing perfectly still, not wanting either Teague or Ossing to take aim at him.

While the three men were keeping track of one another, Alex quietly pulled her right foot out of the clog and put it on the floor next to the shoe, painfully standing on tiptoe so that Ossing wouldn't notice she'd taken it off. Then, bracing herself on the desk next to her, she did the same with the left. Slowly, she lowered herself so that her feet were flat on the floor. She felt the jagged piece of glass in the pocket of her muslin robe. When she had the chance, she could at least try to take a run at Ossing without the clacking of the shoes on the floor.

For a moment, the sound of the helicopter landing nearby disguised the sound of movement in the hall. Castro burst into the room and ambushed Ossing, pointing his Sig at the 187 tattoo on the man's neck.

Kincade, his hands still bound behind him, lurched forward and tried to head-butt the DEA agent. Sig still nuzzled against Ossing's neck, Castro stepped down hard on Kincade's instep, sending the man into spasms of pain. Dr. Teague aimed his gun at Kincade.

"Drop the Webley or I'll remove this tattoo with a through-and-through," Castro said to Ossing. The man complied. "Alex, get Matthew and the doctor out of here. The goons from Homeland Security are on their way."

But the words were barely out of his mouth when he dropped to the floor between Ossing and Alex. The collapse sent his Sig vaulting across the floor as his face swelled and he started spewing blood.

"Jesus," said Ossing, jumping away from the dying man. "That some kind of epileptic fit?" Then, while Teague stood transfixed by Castro's seizures, Ossing reached down, grabbed the Webley he'd dropped, and pointed it at the doctor.

Alex took three unsteady steps toward Castro. In her panic over his condition, she refused to give in to the pain as her kneecap popped to the right when she knelt down. She pulled the glass out of her pocket, cut off a section of her fabric belt, and wadded it into his mouth so that he wouldn't swallow his tongue. Tears filled her eyes. She said to Teague, "This is what you've done. This is where your research has taken us."

Teague couldn't get his eyes off Castro. "I . . . I . . . I . . . had no idea. I didn't mean . . ."

With the Webley still aimed at Teague, Ossing bent down, picked up Castro's Sig Sauer, and jammed it into his belt.

Alex quietly ran her hand down Castro's pants leg. He had handcuffs in his pocket, but she couldn't find the knife. Maybe it was still in the SUV.

To Ossing she said, "You can't go near Matthew or the other kids. You'll kill them all."

Matthew put his hands on Alex's shoulders. "I can help him," he said, looking down at Castro. He reached over to a plant growing on a counter, then knelt next to Castro and said, "Chew this."

Castro turned his swollen face toward Alex. She looked directly into Matthew's eyes. She remembered the equations, his scientific genius.

"Do it," she said to Castro.

He hesitated for a moment and Alex yelled, "Do it *now,* before your throat closes and it won't help you."

Castro chewed and then his head dropped back and he suddenly became still.

Alex's angry eyes flashed on the boy. She had trusted Matthew and the boy had killed him.

"I'm sorry," said Matthew. "He must have been too far gone."

The boy was looking at her imploringly. The way he had his body tilted, only she could see that the fingers of his left hand were crossed. He was telling a lie.

"Perhaps the acetylcholinesterase inhibitor and antihistamine in the plant was too much for him."

He was sending a signal to Alex. The plant contained a neuromuscular blocker that would slow down his respiration and heartbeat, putting Castro into a temporary coma that would last anywhere from a few minutes to a few hours. It was brilliant. It would delay further inflammation and buy time for the antihistamine in the plant to treat him.

Matthew looked at Ossing. Alex saw longing in his eyes. Ossing said to him, "It's time for us to go now. You said on your Face Space page that you'd like to leave the Colony, that there are things you want to see."

Matthew didn't dare look at Teague. Instead, he focused his gaze on Ossing. Alex saw that he was tempted to go with him.

Teague said, "Matthew, you know you can't live out there."

"I'm your real dad," said Ossing. "I've got a plan. Do you know how much money we can make out there, how much people will pay to see you? I'll get you the best doctors. I took real good care of you when you were a kid. I even bought you a tricycle."

"You weren't even around," said Teague. "Matthew, your mother brought you to the hospital. She had bruises on her face and at first I thought she had a milder case of the disease. But then I realized your so-called father here had beaten her. She was busy caring for you. He attacked her for not paying enough attention to him."

"But," Matthew's voice cracked, "why did my mother give me away and never visit?"

Teague's voice softened. "She did it to save your life. It was like those slave mothers who floated their babies down the river. Staying with her meant certain death for you. Coming with me meant you had a chance to live."

"I would have taken you home," said Ossing. "I would have hired someone to take care of you."

Teague turned to Ossing. "You never even came to the hospital. You didn't even bother to show up to sign the adoption papers."

"I risked my life to come here and find you," Ossing said to Matthew. "You owe me. You wouldn't have been born without me. We'd do great together. I can get you television and movie deals. You know how much you liked that tricycle, that blue trike I bought you. Now we can get ourselves a blue Maserati. You can make appearances at Universal Studios, Disneyland. You could even be an action figure—Matthew Brunner Ossing, instead of G.I. Joe."

Teague took a step closer to Ossing, aiming his gun at the man. "I've given my life to keep them from being a sideshow, like the Dionne quints."

Ossing shot first. Teague fell to the floor, blood spurting out of his left shoulder. His gun bounced under the desk.

"Dad!" Matthew yelled to Teague, dropping to his knees to protect him.

Ossing took a few steps closer to Teague to finish him off.

Ossing's kneeling son lunged at him, grabbing him by the legs. Ossing's shoes skidded on the melted ice from Alex's ice pack and he fell forward, hitting his head against the desk. As his neck broke from the force, the Webley skittered across the floor. Alex took a few steps forward, feeling for a pulse in Ossing's neck. He was dead.

She looked up and saw Kincade inching toward the gun on the floor. "Stop him," Alex said to Matthew. The boy grabbed the Webley first and stood up, aiming it at the older man. Alex knelt next to Castro, silently praying that he was still alive. Then she reached into Castro's pocket and pulled out the handcuffs. She used them to hook the director of Homeland Security to a hot-water pipe that brought sterilized water to the lab.

"We have to go *now*," Alex said to Matthew. She pointed to the men jumping out of the helicopter, just a couple of hundred feet from the building. "We've got to protect the other children."

The boy looked frightened. Who wouldn't, in his position? Until this day, his life had been, if not idyllic, at least peaceful. And now all the violence of the outside world had broken through the Colony's doors. He crouched next to the bleeding Teague. "I can't leave my dad," he said.

A grenade blew the center window out, making a large hole in the wall. Four men in SWAT uniforms and gas masks ran into the room. The first one easily disarmed Matthew as he crouched over his dad, soothing the wounded man.

Alex turned to Nat, the computer. "Dak To," she said.

The sounds of AK-47s and M-16s filled the room. Three of the agents dropped to the floor to protect themselves. One pivoted toward the door and fired wildly.

In the confusion, Alex reached into the cabinet that Matthew had looked at earlier. She pulled out a syringe of toxin and moved toward Kincade. With the cabinet open, rows and rows of filled syringes were in view.

"Call them off," Alex said to Kincade. "Or I will inject you with the toxin. You've seen what happened to Castro. It's not a pleasant way to die."

She held the needle next to his neck.

Kincade said, "Get out of here, you assholes. Go back to the copter for now."

The apparent leader of the men aimed his weapon at Alex. He said, "Not without the toxin. I'm finishing the job." Then he pulled off his gas mask. His long, black hair touched his shoulders. He looked Alex squarely in the eyes as he aimed.

"Dale Hightower," Alex said. "Or should I say Farim? How did you . . . ?"

"Don't believe everything you see on TV," he said. "If I could pass for an Indian, so could the two guys who looked like they were taking me into custody."

"Stand down," Kincade said. "You're not going to be able to hit her without getting me."

Farim stopped pointing his Uzi at Alex. Instead, he grabbed Matthew, pulled him to his feet, and pointed his gun at him.

"Put the syringe on the counter and back away or I'll shoot the kid," he said to her.

Alex looked at Matthew. He was scared but stoic. He closed his eyes and prepared to be a martyr.

She put the syringe on the counter and stepped away so that the syringe was clearly out of her reach. The boy opened his eyes and took a deep breath.

Kincade yelled to the agent, "Uncuff me."

"No time," the agent said.

Farim put the toxin-filled syringes into a box and ordered the other three men to pick up Dr. Teague's gun and the Webley. He sent them back to the helicopter.

Kincade said to his remaining agent, "You can't leave me to die. I'm in charge."

The fake Indian just smiled. "I came to work for you for the money. But with this," he said, holding up the toxin, "I can write my own ticket, anywhere in the world."

He followed the other three men out the hole in the wall, then lobbed a grenade into the room.

Alex watched Castro's eyes flutter as it rolled toward him. Then she saw him reach over, pick it up, and throw it back out the window toward the fleeing man. It whizzed past Farim, but fell far short of the helicopter. It rolled and hit the Colony's backup generator, causing an explosion that enveloped the copter in flames.

The jolt of the explosion knocked Farim to the ground. As the flames headed in his direction, he picked himself up and ran back toward the Colony, his Uzi aimed at the lab.

"Alex, get down!" Castro shouted as he crawled toward Ossing, rolling him over and grabbing the Sig from under him.

Farim was firing wildly into the room. A hail of bullets burst chemical bottles on the shelf.

Castro crawled across the floor and rose slowly, flattening himself against the wall near the hole. Then he pivoted quickly and aimed out the broken window. The first and second shots went wild. Castro was still woozy. But the third shot connected and the man crumpled to the ground.

The wind shifted, and Castro ducked down as flames and smoke blew into the room.

"Get the other kids!" Alex said to Matthew. "Is there a safe place?"

But Matthew was glued to Teague's side. The older man said hoarsely, "Matthew, you've got to take the children to the basement of the barn."

Matthew looked uncertain as Alex gestured frantically for him to leave. The doctor weakly tried to stand. Alex said, "I'll help him. You get the other children."

As Matthew turned his back toward them and headed for the door, Alex slid her hands under the man's armpits. She cried out in pain. The man's weight was too much for her bum knee.

For a split second, she considered letting him drop back to the floor so she could save herself. But he lashed out with his good arm, grabbed the desk, and steadied himself. Teague was almost completely upright when the heat from the flames caused an unlabeled bottle of chemicals to burst. Castro pulled Alex out of the way of the mist and, with her and Teague leaning on him, led them out the door.

Alex heard Kincade's screams as the fire came closer to him. She said to Castro, "We've got to go back for Kincade."

"He doesn't deserve it," he said.

"If you're not going in, I will." She put her hand out for the handcuff key.

"I guess he'll burn in hell anyway," said Castro, as he reentered the room to save the man.

CHAPTER   69

When Dan, Grant, and the Colorado State Police pulled up, Castro was leading the handcuffed director of Homeland Security to the road. The EMTs didn't know whom to focus on first. Half of Kincade's face was burned and a tourniquet hugged his arm above a bloody sleeve and his exposed basilica vein. But Castro didn't look any better. He was bruised and scratched from his fight at the gas station and his shirt was covered in his own blood. The swelling hadn't entirely receded, so he looked like a chunkier version of himself. "Jennifer?" he asked Dan.

The major smiled and nodded. "We got her back."

The emergency workers cleaned and stitched the wounds on both men. Grant, gun in hand, jumped into the ambulance with Kincade. Castro refused to go to the hospital just yet. "I want to see this through," he told Dan, waiting expectantly for Alex to emerge.

Alex was in the basement of the log cabin, cleaning and stitching Dr. Teague's wound. Matthew spoke soothingly to the twenty-six kids, who seemed less upset by the explosion and fire than by the blood coming from their "dad."

"He's going to be alright," Alex yelled to the group. "I'm a doctor, like your father, and I will make sure that nothing happens to him."

She felt compelled to do that much. He was the only parent these children knew, the only relative, in fact, other than each other. She couldn't imagine their psychological devastation if they lost their father.

Matthew walked over to her, leaving a girl who looked about 18 in charge of the young ones. He held Andover Teague's right hand as Alex put the final stitches in the older man's left shoulder. Matthew said softly to Alex, "Please say you won't put him in jail."

Alex turned to Andover. "Are you testing the vaccine someplace else now?"

"No," he said faintly.

"Did anyone help you with this?" she asked.

Another no.

Matthew said, "I swear, if I'd known he was doing this, I would never have let him leave the Colony."

She looked at the boy, whose intelligent eyes were brimming with tears. "A lot of people died," she said. "The whole country suffered. I can't wave this aside."

"He's not well. He hasn't got that much time. Please. He was just trying to help other kids."

Alex took a deep breath. Matthew had saved Castro's life. "Let's buy time to think about it," Alex said. She looked over at the children. It was as if the photos in the hallway had come to life. Matthew's pictures had captured their essence. Their healthy joy. Their angelic innocence.

She walked out of the cabin and told everyone to stay back. "We found the poisoner. He was Jeffrey Ossing. He's dead. Three mercenaries hired by Kincade perished in the explosion. The fourth—who you may know as Dale Hightower—is in back and is wounded."

"He's wanted for murder," Dan told the troopers, who unholstered their weapons.

"But you have to stay away from the log cabin," Alex said. "If you go in there, you could cause the children to die."

A couple of troopers ran to the back to find Hightower. In the distance, Alex heard fire trucks rushing to the scene to douse the flames. Castro approached Alex. "Are you going to be alright?" he asked.

Alex knew he was asking about more than her bum knee. Who knows if I'm going to be alright? she thought. But she said, "I'll be fine."

"Are you sure the threat is over?" Dan asked.

Alex thought of the doctor, now in the care of Matthew. "Yes, I am."

EPILOGUE

When the news of the attack on the Colony broke, people were not ready to believe that the plague had ended. But as several weeks passed without additional cases, the public began to feel comfortable. In his own egotistical way, Teague had thought he could wipe out the disease entirely through a vaccine that affected primaries and secondaries. He'd programmed the vector to die out after those two generations. There wouldn't be a third generation of disease. Alex would not die from Elena's bite.

Kincade had lawyered up, but between Alex's statement and information collected by Dan's coffee-buying source in Homeland Security, the full story began to emerge. Three of Kincade's handpicked crew were dead and the little off-the-books mission he'd authorized (decimating a community that no one knew existed) had become horribly public.

In the business world, it would have been described as a "mutuality of interests." The Coalition of American Gaming Executives—a national organization representing casino owners in Vegas and Atlantic City—was chaired by a vice president of Levanthal Industries. He had persuaded the organization to fund Kincade's venture. By putting Farim undercover as a Red Rights activist, Kincade would get a credible enemy for Homeland Security to fight and the Coalition would scare gamblers away from the tribal casinos.

It seemed a lucky break for Kincade when the poisonings began. Although his agency had nothing to do with them, he'd gained political currency by labeling them the work of Red Rights. But Farim, posing as Dale Hightower, had taken his role one step too far. He'd killed Chief Son when the Indian was about to expose him.

The story was eventually pushed off the front page by a cheating scandal in the NFL and the sixth marriage of a famous star. But one group continued mulling over the news about a young man with a scientific mind who had created a system for treating his family of twenty-seven people with medicines based on common plants and insects.

TOTEM, the Native American conglomerate that had dealt with Renfrew, got in touch with Matthew. They offered him the job of directing research in a company they were starting, following *The American Way,* treating people with natural substances. But they offered him something else as well. A large tract of land in New Mexico where he could establish a new Colony. In Colorado, towns had been encroaching closer and closer. Plus, Matthew knew that living on Indian land, he would be in a separate nation. There would be no chance that Andover Teague could be compelled to go off the reservation to stand trial.

Through the efforts of the tribes, the new facility was put up in less than two weeks. Matthew transferred to the tribes his files of the plant substances he had tested. In another few weeks, they would finish building a separate laboratory on the children's land. Matthew was calling it the Del Ray Institute.

Alex asked Barbara to read over the contract that the Native Americans offered Matthew. The young boy wanted little compensation for himself in the deal. Instead, he asked that money be given to the families of those who had been harmed, like Elena's surviving daughter.

"Don't you find it odd," Barbara said, "that Matthew feels a responsibility for the families that Ossing harmed? He hadn't even seen Ossing since he was two."

Alex paused for a moment. Should she tell her best friend that Teague had committed the crime? She knew that the lawyer in Barbara wouldn't let the matter rest. Instead, Alex said, "Well, you know, the sins of the father haunt the child."

Waverly had fired Renfrew for acting against its interests in his earlier dealings with the Native American conglomerate. His post-docs—even Julianna—had soured on him by then. Seeing as how they were first-rate scientists, even the arrogant Buck, Alex suggested that Matthew hire them at the Del Ray Institute, which was now a division of TOTEM Therapeutics.

TOTEM was going by the book, following every FDA regulation for clinical trials in testing the active agent in the plant that Matthew had used to treat Castro. Matthew hadn't been entirely sure it would work when he'd given it to Castro, but, at that moment, there had been no other option. The conglomerate was proud that their first product would not be a pill for baldness or impotence that would benefit only the richest countries. Instead, they would launch their new company with a medication—which Matthew insisted they call "Teague"—that would help babies with *Inflatus Magnus* who would otherwise die in the developing world. Their business model was different from the rest of Big Pharma. Now that it was clear that Native Americans had not been responsible for the deaths, business was again booming at the tribal casinos. Gambling money provided an unlimited fund for research and development. They didn't need to charge an arm and a leg for the drugs once they were ready for market.

Matthew and Alex had long discussions about what to do when the drug cleared FDA scrutiny as being safe and effective. Once the medication became available, the children who took it would no longer be at risk of *Inflatus Magnus* and could leave the Colony. She was helping Matthew get them ready for that possibility. With Chuck's aid, she'd tracked down the mothers and other relatives of the children Teague had adopted and some began to visit their children in the new facility that the Native Americans had built, even though they needed to go through the bothersome decontamination facilities in order to see them.

Other people, like high-profile actors, wanted to visit as well. But Matthew, like Teague, was insistent that the new Colony be a sanctuary and not a tourist destination.

When the drug was ready, the children would be given the option of staying or going. Some of the older ones had already decided to stay. But they would be able to study with tutors and visiting scholars who would stay in the guest facility that was adjacent to the new Colony. They could learn and explore with live teachers.

The children had voted for another construction project. They would put up a building for disabled children whose families didn't want them. Already, kids with different physical and medical maladies were flooding Matthew's reestablished Face Space page with great ideas for the design of the rooms of the building to be more accessible to people with their particular needs.

"We'll keep a room for you in the experts' house, Dr. Blake," Matthew said to Alex when he called her after he and his siblings moved to the New Mexico site. He asked her to fly to the new Colony to see it.

On the flight to New Mexico, Alex thought about the trip to Taos she'd made weeks earlier, when she mistakenly believed she was dealing with a medical mystery that could be solved in a day or two. She recalled how intrigued and excited she'd been to meet Castro Baxter at the Hotel La Fonda. So much had happened since then, revealing so many sides of him. And then that ultimate revelation—the one she'd never seen coming. He was married.

Since that day at the Colony, Castro had vowed not to keep secrets from Alex, to tell her about everything in his life, to not hold back. Last week, he'd told her that he had been giving thought to getting back together with Jennifer, for the sake of the baby. Then, last night, Jennifer had dropped a bombshell on him. The baby was not his. He dutifully reported this to Alex as well. But what was Alex to make of it? She had no desire to be a rebound lover for a spurned husband. She wasn't sure how to help him process this information; even Emilie Londine might have a rocky time helping Castro to sort out his life just now.

On the professional front, the DEA had offered Castro his job back. How could they not, after both *Time* and *60 Minutes* had done pieces on him and tributes to Ted? But Castro didn't want to go back. Galloway was the one who'd arranged for the cremation of Ted's body. He'd asked his own secretary to pose as Ted's mom. Galloway didn't think his agency could survive another Congressionally mandated investigation of an agent using illegal drugs. Alex couldn't believe that this act of hubris was what had triggered an investigation of a much larger magnitude.

And Alex wasn't quite sure how she felt about the overtures Castro had made to Dan, inquiring about the possibility of joining the AFIP team. She'd been attracted to Castro, but how could she trust him? And she still felt a nagging guilt about how, if it hadn't been for him, she might have reached Tommy Teague in time. Ah, Castro, she thought. Just like it took a while for an infection to work its way in and then out of the population, she needed a while to figure out whether she wanted him in or out of her life.

When she reached the new Colony, Alex washed off in the Welcome Center's new decontamination chamber, changed into muslin, and stepped outside, dazzled by the vastness and beauty of the children's homes and the outbuildings. She turned to see if Matthew was around and saw him in the doorway of the old, octagonal log cabin.

He smiled and reached out to shake her hand. "Like it? We moved it here from Colorado."

She viewed the metal mobile. "Your uncle made this, no?"

He nodded. "Poor Uncle Tommy. He was my eyes and ears to the world for so long. I miss him terribly."

Alex knew how hard it was to lose someone close to you. "Your uncle would be proud of how you've expanded on his dream."

Matthew took Alex's hand and led her to a natural pathway of flowering cacti. Even during their animated conversation, he couldn't resist stopping now and then to cut a piece off a plant here and there, label a bag, and put the piece inside it for further study. "How's your dad?" she asked.

Matthew smiled. "Thanks for asking. He's in a wheelchair now. He's had a series of small strokes. The younger children take turns reading to him. I think he's pretty happy, actually."

They climbed up a jutting rock formation about twenty feet off the ground and sat on the edge. They sat comfortably in silence, watching the sun drop slowly in the sky, spreading a rose-colored tinge over the entire desert. The peripatetic Alex felt at peace. She could almost feel the dark spirits of the investigation washing out of her. Not that she would ever forget Elena dying in her arms or the horror she'd felt when she realized that Homeland Security was planning to demolish the Colony and kill the children. But she was beginning to feel healed, like the terror of those incidents was being replaced by wisdom.

"I have a big favor to ask you," started Matthew. "I'd like to visit both my mothers' graves."

At first Alex was confused. Both? Then she realized he was referring to Bree Christalink as well as his birth mother. "I don't know if you can risk it," she said. "There are many more chemicals and man-made substances out there than fifteen years ago, when you went into the Colony. You can hardly buy a piece of fruit now without it being genetically modified. And most men's slacks are woven with nanoparticles to make them stain resistant. Who knows what would trigger you."

"You'll be my doctor. You'll come with."

"Matthew, that's a lot to ask of anyone. Not to mention that I was useless when Castro went into an attack."

"That's what I wanted to talk to you about. How do you think I knew what plant to give your friend when he was dying? I'd tried it on myself."

"Matthew!" Alex was stunned. "What were you thinking? You could have killed yourself."

He looked her straight in the eyes. "Science is about risk. You know that. I waited until Tonya was eighteen, so that she could be in charge if anything bad happened to me."

"Did Dr. Teague know?"

"Uh-uh. But there's nothing unethical about a researcher trying a drug on himself. Think of the Nuremberg Code."

Alex reflected on the code of medical ethics developed by a court in response to the Nazis' inhumane experiments. It was still a guiding force for researchers today. The Code prohibited research on people without their informed consent. It forbade research where there was reason to believe that death or disabling injury would occur. Teague had violated the Code a million times over. But the Code had an exception. It allowed risky research, even potentially fatal research, if the researcher himself was willing to serve as the subject. Like Matthew.

"When would you like to go?" Alex asked.

"Tomorrow," he said.

As Alex and Matthew cabbed into Boston from the airport, the boy's eyes grew wide as saucers at every sight. The buildings. A hot dog vendor. A Great Dane. Simple things that any urban dweller took for granted.

Before their journey, he'd printed off satellite photos of every location they would visit. He had them on his lap in the cab. But, within a few minutes, he'd crumpled them up. "It isn't the same," he said to Alex. "The noise. The smells. It's not at all like I imagined."

The cab dropped them off in front of a church, not far from the capitol building. Behind it was a small cemetery, the final resting place for the founders of the city. Alex led Matthew to the section where generations of Christalinks were buried.

Matthew approached Bree Christalink's grave, taking great care not to step on the grass that covered the area where her body was buried. Alex couldn't help but smile. Here he was, a noted scientist and head of research at a biotech company, but he still was a superstitious kid.

He was lost in thought, staring at the headstone, when an older man with a walrus moustache approached. "She was very special," the man said to Matthew.

The boy turned to him and the man enveloped him in a hug.

"I remember when you came to the hospital to see me," said Matthew.

They awkwardly withdrew from the hug and knelt before the gravestone. "Yes, my daughter was very special indeed," Christalink said.

"She was my other mom," Matthew said, tears running down his cheek. "She used to read to me. *''Twas brillig, and . . .* '"

Christalink joined in. They said in unison, *". . . the slithy toves."*

Alex took a few steps back, allowing the men to be alone. Family, she thought. It can take so many forms. Ties of blood, ties of friendship, and shared links to someone who was no longer around. And through it all, you muddled through the sort of person you wanted to be. Matthew would have made both his mothers proud.

ACKNOWLEDGMENTS

Although this is a work of fiction, many of the technologies and challenges faced by Alex Blake are real. Date rape drugs are a growing problem. Monoclonal antibodies are being tested in humans, sometimes with catastrophic side effects. And research on DNA computers is under way, although no one has yet created one like Sam. My website, www.loriandrews.com, provides information about the startling facts behind this imagined story.

I couldn't have written this book without the help of many people: Lesa Andrews, Danielle Bochneak, Julie Burger, Katharine Cluverius, Richard Fitzpatrick, Bob Gaensslen, Debra Greenfield, Florence Haseltine, Hal Krent, Gary Kubek, Adrianne Noe, Bruce Patsner, Kelley Ragland, Christopher Ripley, Clements Ripley, Mark Rosin, Laura Shackelton, Harriet Stark, Jim Stark, Darren Stephens, and Amanda Urban. These extraordinary individuals have a range of talents among them—medical and law degrees, experience tracking date rape drugs, familiarity with medical research, expertise about viruses, military service, editorial wisdom, high ideals, and common sense. Without their generosity in returning my calls and answering my questions, this book would have never come to pass.